KT-462-073

30130503645980

STONE COLD

Everything about the ranch is a mystery. Rumours abound about the reclusive millionaire who owns it, the women who live with him, the private airstrip, the sudden disappearances. And, most persistent of all, that it is all funded by murder.

Joe Pickett is tasked by the governor to find out the truth. But he soon discovers a lot more than he'd bargained for.

There are two other men living up at the ranch. One is a stone-cold killer who takes an instant dislike to Joe. The other, Joe knows all too well. The first man doesn't frighten him. But the second is another story entirely.

SPECIAL MESSAGE TO READERS

THE ULVERSCROFT FOUNDATION
(registered UK charity number 264873)
was established in 1972 to provide funds for
research, diagnosis and treatment of eye diseases.
Examples of major projects funded by
the Ulverscroft Foundation are:-

- The Children's Eye Unit at Moorfields Eye Hospital, London
- The Ulverscroft Children's Eye Unit at Great Ormond Street Hospital for Sick Children
- Funding research into eye diseases and treatment at the Department of Ophthalmology, University of Leicester
- The Ulverscroft Vision Research Group, Institute of Child Health
- Twin operating theatres at the Western Ophthalmic Hospital, London
- The Chair of Ophthalmology at the Royal Australian College of Ophthalmologists

You can help further the work of the Foundation
by making a donation or leaving a legacy.
Every contribution is gratefully received. If you
would like to help support the Foundation or
require further information, please contact:

THE ULVERSCROFT FOUNDATION
The Green, Bradgate Road, Anstey
Leicester LE7 7FU, England
Tel: (0116) 236 4325

website: www.foundation.ulverscroft.com

STONE COLD

C. J. BOX

ISIS
LARGE
PRINT

First published in Great Britain 2014
by
Head of Zeus Ltd.

First Isis Edition
published 2015
by arrangement with
Head of Zeus Ltd.

The moral right of the author has been asserted

Copyright © 2014 by C. J. Box
All rights reserved

A catalogue record for this book is available
from the British Library.

ISBN 978–1–78541–056–7 (hb)
ISBN 978–1–78541–057–4 (pb)

Published by
F. A. Thorpe (Publishing)
Anstey, Leicestershire

Set by Words & Graphics Ltd.
Anstey, Leicestershire
Printed and bound in Great Britain by
T. J. International Ltd., Padstow, Cornwall

This book is printed on acid-free paper

In memory of my dad, Jack,

And Laurie, always . . .

It's not inequality which is the real misfortune, it's dependence.

— VOLTAIRE

I've got a shotgun, a rifle and a four-wheel drive
And a country boy can survive

— HANK WILLIAMS JR.

CHAPTER ONE

Fort Smith, Montana

Nate Romanowski pushed the drift boat onto the Bighorn River at three-thirty in the morning on a Sunday in early October and let the silent muscle of the current pull him away from the grassy bank. Eight miles downriver was the fortified and opulent vacation home of the notorious man he was going to kill.

It was twenty-four degrees and steam rose from the surface of the black water in thick tendrils, and he was soon enveloped in it. The craft floated quietly and he manned the long oars to keep the upswept bow pointing forward. Gnarled walls of river cottonwoods closed him in, their bare branches reaching overhead from both banks as if to try and join hands. For ten minutes between Third Island and Dag's Run, he couldn't see a damned thing and operated exclusively on feel and sound and experience. He kept to the main channel and avoided the shallows so he wouldn't scrape bottom and could float as swiftly as possible.

He'd made the run before in preparation — so many times, in fact, that the rhythm, mood, and temperament of the river was as familiar to him as his falcons, his weapons, and his code. Or what was left of his code, anyway, he thought, and grinned bitterly to himself in the dark.

While doing night reconnaissance, he'd worn the narrow compression pack on his back that he wore now, and he was so used to the dead weight of the gear inside that he almost forgot it was there. His .500 Wyoming Express five-shot revolver, the most powerful handgun on earth, hung grip-out from its shoulder holster below his left ribs, its security tether unsnapped.

Over his shoulder, the massive concrete spillway of the Yellowtail Dam glowed light blue in the muted light of the stars and the scythelike slice of moon. A single cumulus cloud, its rounded edges highlighted by starlight, moved from north to south, blotting out the continuity of the brilliant Milky Way. It would be hours before fly-fishing guides and anglers — men, women, but mostly men — arrived at the launch near the dam and started their half-day or daylong drift floats down the legendary Bighorn. Nate slipped a cell phone from his breast pocket and powered it on. When he had a signal and the screen glowed, he called up the only number stored in it and texted: *It's a go*. And sent the message.

Within a minute, there was a response: *Go do some good*.

Nate turned off the phone and slipped it back into his pocket.

Nate was tall, angular, and rangy. He didn't row with the oars but used them to steer the boat by lowering one or the other into the current to bring the bow around. He had worked on his technique so it was smooth and he wouldn't splash. The oars were an extension of his arms, and his movements were smooth and unhurried.

His friend Joe Pickett had once described his face and eyes as "hawklike." His blond ponytail, constrained by leather falcon jesses, had grown to midway between his shoulders. It was tucked into the collar of his tactical sweater so it wouldn't be noticed. His eyes were blue and piercing, and the planes of his face were flat, severe, and aerodynamic. He wore a dark camo slouch hat, and his sharp cheekbones were darkened with soot so the moonlight, such as it was, wouldn't reflect.

There was no doubt, Nate had been told, that the world would be a better place without Henry P. Scoggins III in it.

Scoggins was short, fleshy, stooped, and walleyed, and was the last direct heir of the Scoggins pharmaceutical empire of Newark, New Jersey. Unlike his grandfather, the senator and ambassador, or his father, the well-intentioned philanthropist, Henry the Third, as he was known, used his billions to manipulate monetary currencies around the world, corner the market on fourteen of seventeen rare earth metals, and lavishly fund activist groups that advocated legalized prostitution, drug use, and polygamy. He enjoyed the company of corrupt machine politicians, gangsta rap artists, foreign dictators, and domestic organized-crime figures. Several of his lurid divorce proceedings were front-page news over the years, as well as the Los Angeles murder trial where he'd been accused of shooting a hooker in the face and killing her on the front porch of his mansion. He had been found innocent when the jury bought his lawyer's claim that Scoggins mistook her for a homicidal home invader threatening his Beverly Hills neighborhood at the time.

In video clips, Scoggins spoke in a deliberate mid-register timbre that belied his habit of constantly and furtively looking over the heads of the listeners, as if searching for someone more worthwhile, better-looking, or less threatening in the room. He had the arrogant look of a bully who had insulated himself so he'd never have to directly confront a challenge, the kind of man comfortable with rewarding his friends in person and punishing his enemies from a distance.

Isolating the man was the problem. Scoggins surrounded himself with armed bodyguards, and his five U.S.-based homes — Newark, Manhattan, Aspen, Palm Beach, and the infamous Beverly Hills manse — were set up with elaborate security systems. His overseas properties in Caracas, Abu Dhabi, and Grand Cayman were protected by security contractors who were ex-Black Ops.

Few people were aware of the six-million-dollar log home Scoggins had recently purchased through a holding company on the bank of the Bighorn River. The reason: he wanted to learn to fly-fish. The rumor was that Scoggins *thought* he was buying the river itself.

For the past week, in addition to the late-night reconnaissance floats, Nate had scouted the Scoggins property on the ground by trespassing through an adjoining landholding and avoiding the caretaker. There were very few private residences in the river valley, and the few that were there were massive and expensive. They were accessed by a private road that paralleled the bends of the river. Only a couple of the structures could be seen from the road itself, due to high stone walls and steel security gates. The Scoggins property had not only a swinging gate operated by remote control but also a small guardhouse manned by an armed employee during daylight hours. At night, visitors — mostly delivery trucks — had to identify themselves via the closed-circuit camera at the gate to be buzzed in. Additional closed-circuit cameras that swept the grounds were mounted on poles within the compound, and Nate counted two men — one openly armed with a combat shotgun — lazily patrolling the grounds. He had dubbed the gate operator Thug Two, and the men on patrol Thug Three and Thug Four. All wore loose-fitting untucked shirts and cargo pants.

Nate noted the disparity between the massive homes built of logs, stone, and glass, complete with guesthouses and outbuildings and sweeping manicured lawns, and the utter squalor of the Crow Indian Reservation just beyond the fence.

On Friday he'd caught a glimpse of Scoggins in person. He'd been glassing the grounds through his spotting scope, memorizing the layout of the buildings and internalizing the contours of the ground, when a thick metal door opened and two women tumbled out. They had long brown legs and jet-black hair and they were wearing only lingerie. As Nate focused in, he felt the hair on the nape of his neck rise. They were Indians, likely Crows from the reservation. They wore too much makeup and they clutched bundles of their clothing under their arms, as if they'd been in a hurry to gather it up before they were thrown out of the house. The taller one reminded him of a woman he'd once loved named Alisha, who was a Shoshone and a teacher on the Wind River Indian Reservation in Wyoming. It jolted him to his core. She wasn't Alisha but a prostitute, obviously, and she was being unceremoniously kicked out of the house before she could even get dressed.

The shorter of the two women spun on her heel and shouted something Nate couldn't hear at someone out of view inside the house. The taller woman paused, dropped her head in fear or panic, and reached out to the shorter woman to urge her on.

Then Scoggins appeared, flanked by a barrel-chested younger man who had the build of a weight lifter and a smirk on his face. He also wore an oversized shirt and cargo pants. Nate had deemed him Thug One because he rarely left Scoggins's side.

Scoggins wore a loose-fitting robe and oversized slippers on his feet. Two thin white naked ankles could be seen beneath the hem of the robe. Maybe it was Scoggins's hunched slouch and widespread eyes that, even at that distance, reminded Nate of a toad. He was

6

smirking as well, but also flipping his fingers at the women, obviously urging them to go away.

When the shorter woman kept talking and gesticulating and wouldn't leave, Thug One shouldered around Scoggins and rushed her with three long and quick strides. As she turned to run, the big man kicked her hard enough beneath her buttocks to lift her off the ground and send her sprawling. When she scrambled to retrieve the clothes that had flown into the air, the thug wound up for another kick and the taller hooker yanked the shorter one down the pathway, leaving the clothes strewn on the grass.

Nate could only guess the cause of the altercation. Maybe the hookers had objected to what they were asked to do, or they'd tried and didn't satisfy their customer. Maybe one of them got mouthy or tried to steal something. Or maybe Scoggins decided to throw them out instead of pay them. Nate planned to find out.

What he did know was that the altercation made his blood boil. It wasn't Alisha, of course, because Alisha had been murdered. A lock of her hair hung from a beaded band on the barrel of his .50 caliber revolver. But she looked like Alisha and it brought back a wave of guilt, shame, and lethal rage. And when the thug kicked the girl hard enough to send her flying, Nate barely resisted drawing his weapon and charging down the hill to what would likely have been his certain death.

Later, he watched through his spotting scope as Thug One came back out of the house and gathered the scraps of clothing the prostitute had left behind. He walked them over to a trash barrel behind a storage shed and burned them.

"You bastard," Nate whispered.

He caught up with the two prostitutes walking up the middle of the narrow two-lane highway in their bare feet. The taller one dangled a pair of spike heels from her index finger. The women were cold and disheveled, and when they heard him approach in his rented SUV, they turned and grinned desperately, hoping for a ride. Nate slowed and drove around them and signaled them in.

"Car break down?" he asked.

"Something like that," the shorter one said, taking the backseat.

"You are a sight for sore eyes," the taller one said, jumping up into the passenger seat and dropping her shoes on the floorboard. The interior of his vehicle was suddenly filled with a combination of sweet perfume and musky sweat.

The short one was named Candy Alexander and the tall one who looked less like Alisha than he thought previously said her name was D. Anita LittleWolf. Both were from Crow Agency on the reservation, but they wanted to get to Hardin to the north because that's where they'd left LittleWolf's pickup.

"It's parked on the side of a bar," LittleWolf said. "I'm really happy you picked us up. Thank you."

"Yes, thank you," Alexander said from the back. He glanced up and saw her dark eyes in the rearview

8

mirror. Streaks of black mascara ran down her face from her lashes and she rubbed it clean with the heel of her hand.

As he drove to Hardin, he made small talk with them about the weather, about fishing, about how odd it was to find two women in their underwear walking up a deserted highway in southern Montana. Although they didn't get specific, they said they'd been invited to "party down" at a big house on the river, but the host had kicked them out and not even offered to drive them back to where they'd been picked up. Alexander was still fuming about it, but LittleWolf was serene and seemed to take it in stride.

"So the owner of the house invited you to his place and then kicked you out?"

"It wasn't the owner who took us out there," Alexander said, and described Thug One. "We didn't meet the owner until we got there."

"He said he doesn't like dark meat," LittleWolf said without a hint of irony.

"He sounds like a jerk," Nate said.

"He's an asshole," Alexander said, nodding. "They're both assholes. I'd like to round up some friends of mine and go back there . . ."

"Forget about it," LittleWolf said. "You'd never get in that place again."

Nate feigned ignorance and asked her why she said that.

After putting on clothes from overnight bags they'd left in their vehicle, LittleWolf and Alexander loosened up over beers in the bar and told Nate about their adventure, from being contacted by Thug One to being met by him at the bar and transported to the big house on the Bighorn River. How the man asked the gate guard to buzz him in. How he punched a keypad on the front door to unlock it. How the owner of the house had come down the staircase and disapproved of their looks and sent them away, the scene Nate had witnessed. Now that they were safe and warm and their pickup was just outside, they laughed about the details. LittleWolf said she was glad they were gone, because the owner of the place gave her the creeps.

Nate asked them to back up to when they entered the main house.

"There was a keypad?" he asked, and slipped his notebook out from his pocket.

Nate asked D. Anita LittleWolf and Candy Alexander to close their eyes and recall what Thug One had done when he opened the door while it was still very fresh in their memory. LittleWolf said she couldn't see the pad from where she had stood on the porch, but Alexander smiled and described the scene. The keypad was metal and had three rows of numbers: one-two-three on top, four-five-six in the middle, seven-eight-nine on the third row, and a single zero button on the bottom. Nate had sketched out the sequence of the pad on a napkin and handed it over. Alexander closed her eyes in recall, and punched 4-2-2 and another button in the third row. It was either an eight or a nine, she said. She wasn't sure.

When Nate asked her how she could recall the sequence, she said she learned it by looking over the shoulders of rubes using the ATM at the convenience store on the reservation across from the Custer Battlefield, where she used to work. Both women collapsed in laughter.

"It eventually got me fired," Alexander squealed. "But not before I scored a few hundred dollars from *turistas*."

Later, after two more rounds, LittleWolf invited him to follow them back to Crow Agency. "We've got a place where we can party," she said. She looked into his eyes without a hint of guile, and for a moment he saw Alisha again.

"I'll have to pass," he said.

"You don't like dark meat, either?" Alexander said, teasing him.

"Actually, I do," Nate said. "But I don't like that term. There's no dignity in it."

Chastened, they gathered their purses and shoes. He saw them to their pickup but didn't follow.

The previous night, Saturday, he'd stayed hidden with his spotting scope and noted the routine of the Scoggins compound. There had been no more women brought in, and there were no outside visitors. The three outside thugs went into the main house as the sun set, and apparently had dinner at the same time as Scoggins and Thug One. They remained there for an hour, then drifted away one by one to a guesthouse located between the main house and the gate. The lights remained on in the guesthouse until twelve-fifteen a.m.

Not surprisingly, there were two house staff who exited the main house after the three thugs had gone. A middle-aged man and woman crossed the grounds from the house to a tiny cottage on the edge of the property. Nate guessed by their dress that the woman was the cook and the man was her assistant, and possibly an all-around maintenance staffer for the property. They held hands as they walked under an overhead light. Nate was charmed, and vowed to himself that no harm would come to them.

It took longer for Scoggins and Thug One to go to sleep. Light from the second-floor windows — Nate guessed it was Scoggins's room, since it took up the entire floor — remained on until one-thirty. A ground-floor light in the corner was off at midnight. It made sense that the primary bodyguard, Thug One, would be located between the front door and the stairs to Scoggins's floor. On the other corner of the main house opposite from Thug One, a dim light remained on the entire night. Nate guessed it was the security center, where someone sat awake with the CC monitors flickering from all the cameras on the grounds. He wondered about motion detectors, and assumed they were there somewhere.

With a choked-down mini Maglite clenched between his teeth, Nate drew a sketch on a fresh page of his notebook. He outlined the main house, the outbuildings, the guesthouse, the cottage, the wall, and the gate. Within the grounds, he drew circles with a *CC* inside to designate each camera. Then he scratched three large X's to symbolize the three thugs in the guesthouse, two

12

more for Thug One and the security administrator in the main house, and a dollar sign for Scoggins himself.

Nate had determined by his surveillance there was no way to access the Scoggins property from the road without a small army, which he didn't have and didn't want. And there was no way to sneak across it in the dark without being captured by video or confronted by bodyguards. If motion detectors were installed, Nate guessed they'd be concentrated between the wall and gate and the compound.

But like the other huge homes along the small strip of private land, Scoggins's home fronted the water. That way, he could sit inside with a drink behind car-sized sheets of glass and see the river as the sun set or rose. Guided fly fishermen could look at his place with envy and wonder as they floated by. The ABSOLUTELY NO TRESPASSING, DON'T EVEN THINK ABOUT GETTING OUT OF YOUR BOAT and VIOLATORS WILL BE PROSECUTED signs — plus the rotating closed-circuit video camera and five-strand razor-wire fence — kept them out.

Having the magnificent log house on open display to the river was an act of vanity.

And it was Nate's means of accessing the property.

Or, as his employer would say, *Go do some good*.

Nate maneuvered the drift boat into the slow current that hugged the right bank of the river as he approached the Scoggins compound. Thick willows bent overhead and created a black shadow that he

13

floated through. His senses were tuned up high, and he felt more than saw or heard the presence of the compound around the next slight bend to his right. He eased the boat against the willows until the hull thumped against the grassy bank and he reached up and grabbed a handful of branches to pull him in tighter. Slowly, quietly, he grasped the rope between his feet and lowered the anchor in back until it held and stopped the boat. He swung his boots over the gunwale and stood in the cold water. It was knee-deep.

He stayed hard against the wall of willows as he waded silently downstream. After no more than a dozen steps, lights from the compound strobed through the brush and he knew that the stand of willows would end to reveal a long grassy slope all the way up to the log home. He was already behind the river fence. If he walked out in the clear, he could be seen by the closed-circuit camera that swept back and forth along the bank. It was mounted on the side of a river cottonwood and accompanied by a motion detector. Because of the roaming wildlife that hugged the river, Nate guessed the motion detector sounded off periodically throughout the night and would likely not alarm the technician inside. But a screen shot of him on a monitor certainly would.

In the shadows, Nate unbuckled his compression pack and reversed it so it covered his chest. He unzipped the top. For easy access, the items inside had been packed in the reverse order they were to be used.

For seven full minutes, Nate stood hidden in the river with his eyes closed, going over his plan. Not that something wouldn't go wrong — it always did. The trick was to try and anticipate the surprise problems as best he could and come up with options on the fly. His assignment was to kill Henry P. Scoggins III, but with a twist of his own. The twist was important to him.

And if his plans blew up once they were under way, he had to keep the endgame in mind. Even if the result was a bloodbath he hoped to avoid.

When he opened his eyes, the night seemed lighter, brighter, and suddenly charged with anticipation. The river sounds behind him were louder and more full-throated. He could distinctly smell the odors and perfumes of the world around him: the tinny smell of the moving river, the decayed mud that swirled in the current he'd stirred up along the bank, sage from the hills beyond the river, even cooking smells that lingered from the log house itself. He took a deep breath, held it, and slowly expelled it through his nostrils.

It was then he realized he was not alone in the stand of brush.

Less than three feet away was a heavy-bodied mule deer doe, her big eyes fixed on him and her large ears cupped in his direction. He instinctively reached across his body for his weapon, but paused as his hand gripped the butt of his revolver. Now that he saw her, he noticed he could smell her as well; musky, dank, sage on her breath. His movement had not spooked her out of the willows.

In falconry parlance, the state of *yarak* is defined as: "full of stamina, well muscled, alert, neither too fat nor too thin, perfect condition for hunting and killing prey. This state is rarely achieved but a wonder to behold when observed."

Nate was as close to *yarak* as a human could be.

The mule deer could help him. She could be his partner. He noticed she was trembling, ready to spring away.

He whispered, "Go."

She did, and with a crash of snapped willows the deer bounded from the brush into the clearing.

Nate moved swiftly, emerging from the brush right behind her, keeping the trunk of the tree between him and the CC camera. The boxy snout of the camera was pointed downriver but rotating in his direction as he approached it. The deer veered away from the tree and continued bouncing — *boing-boing-boing* — along the fence. As Nate ran straight toward the camera, he reached into the top of his pack and unfurled a black cloth sack that he threw over both the camera and mount before it could view him. It was like placing a hood over the head of a falcon, and he cinched the drawstring tight and stood back. The camera still rotated inside the sack, and it resembled the head of a man looking from side to side.

There was another distant snapping of willows and cattails as the mule deer vanished into the brush on the other side of the clearing. No doubt the motion detector had signaled the intrusion. Perhaps the camera had caught a fleeting look at the doe — his partner — as she bounded through its field of view.

"Thank you," Nate said to the deer.

Then he stepped back into the shadows of the willows and checked his watch and waited.

It took twenty-two minutes, much longer than he had estimated, before he heard the slamming of a door at the log house and heavy footfalls on their way down to the river. That it had taken the technician so long to realize his riverside camera was out confirmed to Nate that the man wasn't anticipating trouble. Or he was simply incompetent. *That bodes well*, Nate thought to himself. He hoped the other thugs would be as thick.

A harsh orb of white light from a flashlight moved down the sloping grass lawn in front of the technician. Nate squinted and turned his head and followed it in his peripheral vision. It was a trick he'd learned years before in the Third World for maintaining his night sight. A blast of the flashlight in his eyes would blind him momentarily if he let it happen, and he couldn't risk it.

He heard the footfalls stop less than twelve feet away, and heard a man say to himself, "What the *fuck*?"

Meaning the technician was illuminating the black hood covering the camera with the beam of his flashlight and probably wondering what it was.

Nate hurled himself from the willows like a blitzing linebacker going after the quarterback on his blind side. He dived low so his full weight would take out the legs of the technician.

The man made an *umpf* sound as he was hit and his flashlight flew into the air. The butt of a shotgun grazed

Nate's shoulders as he took the man down, and he quickly turned and swarmed him and wrenched the long gun away and threw it aside.

Before the technician could cry out, Nate jammed a spare black hood into his mouth with his left hand and chopped hard across the bridge of the man's nose with his right. He heard the muffled crack of bone and smelled the hot metallic flood of blood.

The technician didn't put up much of a fight — that usually happened from the immediate result of a broken nose — and he went suddenly limp with shock and pain. Nate rolled the technician over on his stomach and bound his hands behind his back with one of the plastic zip-tie cuff restraints he kept in the side pocket of his pack. He pulled it tight. He did the same with the technician's ankles, and used an additional thirty-inch zip tie to hog-tie the man so he couldn't move. Nate had done it all very quickly, he thought, and with the speed and panache of a steer roper used to winning money at the rodeo.

Nate rifled through the technician's cargo pants and baggy shirt. There weren't any more weapons, and Nate found a cell phone, a small walkie-talkie (turned off), loose change, a billfold, two loose marijuana joints — *the reason it had taken him so long to respond?* — and tossed it all into the willows. The technician's clothing and thick hair smelled of weed.

Nate rocked back on his haunches and surveyed the slope up to the log home and the outbuildings beyond it. There was no sound or movement, no lights suddenly coming on from Thug One's level or from the guesthouse.

He dragged the limp body of the technician out of the moonlight and left him in the shadows of the willows, then ducked inside the cover to circumnavigate the compound from the wooded right side.

When Nate reemerged from the tangle of downed timber and river cottonwoods, the guesthouse was before him. He paused and let his breathing slow, noting the lack of movement, sound, or lights from within the building. It was a log-constructed home in the same style of the main house, only much smaller and on one level. He kept the guesthouse between himself and one of the lawn-mounted cameras he'd noted during his reconnaissance and flattened himself against the exterior wall on the left side of the front door. It was a steel door in a steel frame but had been painted to look like wood. He could hear rhythmic snoring from inside.

He drew a glue gun with the long tube of aircraft adhesive from his pack and uncapped the nozzle. The substance was strong enough to be used to bond ceramic tiles to the space shuttle. He could smell a strong whiff of the quick-drying epoxy in the still night air as he carefully wedged the tip of the tube between the door and doorjamb, then worked a glistening bead of it across the top of the threshold and down the side of the door itself. He pumped a little extra near the latch and strike plate to figuratively weld the mechanism in place.

Nate left the porch and kept his head down as he circled the house, leaving snail tracks of epoxy along the bottom of all the closed windows in their frames. He replicated the procedure on the back door, and waited a few minutes for the glue to dry. He risked tugging on the back door and found it bound tight.

He capped the glue gun and stowed it away in his pack and turned toward the main house. Nate had decided to not worry about the older couple in the bungalow.

Although he approached the front door of the main log house by zigzagging from tree to tree across the lawn, Nate had no doubt that his image was being captured by video sweeps from the closed-circuit cameras, and that additional motion detectors were noting his movements. But since the technician was bound up near the river and there was no clicking on of lights or discernible movement from within the main house, he banked on the assumption that the technician had been alone with no backup.

Nate paused at the heavy front door and stared at the keypad. A wrong combination might trigger an additional alarm that could wake Thug One and Scoggins inside.

He reached down and punched 4-2-2-8.

A tiny red light pulsed on the side of the keypad, but there was no internal sound that indicated the door had unlocked. He could hear no alarm inside.

Nate drew his .500 Wyoming Express with his right hand and held the long-barreled weapon tight against his right thigh and punched 4-2-2-9 with his left index finger. There was a *thunk* from the locking mechanism, and Nate pushed the door open as a single high chime rang out inside.

He entered quickly and eased the door shut behind him and raised his weapon. He hadn't been able to see inside the home before, and had only guessed at its layout. He found himself in a dark vestibule at the mouth of a great room. Coats and jackets hung from pegs on the vestibule wall, and there was a neat row of shoes and boots.

Because of the chime, his senses were on high alert. *Who would have guessed a chime would ring out when the door was opened?*

Nate entered the great room and felt it open up above his head. There were sconces on the walls emitting very dim light, and he took it in: heavy leather furniture draped with Navajo rugs, pine interior walls, framed paintings of fish and wildlife, a huge hoary bison head above the fireplace — all very western chic. A wide carpeted staircase rose up from the ground floor to the second, and on the second level a railed walkway rimmed the opening. A massive elk antler chandelier dropped from the roof in the center of the opening.

He glanced right and saw light leaking out from under a door at the end of a hallway: the technician's security room. Then he glanced left, where he had guessed Thug One slept. But instead of a closed door at the end of the hallway, he saw one that was ajar.

Nate swung in that direction and cocked the hammer of his gun with a single upward motion. Would he be able to close the door and seal it with the man sleeping inside?

That's when he heard the slap of bare feet on the other side of the great room, where the kitchen was. And a growling, "Who the fuck is coming in here for a midnight snack?"

Thug One stood in the entryway of the kitchen, naked except for boxer shorts and a shoulder holster, with a bottle of beer in one hand and a pork chop in the other. His hair was matted on the right side of his head from sleeping, but it took only half a second for him to realize what was happening.

Thug One threw the chop one way and the bottle of beer the other and went for his pistol. No *Who are you?* or *What are you doing here?* The beer bottle smashed against the stone of the fireplace.

Nate said, "Don't do it."

Thug One froze, his fingertips an inch from the butt of his pistol. He was in a slight crouch, his thigh muscles taut, his eyes locked with Nate's.

"If you pull the weapon, I'll blow your head off," Nate said softly.

Thug One blinked, and Nate sensed the man had made the right decision.

"Take off the holster and lower it to the carpet."

Thug One stood up straight and glared at Nate, his head cocked slightly to the side, his face hard. His eyes shifted from Nate to the gaping hole of the muzzle.

22

"Why are you here?" Thug One asked. He had a saw-blade Boston accent: *Why ah you he-ah?*

"I'm here for your boss. He's all I want."

"How'd you get in?"

"Through the door."

Thug One shot an inadvertent glance down the hallway toward the closed security room door, then made a face.

"Fuck you," the man said, turning back. "You ain't gettin' back *out*."

Nate sighed, tired of the game. He chinned up toward the second floor, said, "Are you willing to lose your life to save his?"

Thug One didn't answer.

"Two seconds," Nate said in a whisper.

Just as Nate began to repeat himself, the man slipped the leather strap off his shoulder and let it slide down his arm so he caught it in his hand. He bent and put the gun on the floor.

Nate gestured with his weapon toward Thug One's open bedroom door.

After a glower that seemed more obligatory than dangerous, the man did a shoulder roll and padded down the hallway with Nate behind him. "He's an asshole, anyway," the man said.

"I'm going to close your door," Nate said. "Stay inside and you'll keep breathing. Open it and you won't."

Thug One walked to the foot of the rumpled bed and stood with his back to Nate.

"Put your hands behind your back and don't turn around," Nate said.

Because he was so muscle-bound through the shoulders and lats, Thug One could barely reach backward. Nate looped a zip tie around Thug One's wrists and wrenched it tight, pulling the man's hands together.

"That hurts," Thug One said through clenched teeth.

"It's supposed to," Nate said, backing away and closing the door tight. He slid the glue gun out of his pack and sealed it. The fumes were sharp and acrid in the closed hallway.

Nate grimaced and thought, *Boxer shorts and a shoulder holster?*

He paused before going back into the great room, listening closely for any stirring upstairs. How could Scoggins have slept through the door chime, the broken bottle, *and* the conversation?

Nate worked fast, cognizant of the three sleeping thugs in the guesthouse, the couple in the cottage, and Thug One fuming in his room. He ran down the hallway into the security room and located the Mac Pro server the technician used for the outside surveillance network. After yanking out all of the cords, he carried the machine back into the great room and unfurled a military-style body bag from his pack and stuffed it inside.

He left the body bag open.

Nate stood in the middle of the room and looked up at the four closed doors along the walkway and wondered which one Henry Scoggins slept behind. He could try them one by one.

Or . . .

The incredible *BOOM* of Nate's gun was concussive in the closed house. The .50 caliber slug blew through the chain that held the elk antler chandelier aloft, and he stepped aside as it crashed to the floor.

Out in the compound, he visualized the three other thugs awakening from their stupor, having heard the shot and the crash. He guessed the cook had rolled over in her bed and roused her husband at the sound. Thug One must be glaring at his closed door, guessing what had happened on the other side and wondering if he'd ever again land a personal security job.

Nate stepped back into the dark vestibule. What happened next was important. He couldn't kill an unarmed man — that was the twist. It was the reason he'd created the distraction instead of searching for Scoggins room by room.

He expected Scoggins to come rushing through one of the doors. Instead, there was an angry shout.

"Jolovich, what the hell just happened?"

So Thug One was Jolovich, Nate thought.

"Jolovich, goddamn you — you woke me up. What were you doing? Cleaning your damned gun again?"

Nate determined the voice was coming from one of the doors on the east side.

"Jolovich?" This time, there was a hint of panic with the anger.

Scoggins threw open an east door and staggered out to the railing. His sleep mask was pushed up on his forehead and he was in the process of digging a foam earplug out of his right ear — the reason he hadn't heard the door chime. He wore the open robe Nate had seen him in earlier, and his thin legs and basketball-sized naked belly were shockingly white.

As Scoggins clutched the railing, Nate noted how the robe sagged more on the right than the left because of something heavy in the pocket.

"Jolovich, where the hell are you? Peterson?"

The technician must be Peterson, Nate thought. He stepped out into the dim great room.

When Scoggins saw him, he instinctively did a little knee-dip of surprise.

Scoggins fired questions: "Who the hell are you? How did you get in here? Where's Jolovich?"

"Nate Romanowski. Used the keypad. Hiding."

"Hiding?"

"It's tough to find good help these days."

"But . . ." Scoggins sputtered, gesturing toward the security room down the hallway.

"Peterson isn't doing so well, either," Nate said.

Scoggins shook his head, puzzled. "Why are you here?"

Nate said, "Guess." He raised his weapon and said, "Come with me."

Scoggins shook his head. "No."

"Then you'll die where you stand."

Scoggins started to argue, then narrowed his eyes and squinted down through the dim light. Nate guessed all he could see was the gun.

"I can pay you more than they pay you," Scoggins said.

"I'm sure you can."

"Are you a reasonable man?"

"Never have been," Nate said. "Now come down."

Scoggins sighed and groaned and slowly made his way down the stairs. He was wheezing from the exertion, and when he got close Nate was shocked by how small and froglike he was just a few feet away. The sleeves on Scoggins's robe were long and hung past his hands, and he kept his arms at his sides. As the man passed, Nate again noted the weight pulling down the material of the robe from the right pocket.

"Are you going to let me get dressed, at least?"

"No."

"Jesus Fucking Christ," Scoggins said, looking up toward the ceiling. "Which one of my enemies put you up to this?"

Nate ignored the question and prodded Scoggins with the muzzle of his gun, then followed him through the vestibule and outside. Nate paused on the porch while Scoggins walked a few steps ahead and fumbled for the ties of his robe against the night chill.

"It's fuckin' freezing out here," Scoggins said, cinching his robe with his back to Nate, but actually reaching for his semiautomatic pistol in his pocket. He turned clumsily with the gun raised and Nate shot him in the heart. The impact lifted the man completely off his feet, and he collapsed in a half-naked tangle. The gun skittered across the flagstone portico.

⋆ ⋆ ⋆

He dragged the body bag with Scoggins, the server, and the pistol around the side of the house. Scoggins didn't weigh as much as he looked, and the nylon of the bag sizzled along the manicured grass toward the river. In the distance behind him, Nate could hear shouting and pounding from the three thugs trying to get out of the guest cabin. Other voices — from the cook and her husband — melded with the noise. Jolovich remained in his room and stayed quiet.

"I can't get the door open!" a man's voice shouted from the compound.

"Don't you think we know that, old man?" one of the thugs yelled back.

A woman's voice: "Go find Jolovich, Ron."

Ron: "*You* go find him. You know how he is."

Nate left the body bag on the bank and an opening in the wire fence. He splashed in the shallow water upriver to unanchor his boat. He pulled it behind him to the lawn, then lifted the body and the contents onto the floor of the boat and swung in.

Within a few minutes, river sounds overtook the shouting and thumping from the Scoggins compound. He withdrew his cell phone and powered it on again. When he had reception bars, he made the call.

It was answered after one ring. Nate could hear the whine of an engine in the background.

"Did you do some good?"

"Affirmative."

"Good man! How far out are you?"

28

"Forty-five minutes."

"Splendid! Magnificent! I'll be there."

Nate punched off.

The drift boat was slightly more sluggish because of the dead weight inside, but he stuck to the swift channels. The eastern horizon was banded with a creamy rose color, and the stars in that quadrant of sky were fading in intensity.

The temperature dropped as he powered the boat downriver, and the steam got thicker. He could feel waning body heat on his legs from the bag at his feet.

Nate tried not to dwell on what had just happened at the compound. He could sort that out later. Leaving Peterson and Jolovich alive were wild cards.

As he cruised in a fast current that took him down the center of the river, he saw the falcon watching him from the gnarled dead branch of an ancient cottonwood. It was a peregrine with a mottled light breast and sharp black eyes. He knew how unusual it was to see a peregrine in the open, and it chilled him how the bird seemed to focus on him as he passed, as if assessing his worth. Peregrines, as Nate intimately knew, were killing machines — the fastest predators in the sky.

That bird, Nate thought, had no *right* to pass judgment on him. Peregrine falcons, unlike other raptors, would target any kind of prey, whether ducks, rabbits, geese, cats, or mice. They were stone-cold killers.

So what was *he* now? He had no idea anymore, and shoved the thought aside. Unbidden, the image of his friend Joe appeared, an unreadable expression on his face. He shoved that aside, too.

In the distance, he could hear the buzz of a small plane approaching. Right on time. The old asphalt airstrip was less than a half-mile downriver.

CHAPTER
TWO

Saddlestring, Wyoming

A month later, Wyoming game warden Joe Pickett winced against an icy wind in his face as he stood with his hands jammed into his parka pockets on the top of a treeless mountain in the Bighorn Range.

"*Come on,*" he shouted to the tow truck driver, "you can do it." He knew his words had been snatched away by the wind.

The driver was named Dave Farkus, and he'd had no idea when he took the part-time job at a local towing and recovery company in Saddlestring that it would mean taking his leased one-ton up a steep mountain switchback road to the very top as the first big snow of the winter rolled across the northern horizon, headed straight toward them. Farkus had managed to get his 1997 Ford F-450 truck turned around and had backed up to the edge of the snowfield, but he was obviously having second thoughts about trying to retrieve the vehicle that was buried deep seventy yards away. All that could be seen of the buried pickup — Joe's departmental vehicle until he'd sunk it to the top of the wheel wells on an ill-fated run across the field two years before — was the dented top of its green cab and several radio antennas whipping back and forth in the wind. Farkus looked over at Joe through his closed passenger-side window and gestured with a *what-can-I-possibly-do-now?* shrug.

"Unwind the cable," Joe shouted, using his hands to mimic the action so Farkus could understand. Farkus pretended he couldn't and looked at Joe with the uncomprehending stare of Joe's yellow Labrador, Daisy.

Joe and Farkus had spent the last hour digging with shovels through the hard crust of snow around the back of the pickup until they located the rear bumper. While Joe continued digging until he uncovered the rear wheel, Farkus had walked back to his truck to bring it closer. He had taken an inordinate amount of time while Joe labored. The snow beneath the crust was grainy and loose, and for every shovelful he threw out, a half-shovelful filled in the hole. Beneath his insulated Carhartt overalls, Wranglers, red uniform shirt, and parka, he was sweating hard by the time Farkus showed up. The wind was cutting through it all, though, and he was chilled as he waited for Farkus to *do something*. He was afraid the strong wind was sifting the snow back into the hole he'd dug and would fill it up, at the rate they were proceeding.

Joe groaned and made his way to the tow truck and climbed inside. It felt good to get out of the wind into the warm interior, although it smelled of fast-food wrappers, grease, diesel fuel, his own sweat, and Farkus.

The view through the windshield was stunning, now that he could look at it clearly without squinting his eyes against the wind. Frozen blue-black waves of mountain summits stretched as far as he could see at eye level. Many were topped with white skullcaps of snow that had not melted during the summer, and between the ranges were deep wooded ravines and canyons that dropped out of sight. They were at least nine and a half thousand feet in elevation, above the timberline, where the only life was the scaly blue-green lichen on the sides of exposed granite boulders. The approaching storm clouds, rolling from the north with black fists, looked ominous.

He pulled his parka hood back and said, "We're going to need to take your hook and cable out there and wrap it around the rear axle. Then you can power up the winch to pull it out."

"That truck is buried *deep*," Farkus said, bugging his eyes with exasperation. "What if we try and it pulls my outfit into the snowfield with that storm coming? We might never get out."

"There's only one way we'll find that out."

Dave Farkus was fifty-eight and pear-shaped, with rheumy eyes, jowls, thick muttonchop sideburns that had birthed a full beard, and a bulbous nose. He worked hard at not working hard, but he'd shown an uncanny ability to get caught in the middle of several conflicts that had involved Joe as well. He wore a thick grease-stained down coat and a flocked bomber hat with earflaps that hung down on each side. Tributaries of frozen snot ran down his whiskers from his nostrils from helping Joe dig out the back of the truck.

"Joe . . . if I wreck this truck or leave it up here like you did . . ."

"No whining," Joe said. "You owe me this, remember?"

"Aw, jeez," Farkus said, sitting back and shaking his head. "That's not even fair."

Fifteen months before, Joe had helped Farkus by shepherding him out of Savage Run Canyon during an epic forest fire that had blackened thousands of acres of timber. Farkus had been injured at the time, and Joe's actions had saved his life. Joe didn't particularly like Farkus, and Farkus didn't particularly like Joe. But in the hospital under sedation, Farkus had said to Joe, "If there's anything I can ever do for you, just ask."

And Joe had asked, once he found out Farkus had had to go back to work when his disability claims had finally been denied by the state workers'-compensation division.

"How long has the damn thing been up here?" Farkus asked.

"Two years," Joe said. And one month.

"I'm sure the state has written it off by now. Who the hell cares if we even get it out?"

"I do," Joe said.

Joe had been at the wheel, trying to drive across the perennial snowfield to connect with his friend Nate Romanowski when he'd buried his departmental vehicle. The ridge overlooked the South Fork of the Twelve Sleep River far below, where Nate was about to

34

get into a gun battle that would change the course of his life. Joe had to abandon his vehicle and climb down the mountain on foot. The snows had come before he could convince a vehicle-recovery company to try and retrieve it. The summer before, another recovery company had made it as far as the summit before turning back, saying they couldn't risk damaging their equipment on such a foolish mission. Joe had lost another entire year because the fire the summer before had blocked the access road and littered it with downed burned trees.

Joe wondered again, as he had constantly over the last year, where Nate was now, what he was doing. And whether he would ever see him again.

Farkus tried again: "Why don't we say we tried and go home before this storm hits?"

"That wasn't the deal."

"Why in the hell do you care so much about a wreck on top of a mountain?"

"It doesn't matter," Joe said. He wasn't willing to tell Farkus that he was on very thin ice with his new director, Lisa Greene-Dempsey, who never failed to mention that Joe Pickett was responsible for more real actual property damage than any other employee of the agency. She'd soon issue another year-end report with his name at the top of the list unless Joe could mitigate the cost by bringing back at least the last of his wrecked pickups.

"I'll go with you, come on," Joe said. "Let's go hook that cable on and get it out of here. Then we can get off the top before the storm hits."

As he spoke, he felt the vibration of his cell phone deep in his breast pocket beneath the parka. Cell service was spotty in the mountains, and it surprised him. A few seconds later, there was another call. He didn't want to take it, though, because he didn't want to give Farkus another excuse to delay.

"If I wreck this truck, my boss will take it out of my hide," Farkus said. "I could lose my *job*."

"Since when have you wanted a job, anyway?" Joe asked. "Now, let's go."

"That was mean," Farkus said.

It took nearly an hour of winching, digging, repositioning the tow truck, and reattaching the hook and cable to free the pickup and drag it out of the snowfield and position it on the wheel lift of the truck.

Joe's satisfaction on getting his old pickup out sank by degrees when he watched it get winched through the snowfield. The pickup was a wreck. The windows had been crushed inward by the weight and pressure of the snow, and the cab was packed with it. He couldn't even see the steering wheel inside. The sidewalls were dented and the rear left tire was flat. He could only guess at the condition of the motor and drivetrain after being encased in ice for two years. If anything, the pickup might provide some parts, but it would likely never be put into service again. Meaning he'd still top the list.

Farkus cursed under his breath as they cinched the nylon web ties on the rear wheels of the pickup.

"Okay," Farkus hollered, when the straps were tight. "Let's get out of here."

"Give me a minute," Joe said, stepping back to the cab and opening the driver's-side door.

"What in the hell are you doing?"

"Checking something," Joe said, digging out handfuls of snow from inside until he could reach behind the bench seat and feel around. *It was still there.*

He closed the door and climbed back into the cab of the tow truck with Farkus.

"What was that all about?"

"Never mind," Joe said, relieved.

"We're getting off this damned mountain with our lives," Farkus said.

"We've done it before," Joe smiled.

"It's barely November. And it's *snowing*."

"It always snows up here."

"But I'm sick of it!" Farkus said, hitting the cracked dashboard with the heel of his hand in anger. "I want to move someplace where it's warm and flat. I'm sick of mountains and this damned horrible weather. I want to see long-legged women in bikinis! Most of all, I'm sick of having guns pointed at me and animals falling out of the sky and nearly drowning. Do you know how much my hospital bills are?"

"No. But when did you start paying your bills?"

"Just stop it, Joe, goddamnit."

As Joe scooped packed snow from his cuffs and the collar of his shirt, he remembered the calls he'd received earlier and dug out his phone.

One from Governor Rulon's office. The other from his oldest daughter, Sheridan, a junior at the University of Wyoming. Rulon had left a message Joe wouldn't be able to retrieve until they cleared the timber and got back on the highway, where there would be cell reception. Sheridan, typical of kids her age, hadn't. In fact, Sheridan rarely used her phone as a phone. It was more of a texting device.

Both calls had come completely out of the blue.

The falling snow lightened in volume as Farkus maneuvered the tow truck down the mountain. Because the wreck on the back made the truck longer, Farkus had to carefully negotiate sharp turns in the burned timber to stay on the road. Twice, Joe could hear the body of the old truck scraping against tree trunks and damaging it further. Because many of the trees were standing dead, Joe feared the impact might knock them over and crush the cab of the tow truck. He told Farkus to slow down and be more careful. Farkus threw up his hands and complained that they may not make it to the highway before it got dark.

"That's why you have headlights," Joe said.

"Still . . ."

"Try not to beat up that pickup or knock down any trees until we get on the road, please."

"If you think it's so damned easy, you can drive," Farkus huffed.

Joe dismissed him and thought about Sheridan. For the past two months, she'd been the resident assistant at her dormitory at UW and they hadn't heard much from her. She claimed to be wildly busy with school, activities, and managing a coed floor of freshmen.

38

Sheridan's tuition was paid by a trust established under duress by her grandmother Missy — Marybeth's mother — although there were additional expenses Joe and Marybeth were responsible for. Sheridan communicated primarily through cryptic texts and cell phone photos of herself at football games and parties, which made Joe wince every time. It was unusual for her to actually call, and more unusual for her to call *him*.

"Finally, thank God," Farkus muttered, as they turned from the rough mountain trail onto the two-lane state highway. "Where do we drop off this wreck?"

"My house."

Joe lived in a small state-owned home on Bighorn Road, eight miles from Saddlestring. It was en route from the mountains.

"So who is going to pay me for this?"

"Give me your bill and I'll send it in," Joe said, distracted. He was waiting for the NO SERVICE indicator on his phone to give way to cell phone reception.

"Shit," Farkus groaned, "I have to wait for the *state* to pay me? That'll take months."

"Maybe. Sorry."

"Do I at least get a tip?"

Joe said, "Never trust a man who wears white shoes. There's your tip."

"Very fucking funny."

Joe nodded.

"At least say we're square now?" Farkus said.

"We're square."

Joe waited, staring at his phone.

"I've got to get on the Internet and look for someplace warm to live," Farkus said. "Someplace with sun and an ocean I can look at. Maybe I can hook up with a boat captain and take rubes out deep-sea fishing. I haven't tied a fly in months, but I could learn some of those exotic patterns and —"

"Excuse me," Joe said, turning away. Two reception bars had appeared on the display screen of his phone, and he called Sheridan first.

The message said, "Please enjoy the music while your party is reached," and launched into a bad song from a bad group Joe had never heard before. He sighed, waited, and left a brief message that he was returning her call and that she should call him back or wait twenty minutes and call the house. She *never* answered her phone on the first attempt, and like every college student Joe knew, she didn't have a landline in her dorm room.

As soon as he rang off, Farkus continued on as if he'd never stopped. "I've been reading about these bonefish out in the salt flats. They feed on little crabs, I guess, and all a man needs to do is learn how to tie an imitation crab on a big-ass number-two or -four hook. It looks easy to me, much easier than these complicated little trout patterns on a size-twenty-two —"

Joe said, "Give it a rest, Dave. I've got to check a message from the governor."

Farkus shut up mid-sentence. "Our governor? *Rulon?*"

"Yup."

"Well, ain't you the big shot?" Farkus said, whistling. Then, as Joe punched in his message code, Farkus mocked him: "*I'm Joe Pickett and I'm so important I've got to check a message from the governor —*"

"Please shut up."

Joe listened to the message.

"This is Lois Fornstrom from Governor Rulon's office." She was the governor's personal secretary. "Governor Rulon requests the pleasure of your company — that's how he put it — tomorrow morning in his office. He said to tell you he's sending his plane to the Saddlestring Airport at nine with a return to Cheyenne tomorrow and he'd like you to be on it. He said the matter was important and he doesn't really care if you don't like flying. You're to meet with the governor for twenty minutes and you'll be flown back in the evening so you can pack."

That was all. *Pack? For what?*

Joe said, "Uh-oh."

"Sounds like trouble," Farkus said with a wicked grin.

"Yup."

Joe stared out the passenger window of the tow truck as Farkus drove down Bighorn Road. Small herds of mule deer looked back from just inside the trees as dusk melded into darkness, and for a quarter of a mile a coyote ran parallel to the truck in the borrow pit before veering off into the brush.

He'd been wondering when Rulon would call.

It had been over a year since he'd quit his job with a combination of anger and sorrow, thinking he could no longer work for the bureaucracy. That, and his new director, LGD, who had told him of her plans to modernize the agency and bring him in from the field to work at her side at a desk in Cheyenne. Leaving law enforcement had also allowed him to complete a case against a federal official who would have been tough to nail within the system.

When it was done, he'd looked up and considered his family finances — his wife, Marybeth, had just lost a business opportunity to renovate a grand old hotel in the heart of town and would return to her part-time job at the library; he had one daughter in college, and both their ward April and youngest daughter, Lucy, were on the way; their savings would last them three months at the most; and he couldn't imagine starting over in a new career at his age. Joe refused to even consider public assistance of any kind, or unemployment benefits. Plus, he loved his job as a game warden — being out in the field every day in his pickup or on horseback or in a boat. He knew the land, the wildlife, and the rhythms of his district as if they were his second family. Every morning, he looked forward to pulling on his red uniform shirt with the pronghorn antelope patch on the sleeve, clamping on his weathered Stetson, and gathering his gear and weapons — and his dog — to take out to his pickup in the predawn light.

Luckily for Joe, Governor Rulon had always had a soft spot for him, even though he wasn't sure why. And once again, the governor had slipped him his card in a moment of crisis and said, "Call me."

Joe had. Within a week, he was a game warden again and had retained badge number twenty-one, meaning his seniority in the department was twenty-first of the fifty-two wardens working in the state. Over the objections of Director LGD (Joe had heard through the grapevine), Rulon instituted a fifteen percent salary increase for Joe from his own discretionary funds and added the title *special liaison to the executive branch* to Joe's job description. He'd called the governor's office at the time to ask what that meant. Joe recalled the conversation as if it had just happened.

"This new title —" Joe started to ask, but he was cut off by Rulon, who was doughy, red-faced, charismatic, unpredictable, and a year into his second and final term of office.

"Fancy, huh? Sounds official as hell, doesn't it?" the governor said so loudly Joe had to move the phone away from his ear. Joe had learned years before Rulon didn't simply talk. He *boomed*.

"But what does it mean, exactly?"

"Hell if I know. I'm still figuring it out."

"Do I report to you, or to the director, or what?" Joe asked.

"You still report to your director. Nothing changes, except I'd like you to stay out of trouble with her so you don't make me look like a buffoon for this. Can you do that?"

"I hope so."

"Keep your nose clean, Dudley Do-Right," the governor said, chuckling at his own joke.

"I do appreciate this."

"You should," Rulon said. "It's one of those things I probably never should have done. But hell, I only have three years left and what can the bastards possibly do to me now?"

Joe didn't know which bastards. Rulon faced lots of them, according to Rulon. Legislators, environmentalists, lobbyists, industry hacks, but most of all the Feds. According to Rulon, they were assaulting him in human-wave attacks, even though he was of the same party affiliation. Democrats were a rare breed in Wyoming, but Rulon was immensely popular.

"So," Joe asked, "why me?"

"Ha!" Rulon laughed. "Why do you think? I'm a terrific judge of men and character. That's how I got where I am. And you, Joe, have the uncanny ability to irritate the right people and cause havoc when you bore in like a pit bull. I want you to do that for me if I ask."

Suddenly, it was clear.

"Think of yourself, once again, as my range rider," Rulon said. "I'm the benevolent and kindly ranch owner, and you're the hired gun I send out to solve my problems. You did it before, and you can do it again."

Joe said, "You exiled me last time, if you'll remember."

"Had to!" Rulon said, as if it were the most natural thing in the world. "It was reelection time and you were stinking up the joint with your hijinks. We had to hide you for a while. But that's behind us now."

44

Joe was speechless.

"Just be ready," Rulon said, already distracted with something else on his desk by the way his attention had flagged. "If I call, you need to respond. It could be anything and at any time. LGD will understand — sort of. So cowboy up and be my range rider and make me proud!"

With that, the governor slammed down his phone.

Joe had been waiting ever since.

They released the old truck on the side of Joe's garage and Farkus roared away toward town on Bighorn Road. When he was gone, Joe opened the driver's door again and dug out the frozen urn of his father's ashes that he'd left behind the seat years before. He'd never known where to spread them — no place seemed *right* — and he'd stashed them behind the seat until he could figure it out.

It was his father's last dirty trick, sticking his son with his ashes and not enough good memories to determine a proper place to leave them. Even so, Joe didn't want the urn to be discarded or sold by a used-parts dealer somewhere.

He put the urn on his workbench in the garage to deal with later.

A gleaming black late-model pickup with Texas plates was in front of Joe's house. He'd never seen the truck before, and his guard was up as he pushed through the front gate toward the door. All the lights were on in the house and Marybeth's van and April's new acquisition

— a fifteen-year-old Jeep Cherokee — were parked on either side of the Texas pickup.

He never knew who might be waiting for him at his house because it also served as the local game warden station. Hunters, fishermen, and locals often simply dropped by, wanting him to personally explain regulations, mediate disputes, or lobby for some kind of action. It was a burden on Marybeth because she had to serve as a kind of unpaid receptionist and assistant, and something his girls had grown up with: having strangers — sometimes covered with blood — simply show up at their door.

There was an animated conversation going on in the living room when he entered the mudroom and hung up his parka and unlaced his Sorel winter pac boots. April was chattering away, and a male voice was laughing and urging her on.

Joe didn't like that.

April had recently turned eighteen and was a senior at Saddlestring High. Despite a very troubled past and an antagonistic relationship with both Joe and especially Marybeth, she had turned a corner the year before and become . . . a cowgirl. She worked after school at Welton's Western Wear, one of the oldest retail stores in operation in Saddlestring, selling hats, boots, belts, yoked cowboy shirts, jeans, and outerwear to locals and tourists alike. She'd gone from troubled Goth to bubbly cowgirl so quickly it'd left both Joe and Marybeth almost breathless. Joe had expected the phase to end, but it hadn't. In fact, April had embraced the new April to the point that she now socialized almost exclusively with the cowboy clique at school and seemed to have withdrawn from the Goth and slacker cliques entirely. It was as if she'd stepped out of an old uniform and pulled on a new one, and her persona had changed as well. She had blossomed from a morose and bitter girl with black fingernails to one who wore Cruel Girl jeans, square-toed turquoise Fatbaby boots, bejeweled belts, and tight western tops that showcased her buxom figure in a way Joe found alarming. The young cowboys felt otherwise. They flocked around her at school and work and sometimes drove by the house at night, hoping to catch a glimpse of her through her bedroom window.

Warily, Joe entered the living room.

April sat sidewise on one end of the couch with her legs tucked under her, leaning forward attentively toward a compact young man in a black cowboy hat on the other end of the couch as if at any moment she might spring at him.

She looked at Joe and her eyes brightened and she said, "Daddy!"

April had never called Joe Daddy before in his life. He was taken aback.

"Daddy, this is my" — she giggled at her hesitation — "*friend* Dallas. Dallas Cates."

She said the name with a triumphant whoop.

The young man jumped to his feet and turned with a practiced grin on his face. He was shorter than Joe but had wider shoulders and biceps that strained at the fabric of his snap-button western shirt. He was lean and hard, and his face looked to be constructed of a series of smooth, flat white rocks — sharp cheekbones, wide jaw, heavy brow. There was a two-inch scar on his left cheek that tugged at the edge of his mouth in an inadvertent sneer. His neck was as wide as his jaw and projected raw physical power.

Cates's belt buckle was the size of a silver saucer, Joe thought.

The young man removed his hat with a graceful swoop of his left hand and pressed the brim to his breast while he reached out with his right to Joe.

"It's a real pleasure to meet you, Mr. Pickett," he said as he gripped Joe's hand a little too hard.

Dallas Cates was a local legend, and Joe had run into him before. Cates had graduated from high school a few years before after winning the National High School Finals Rodeo three times in a row in bull riding. He was also a former state wrestling champion. An amazing athlete, Cates had had his pick of rodeo scholarships and had chosen the University of Nevada, Las Vegas, where he won the College National Finals Rodeo his first two years before quitting and going pro and moving to Stephenville, Texas, where so many other national rodeo cowboys lived. People in Saddlestring and throughout the state followed and tracked his weekly winnings the way southern NASCAR fans followed the Sprint Cup Series.

But that wasn't all there was to Dallas Cates.

"What are you doing in my house?" Joe asked without a smile.

48

Cates's grin didn't lose its wattage, but something hardened in his eyes and he didn't let go of his grip on Joe's hand.

"Daddy!" April cried, jumping up to intervene as if she planned to wedge herself between them. "Don't embarrass me like that. Dallas came into Welton's this afternoon to say hello to everybody. Wrangler has him touring stores in the country for its boot-cut jeans. He stood right next to that life-size promotional display we have of him and took pictures with everybody. I told him about Mom's horses and he said he'd like to see them someday, so I invited him out tonight. That's all." Somehow, she remained cheerful during the explanation, Joe thought. Where had the old April gone?

Joe said, "So if you've seen them, I guess you'll be going."

Cates looked to April and arched his eyebrows in a questioning way.

"Of *course* he won't be going right away," April said, playfully prying Joe's and Cates's hands apart. "He might even stay for dinner."

"That sounds like a nonstarter," Joe said flatly.

Lucy, their sixteen-year-old high school sophomore and a blond, lithe dead ringer for a younger Marybeth, appeared in the hallway with a textbook and her homework, likely on her way to ask Marybeth a question. When she saw April and Dallas Cates, she haughtily rolled her eyes, spun on her heel in a perfect one-eighty, and marched straight back to her room.

"Don't think I didn't see that, Lucy," April called after her.

Lucy's bedroom door slammed so hard, pictures on the walls jumped.

"She's the annoying one I told you about," April said to Cates, who shrugged. Joe noticed Cates's eyes had lingered on Lucy for a beat too long.

April turned back to Joe, her face expectant: "And there's something I need to ask you and Mom."

"Now probably isn't the best time," Cates cautioned, turning his attention from the hallway to April.

"It's about the NFR in Las Vegas next month . . ."

Before Joe could object or April could make her case for attending the National Finals Rodeo in Las Vegas, Marybeth stepped into the kitchen doorway and said sharply, "Joe, can I talk to you for a minute?"

As he entered the kitchen in a dark rage, she kissed him on the cheek and said, "Welcome home."

Joe grunted.

"The testosterone was getting so thick in there I could cut it with a knife."

CHAPTER
THREE

Cheyenne, Wyoming

Over Chugwater in southeastern Wyoming, Joe leaned over in the passenger seat of the governor's Cessna Citation Encore small jet — dubbed *Rulon One* — and chanced a look outside the window. His stomach was in knots and his fingers gripped the armrests so tightly he was afraid he was leaving permanent impressions.

The terrain below was a sea of taupe and white: high prairie and patches of snow as far as he could see. There were a few skeletal trees choking the riverbeds, and the occasional lonely ranch building. Herds of cattle and pronghorn antelope dotted the terrain. If it weren't for the commas of snow, the vista looked almost African, like documentary footage he'd seen of the Serengeti Plain. He was less than a half-hour from Cheyenne.

The accordion door for the cockpit folded and the copilot looked back at Joe with a mixture of amusement and malice. He looked too young and fresh-faced to be at the controls, Joe thought.

"How's it going back there, partner?"

"Dandy," Joe said sourly.

"Don't like flying much, do you?"

Joe glared his response.

The copilot said with a smile, "There's wind in Cheyenne — imagine that. It might be a little bumpy on the approach. Just pretend you're riding a bull."

"No thanks," Joe said, thinking of the bull rider that had infiltrated his household.

Dallas Cates hadn't stayed for dinner the night before, despite April's begging him. He'd mumbled something about "knowing where he wasn't wanted" and said good night to *Mr. Pickett* and *Mrs. Pickett* and thanked them for their hospitality while he gathered his NFR coat. April went outside with him to say good-bye.

"You remember that character Eddie Haskell on *Leave It to Beaver*?" Joe asked Marybeth.

"I was just thinking the same thing," she said, moving a steaming casserole dish of lasagna from the oven to the range top to cool. "What is it between you two?"

"I don't like him."

"That was obvious."

"Good."

"I'll go let Lucy know we're ready to eat," Marybeth said, trying to stifle a smile. After she passed Joe, she paused in the doorway and looked back.

"There's something else, isn't there?"

"I have to go to Cheyenne tomorrow."

"The governor called?"

Joe nodded.

He felt her eyes on him.

52

"Let's talk about this tonight," Joe said, not wanting April to return in mid-conversation.

Dinner had been frosty. April sat fuming and pushing bits of food around on her plate after returning to the house. Joe had noted that it took her ten minutes to say good-bye to Dallas Cates, but he didn't remark on it.

Marybeth tried to elevate the mood by saying things like "Isn't this nice to all be around to eat dinner together?" but her words seemed to clunk against the walls. Joe noticed that Lucy warily looked from her mom to April to Joe, waiting for the fireworks to begin.

Finally, Lucy asked if she could go to the movies on Friday night.

"With who?" Marybeth asked.

"Noah."

Joe grimaced. Noah After Buffalo was a Northern Arapaho from the reservation school. He was bright, polite, and handsome. Lucy had met him at a debate tournament where they competed against each other in dramatic interpretation. He seemed like a smart, well-adjusted boy. Still . . .

Marybeth asked, "Is he picking you up?"

"I don't know," Lucy said. "We haven't figured that out yet."

"Is he buying your ticket?"

Lucy shrugged.

Marybeth said, "When you get this all figured out, we can talk."

Lucy sighed a heavy, put-upon sigh.

"Have you heard from Sheridan?" Joe asked Marybeth.

"A couple of texts," she said. "She needs me to send her winter coat. I don't know how she forgot it. And she needs some money for books."

Joe waited for more, but that was it.

"She called me this afternoon and didn't leave a message," he said. "I was wondering if you knew why."

Marybeth looked up, concerned. "No."

"I'll try her again later," Joe said. "She never answers her phone."

"Try texting."

"I hate texting," Joe grumbled.

After a beat of silence, April slammed down her fork and glared at Joe.

"Tell me why I can't go to the NFR." She leaned forward and bared her teeth. *"Tell me why."*

"You'll miss school," Joe said.

"I'm getting all A's and B's," April said. "I can take a few days off. I'm a senior, you know. I'm going to graduate."

Joe looked at Marybeth for support.

Marybeth said, "April, how would you even get to Las Vegas? Where would you stay? How could you afford it?"

"Don't worry about that," April said. "I've got it covered. It won't cost you a dime."

"That's not it," Joe said, trying not to let his anger show in his voice. He knew she had a point.

"No, it isn't, is it?" April said. "This is about Dallas."

Joe said, "Yup."

Marybeth said, "April, you need to give us some details. You need to have a plan before we can even consider it. So far, I haven't heard anything."

Joe noted the crack in their united front.

"You and your *plans*," April said, rolling her eyes. Then: "Look, I can take care of myself. I've got a job and a car. You people forget I'm friggin' *eighteen*."

"And he's twenty-four," Joe said.

April turned on him and shouted, "*Aha!* I knew that was the reason."

"It's a big one."

April sat back in her chair and shook her head as if she couldn't believe the incredible ignorance she was hearing. She said, "This is Dallas Cates, PRCA champion bull rider. He could have asked any girl on the planet to go to the NFR and watch him ride, and he asked me. *Me!* And you two act like I'm too stupid and immature to know what I'm doing."

Joe said, "Well . . ."

"The hell with both of you," April cried out, and pushed away from the table. She rose and did an aggressive shoulder roll before stomping down the hallway toward her room. The slam of the door made the pictures on the walls jump — again.

"I'll go talk with her," Marybeth said, getting up.

When she was gone, Lucy looked to Joe with her eyebrows arched and said, "April. She's *b-a-a-a-a-ck*."

In bed, Marybeth put down her book and asked Joe what it was about Dallas Cates, besides the age difference, that bothered him.

Joe said, "Do you remember the name Serda Tibbs?"

Marybeth's reaction indicated she did.

Eleven years before, when Joe had been on the job in the Saddlestring District for only two years, he'd heard the call from the sheriff's department over the mutual aid channel. A half-naked girl had been picked up by a deputy while walking away from town down a rural county road. The few clothes she had on were ripped and dirty, and she was bruised and appeared to be in shock. If it hadn't been in September when the weather was mild, she might have died of exposure out on that road.

Serda Tibbs was a sophomore and new student at Saddlestring High School. Her parents had recently moved from the Deep South, and her father was out of town on a roughneck crew. Under questioning, she said she could barely remember what had happened to her after she'd left after school with a group of local boys who said they were going to show her around the county. The boys were popular and well known, all of them athletes and older than her. Her blood alcohol level indicated she'd been drinking heavily, but she said something had happened to her beyond that. The medical tech at the hospital suspected she'd been slipped a date-rape drug although the testing was inconclusive. They did confirm, though, she'd been assaulted and left on the side of the county road.

Because she was new and didn't know where she was, she had walked the wrong way to get back to town.

Four boys were arrested, all members of the football team. Joe had no involvement in the investigation, but he knew how the crime rocked the community. The boys eventually confessed and the two younger perpetrators were sent to a juvenile facility and the older two to the state prison in Rawlins. Serda Tibbs withdrew from high school and her family moved to Oklahoma.

"How does Dallas figure into this?" Marybeth asked Joe.

He said, "Serda never named all the boys involved, because she was so damaged by it, but Deputy Reed told me he suspected it was five of them, not four."

Reed was now the sheriff of Twelve Sleep County.

"He always thought the fifth was Dallas Cates," Joe said. "Dallas wouldn't admit to it, and the other boys didn't name him. Reed said he thought they were scared of what he would do to them, and he could never make a case. Dallas was *the* big shot at the school then, if you'll remember. That's when he was winning the high school finals and state wrestling. He had an ability to intimidate his competition then, and he still does. Reed suspected he intimidated those other boys to keep their mouths shut."

"My God," Marybeth said. "And he was in our house."

Joe nodded. "We need to keep him away."

"Should you tell April?"

Joe nodded.

Marybeth was still for a long time. Then she said, "Do you think it will make any difference?"

"I'm not sure," Joe confessed.

He hadn't slept well the rest of the night, and was at the airport looking at the sky for *Rulon One* an hour before he needed to be there.

"Magic City of the Plains dead ahead," the copilot announced through the open accordion door. "Welcome to Cheyenne — the three hundred fifty-fourth most populous metropolitan area in the United States."

Joe nodded grimly and gripped the armrests.

"As I said, it's likely to be a little bumpy."

"I'm getting used to it," Joe said, as much to himself as to the copilot.

That morning, before leaving his house, he'd stuffed Sheridan's winter coat into his backpack.

The director of the Wyoming Game and Fish Department, Lisa Greene-Dempsey, was inside the cinder-block state terminal to greet him. Joe was surprised. Director LGD, as she preferred to be called, had been in her job for a little over a year, and her philosophy and policies were beginning to take effect throughout the agency. Her goal from the beginning was to "modernize" the agency, turning it from what some called the Wyoming "Guts and Feathers" Department into a more progressive body that embraced diversity, wildlife appreciation, and environmental stewardship. Nearly a dozen longtime game wardens and fifteen percent of the headquarters administration had retired.

Director LGD was wiry, fidgety, and wore rimless glasses that made her eyes look bigger than they were and gave her a perpetually startled look. She had short, straight brown hair parted on the center-left and a habit of waving her fingers like a pair of flushing birds when she talked.

She strode up to Joe as he entered the terminal and grasped his hand with an exaggerated motion and said, "How are you doing, Joe?"

"Fine, boss," he said warily as she pumped his hand.

"When I heard you were coming today, I thought I'd take the opportunity to ride with you to the capitol."

He nodded politely.

She grasped his arm and steered him through the terminal toward a waiting green departmental SUV. Her administrative assistant, named Brandi Forgey, was at the wheel. LGD climbed into the backseat with Joe.

"Brandi," LGD said, "take us to the capitol and use the scenic route, please."

Forgey nodded and put the SUV into gear. The ride to the governor's office normally took less than ten minutes.

"We don't have much time before we get there," LGD said, leaning toward Joe. He fought an urge to recoil.

"I need you to give him a message for me."

"Does this mean you're not going to be in the meeting?" Joe asked her.

LGD shook her head abruptly and forged on. "I haven't been asked. This arrangement the governor has with you is very unusual, and I can't say I like it. The governor doesn't seem to honor our system of chain of command and structure. Neither, frankly, do you."

Joe shrugged with a *what-can-I-do?* gesture.

"We're not close, the governor and I," she said, looking away from Joe. "I've been instructed to communicate with the governor's staff via email. He prefers it that way."

"Oh?" This was news.

"He's a busy man. Anyway, our agency desperately needs a new appropriation the next fiscal year to open our pilot WAC."

Joe looked back, puzzled. "WAC?"

"Wildlife Appreciation Center," she said with irritation. "Haven't you been keeping up with my 'Memos from the Director'?"

He was caught. Since taking over, Director LGD had been sending out electronic memos to all employees about her plans for modernizing the agency. Joe had stopped reading them months ago.

"Sorry," he said. Then: "But I did finally retrieve that pickup from the top of the mountain . . ."

She dismissed his sentence with a wave of her hand. "Not now, Joe."

"I thought that was important to you," Joe said.

"Not as important as the WAC program," she said. "Anyway, we sent the proposed language to the governor's office six weeks ago so he could request the funding from the legislature and put it in his State of the State address. He hasn't even responded. We really need him on board with this."

Joe shook his head. "So you're asking me . . . *what?*"

She bore in. "To urge his support for the program. We can't expand our mission beyond blood sports unless the governor is behind it."

He cringed. Joe hated when hunting and fishing were called "blood sports." Most of the hunters and anglers he knew, both male and female, did so out of tradition or for subsistence or taste for wild game. Blood was a by-product. Plus, a growing number of anglers practiced catch-and-release.

"Oh, look," Brandi Forgey said as she eased to the curb in front of the gold-domed capitol building. "We're here already."

Something dark passed over Director LGD's face, and she turned toward her driver.

"You were supposed to take the scenic route."

"Sorry," Brandi Forgey sang.

"Well, I had better be going," Joe said. As he did, he saw a twinkle in Brandi Forgey's eye reflected in the rearview mirror. It was in that little signal that occurred silently between staffers that they recognized that neither had much respect for their mutual boss. Joe tried not to wink back.

"Don't forget to ask him about the WAC program!" Director LGD called out to Joe while he quickly gathered his backpack and climbed out of the SUV. There was a real strain of desperation in her voice.

As he walked across the brown grass toward the steps of the building, he again thought there was no way he could ever work among the politicians. He'd rather be on top of a windswept mountain with the likes of Dave Farkus.

Lois Fornstrom, the governor's personal secretary, recognized Joe immediately and waved him through the anteroom to Rulon's office. Several people sat in worn lounge chairs, obviously waiting for a word with the governor. A stocky man in an ill-fitting suit with a briefcase on his lap objected, saying he had been waiting for two hours. To Joe, he looked like a lobbyist of some kind — a slickster.

"He's come all the way from Saddlestring," Fornstrom said without sympathy.

"I came from Arlington, Virginia!" the man said, red-faced.

Joe stayed out of it and smiled at Fornstrom and entered Rulon's private office. He closed the door behind him.

The governor was on the phone when he entered, and he looked up and waved Joe toward one of two chairs in front of his desk. Joe took off his hat and put it crown-down on the other chair and waited.

The governor had two offices — a larger public room used for bill signings, press conferences, and small groups, and this close and intimate office, which was dark, book-lined, and cluttered with memorabilia. A buffalo skull embedded with an ancient stone arrowhead dominated the wall behind the governor, and a tooled John Wayne Winchester Model 1873 lever-action carbine rested on a deer antler mount.

Rulon had once told Joe he kept it loaded. Joe didn't doubt it.

Rulon said into the phone, "You read the legislation, so why are you asking me? It says if you send any of your agents into our state to enforce federal gun laws, we'll arrest them and throw them into the pokey. That's what it says, that's what I signed, and that's what we'll do."

Rulon looked up at Joe and shook his head, exasperated. He *loved* giving it to the Feds. And the voters loved when he did it.

"That's right," Rulon said to whoever was on the other end, "and don't start with the 'gun culture' canard. We don't even have a *gun culture* in Wyoming. It's just part of who we are. Our murder rate is damned low, too. You folks might learn something from that where you are. So spare me your lectures."

Joe could hear a raised voice on the other end of the phone, and Rulon rolled his eyes and studied the ceiling. Joe looked up, too, and for the first time saw the dozens of pencils stuck into the ceiling tile. They looked like icicles hanging there. No doubt the governor had tossed them up there over the years, and many stuck.

"Our time is up," Rulon said, suddenly impatient. He leaned forward in his chair, and the person on the other end continued to make his case.

"Tell you what," Rulon said, "send them up here. Try me out to see if we're serious. How about *that?*"

The governor slammed down the phone and said to Joe, "ATF bastards."

"Ah," Joe said.

"The damned Cowboy Congress hung me out to dry with this one. Sure, I signed it. But the Feds aren't pleased."

Joe knew Rulon's description of the Wyoming legislature was *Cowboy Congress*. But he said it with some affection.

The moment the phone was cradled, Rulon had punched the DO NOT DISTURB button. And just that fast, the issue with the man from the Bureau of Alcohol, Tobacco, and Firearms was behind him.

"Good to see you, Joe."

"Thank you, Governor."

Rulon asked about Marybeth, about Saddlestring, about Sheriff Reed in a perfunctory manner. It was how he always established common ground. Wyoming had so few residents the governor practically knew them all, and familiarity was essential to his success and popularity, Joe knew.

"How are you getting along with your new director?" Rulon asked, probing Joe's face with intensity.

"Fine, I guess. She picked me up at the airport this morning."

"Really?" Rulon asked, immediately suspicious.

"She asked me to relay a message —"

"*Auuugh,*" Rulon groaned, cutting Joe off. "Is it about those damned Bambi-hugging stations of hers?"

"She called them Wildlife Appreciation Centers."

Rulon rolled his eyes. "She thinks I'm made of money. Everybody does. I wish I could relive the day I let the fetching Mrs. Rulon convince me to name her good friend and fellow rabble-rouser Lisa Greene-Dempsey as the Game and Fish director. It was kind of a difficult time in our marriage, and . . . enough about that. We all make mistakes. Even me, as surprising as that may sound."

Joe bit his tongue.

"Okay, to the business at hand," Rulon said, shooting out his sleeve to check the time on his wristwatch. Joe knew it to be a signal to be quiet and listen.

"We have ten minutes before we're interrupted," Rulon said.

"Okay."

"How much do you know about Medicine Wheel County?"

Joe's heart sank. For a game warden, it was a district that was assigned as punishment.

"Am I being sent there?"

"So you've been there?"

"Passed through it on the way to South Dakota years ago," Joe said.

Rulon said, "Those people up there . . . are peculiar. I don't say that about many places in this state, and what I say in this room stays in this room, right?"

"Right."

The governor swiveled in his chair and addressed the top right corner of a huge framed state map on the east wall.

"Those people up there are insular, inbred, cranky, and they didn't vote for me in the last election. So to hell with them, I say. They remind me of hill people from somewhere else. More of them are on welfare and assistance per capita than any other county in the state. I don't like them, and they don't like me."

Joe nodded that he understood what Rulon was saying even if he didn't necessarily agree with it.

"It's a shame, too," Rulon said, "because that country up there is damned beautiful. It's just too bad those cranky bastards live in it, collecting government checks. I'd just ignore them the best I could, except there's a problem up there.

"Have you ever heard the name Wolfgang Templeton?"

Joe felt a twinge. He *had* heard the name, but he wasn't sure he could recall the details. It wasn't an easy name to forget. Rulon didn't wait for Joe to conjure up his recollection.

"Templeton is a mystery man, an enigma," Rulon said. "Nobody seems to know where he came from or where he got his money. But six years ago, he bought this magnificent old place — the only way I can describe it is as a castle — deep in the heart of Medicine Wheel County. It's called Sand Creek Ranch. I've never seen it, but I've heard plenty. You can research the history of it later. We don't have time for that now.

"Anyway, this Templeton has bought up most of the private holdings up there. He's got his own little fiefdom, but he keeps completely to himself. No one up there — those cranky bastards — will say much about him other than they seem to revere the guy. Or they're scared of him — one of the two."

Joe was intrigued. Not that large landholdings weren't often purchased by wealthy out-of-state owners

— they were. But an extremely wealthy man buying up most of an impoverished county — that was unusual. Then it came to him, what he'd heard . . .

"The Feds suspect Templeton of being involved in organized crime," Rulon said. "Actually, that's not exactly right. They have suspicions that Templeton is operating some kind of extremely high-end murder-for-hire business. They're very vague about what it is they think he's involved in or what he's under suspicion for. But for the last three years, they've been sniffing around and asking questions and bothering me. They assume since he lives in Wyoming that we must know about him, and they wonder why we don't cooperate."

Rulon let that hang there for a moment.

"So why don't we cooperate?" Joe asked.

Rulon whacked the top of his desk with his open hand. "Because we don't know a damned thing about him other than what I just told you. This Templeton pays his property taxes, licenses his vehicles, and minds his own business. No complaints have been brought against him, so there's been no reason to investigate the guy. Apparently, he has an airstrip and his own plane, and he leaves for days and weeks on end — but we don't know what he does. Normally, I wouldn't care. Wyoming citizens can do whatever the hell they want as long as they don't hurt anyone else, as far as I'm concerned. But you know how it is here. There is just enough talk — and these federal suspicions — that I'm getting a little nervous about it."

Joe was surprised. He said, "I thought you were generally at war with the federal government."

"I am," Rulon said emphatically, "and that isn't going to stop. It's one thing to be independent and tell them to leave us the hell alone and to go piss up a rope because we have plenty of mineral wealth. I have no problem doing that. But I have to pick my battles, you know? I can't let it be insinuated that we're harboring some kind of criminal threat, or that I'm letting this state be used as the base of operations for organized crime. We can't give those bastards any more reason to go after us."

Rulon sighed and leaned forward and lowered his voice. He said, "The theme out of Washington these days is 'reward your friends and punish your enemies.' I give them fits on all kinds of issues, but I do it to protect the citizens of this state. I can't give those bastards a justification or excuse to marginalize us any further, or punish us. We've got to make sure our own nest is clean, if you know what I'm talking about."

Joe thought he did. He said, "Where do I come in?"

The governor steepled his fingers together and peered at Joe over them. "You've always had this ability to get into the middle of things. And when you do, you look at the situation in a clear-eyed way. At times, it's annoyed me and I just wished you'd gone on with your business. But it is a unique gift, and I recognize that.

"Joe," Rulon said, "you're my range rider — a seeker of truth. You're my man on the ground, like before. Only this time, you can't get directly involved in the situation and you need to be wary not to embarrass me."

Joe felt himself flush.

Rulon said, "To be honest, Joe, you weren't my first choice."

"Oh?"

The governor's face was grave. "Two weeks ago, I asked my Division of Criminal Investigation to send a man up there to gather information. Not to storm the castle or throw his weight around — just to get the lay of the land and report back. It was done on the sly, but my guess is it didn't take long for those cranky insular hill people up there to figure out there was a stranger in their midst. It didn't work out, and now I have blood on my hands."

Joe sat up. A state DCI agent had been murdered?

"We can't prove anything," Rulon said. "But the poor guy burned to death in a motel fire."

"Okay, I read something about that," Joe said. "A fatality in a unit of some mom-and-pop motel. But no mention that he was with DCI."

"It took some real arm-twisting to contain that story," Rulon said. "We wanted to wait on revealing his identity until it was proven the fire was arson or an arrest could be made. We even asked the FBI for help with the investigation, but they couldn't determine any kind of foul play. It was a fire caused by our man smoking cigarettes and falling asleep in bed, they said. Nobody up there talked, and there is nothing to go on to prove it wasn't a stupid tragic accident."

"But you don't believe that?" Joe said.

"I don't know what to believe," Rulon said. "I just know I don't think the best way to find out about

69

Templeton or what's going on up there is to walk around with a state DCI badge, asking questions."

Joe said, "Ah, now I get it."

"Thought you would. Do you know the game warden up there?"

Joe said, "Jim Latta. I don't know him well."

Said Rulon, "No one in Medicine Wheel County will suspect anything if Jim Latta gets some help from a fellow game warden. Happens all the time, as you know. That way, you can get access to that county in a way no one else could."

"Do we let Latta know what's going on?" Joe asked.

"Your call. I'd suggest you wait to see if you can trust him. I'll let Lisa know that you're being sent up there to give a hand to Jim Latta, and she can let him know to expect you."

Joe was taken aback. Was Latta under suspicion as well?

Rulon said, "I've asked our man at the FBI to fill you in on all the details of what they've got, and he's supposed to be here any minute."

"Your man?" Joe prompted.

"Special Agent Chuck Coon. I believe you know him."

Joe smiled. He'd worked for years with Coon.

"He thinks you can be a loose cannon," Rulon said. "I couldn't disabuse him of that notion with a straight face."

"He's a good man," Joe said, and meant it.

"Too damned tightly wrapped, if you ask me. But a lot of those lifers are like that. Anyway, he said he'd brief you on what they know and establish some kind of line of communication and support if you need it."

Joe nodded, then asked, "If the FBI has these suspicions, why don't they send one of their own?"

Rulon snorted. "If those cranky hill people up there identified my undercover DCI guy, how long do you think a Fed in sheep's clothing would last? Those guys might as well have *FBI* tattooed on their foreheads."

"I see your point," Joe said, slightly overwhelmed with the implications of his assignment.

But this was Rulon's way: he was to work *for* the governor but *through* the FBI, with his own agency director providing bureaucratic cover without even knowing it. Thus, several layers of deniability were established if the situation went sour.

Rulon said, "For damn sure don't clue in the sheriff up there. That might have been the DCI agent's first mistake."

Joe nodded and gulped.

Rulon again shot out his sleeve. "And we're out of time." He stood and shrugged on his suit jacket. He said, "Thanks, Joe."

"Hold it," Joe said, standing. "I have a hundred questions."

"I'm not surprised. Maybe somebody can answer them for you."

"Governor . . ."

Rulon turned as he reached for the door handle. He said, "Joe, you know how this works. I smoothed the way for you to come back and even goosed your salary.

And I left you completely alone. Now I need your help."

He narrowed his eyes and said, "I'm not asking you to get involved in anything up there, and I damned sure don't want you risking your life. I can't have any more casualties on my conscience. But find out what the deal is with Templeton, and let us know. Stay in the shadows, or the sagebrush, in your case. Just report back. Don't let things get western, okay?"

With that Rulon left Joe in his office, clutching the brim of his Stetson. He could hear the governor booming welcomes and homilies to a group of visitors in his larger office.

As he turned to exit, Lois Fornstrom stuck her head in the doorway and said, "Mr. Coon of the FBI is waiting for you."

Joe clamped on his hat and shook Coon's hand in the anteroom, careful not to make eye contact with the citizens and lobbyists still waiting for a session with the governor.

Coon had aged since Joe last saw him. His chest and neck were thicker and his boyish face was cobwebbed with stress lines. He wore a dark blue suit, a red tie, and loafers.

He said, "Long time, Joe."

"Yup."

"Even longer would have been better."

"Good to see you, too, Chuck."

"Follow me. I have a feeling you're not going to like what I'm about to show you."

CHAPTER
FOUR

Who is Wolfgang Templeton?

Joe and Special Agent Coon spent the ten minutes it took to drive from the capitol to the Federal Building updating each other on their families. Although he was the same age as Joe, Coon had started his family later in life and was going through situations Joe found strangely nostalgic. Coon's oldest daughter was in her second year of high school and had turned sullen, spending all of her time with her friends or texting with them in her room. Joe laughed, saying it sounded familiar. Coon's son was in the eighth grade and was a struggling point guard for the McCormick Warriors.

"He assumes he'll get bigger, faster, and quicker," Coon said. "How do I tell him it may not happen?"

Joe shrugged. "Just go to the games and cheer him on. Believe me, he'll be the first to know."

Joe outlined what was happening with Sheridan, Lucy, and April. As he did, Coon shook his head.

"Three teenage girls," he said. "And I thought *I* had trouble."

"They're not trouble," Joe said. "But they're weighing on my mind right now."

* ★ ★

Inside the ugly Federal Building in central Cheyenne, Joe surrendered his weapon, cell phone, badge, cuffs, and bear spray, and argued with the officer to keep his hat. Coon intervened and told the security officer it was all right. Joe traded his possessions for a VISITOR laminate that he clipped on the breast pocket of his uniform shirt. They rode the elevator together — Joe's normal life was without elevators — and he followed Coon through a large room filled with cubicles and out-of-date computers to the supervisor's corner office.

Joe liked Coon, and they'd been involved in several situations over the years, although from different angles. Coon was professional, straight-up, and generally by-the-book. He'd chosen to stay and work in the Mountain West and not use the smallest state FBI office as a stepping-stone to a more high-profile post, unlike his predecessors. When Joe sat down, Coon outlined the agreement he'd reached with the governor's office: Joe would go to Medicine Wheel County and report directly to Coon, and he'd advise Rulon; Joe's role was not law enforcement or investigation but information gathering; Joe was *not* to represent himself as either an agent of the FBI or the governor's office; Joe was to extricate himself immediately if the situation turned dangerous.

Joe raised both of his hands shoulder height and dangled them and said, "Do I look enough like a puppet to fit the bill?"

"Very funny," Coon said. "The idea here is Medicine Wheel County locals are used to seeing their game

74

warden poking around. Your presence won't stir them up. And if they get an idea to check out your credentials, they'll find out that you are indeed a Wyoming game warden of many years."

Joe lowered his arms to his lap. "This is unusual," he said, "you working with the governor instead of against him."

Coon said, "I know it appears that way sometimes, and believe me, I have higher-ups who don't exactly like your governor. But I'm trying to mend some fences here. This antagonism between the national government and the states out here can't last forever. And if we can work together on this, everybody wins."

"Gotcha."

"So, who is Wolfgang Templeton?" Coon asked rhetorically from behind his desk. "Answer is: we're not sure."

For the next half-hour, Chuck Coon leafed through a file on his desk and hit the highlights. When Joe reached for his spiral notebook to take notes, Coon said it wasn't necessary, that the file in front of him was a redacted copy and that he'd give it to Joe to take with him to study when they were done. Joe sat back and listened, shaking his head several times.

Wolfgang Peter Templeton was born on a country estate between Porters and Pickerel lakes in eastern Pennsylvania to a father who was a college dean and a pediatrician mother. He'd been sent to private schools and appointed to West Point. Templeton had served as an officer in the army and was decorated for heroism for acts during the invasion of Grenada in 1983 when he was a commander in the army's Rapid Deployment Force, consisting of the 1st and 2nd Ranger Battalions and the 82nd Airborne Division paratroopers. His niche was Special Ops. After twenty years in the service, Templeton had retired from the military and founded one of the first hedge fund companies in New York City and was wildly successful and an influential leader in global high finance and an annual participant in the World Economic Forum in Davos, Switzerland. Templeton had married Hillary (Rothschild) Swain of Sagaponack in the Hamptons, New York — she was one of two heirs to the Allegheny Group, a consortium of defense contractors. The wedding had taken place at St. Patrick's Cathedral with a massive reception at Tavern on the Green that was covered by the *New York Times*. He was a Republican and rumored to have political ambitions and had given the green light to an exploratory committee in his home state of Pennsylvania, with his eye on the U.S. Senate.

Coon slid four eight-by-ten photographs across his desk, and Joe caught them. In the first and most dated, Templeton wore combat fatigues and cut a striking figure on a beach — probably Grenada. In the second, he wore a tuxedo and stood arm in arm with a beautiful woman — Swain, no doubt — in a flowing white wedding gown. In the third, he stared straight at the camera lens from behind a desk with the Manhattan skyline visible through the window behind him. The last photo was of Templeton at a lectern with other well-dressed men and women, obviously signaling the morning opening of the New York Stock Exchange.

Templeton was lean and angular, with an almost old-fashioned regal bearing, Joe thought. He had a strong jaw, an aquiline nose, large hands, and wide shoulders. His eyes exuded intelligence, competence, and warmth. In the most recent photographs, Templeton wore a thin mustache that gave him a rakish air, like a 1930s movie star.

In 2001, Coon read, Templeton divorced and suddenly sold his firm for millions just prior to 9/11 and seemed to vanish. There were short items noting his sudden departure in the *Wall Street Journal* and *Investor's Business Daily*, with one of the journalists speculating that Templeton, like Icarus, had perhaps "journeyed too close to the financial sun" during his meteoric rise. Joe thought perhaps that was when he'd first heard the name — while reading the *Wall Street Journal* in his dentist's office.

Coon paused and looked up at Joe and said, "I feel like I'm reading about the interworkings of an entirely different planet."

"For the first time in my life, I feel like James Bond," Joe said.

"The bureau had no interest in Templeton during his military career, his rise in business, and his decision to move on with his life," Coon said, nodding at the materials on his desk. "In case you were wondering."

"I was," Joe said. "Then why the file?"

"This was all assembled later, after 2006," Coon said, thumbing back. "The backstory was put together by staffers in Washington."

"So what's the front story?" Joe asked. "Why was a file on him even opened?"

Coon explained that Wolfgang Templeton's name first came up in an interview with a confidential informant seven years prior, during an investigation of a U.S. senator who was suspected of accepting bribes from Middle Eastern governments. The CI knew the senator from their mutual participation at the World Economic Forum in Davos, and during the interview he brought up an unrelated event: the still-unsolved kidnapping of a scion of a privately held brewery fortune in Saint Louis in 2004. The heir to the fortune, Jonah Lamprecht, was bad news on wheels, Coon said. Lamprecht was a forty-six-year-old playboy who'd been arrested twice for aggravated assault and forcible rape but had lawyered up and beat the charges both times.

"Lamprecht was high-profile," Coon said, "and sort of a poster child for slipping date-rape drugs to young women and assaulting them. One victim finally came forward and three other women said, 'Me too.' You can imagine how the Lamprecht family felt. Jonah was also supposedly involved in sex-tourism rings and excursions to Thailand and the Dominican Republic."

Coon said Lamprecht had enough underworld connections — and enemies — that when his Lamborghini Aventador was found parked and empty on a tree-lined road at the St. Louis Country Club, no one was shocked. When a ransom letter arrived

78

demanding $5 million for his safe return, the extended Lamprecht family had brought in the FBI. A second letter arrived three days later, saying that because the family had disobeyed instructions not to involve law enforcement, Jonah would be killed.

Coon said, referencing the file, "No suspects were ever found, and no body. The letters were analyzed and provided zero evidence of any kind — no fingerprints, DNA, nothing. They were postmarked from Saint Louis and printed on a laser printer with Microsoft Word. The case remains open. But this CI told our people that it was whispered among the big shots at Davos that members of the Lamprecht family had hired someone to disappear Jonah two years before. The name he floated was Wolfgang Templeton. According to the CI, it was understood among the hoity-toity Davos types that if any of them needed something done in their private lives or businesses and they were willing to pay a ton of money to get it done right, Wolfgang Templeton was the man to contact.

"That's when the file was opened," Coon said, thumbing ahead. "Now jump to 2008. Two Columbia grad students launched a computer application in their dorm room that supposedly, through some kind of voodoo algorithm, would go out and search the Internet and assemble an email list of like-minded consumers based on their social network posts and Internet searches and crap like that. They claimed they could create surefire customer lists for specific products. When the word got out, all the big Internet companies beat a path to their door because no one else had been able to figure it out yet so specifically. Everybody wanted to buy their little start-up, and the bidding began. We're talking billions of dollars here —"

Joe said, "I know the rest. I remember reading about it. Just a week or so before the auction, a third grad student named Brandon Fonnesbeck pops up and says the two guys stole the algorithm from *him*, and he claims he has emails from them to prove it. Then, before he can reveal the evidence, Fonnesbeck's boat is spotted off of Long Island and he's not on it. His body is never found."

Coon raised his eyebrows, impressed. "And here I thought you spent all your time checking fishing licenses."

"What do *you* know?" Joe said sarcastically. "Continue."

Coon smiled. "So three years ago, another CI is in a bar in Silicon Valley, drinking vodka with a group of high-tech CEOs. They're railing on and on about Apple — how they hate Steve Jobs, who they say keeps stealing stuff out from under them and making billions of dollars from their work. One of these guys jokes that they ought to get together and pool funds and hire somebody to disappear Jobs. It's a joke, and they never did anything. But when Jobs died of natural causes, our CI remembered the conversation. Guess what name came up that night?"

"Wolfgang Templeton," Joe said.

"Correct," Coon said. "Which says to me there is a certain name recognition of this guy among a certain level of people. The kind of people who travel on private planes and own multibillion-dollar firms. We're talking about a level where high-finance types and politicians mix together — the *elite*. They interact with one another at conferences and forums like Davos. And when they talk off the record to each other about their problems, apparently the name Wolfgang Templeton comes up."

Joe nodded and sat back. The hook was set.

"Have you ever questioned him?" Joe asked.

"Me personally, no. I've never laid eyes on him. But after his name came up on the Lamprecht kidnapping, two agents from our New Orleans office — Templeton was living in one of those old plantation mansions at the time, I guess — went and knocked on his door. He said he had no relationship at all with the Lamprecht family and had no idea what they were talking about. They described him in the file as very courteous and helpful, but useless in their investigation. The agents had nothing to pin on him — no witnesses, no evidence — just that his name had come up. Reading it, well, it's kind of embarrassing. Templeton had alibis for the date of the kidnapping, and those agents were sent home with their tails between their legs."

"And now he lives in Wyoming?" Joe said, shaking his head. "How'd that happen?"

"That's what we'd like to know," Coon said. "Apparently, he sold out in New Orleans shortly after that visit by our guys and quietly bought the place in Medicine Wheel County. He did it under the radar, through third-party firms. Nothing illegal about that, but it indicates a penchant toward secrecy."

Coon paused, looking over the transaction records. "But again, I guess it isn't so unusual among the rich and well connected. They know if word gets out that they're interested in a certain property, the price might go up. So they conduct an anonymous transaction that keeps their name out of it until it's done. And when he relocates to Wyoming, the file goes cold. The bureau has so much on its plate these days we couldn't devote any manpower to what really amounts to snippets of gossip."

Joe waited for the other shoe to drop. It did.

Coon said, "But now there's something else much more recent. In fact, just a month ago, and I'm sure you've heard of it."

Joe waited.

Coon said, "The disappearance of Henry P. Scoggins the Third."

Joe sat up. Of course he'd heard about it. Scoggins had vanished from his own fishing lodge on the Bighorn River under the watchful eyes of a private security team. Speculation had run from kidnapping — which seemed unlikely, even though the questioning of locals and members of the Crow tribe had brought accusations of harassment and racism — to the possibility that Scoggins had sleep-walked into the river during the night and drowned. His body had never been found.

"What do you have that might tie Templeton to Henry Scoggins?" Joe asked.

82

"Practically nothing," Coon said, and rubbed at his face with his hands, "except Scoggins seems to fit the profile. Extremely wealthy. Hated bitterly by his enemies, who are also extremely wealthy and connected, and among that elite set we just identified. No explanation for his disappearance. No body. Except this time we might have a lead, although it's a damned thin one."

Coon paused for a long time.

Joe said, "Now comes the part I may not like, right?"

Coon nodded wordlessly and flipped to the last few pages of the file.

"The affidavits from the security team seem hinky to me, but you can be the judge of that when you read them over. Something happened that night they're not being truthful about, is my intuition. That's all it is — intuition. I'd like to question them myself — especially this Jolovich guy, who was the head of the security detail. But right now, I don't have enough backup to call him in or make the trip.

"But we have two other pieces that interest me and I think will interest you."

Coon said, "A member of the Crow tribe named Benny Black Eagle was bait-fishing on the river before dawn the morning after the disappearance. He said he saw a private plane land on an old abandoned runway about a mile upriver from where he was. He saw a man carry a big duffel bag of some kind from the river to the plane, and then the plane took off, heading southeast."

"Could he identify the man or the pilot?"

Coon shook his head. "Too far and too dark. He could barely see them at all. But we know there was no FAA flight plan filed by anyone for that morning for that airstrip."

"The bag —"

"Could have been the size of a body. But maybe not. He wasn't sure. But we do know Templeton has a pilot's license and at least one private plane, maybe two."

Joe was confused. "Where is this headed?"

Coon said, "The tribal police up there talked to a couple of members — girls — who told them about meeting a Caucasian a couple of days before Scoggins disappeared. The guy gave them a ride from the Scoggins compound to a bar near Hardin. They really liked him, but they didn't get his name. A police artist was called in, and here's what he came up with." He handed a rough composite across the desk to Joe.

He looked at it. A rough face, hawklike nose, piercing eyes. Joe felt a chill roll down his back.

"Something else," Coon said, sliding over a mottled black-and-white photo. "All the electronic surveillance of the Scoggins compound was disabled and the hard drives were missing from the computers. But there was an old trail cam mounted on a tree the bad guys must not have known about."

Joe was familiar with trail cameras that were used by landowners and hunters to get nighttime images of passing wildlife. He'd used trail-cam images to implicate poachers on private land as well.

The photo was grainy and of poor quality, and had obviously been enlarged. Tree trunks were brilliant white stripes against black, and the brush looked haunting and skeletal. The single image was unfocused, but in the distance he could clearly see the form of a man who appeared to be leaning forward as he walked, as if dragging something heavy behind him.

The side of his face couldn't be clearly seen, but the set of his shoulders and the outline of his frame were familiar enough.

"You know him best," Coon said. "Is that your pal Nate Romanowski?"

"Can't say for sure."

"How in the hell did he get mixed up with Wolfgang Templeton, is what I'd like to know," Coon said.

"Me too," Joe whispered.

"When was the last time you saw Nate Romanowski?" Coon asked.

Joe looked up. The FBI had been trying to find Nate for years to question him about several unsolved disappearances. Coon had not pursued the search with the intensity of his predecessors, but Nate was still listed as a federal fugitive.

"Last year," Joe said. "He showed up at my home and helped me out with that train wreck of a search for Butch Roberson."

"I can't recall you reporting that to me," Coon said icily.

"That's because I didn't."

"But you've not seen him since?"

"No," Joe said. "Nate is . . . unusual in his habits. He'll just show up, and we never know where he goes when he leaves."

"Any idea where he's been living?"

"No. I assumed Idaho, but I might be wrong."

"My guess," Coon said, "is he's now based in Medicine Wheel County."

Joe took a deep breath. "Nate has his own style. But he's not a kidnapper or a hired killer."

"Are you sure about that?"

Joe took a moment to answer. "Somewhat."

Joe recalled the last time he'd seen his friend. Nate had come across as slightly unhinged — more excitable and more violent. Joe attributed it to what Nate had gone through the year before that, when he'd been tracked down by an old mentor.

Had Nate discarded his unique set of principles and gone off the deep end?

Coon said, "Take the file and study it. I've got a conference call with Washington in five minutes on another matter. Call me if you've got questions, and keep me informed on what you find out when you get up there. And, Joe, don't do anything stupid."

Joe didn't respond. He was still reeling from the revelations.

"Joe?" Coon prompted.

Joe looked at his watch. It was nearly noon. He had four hours before *Rulon One* was scheduled to take him back to Saddlestring.

"Can I borrow a car?" Joe asked.

"You want to borrow a government car? You? With your track record?"

Joe grinned. "My daughter needs her winter coat and you have a motor pool full of government cars."

"I swear, if anything happens to one of our vehicles, I'll take it out of your hide," Coon said, shaking his head.

"What could possibly go wrong?" Joe asked with a slight grin.

CHAPTER
FIVE

Laramie, Wyoming

His plastic tray slid along the tubed aluminum railing, and Joe followed Sheridan through the buffet line of the Mongolian Wok food station in Washakie Dining Center at the University of Wyoming. The cafeteria was bustling at lunchtime, and Joe knew how much he stood out by his uniform — and his age — by the number of interested and appalled stares he received from students. Sheridan noticed it as well and smiled in sympathy over her shoulder while taking a plate of thin noodles with strips of beef and Mongolian hot sauce.

They'd passed up the burger bar, the sandwich bar, the salad station, and four other offerings that Joe preferred as he followed the lead of his daughter.

Joe leaned toward her and said, "Things have changed in this place. When I went to school here, we had a choice of Spam with green beans or macaroni and cheese."

"Yuck," she said, rolling her eyes.

Sheridan was dressed like most of the other students: UW hoodie, skinny jeans, boots, backpack. She was blond and clear-eyed and striking, Joe thought, more mature for her age than most of the students that

88

gawked at him. He admired her self-assurance, and she seemed no longer embarrassed by the presence of one of her parents, which had been the case in her first two years. He understood.

He stared at his plate and said, "I don't know what I'm eating."

"Stir-fried noodles with beef, shrimp, and veggies," she said, since she'd ordered for him. "Give it a try."

He grunted and stabbed at the strips of beef with a fork. Sheridan used chopsticks. The food was better than he'd imagined it would be.

"Thanks for bringing my coat," she said.

"You'll need it."

"No kidding." She gestured with her chopsticks through the windows toward Grand Street. It was spitting snow.

"So April has a boyfriend?" she asked, looking at him slyly.

"How did you know?"

"Facebook. She decided to friend me again, and I read about it last night. Is it really Dallas Cates?"

"Yup."

"He's trouble with a capital *T*," she said. "I'd try and tell her that, but she'd just think I was being bitchy and trying to tear her down. Or accuse me of trying to steal Dallas or something like that."

Joe nodded. Although the relationship between Sheridan and April had thawed a bit, it was still contentious. April was a hard customer.

"She's not real happy with you and Mom right now," Sheridan said.

"Tell me about it. That was on the Internet, too?"

She nodded.

"I hate Facebook," Joe said.

Sheridan chuckled.

Before he could ask why she'd called, Sheridan said, "So what brings you down here?"

He hesitated. The words that came to mind — *mission, special assignment* — sounded too fraught with intrigue. He said, "The governor asked me to help with an investigation up in the Black Hills. He could have asked over the phone, but he brought me down here instead."

She paused and studied his face, looking for clues beyond what he'd just said.

"Don't do that," he said. "Your mother does that."

"It's so we can figure out what you're really saying," she said breezily. "So you can't really talk about it, huh?"

"That's right."

She smiled to herself for getting to the heart of it.

He asked, "Have you happened to have heard anything from Nate the last couple of months?"

"Nate?" she said, looking up, surprised. "No. Why?"

Sheridan was Nate's apprentice falconer, and the previous year she'd started flying her first bird. The kestrel had performed as it should and reconfirmed her fascination with the sport. She'd mentioned from time to time that Nate had sent her emails and offered tips on flying the bird. They'd released the bird prior to

90

school starting, with the hope that Sheridan could get another in the future.

"Just wondering," Joe said.

"Does this thing you're doing involve Nate?"

Joe shrugged. "I hope not." But the black worm of dread that had formed in his stomach when he saw the trail-cam photo had grown over the past hour.

"If you see him, well, tell him hello from me," she said. "Tell him he's been a bad master falconer lately."

Joe smiled. "I'll tell him."

They ate until the silence became an issue. Then Joe said, "You called me yesterday. Was it a real call or a pocket call?"

"A real call, I guess," she said, avoiding his eyes.

"It's okay to leave a message," he said. "In fact, if you left a message I'd have some idea what was going on and not worry about it."

"I *know*," she said.

"So leave a message next time. What were you calling about?"

She took a deep breath and seemed to weigh her response. "It seems kind of stupid now."

"Try me."

"There's this guy on my floor," she said, and Joe immediately felt himself tense up.

"He's a transfer student from California," she said. "Los Angeles, according to the directory. I don't know much about him, but he gives me a really bad vibe."

Joe lowered his voice and said, "What kind of bad vibe? Like stalker vibe, or predator vibe, or what? Is he harassing you?"

"No, no, nothing like that," she said, moving her hands as if erasing his implication from the air. "He hasn't said two words to me since the semester started. He hardly talks to *anyone*."

Joe pushed his plate aside and urged her on. He knew she had second thoughts about involving him by the way she hesitated with the details. He didn't want to come on too strong so she'd back off.

"Okay," she said. "His name is Erik Young. He's a junior, which is weird right there. All the other kids on my floor are fresh men. Everybody else lives off-campus. When he didn't come to the mandatory orientation at the dorm, I thought, 'Okay, he's been through all this stuff before, so no big deal. Maybe he's shy.' When I saw him in the hall, I introduced myself as the RA and he just stared at me. His eyes reminded me of falcon eyes — black and kind of dead. Do you know what I mean? Then he walked right past me as if I wasn't there."

"Does he speak English? Is it possible he's an exchange student who doesn't know the language?" Joe asked.

"That's what I wondered at first, too. That he was just shy or not comfortable with the language. But that's not the case. His roommate told me Erik had talked to him a little, but what he'd said weirded him out. In fact, his roommate said he was crazy and transferred out of the dorm the first week. Now Erik lives as a single in his room. All he does is play first-person shooter games on his computer. I had to knock on his door a couple of times to ask him to turn the volume down. Erik turns the sound down, but he won't open the door or apologize or anything."

Joe said, "First-person shooter games?"

"Yeah. If you stand outside his room, all you can hear is *BLAM-BLAM-BLAM* and explosions going off."

She sighed. "You know, I've really tried with him. I'm not trying to be his best friend, but it just gets to me when I say hello or ask him a question and he just puts those eyes on me and moves on. He has no friends, dresses in all black, and totally keeps to himself. In fact," she said, as her voice dropped to a whisper and she looked over Joe's shoulder, "there he is."

Joe instinctively started to turn in his seat, when he felt Sheridan's hand on his.

"Don't stare," she said. "He'll know we're talking about him."

"Gotcha."

Instead, Joe gathered his plate and stood with his tray, looking around the room as if to locate where to deposit it.

Erik Young stood a few feet inside the entrance to the cafeteria, as if looking for a place to sit. Students flowed around him, but he was still, an island in a sea of motion. He was thin and had a pinched face with no expression. He wore a long dark coat that reminded Joe of a duster, but he was hatless. After a moment, Young backed out of the room without looking over his shoulder and nearly ran into a couple of female students who were entering. They glared at him, but he ignored them, and he continued backing away until he was gone.

Joe felt a chill run down his spine. He sat back down.

"See what I mean?" Sheridan said. "I can't believe he just showed up like that when I was telling you about him."

Joe said, "Have you talked to anyone?"

Sheridan nodded. "It's kind of embarrassing, you know. But yeah, I talked to the dorm administrator and even a guy from campus police. But all I could honestly say was that the guy just made me uncomfortable. They asked what you asked — has he said or done anything to me or threatened anyone — and I had to say no. See, he hasn't *done* anything. There are rules and procedures for this kind of thing, I guess. They can't really do anything or infringe on his civil rights unless he acts out in some way. That's what they told me."

"Does he have a gun?" Joe asked.

She shrugged. "It's against the rules, of course, but how would I know? The residents aren't supposed to have guns in their rooms, but a lot of these guys are hunters. Some RAs just kind of look the other way if they know the student is, you know, *normal*."

Joe sat back and looked at his daughter.

She said it first: "Let's just say if there was a mass shooting on this campus, he would be the first guy who would come to my mind. I know that's judgmental and not fair because I really don't even know him. But you saw him . . ."

"I did," Joe said. "Judging is fine with me. I trust your judgment and you should, too. Sheridan," he said with emphasis, "you've always been judgmental. You've seen a lot, and it's okay. Don't let college make you doubt your instincts."

"So what should I do?" she asked.

"It's a tough one. Keep your eye on him, that's for sure. Make sure your concerns are in writing and the administration has a record of them. That way, they can open a file of some kind. And if there is anything — *anything at all* — that he does or says or you suspect, you call the campus police and you call me one second later. Do you promise me you'll do that?"

She hesitated for a moment. Then: "Yes."

"Do you still have that pepper spray I gave you?"

She nodded.

"Keep it with you every second of the day."

"I will."

"Where is it now?"

Sheridan cocked her head in a way that indicated *Somewhere in my room*.

"Find it and keep it with you. And if you need to call me and I don't answer that second, *leave a message*."

She said, "What can you do if you're hundreds of miles away?"

Joe said, "You'd be surprised how fast I can get here."

After a beat, Sheridan said, "Now I feel kind of stupid. I didn't mean to get you worked up based on, you know, my *feelings*."

Joe reached out and grasped his oldest daughter's hand. "I'll do some background checking on this guy. I may involve the university folks if I learn anything. I'll try not to bring your name into it unless I have to. But in the meanwhile, don't feel guilty for telling me. You've done the right thing."

"Dad . . ." she said, and for a moment he could see in her face the little girl he remembered. "Thank you. I feel a little better."

"That's my job," he said.

"Please don't tell Mom. You know how she worries."

"I can't promise that. We don't keep secrets," Joe said. "But I'd suggest *you* let her know about our talk before I get home."

"She'll want to move in with me," Sheridan laughed, breaking the tension. "Then who would keep an eye on April and Dallas Cates?"

Joe groaned.

Sheridan said she had to go to class, and Joe accompanied her as far as the outside doors. She gave him a quick hug and a peck on the cheek, and as she left and joined the river of students headed toward the classroom buildings, he thought, *I won't let anything happen to you.*

Instead of walking to the U.S. government Crown Vic he'd borrowed, Joe joined the flow of students on an inner walkway toward the dormitories and, beyond that, the classroom buildings. He ignored a couple of young yahoos who said, "Hey, Game Warden, want to see my fishing license?" He kept his anger at bay as he walked, and he spotted Erik Young a hundred yards ahead on the walkway. The boy stood out in his

96

all-black clothing and by the way other students gave him space as he walked. Joe noted that: students who likely didn't know Young or had likely never seen him before instinctively stepped aside to let him pass. The boy had an aura about him.

And, Joe thought, there was nothing anyone could — or should — do about it. Yet.

Rather than continue on across the street toward the classroom buildings, Young branched off the sidewalk across the dying lawn toward White Hall. Keeping his distance, Joe followed.

Two girls were inside the vestibule of the building, passing their student IDs through a card reader to unlock the front doors. He pressed close enough to them so he could enter the building due to their access. When one of them glanced over her shoulder at him, the look of worry on her face vanished as soon as she made him: *a lost parent*. He knew he looked the part.

Young wasn't inside the lobby or near the dorm administration desk. Joe turned toward the double elevators to see one of them was occupied, and the lights indicated whoever was on it had taken it to the fourth floor. Sheridan's floor.

When the next elevator doors opened and three freshman boys stepped out, Joe went in. He instinctively rested his right hand on the butt of his .40 Glock as the doors closed and the car rose.

The fourth floor was quiet and empty. As the doors whooshed closed behind him, Joe cautiously walked down the hallway. Sheridan's room was at the end of the hall, emblazoned with a red RESIDENT ASSISTANT sign as well as a collage of photos and notices. He paused at her door. There was a photo of the Pickett family from the summer before in front of their house. He looked taciturn, Marybeth looked lovely, and the personalities of all three girls showed clearly in the shot: Sheridan attractive and self-assured; April smirking with the devil in her eyes; Lucy beaming as if she were in a pool of her own personal sunshine.

He turned and slowly walked down the hallway. The personalities and quirks of the freshmen were also displayed outside of their doors: photos, clippings, sports logos, quotes running from childish to profound. Except for one door halfway down. On that door there was a single white sticker with a name in a tiny font. He bent to read it. *Erik "fuck" Young*. The *fuck* had been scrawled by the same pen that crossed out the letters *n* and *g*. Joe wondered who had written it — another student or Young himself?

As he bent toward the door, he heard the sounds from inside that Sheridan had described: single gunshots, automatic fire, cries of pain, the roar of engines and helicopters.

He knocked on the door. No response. Then he rapped sharply, so there was no way the boy inside couldn't hear.

Joe wasn't sure what he was prepared to do or say. He settled on his standard opening when he visited a potential suspect, one that had elicited both immediate confessions and surprising information. He'd say, "I guess you know why I'm here."

But instead of answering, the game was reduced in volume. Erik Young refused to respond or open the door.

Joe left after five minutes.

Both the head of campus security and the vice president of student affairs confirmed Joe's worst fears: nothing could be done until Young actually *did* something. So far, he'd broken no rules or procedures. The fact that he dressed oddly and kept to himself violated no policies. While they could keep an eye on Young and he was now officially on their radar, they had to stay on the proper side of the line and not cross over into anything that would be perceived as harassment or discrimination. Joe left Laramie sympathetic but frustrated, and with a shadow of foreboding hanging over his head.

On the drive back to Cheyenne, again sandwiched between eighteen-wheelers, Joe called Coon's private cell number, and the call went immediately to voicemail.

"This is Joe Pickett," he said. "I'll leave your car at the airport with the keys at the counter. Thanks for lending it to me. So far, I haven't caused any damage, but I still have an hour.

"And I need you to run a name for me. Erik Young. Los Angeles, California. I'll spell that . . ."

CHAPTER
SIX

Saddlestring, Wyoming

That night, Joe stood near the stove in his kitchen and idly watched a musical performance taking place in the living room. He ate a grilled cheese sandwich Marybeth had whipped up and drank a Shiner Bock beer. He'd missed dinner — again — because of the flight from Cheyenne.

The living room furniture had been pushed back against the walls to create enough floor space for the show. Lucy had the lead. She had an earthy, lovely tone to her voice. Harmonizing — and interjecting clever scripted phrases — were fellow students LeeAnne Dow and Hannah Roberson, Lucy's best friend. They had all landed parts in a high school musical and had gotten together to practice their numbers. Marybeth told him LeeAnne and Hannah had made arrangements to spend the night as well.

April was bunkered in her room and had not eaten dinner or spoken to anyone since she got home from her shift at Welton's Western Wear. When Joe had knocked on her door, April yelled, "Go away!" He'd decided to leave her alone, although he did hope he'd have the chance to say good-bye in the morning.

As he finished his sandwich, the girls harmonized the chorus:

Black, yellow, brown, and white
Diversity is what makes the world seem right
Diversity, Dee-verse-i-teeeeee

"What are they singing about?" Joe whispered to Marybeth over his shoulder.

"Diversity."

Joe said, "Well, I got *that*. Is this for that *Rainbow*-whatever production?"

"*Rainbow Dreams*," Marybeth said. "Written and choreographed by the new music teacher, a Miss Shirley Lemmex, who is twenty-four and," she continued in a dramatic stage whisper, "*very enthusiastic.*"

Joe nodded. He didn't know LeeAnne well, but he certainly knew Hannah Roberson. Hannah visited her father, Butch — convicted of a double homicide the year before in the case Joe had been squarely in the middle of — once a month when she and her mother, Pam, made the long drive to Rawlins and the Wyoming State Penitentiary. Hannah had a secret she shared only with Joe, Marybeth, and perhaps Lucy. She'd weathered the last year, and Marybeth had gotten her into professional counseling and done her own kind of counseling as well: teaching Hannah how to care for and ride horses. She seemed to have taken to it, according to Marybeth.

There is no right, there is no wrong
It's our different cultures that make us strong
Diversity, Dee-verse-i-teeeeee

Joe cringed. "Is that all there is to the lyrics?" he asked.

Marybeth patted him on the shoulder and said, "I'm sure there's more to it."

"I hope so. I mean, don't we believe in right and wrong?"

"Don't be a grump," Marybeth said. "Appreciate how well they're singing, not *what* they're singing."

He drank the last of his beer in silence.

"I'm going out to feed," she said, patting him on the shoulder.

He nodded. It was her nightly routine.

He watched Marybeth pull on her canvas barn coat and slip into her high Bogs boots. Hannah broke from the song and asked her if she needed help with the horses.

Before Marybeth could answer, Joe said, "Thanks for asking, Hannah, but I'll go out with her tonight. You girls keep practicing."

"You will?" Marybeth asked him, surprised. Then she got it: Joe wanted to talk to her away from the singers.

The single bare lightbulb in the small barn threw harsh shadows through the bars of the sliding horse panels, making the inside where the horses shuffled look like a film noir jail. Marybeth measured out thick sections of hay between her hands from fifty-pound bales and pushed each through the hinged feeder panels into black rubber tubs on the other side. The three horses reestablished their nightly pecking order of who ate first: Rojo, Toby, and Poke.

Joe hung back near the barn door and admired his wife. When she was done dropping the feed into the stalls, she closed the panels and said, "How is Sheridan doing? You gave her that coat, right?"

"I did," he said.

Obviously something in his tone made her pause and look at him with concern.

He told her about Erik Young, and how he'd talked to the university administrators and asked the FBI to run his name through their database. Marybeth listened with worry in her eyes. Joe said he'd told Sheridan he would be there as fast as he could if she called.

"I wish I — we — weren't five hours away," she said, lowering her head and hugging herself in an involuntary gesture of mother's fear. "This is the kind of thing I have nightmares about."

Joe said, "Sheridan's smart, and she's aware of her surroundings. Much more so than I would have thought, to be honest. She'll do the right thing."

Marybeth quizzed him on the steps Sheridan had taken so far and who she'd talked with. She agreed the bases had been covered but wondered if Sheridan would consider stepping down from her RA role and possibly moving. As she speculated, she shook her head. "No, she'd never do that. She's like you," she said to Joe. "She doesn't have the sense to get out of the way of trouble."

Joe shrugged.

"I'm going to call her tomorrow morning," Marybeth said.

Joe said, "She made me promise I wouldn't tell you so you'd worry. So this has to be between us."

She winced. Joe was reminded of the special mother-and-daughter bond, and that by Sheridan reaching out to Joe first it would worry Marybeth even more.

"I guess she figured it was more up my alley," Joe said, looking at his boots.

"I understand," she said. "But that doesn't mean I'm not going to look into this Erik Young myself."

Marybeth often used library computers to access state and federal criminal databases. She wasn't supposed to know the passwords, but she did. Her skill at research and investigation had aided Joe countless times.

She said, "If Erik Young fits the profile, he's probably got a Facebook page or he's posted some things online. If I can find them and they're threatening, well, the university might have something to go on. These types don't operate in complete secrecy, from what I understand. They generally telegraph what's going on inside their heads.

"I won't tell Sheridan I'm doing it," Marybeth said, "but I'll let you know what I find. And Joe, if I find something, you've got to drop whatever you're doing and follow up *that minute*."

Joe said, "Yup."

"Oh," she said, smiling wistfully, "life was so much easier when they were all my little chickens and I could keep an eye on them because they were close. Now Sheridan's in another town, April's going off the rails because of a cowboy, and Lucy wants to start dating. I feel like they're all drifting away from me."

There were tears in her eyes, and Joe pulled her close. He said, "We've done all we can. You're the greatest mother I've ever been around — better than both of ours. Especially yours. They'll be all right. *You'll* be all right."

"But I've lost control," she said into his shoulder.

"That's part of the deal, I think," he said.

When she stepped away and wiped the tears from her cheeks, he outlined the assignment from the governor without going into many specifics and told her he was going away for a while and he didn't know for how long. He left out names but explained that there was a suspicion that a wealthy rancher in Medicine Wheel County might also be a high-society hit man.

"That's nuts," Marybeth said, shaking her head. "In Wyoming?"

"They suspect he uses his ranch as his base. As far as I know, he hasn't operated in the state. But I agree — it sounds nuts."

"What if they're right?"

He said, "Then maybe I can help bring him to justice. But like I told you, I'm under strict orders not to get too close. My job is to serve as eyes and ears only and to get out if the situation gets western."

Her shoulders dropped and she said, "You've never been able to do that, Joe."

It was cool enough in the barn that their breath puffed out in clouds of condensation. On the other side of the metal gates, the horses ate their hay in a methodic *grum-grum-grum* chorus.

"This time I will," he said. "Count on it."

She looked at him sadly, as if she knew more about him than he did.

Then he told her about the photos.

"It couldn't be *our* Nate, could it?" she asked, incredulous.

"Sure looked like him."

"There has to be an explanation," she said. "Maybe he was somewhere where he wasn't supposed to be, or it was someone who just looked like him from a distance."

"Could be."

She paused. "When he was here last year, there did seem to be something different about him. He seemed kind of unmoored, don't you think? Like he was really struggling with his own code?"

Joe nodded. They'd talked about it several times. He tried not to get miffed when Marybeth's thoughts turned to Nate after she'd had several glasses of wine, but they often did.

She said, "I know he's been through a lot and I can't even imagine what that would be like. But still, I can't see him turning into some kind of killer, can you?"

Joe said, "That's what I hope to clear up."

"I hope you do," she said, gathering the thick plastic grain buckets and stacking them together near the hay bales.

106

While she did, Joe turned and pulled down a thick turnout blanket Marybeth used to cover her horses in cold weather after she rode them. The blanket was wide and covered with canvas on the outside but had soft fleece on the inside. He flipped it inside out and unfurled it with a gentle snap.

The sound made Marybeth turn around.

"What are you doing?" she asked.

He spread the blanket over a two-foot-high shelf of hay bales.

She said, "You're not thinking what I think you're thinking."

When he didn't respond, she said, "Are you?"

He reached behind him and turned off the light. It was suddenly dark, and the only light was from starlight outside the stall doors. The horses continued with the *grum-grum-grum* sound.

"Joe," Marybeth whispered, "this is *crazy*. What if one of those girls comes out to check on us?"

He said, "Listen."

From inside the house, he could faintly hear:

Black, yellow, brown, and white
Diversity makes the world seem right
Diversity, Dee-verse-i-teeeeee

Joe said, "Our house is filled with girls and I'm going to be gone for a while. Watching you and listening to you tonight . . . well, you know."

"Oh, Joe," she said. But she wasn't angry.

When they were through, Joe buckled his belt in the dark and helped Marybeth find her missing boot. The singing inside still went on.

She said, "I can't believe we just did that. I think I have hay stuck inside my pants."

He laughed.

"And my horses probably watched the whole time. They probably thought you were attacking me or something."

Joe pulled her close and tilted her head up and kissed her.

They held hands on the way to the house and didn't let go until they reached the back door. Marybeth took a moment to comb bits of hay out of her hair with her fingers and smooth out her coat. She reached up and brushed several stalks of hay from Joe's shoulders.

"I think we're presentable now," she said. Before going inside, she said, "I hope it's not Nate."

Slightly deflated, Joe said, "Me too."

"And you promise you'll get out of Medicine Wheel County if it gets dangerous?"

"Of course."

"By the way," she said, swatting him gently on his backside, "thanks for the roll in the hay."

"My pleasure, ma'am."

"Don't make it a habit," she said, with gentle admonishment. "I don't want you to get the impression I'm easy."

CHAPTER
SEVEN

New York City

The same night, 1,927 miles away, Nate Romanowski sat behind the wheel of a white panel van outside a closed florist's shop on 74th Street on the Upper West Side of Manhattan. Since this was the third night in a row he'd been there, he had begun to recognize a few of the occupants of the brownstone apartment buildings on the street. They couldn't see him, though, due to the dark tint of the windows. There was the skinny lady with large, round sunglasses who left her building every night at six forty-five p.m. sharp, who would blast out the door as if the block were on fire and charge toward Broadway or Amsterdam to find a restaurant, he guessed, since she didn't return until after nine. There was the professorial-type man in his mid-fifties who came outside and stood on the stoop and furtively smoked a cigarette in obvious fear of being seen by passersby on the street or his wife inside. There was the balding middle-aged Wall Street type who walked his tiny but manically energetic toy fox terrier and looked as if he'd just hooked into a leaping trout.

Twice he'd seen Jonah Bank, the infamous New York stockbroker, financial adviser, and "wealth-management executive" who had bilked investors — many of whom lived within blocks of where Nate was parked — of over $9 billion in one of the largest Ponzi schemes in American history. That a banker was named Bank lent the scandal a twirl of irony.

But both times, the operation had been called off at the last minute.

Nate hoped tonight was the night. He was sick of New York and it made him tired. The thick air was filled with smells — taxi fumes, exotic cooking, the Hudson River, steam from the sidewalk grates — and sounds — blaring horns, sidewalk conversations, the throbbing hum of the city itself. It was sensory overload.

He missed thin air, big skies, vast quiet, and his falcons. He also missed his sense of righteous purpose, and yearned for it in the same way he yearned for Alisha Whiteplume and Haley. He wished that instead of being behind the wheel of a panel van in the middle of more than eight million people he was sitting naked in a tree watching the Twelve Sleep River roll by.

It wasn't the first time in his life he was completely out of his comfort zone. He could do the job. But he couldn't convince himself that he would take any satisfaction from it.

Nate had been sent to assist in the operation, which had been in the planning and reconnaissance phases for weeks. He was not the primary on the job. The primary, code-named Whip, had been in New York for over a month shadowing Bank and casing his habits and movements. Bank was in the midst of his first trial for

110

security fraud and was free for the time being to return to his home in The Dakota on West 72nd each night. Nate had never met Whip, although he'd seen a photo and had been briefed on him.

Whip was a longtime associate in the enterprise, and for most of it the only operator. As far as Nate could discern, Whip knew as little about him as he knew about Whip. They referred to each other by the code names given to them: Whip and The Falcon. Nate wondered if Whip liked the idea of an additional operator in the firm.

So far, Nate's communications with Whip had been via prepaid throwaway cell phones — a new phone and a new number every day — so neither could be tracked or monitored.

Upon Nate's arrival in New York, Whip had told him that Bank was literally untouchable during the daytime. He was picked up by federal marshals each morning and delivered to the courthouse of the Southern District of New York, and returned to The Dakota by two private bodyguards. Breaching the security at the building was nearly impossible, Whip said, and the problem with taking down Bank on the street was the proliferation of closed-circuit security cameras in the neighborhood: they were everywhere. Whip said he'd never seen so many cameras anywhere else except London.

Whip's voice was low and flat, and with a hint of a southern accent that Nate guessed was western Kentucky. Whip didn't try to get familiar with Nate in anyway, and used as few words as possible to convey information. Nate was fine with that, and he guessed Whip had a similar Special Ops background because he used the same jargon.

Whip said he'd discovered a vulnerability in regard to Jonah Bank. Nate knew there was *always* a vulnerability, if the time and effort was spent to discover it. No human being could be one hundred percent secure. There was always a way to get close enough to a target to do the job.

Every night between seven and seven-thirty, Whip said, Bank left The Dakota alone on foot without minders or bodyguards. He changed out of his $3,000 Dolce & Gabbana three-piece courtroom suit into a baseball cap, a worn leather bomber jacket, baggy jeans, and Nike running shoes. Bank's destination was Zabar's, an eclectic specialty food store eight blocks away at Broadway and 80th, where he'd buy the "Nova Scotia" — a bagel with scallion cream cheese — and a single black-and-white cookie. Bank would return to the building before eight. Whip speculated that Bank's bodyguards weren't aware of his nightly sojourn, or they'd accompany him or insist on fetching the snack themselves.

Bank didn't deviate from his established route on the round trip. After leaving The Dakota, he'd walk up West 72nd to Broadway and blend in with the crowded foot traffic for the remaining eight blocks to Zabar's. But on the way back, while he was eating, he'd return by a different route: 80th to Amsterdam, then 74th to Columbus Avenue, then to 72nd and The Dakota, where he'd enter the same side door from which he'd departed.

Whip had identified one block on the return route that was poorly lit and not bristling with closed-circuit cameras. It was on 74th, between Amsterdam and Columbus. The block was quiet and residential, with only one storefront retail business — Abraham's Florist Shop, where Abraham's white panel delivery van was parked out front during business hours. The single CC camera Whip identified was across the street from the florist's shop.

Many nights, Abraham took his van on final deliveries and never returned it. Whip guessed Abraham took it to his home in Brooklyn. Other nights, Abraham left the van parked and locked and rode the train home. There didn't seem to be any way to predict whether the vehicle would be left on the street or gone for the night until Whip figured it out: it depended on the location of Abraham's last delivery. If the delivery was in the direction of Brooklyn or in Brooklyn itself, Abraham kept the van. If it was somewhere else or there were no more deliveries at all, the owner would ride the train home.

So for the past three nights, Whip had placed anonymous orders via the Internet for deliveries after six to three different addresses on the way to Brooklyn, each time specifying that the flowers be left on the stoop if the recipient wasn't home. He paid for each with a valid but stolen credit card number from a list he'd been provided.

Whip had taken a photo of the florist's logo on the side of the van with his cell phone, and had a vinyl replica made uptown. Then he'd found a nearly identical 2009 Chevy Express Cargo Van at a location near LaGuardia Airport and reserved it for Nate. Nate's job was to drive the van and slip it into the empty space after Abraham went home for the night and wait for further instructions. If anyone ever reviewed the video history of the block, they'd notice the lack of a pattern to whether the van was there for the night or gone.

The CC camera could clearly view the van on the street, but it couldn't see through it to the opposite sidewalk. There was an eighteen-foot length of pavement blocked by the van. Anything that happened within that eighteen feet couldn't be seen.

On both of the two previous nights, Nate had heard his throw-away phone chirp and heard Whip say, "I've got him. Unlock the doors and get ready." Nate had responded by punching the electric toggle on his armrest and hearing the locks clunk open. He watched the sidewalk via the passenger-side rearview mirror while poising his hand over the door handle, ready to throw open the sliding door.

On night one, Jonah Bank had been wearing the uniform Whip had described and he'd approached in an amble, as if he wanted the walk back to his home to last as long as possible. In the distance behind Bank was a rapidly approaching figure hidden in shadow. Nate guessed it was Whip.

114

As Bank neared the rear bumper of the van, Nate heard a cacophony of enthused voices and looked up to see ten or twelve well-dressed people coming down the sidewalk in a writhing knot. They'd engulfed Bank just as he approached the sliding side door of the van.

"Abort," Whip said softly, and melded back into the darkness.

The group of people were clutching tickets and talking about the last time they'd heard Diana Krall sing at the Beacon Theatre a block away. They unconsciously parted to let Bank pass through them going in the other direction, and re-formed when he was through. By then he was twenty feet away on the sidewalk, strolling toward The Dakota, and two steps away from a pool of overhead streetlights and back in the field of vision of the CC camera.

The night before, Bank had appeared at the exact same time and place. Nate had glanced up the street — no concertgoers this time — and unlocked the doors to the van. Again, he saw Bank approach in his rearview mirror and the dark form close on him from the shadows, on pace to overtake Bank when he was shielded by the van. But there was someone else — a woman who had passed Nate's vehicle thirty seconds before, en route to Broadway. Something had made her turn around, and she was now jogging back the way she'd come. Her heels clicked on the pavement with sharp percussion, and Bank heard them and paused to look over his shoulder.

She was suddenly in Bank's face, screaming.

"It's you, you bastard!" she shrieked, jabbing a finger in his face. "It took me a minute, but I realized it was you, you putrid piece of shit."

Because Bank was only half turned, Nate could see the weary look of bemusement on his face. When Bank said, "I'm sorry, I don't know what you're talking about. You must be mistaken, lady," Nate saw Whip's form freeze on his approach.

"You're Jonah Bank, you wicked prick," she screamed. "You stole my grandmother's *last dime*. You stole every penny from the sweetest woman I've ever known, and I hope you go *straight to hell and burn for a thousand years.*"

Bank shrugged unconvincingly and turned away from her. He was then next to the sliding door of the van and for a moment Nate couldn't see him. Then Bank walked by the driver's-side window, head down and determined, with the woman skipping alongside, jabbing her finger and cursing.

"It's him, everybody!" she shouted, trying to rouse the residents of the quiet buildings. "It's Jonah Bank. Right here, the pathetic douche-bag thief of New York! The predator!"

No curtains rustled from the windows of the brownstone apartments.

There was a whisper from the cell phone: "Abort."

"It's him!" she yelled, still keeping pace with Bank. "Here he is, the bastard."

The two of them entered the pool of light on the corner, and she stayed with him, skipping alongside and jabbing at him with her finger until he was out of sight.

116

"I've got him. Unlock the doors and get ready."

Bank's only concession to the events of the night before was to flip up the collar of his bomber jacket and pull his cap lower to further obscure his face. Plus, he seemed to be walking more rapidly, with his head down.

This time, the block was empty. Nate unlocked the door.

Bank approached the van quickly. As he did, and a second before he walked into the blind spot directly next to the sliding panel door, Nate saw Whip close in until the two figures melded into one. Nate threw the van door open and stepped back as both of them hurtled inside. Whip had wrapped up Bank and was on top of him as they hit the van floor, rocking the vehicle. In the next second, Nate saw a stubby revolver in Whip's hand and a flash of Bank's panicked eyes as the muzzle pressed into his ball cap with enough muscle to jam the man's head into the floor. Whip reached back with his free hand and slammed the door closed behind him.

"Look, I don't know who you are, but —" Bank said, and never finished the sentence. Instead, there was an angry *snap-snap-snap-snap*.

The reports from the gun were loud inside the van. Bank made an *ungh* sound and stopped struggling, except for a reflexive tapping of his fingertips on the back of the passenger seat that sounded for a moment to Nate like Morse code. Then it stopped.

The inside of the van smelled sharply of gunpowder. Small-caliber or partially silenced, Nate thought. It was unlikely the neighbors would have heard anything, since the door to the van was closed and the shots had been muffled by the muzzle pressed hard into Bank's ball cap.

Whip looked up, and Nate saw his face for the first time. He was young, boyish, pale, with high cheekbones, brown hair brushed straight back, a red slash of a mouth parting to reveal perfect white teeth, and close-set, piercing eyes.

"Go," Whip said. "Ease out and don't burn rubber."

Nate started the van, pulled out, and drove the half-block through the green light on Columbus and beyond. There were no shouts, no sirens, no one peering out the apartment windows or gathering on the stoops of the brownstones.

He heard the sound of a body bag being unfurled, and felt the van rock slightly as the body was rolled into it. The zipper sang as it was closed, and within half a minute, Whip was in the passenger seat, reaching for the buckle of the seat belt.

"I got him into the bag before he bled on the floor," Whip said. "Still, we'll need to wipe down every inch of this van."

Nate nodded, and noticed Whip still had the gun in his hand, although it was resting on his right thigh.

"You can put that away now," Nate said.

Whip reacted with a slight grin. "I will when I'm ready. You worried?"

"No."

"Are you wondering about this weapon?"

"A little."

118

"Ruger LCR double-action .22," Whip said. "Hammerless, so it doesn't snag on clothes. Eight rounds in the cylinder. I load the first four with .22 smalls. Four through eight in the cylinder are .22 long-rifle hollow-points. Not that I've ever had to use four through eight."

"Why .22 smalls?" Nate asked.

"No one ever uses them anymore, but they're deadly little rounds at point-blank range. Very little noise, as you noticed, so no need for a suppressor. And the bullets don't exit the skull, so there's no messy exit wound. The slugs penetrate and just bounce around in there through the brain like bees in a jar."

He paused and looked down at his gun. Whip said, "No spent casings ejected, of course, because they stay in the cylinder."

Nate grunted.

Whip said, "I hear you use a wheel gun as well, but a hell of a lot bigger."

"Yup."

"Bigger isn't always better."

"No, just bigger."

Whip seemed to be weighing what he said next, then apparently let it go. In a few minutes, he addressed the inside of the windshield without looking over.

"Do you know where we're going in Jersey?"

"Yes."

Whip withdrew his cheap phone and pressed out a ten-digit number and brought it up to his ear.

"It's done," he said. "We'll be there in an hour."

He listened for a moment, then terminated the call.

"What did he say?" Nate asked.

"He said I just did some good."

"Does he always say that?"

"Yes, he does," Whip said softly, while he shoved the Ruger into his outside jacket pocket. "Because he believes it."

"Do you?" Nate asked.

"Take the George Washington Bridge," Whip said, gesturing ahead.

"I said I knew how to get there."

"I've got one question," Whip said after a few moments. "Do we want to get to know each other or not?"

Nate wasn't sure how to answer.

Twenty minutes of silence later — Nate was grateful Whip didn't mind silence, either — at the Hackensack exit onto I-80 from the New Jersey Turnpike, Nate noticed in his rearview mirror that Jonah Bank was sitting up in the back, listing unevenly from side to side inside the body bag, as if he were drunk.

"Hey," Nate said.

"What?"

Nate chinned over his shoulder, and Whip turned around and said, "Oh shit."

Then, without hesitation, Whip unbuckled his seat belt and drew the pistol and turned in his seat and extended his arm toward the swaying head inside the body bag. The single report was much louder than the previous four, and Bank's dead body flopped straight back and landed with a thump.

120

"That never happens," Whip said, turning back around and buckling his seat belt. "Really, it doesn't. We'll not speak of this again," he said, shaking his head.

"That's why I use a bigger gun," Nate said.

On the New Jersey state highway 208 North, Nate said, "Do you know who commissioned this?"

"No," Whip said quickly. "I never ask, and I don't want or need to know. And, frankly, I don't care. Jonah Bank was the lowest of the low, the way he fleeced all those old Jews. He had a lot of enemies, and he probably had some friends who didn't want him talking."

"So you never ask?"

"Never. I know by the time the job gets to me, it's been fully vetted. All I ask is to have enough time to do the recon properly and figure out the vulnerability. Once I'm satisfied I've done both, and only then, do I move."

Nate asked, "Have you ever gone after someone who might be innocent?"

"No," Whip said, as if the question were ridiculous. "Never. That's not what we do."

Nate nodded, but he wasn't sure he was satisfied with the answer.

Whip seemed agitated, though, by the question itself. He leaned forward in his seat and turned his head toward Nate. "What I can't figure out is just why you're even here."

"Me either," Nate said. "I guess because he asked me."

"But why? We do three or four operations a year. Each one requires lots of time, money, and planning. This one took two and a half months. I've never botched a single operation and we've attracted zero attention or heat. The reason it's always gone so perfectly is because the target is completely vetted and we don't try to do too much or rush things . . ."

Nate noticed that as Whip spoke more heatedly, his accent became more pronounced, and he said *thangs*.

"We keep our heads down, is what I'm saying," Whip continued. "We stay under the radar and do good work. But all of a sudden he feels the need to recruit some kind of ponytailed nature boy . . . I don't know what is going on. No offense, of course."

"Of course," Nate said through gritted teeth.

Whip said, "Bringing you on means one of two things. One is that he thinks I'm losing my edge, but that doesn't make any sense. I *have not lost my edge*, as you can see from what happened back in the city. So if he's looking to replace me, he's got to have another reason than that."

Whip raised his hand in the air with two fingers extended.

"The other possibility is he wants to expand operations, double or triple the number of jobs. But more people and more jobs means more chances of exposure. That's too many damned pots to watch over for anyone, and something's going to boil over, if you catch my drift."

"I don't know the answer," Nate said.

122

"I'm sure as hell going to find out," Whip said, sitting back. "I liked it the way it was. I don't need help, and we don't need another operator. That's just what I think. If it comes down between you and me, well, it'll have to be you. No offense, of course."

"Of course."

Hill Top Airport was three miles north of West Milford. It was a tiny, privately owned airstrip without a control tower or normal nighttime operations. Nate parked the van on the shadowed side of a private hangar and they wiped down the interior and exterior of the van and stripped the vinyl ABRAHAM's FLORIST SHOP signage from the sides. Both broke their cell phones into pieces and threw them inside the body bag along with the cleaning rags and zipped it back up. Whip checked for spots of blood on the pavement since he'd shot a hole in the bag's fabric, but said it was clean.

It was a cold night and moisture hung in the air to make it seem colder. Nate could see his breath, and his fingers and toes were starting to get numb.

They heard the airplane approaching at low altitude and it landed in the dark and taxied their way.

Nate and Whip grasped the opposite ends of the body bag and carried it toward the small plane.

Before they hefted the bag inside, Nate said to Whip: "It won't be me."

CHAPTER
EIGHT

Medicine Wheel County, Wyoming

Joe Pickett drove north on U.S. 85 with Daisy sleeping on the passenger seat and a huge crate filled with 150 full-grown ring-necked pheasants in the back. Daisy was exhausted because she'd spent the first hour and a half staring at them through the back window.

Delivering the birds was the, excuse Director LGD and her management team had come up with for Joe to enter Medicine Wheel County without suspicion, once Rulon had briefed her on the special assignment. The northeast corner of the state had had a particularly harsh winter the year before that had annihilated the pheasant population, and it was necessary to supplement the Black Hills with birds so the hunters wouldn't gripe. Jim Latta, the local game warden, was in charge of releasing the newcomers that had been raised at the state bird farm in Hawk Springs; thus, it would appear legitimate for Joe and Latta to link up. That was the idea, anyway, Joe thought. Latta was unaware of the real reason Joe was coming.

Director LGD's brain trust had come up with two cover stories for Joe's sojourn. The first was under a departmental directive to double the number of public

124

walk-in hunting areas on private land by the next fiscal year. Joe had established several in his district by working with local landowners, but there were none yet in Medicine Wheel County. Joe would supposedly use his experience to help Latta to further the directive.

Unfortunately, the second cover story meant he had to drive his truck four and a half hours southeast, load the crate of nervous pheasants with the help of the state biologists, and turn north again, skirting the eastern edge of the state.

The landscape changed character as he drove, from flat farmland to arid steppe. There had been an unusual cold spell and early winter snows the week before that still lingered under overcast skies. Skeletal cottonwoods in the eastern valleys had lost their leaves but were furred with frost even in the late afternoon. It was stark and white and rolling in every direction, and there was little oncoming traffic once he passed Mule Creek Junction and continued north. A single mangy coyote loped parallel to the highway for a while, but then turned as if it were ashamed of something when Joe slowed down to look at it.

Joe had never seen the vast stretches of Mongolia, but he guessed they would look similar under the pall of early winter. He knew the area consisted mainly of huge ranches that were once multigenerational but were now under out-of-state ownership. Scattered, frost-covered Angus cattle watched him drive past with dullards' eyes.

North of Lusk, he'd pulled over to the side of the highway to wrap a canvas sheet from his gear box around the crate of birds. He secured it with nylon straps. The wind was cold and icy, and he feared it would freeze the birds to death before he could deliver them. Daisy watched from the rear window with twin threads of drool stringing from her mouth to the top of the bench seat.

Ten miles later, the highway turned pink. He'd once heard the reason was because the early road crews had used burned underground coal for a base, but the pink wasn't cheery or bright — just strange and otherworldly.

He noted how pockets of isolated pronghorn antelope blended in perfectly in the terrain with its swaths of snow on sparse brown grass. It was almost impossible to see them unless the entire herd moved at once, because they seemed to be a part of the landscape itself.

After he crossed Hat Creek, he looked around for miles without seeing a single structure, and he felt like he was alone on the surface of a distant uninhabited planet. The radio station he'd been listening to began to crackle with static during the newsbreak — something about notorious New York financier Jonah Bank's disappearance after he failed to show up in court. It was one of those stories that seemed to consume the eastern media but had no impact or relation to anything in Joe's world. He'd not followed the story closely except to note that in Wyoming there was an actual Jonah Bank that was a bank. He reached down and shut the radio off.

He felt a pang of guilt for being lifted up by the pure solitude, with the open road and a new assignment out ahead of him. For brief stretches of time, he pushed aside the stress generated by Erik Young and Dallas Cates and thought about a certain Wyoming rancher and what he'd learned about him.

All around him was white isolation and vistas stretched out as far as he could see.

He loved it.

Joe had opened the file Coon lent him at three-thirty that morning because he couldn't sleep. He'd made coffee and sat at his desk in his tiny side office in his robe and had read through the pages in order, trying to make some kind of sense of them.

He found Wolfgang Templeton fascinating. What would cause a man who had it all — it seemed — to give up and move on when everything appeared to be going his way? And if the FBI speculation was valid, weren't there hundreds of other lucrative opportunities available to Templeton that didn't involve creating a murder-for-hire gig? Nothing Joe read about Templeton suggested recklessness or anarchy. In every way, the man seemed measured, honorable, and professional — an American success story. Joe liked those. He'd never envied successful people or wanted them brought down — unless, of course, they turned out to be poachers. Or worse.

As he thumbed through the file, he found a photocopy of a small story in *Investor's Business Daily* about Templeton's last days in finance. Coon had not mentioned it during their meeting. It was called "CEO's Bitter Last Hurrah," and it had appeared the week Templeton suddenly retired.

According to the item, quoting from an anonymous source on the inside of the firm, Templeton had called his senior executives and board of directors together for an emergency meeting, where he declared, "Our free enterprise system is broken and can't be fixed." The source said Templeton was angry and blamed the state of the economy on "untouchable elites" and "crony capitalists working hand-in-glove with corrupt politicians." There was no point anymore, he said, of "competing fairly and with a well-tuned moral compass" because the deck was stacked. According to the insider, Templeton said he could no longer serve as chairman, but would "do the right thing" outside the system. He gave no clues what that meant.

Joe sat back and said, *"Hmmmm."*

But there was obviously a reason why Wolfgang Templeton had chosen to relocate in the most remote and economically depressed part of Wyoming — and it certainly wasn't because the cattle business was booming. If Templeton had a long-term reason for choosing Medicine Wheel County — and he might — Joe couldn't figure out what it was.

Unless, of course, Templeton simply wanted to be left alone. There was nothing wrong with that, and Wyomingites tended to give new people the space they desired and not stick their noses where they didn't belong. Joe felt a little uncomfortable doing exactly that on behalf of the governor.

Unless, of course, Templeton *was* a killer.

Coon's case file didn't reveal much more about the victims than Joe had been told.

Jonah Lamprecht had disappeared in Saint Louis in 2004.

Brandon Fonnesbeck had vanished off the coast of Long Island in 2008.

Henry P. Scoggins III had been abducted — or walked away — from his fishing lodge in Montana the month before.

Several threads connected them, but tenuously. All the victims were extremely wealthy and well connected, and ran with a certain elite international crowd. No traceable ransom demands were ever received by their families or loved ones. Most important, none of their bodies had ever been found. The only dubious connection was that the name Wolfgang Templeton had been brought up peripherally in each case.

Joe shook his head. It was weak, very weak. So weak that he would never take the circumstantial evidence in the file to his own county prosecutor, Dulcie Schalk. Dulcie would hand the file back and tell him she needed more. There were *years* between the incidents — as long as five between Fonnesbeck and Scoggins, which certainly didn't lend weight to the idea of a busy hit man's schedule.

But the FBI, with everything they had on their plates these days, had invested time and interest to build the file. They must have reasons beyond what Joe could see, he thought. It was possible Coon didn't even know what the reasons were.

Joe wondered if there were additional disappearances of similar people that weren't included in the case file — maybe even scores of missing persons where the name Wolfgang Templeton simply hadn't come up. If the FBI's suspicions were correct, there likely were, he thought. And if the whole thing was a wasteful fishing expedition . . .

But there was the DCI agent, whose name had been redacted from the incident report. The man had been sent to Medicine Wheel County to find out what he could about Templeton, and within a few days there had been a fire in his room that killed him.

And there was that photo of the man who could possibly be Nate.

There was a small sign vandalized by bullet holes that read ENTERING MEDICINE WHEEL COUNTY as Joe crossed the Cheyenne River. Within twenty minutes, the landscape changed once again. The flats began to fold into gently sloping hills and then fold again, as if they were a floor rug being jammed into a corner. The folds led into heavily wooded small mountains. The thick spruce that covered the hills was dark under the leaden sky — thus the name Black Hills — and sharp ravines knifed through the surface and chalky bluffs jutted out from the timber like thrust jaws.

It was beautiful and complex country, Joe thought, mountainous, but not severe and dangerous like his

130

Bighorns. The terrain was oddly inviting and accessible, with wide meadows bordered by hillocks. The road itself changed from a straightaway into a winding pink road that hugged the contours of the foothills and sometimes plunged over blind rises.

He glimpsed some structures in the timber as he drove, mainly older houses tucked behind the first wall of trees. They were well situated but looked ramshackle and abandoned. The only homes he saw that were occupied were marked with collections of old vehicles and newer four-wheel-drive pickups scattered around their lots. Wood smoke curled from blackened chimneys and dispersed in the upper branches of the spruce trees before filtering into the close sky.

He didn't slow to read the old markers on the side of the highway as he drove — he could do that later — but he was left with the impression of a place that had once been vibrant and filled with energy and ambition but now held only testimonials to failed enterprise. He did slow down, though, to let a clumsy flock of wild turkeys cross the road. They waddled like fat, drunk chickens.

Medicine Wheel District game warden Jim Latta said he'd meet him two miles south of Wedell, one of three small communities that still existed in Medicine Wheel County, the others being Medicine Wheel itself and Sundance on the far western border.

Latta's green Game and Fish pickup was parked just off the highway on an old two-track trail at the bottom of a wooded grade. As Joe slowed to join him, Latta waved for him to follow.

The road was narrow and muddy, and twisted through the timber. At times, Joe couldn't see Latta's truck because the trees were so dense, but he knew the game warden was ahead of him because there were no other exit roads. Finally, after grinding up a sharp rise, he found Latta's truck parked in a grassy opening and Latta himself climbing out and pulling on a green wool Filson vest identical to the one Joe wore.

Joe parked next to Latta's truck and let Daisy out to romp and relieve herself.

Latta approached with his right hand extended and a sly smile on his face, and as Joe shook his dry and meaty hand Latta said, "Long time, Mr. Pickett."

"It has been. When was it, the Wyoming Game Wardens Association dinner a few years back?"

"Seven years, I think," Latta said. "That's the last time I went."

"Seven years," Joe echoed.

"Time flies," Latta said. "So, you brought me some birds."

"Yup," Joe said, clamping on his hat. "Let's pull that canvas off so you can see 'em."

Jim Latta was a few inches shorter than Joe, thick through the shoulders and chest, with a large round head, cherubic cheeks, and a gunfighter's sweeping handlebar mustache. His eyes didn't give much away as he spoke — he had the cop's deadeye down to perfection — and his voice was surprisingly high for his bulldog features. His badge said he was warden number six, and he had ten years seniority on Joe. Although he'd no doubt moved from district to district around

132

the state as Joe had in his early years, Latta had been in the Medicine Wheel District since Joe had been hired. Latta was a fixture in the northeast corner of the state, and rarely ventured out.

Joe climbed up in the back of his pickup after lowering the tailgate. The metal beaded moisture from a light combination of rain and snow, and the surface of the bed was slick under his boots.

While Joe unhooked the nylon straps, Latta said, "It pains me to say this, but we could save a whole lot of energy by just delivering these birds to about six local yahoos up there in Wedell. Those bastards will have 'em poached out of here by the end of the month."

Joe shook his head to commiserate.

"In fact," Latta said softly, "I think I see one of those reprobates now."

Joe paused.

"Don't look up there real obvious, but I think I see a four-wheeler up there to the southeast on that hill behind you. I'd guess he's scouting so he knows where we release these damned birds."

So he wouldn't turn and obviously look at the potential poacher, Joe sidled to the side of the crate and used the mirror on the passenger side to see. He had to duck a bit before he got a bead on the man Latta had spotted.

Midway up the timbered hill behind and to the side of them, Joe glimpsed a man who appeared to be holding his head. No, he thought, the man was using binoculars.

133

"There's an old logging road up there," Latta said. "He's probably standing on top of the seat of his four-wheeler so he can see us."

"Do you know him?"

"Not sure. But it might be Bill Critchfield. He's kind of the ringleader of the bunch. If it's him, he's probably poached more deer, elk, and birds in these hills alone than any other guy besides Gene Smith, who's his best buddy. They live up in Wedell, but they spend a lot of their time down here."

Joe said, "Have you ever caught him?"

"Twice," Latta said wearily. "Caught him and Smith dead to rights while they were gutting out a dry doe on a sunny day in June, and another time with twenty dead pheasants in the bed of Critchfield's pickup. Judge Bartholomew let them skate both times. You ever run into Judge Ethan Bartholomew?"

"Nope."

"Good thing," Latta said. "He has a way of making a game warden feel . . . kind of useless."

"So what do you want to do now?" Joe asked while he folded up the damp canvas cover.

"Nothing *to* do," Latta said. "Let's release the birds and hope like hell they'll take to cover in the canyons between here and Wedell before Critchfield and Smith wipe 'em out."

Joe paused. "It's that bad around here, huh?" He called Daisy in, and she bounded into the cab of his pickup.

"It's a whole different world," Latta said.

134

"Sounds like a plan. Not a good plan, but a plan," Joe said. "I don't like the idea of releasing these birds so they can be poached out. That just rubs me the wrong way."

"Yeah," Latta said with a shrug. "Used to bother the hell out of me, too. But we can't take these birds home. My backyard isn't big enough."

It was meant as a joke, but Joe didn't laugh.

Joe said, "Maybe we could set up surveillance and catch them in the act. With me here, you've just doubled your forces."

Latta responded with a frown. "Yeah, and we can drag their sorry asses in front of Judge Bartholomew, who will say we entrapped them or some such bullshit. Naw," Latta said, nodding toward the crate, "let's let 'em go."

"You're the man in charge," Joe said, shaking his head and leaning down to open the crate.

Daisy watched and whined as if tortured inside the cab of Joe's truck while 150 pheasants shot out of the crate one by one like fireworks and soared into the dark timber on the north side of the meadow. Within three minutes, the crate was empty. Joe could see a few of the birds perching in the trees at the edge of the meadow, taking in their new surroundings.

"Good enough for government work," Latta said, nonchalantly.

Joe was surprised Latta had chosen to release them all at once in the same place, and not disperse them throughout the drainage. But Latta was the local warden and he was running the show.

When Joe paused at the door of his pickup to take off his gloves before getting in, he heard a distant grinding and then a two-stroke motor fire up. The four-wheeler whined away in the trees.

"There goes Bill Critchfield back to tell his buddies so they can load their shotguns and charge up their spotlights," Latta said with bitter resignation.

"Well," Joe said, puzzled by what had just taken place, "I guess I'll go find my motel and check in before it gets too late."

"Where you staying?"

"The Whispering Pines Motel in Medicine Wheel," Joe said.

Latta nodded but seemed troubled. "That's the place that had a fire a month ago. Maybe you didn't hear about it, but some poor guy from Cheyenne died in one of the cabins when it burned down during the night."

Joe said, "Yeah, I heard about that. But I figure, what are the odds of the same place burning down twice?"

"I hadn't thought of it that way," Latta said. Then: "I live in Wedell. How about I buy you a beer at the Bronco Bar on your way to Medicine Wheel? Believe me, that motel won't be full this time of year. In fact, you'll probably be their only customer."

"I could do that," Joe said. "It's been a long day."

"Yeah," Latta said, putting his hands on his hips and surveying the darkening timber surrounding them, as if looking for additional spies. "Maybe you can tell me why Cheyenne wants you to ride along with me up here for a couple of days. It ain't like I don't have a good handle on my district."

136

Joe nodded. Latta was already suspicious. He had a right to be, Joe thought.

But Joe had some questions of his own.

CHAPTER
NINE

Wedell, Wyoming

The downtown of Wedell was a single block of slumped and decaying storefronts, most of them boarded up. The only paved street was the old state highway that halved the few remaining businesses — a dollar store, a convenience store, a gas station with twenty-four-hour pumps, the ancient post office, a craft store/rock shop/hardware store, and the Bronco Bar, which was situated in the dead center of the block. Unpaved residential roads spurred off the old highway and led to a mishmash of double-wide trailers, clapboard homes, and a few two-story brick Victorian houses that towered over the rest of the community, looking like royalty that got off at the wrong stop.

Hard pellets of snow bounced off Joe's pickup hood and windshield as he pulled in next to Jim Latta's vehicle in front of the saloon. There were few other cars or trucks on the street, and no pedestrians. The pending darkness and the low cloud cover made Wedell seem particularly gloomy, although the neon Coors and Fat Tire Ale signs in the windows of the bar looked inviting.

He told Daisy to be patient, and followed Latta inside. Three patrons, all men wearing ball caps and muddy boots, sat at the long bar that ran the length of the room. They had bottles of beer in front of them, and they were all watching the Speed Channel as if they had money riding on who would win the three-month-old Pure Michigan 400 NASCAR race being replayed on the screen. All three glanced over at the two game wardens in their red uniform shirts, and their looks held just long enough to confirm that none of them were in trouble. When they were assured Latta and Joe weren't looking for them, they shifted back to the race.

The bar itself was typical, Joe thought: dusty elk, bear, deer, and pronghorn antelope heads on the walls, yellowing Polaroid shots of drunken patrons from years before thumbtacked to the rough-cut timber walls, a hand-drawn poster above the bar mirror with the details of a raffle for a .270 Winchester rifle to benefit the local Gun Owners of America chapter. An old sign with frontier-style writing read:

A farting horse will never tire and
A farting man is the man to hire

A jukebox in the corner played Hank Williams Jr.'s "A Country Boy Can Survive."

The woman behind the bar, who had big blond hair and an overfull figure and a wide Slavic face, said, "What can I get you, Jim?" to Latta.

"I'll have a Coors Light," he said, slipping into the farthest of two booths from the bar itself. To Joe, he said, "I'm watching my girlish figure."

"Make it two," Joe said to the bartender.

She plucked bottles from a cooler behind the bar and twisted off the caps. As she did, the sleeves of the black long-sleeve Henley she was wearing slid back to reveal Popeye-sized forearms from opening *a lot* of beer bottles in her career, Joe guessed.

Joe sat across from Latta, They were far enough away from the bar and the NASCAR race was loud enough that they wouldn't be easily overheard.

The bartender came out from behind the bar with four bottlenecks gripped between the fingers of her right hand and hanging down like sleeping bats. In her left she had a plastic basket of bright yellow popcorn. Her shirt read DON'T FLATTER YOURSELF, COWBOY, I WAS LOOKIN' AT YOUR HORSE, and she wore a silver buckle the size of a dinner plate.

"Happy hour," she said, placing the four beers down on the table with a thud. To Latta: "As if you didn't know."

Latta grinned. "Shawna, this is Joe. Joe, this is Shawna."

By the way Latta and Shawna exchanged looks, Joe guessed there was some history between them. He said, "Nice to meet you."

"No problem," she said, as if the pleasure was all his. She assessed Joe with a practiced eye from his boots to his hat. Her eyes caught on his wedding ring and hung there for a long second before regaining momentum and proceeding up his arm to his face. By the time she met his eyes she'd dismissed him.

"Shawna here was the Women's Professional Rodeo Association barrel-racing champion of the world back in 1997," Latta said.

"Back when I was younger and weighed less than my horse, anyway," she said. "Give me a holler if you boys need a reride on them beers." She didn't look back over her shoulder at Latta as she returned to the bar and her high-backed stool to watch the conclusion of the race.

"Quite a charmer," Joe said, sipping his beer. He hadn't expected a glass, and it was the kind of place where they didn't even ask.

"We kind of had a thing a few years ago after my wife left. You know what you hear about barrel racers in the sack? Well, it's true," Latta said with a defensive grin.

"I didn't mean to insult her or you," Joe said quickly.

"You didn't," Latta said. "She's pretty rough around the edges. I get that."

Joe didn't know Latta was divorced. In fact, he didn't know much about him at all. There were fifty-two game wardens in the state, and they were a different lot, Joe knew. Some kept in touch with other game wardens and worked shoulder to shoulder with them, some closely followed the goings-on at headquarters and reported back, and some kept completely to themselves. Latta kept to himself. Divorce was a common casualty within the profession, mainly due to wardens' long hours, remote postings, and poor pay. Joe had expected Latta to make departmental small talk and ask him about their new director, LGD, and the changes coming at the agency, but he didn't.

"So," Latta said, slipping on his stoic law enforcement game face so smoothly Joe felt a tug in his gut, "why are you here? They should know by now I'm not looking for any help. I've been doin' my job up here

141

for twenty-three years without once getting written up. But I do my own thing. I don't even like trainees breathing down my neck. If they got a problem with me or the way I'm doing my job, they should tell me direct. They shouldn't send you up here to spy on me."

Joe said, "I'm not here to spy on you."

Latta probed into Joe's eyes for a tell. Joe let him.

"So why are you here?"

"LGD has a burr under her saddle when it comes to game wardens creating more public access with walk-in areas on private land. She knows there aren't any up here; I guess she thought I could help you out."

Latta looked away. So there was *something* Latta was hiding or suspecting, Joe thought. He didn't have enough information or familiarity with Latta to guess what it was.

"Now I feel kind of stupid," Latta mumbled. "I thought . . . well, it's pretty well known you've done some work on the side for the governor, Joe. You don't exactly have a low profile, with all the stuff you've gotten involved in over the years. So when I hear the famous Joe Pickett is coming to shadow me for a couple of weeks, well . . ."

Joe thought, *Famous Joe Pickett*. He couldn't even comprehend the words.

Instead of letting Latta speculate further and maybe get closer to the truth, Joe said, "Back there when we released those birds you said this place is a whole different world. What did you mean by that?"

Latta paused, then finished his first beer and set it aside. He reached for the second. "I guess every district

142

is unique in its own way. I bet you've got plenty of war stories to tell about yours."

"I do," Joe said, "but we aren't talking about my district right now."

Latta grinned sheepishly, caught at trying to divert the question in a clumsy way. He said, "Well, have you been up here before?"

"Just to pass through."

"It's a tough place to live," Latta said. "In some ways it's got all a certain kind of man could ask for. In other ways, it's got nothing at all."

Joe waited for a moment, and said, "You'll have to unpack that for me."

"It'll take a little while," Latta said, looking over in an attempt to get Shawna's attention. "In fact, it's going to take another round."

"None for me," Joe said.

"*Shawna,*" Latta boomed, "we need a reride."

"There was a time when Medicine Wheel County looked like it was gonna be in the big leagues," Latta said, leaning forward toward Joe across the table. "We're talkin' turn of the last century. There was a big-ass gold-mining operation up here, and coal mines that employed hundreds of people. You passed most of those old places on the road you came on today. The owners of the gold mine were named Eric and Maïda Wedell. They were one of the richest families in the state at one time and the town of Wedell was a big shit. Now look at it."

Joe recalled the historical plaques he hadn't stopped to read.

Latta said, "This place at one time was *booming*. Gold, copper, coal, oil — there were even two big-time lumber mills and a hell of a logging industry. There are old logging roads *everywhere* in the hills. Copper was a big one. All three of the towns grew like crazy — Medicine Wheel and Wedell were rivals, trying to be the biggest. Sundance was the smallest of the three towns in the county then. If you look at the old newspapers, which I've done, you'll see that Medicine Wheel had an opera house and an orchestra, and Wedell right here used to have a dance hall where they brought in big-time entertainers from California and New York. Hell, they had Lily Langtry and Houdini right here in this town at one time. Medicine Wheel had a morning paper *and* an evening paper — one for Republicans and one for Democrats.

"I mean, what did you see when you drove here today?" Latta said. "Pretty mountains, streams, wildlife out the wazoo. The weather isn't as severe as where you live, and the wind doesn't blow like it does in Cheyenne, Casper, or Rawlins. Some people might say these mountains don't compare to the Bighorns, the Winds, the Tetons, or the Snowy Range, and they don't. These are nice gentle mountains. You won't fall off a cliff here or die from exposure, and we don't have all the damned wolves and grizzlies that will chew your ass off. This is paradise compared to them places. Tourists used to come through here on their trips between Mount Rushmore and Yellowstone. Rich guys from the Midwest used to build second homes here because it was just so damned scenic and mild."

144

Four more beers arrived, just as Joe had finished his first. Latta thought nothing of it, and grasped his third by the neck.

"Take it easy, cowboy," Shawna cautioned as she returned to the bar.

"You know me," Latta said.

"And that there's the problem," she countered. One of the patrons at the bar guffawed and turned quickly away.

Latta ignored her and the patron. He told Joe, "Medicine Wheel County in 1920 had a population of seventy thousand folks — bigger than Cheyenne or Casper or any other damned place in Wyoming. There was even an effort to move the state capitol from Cheyenne up here. Of course, the Union Pacific Railroad ran Wyoming then, and they nixed the idea. But the old-timers around here *still* hate Cheyenne for that."

Joe smiled. Old small-town rivalries ran deep.

"I think that's where it started," Latta said, lowering his voice as if he feared being overheard. "They lost that fight with Cheyenne and the people here took it personally. They went around with a chip on their shoulder, and they were convinced the deck was stacked against them. Then damn if they didn't turn out to be right.

"First it was copper. The owners of the mine and mill diversified into Montana and South Dakota and got so overextended their credit got cut off by the banks. The copper mines closed in the 1920s, followed by the gold mines in the 1930s. The coal mines were underground, though, and they seemed untouchable.

Even when the companies learned they could strip-mine millions of tons of coal around Gillette a hell of a lot cheaper than digging it out of the mountain here, the coal mines kept chugging along. There are third-generation coal miners around here, and they are a tough bunch of hombres. But the EPA shut 'em down five years ago. The Feds put new clean-air regulations up and the power plants couldn't afford to finance new scrubbers, I guess. The coal from here was too expensive to burn, and the low-sulfur coal from Gillette won out. All them mines shut down within a year, and folks were dropping off their house keys at the bank on the way out of town."

Joe clicked his tongue in sympathy. It was a familiar story.

Latta said, "The tourism economy died when the interstate highway system routed I-90 north of here so the tourists could shoot right through the top of the county and not pass through these towns anymore.

"Then the only rail spur that could transport lumber from here east went belly-up ten years ago and the mill closed. That shut down the loggers. You know what loggers are like, don't you? Loggers log. They can't do nothing else. They're used to months of downtime when the weather is bad and then balls-to-the-walls work when the snow melts. But when the good weather rolls around and they can't go into the woods — damn. They get grumpy.

"It was one damned thing after another, is what I'm saying," Latta said, looking down at his hands grasping the bottle.

146

"All we got left up here," he said, "is what was here in the first place, meaning big game and some damned fine habitat, and a few really bitter people who decided to stay."

He looked up. "Only sixty people still live in the town of Medicine Wheel. About eight hundred fifty hang on here in Wedell. And Sundance, which used to be the smallest town in the county, has twelve hundred. Them Sundancers keep to themselves and pretend they aren't part of the rest of the county. So I doubt you'll find nine hundred more miserable, angry, or bitter people anywhere in the U.S. of A."

"Where did the people go who left here?" Joe asked.

"All over. A lot of them headed to North Dakota the last few years to get in on that Bakken play. They were the smart ones."

Joe asked, "What keeps those nine hundred people here if there's nothing for them to do?"

"They like it here."

"How do they survive?"

"Hell," Latta said, "transfer payments. They mostly live off the dole. Welfare, Social Security, you name it. There's a doctor over in Sundance who will write a letter for just about anyone, saying he's disabled. Half the men get disability checks. I see a lot of these disabled guys up in the hills during hunting season, and it's just amazing what they can do: pack a quarter of an elk on their back, hike ten miles — it's just, well, you know. Quite a few of them are employed as hunting guides for a few months, and about fifteen work at a wild game-processing plant that's damned good —

state of the art, in fact. Other than that, they do a whole lot of nothing.

"The thing is," Latta said, "no one is ashamed of it. They all think they got dealt a bad hand from the companies, the state, and the Feds. They act like they're owed whatever they can scam. And they've been doing it so long it's a way of life."

"We've got a few of them where I come from," Joe said, thinking of Dave Farkus.

"Yeah," Latta said, consumed with thoughts of his own that Joe couldn't penetrate, as if he had something he wanted to say but wasn't sure whether to say it.

"Like I said, the only thing going anymore is the hunting and fishing. There's plenty of that. I keep busy."

Joe thought about the poachers Latta had mentioned, but chose to steer clear of the subject. Instead, he asked, "Why do you stay?"

"There's a couple bright spots," Latta said, finally.

Joe looked around the bar, then said, "What bright spots?"

"I got a nice house here in Wedell. Did you see those old Victorians when you drove in?"

Joe nodded.

"I bought one of them at a fire-sale price ten years ago. Used to belong to one of the Wedell kids. I never thought I'd live in a house like that in my entire life. Six bedrooms, three bathrooms, a carriage house out back. I'll have to show it to you."

"I'd like to see it," Joe said, puzzled. It was against policy for a game warden to own his own house and not have it be provided by the state, much less a six-bedroom mansion — old or not.

"Plus, my daughter likes it here," Latta said. "She has friends she wouldn't want to leave."

"Your daughter?"

Latta looked up with a wistful expression and a hint of moisture in his eyes.

"My Emily," he said. "Thirteen years old."

"That can be a tough age," Joe said. "I know."

"Ain't nothin' bad about her, Joe. My wife couldn't stand it here, and when she left she didn't take Emily. She just packed the car and took off for Oregon and left me and a four-year-old girl with muscular dystrophy."

Joe felt like he'd been punched. "Jim, I just can't imagine what that would be like. So your daughter is doing okay?"

"She is now," Latta said, averting his eyes. "It was so damned tough when she was trying to walk and she'd keep falling down. My wife said she was uncoordinated — a slow learner. But it was MD. The doctors at the time said she wouldn't live past eighteen or twenty before her muscles got so weak she'd die of respiratory failure. But now they're saying she might live to forty. Forty!"

"That's great, Jim. What changed?"

"Emily got an operation over in Rapid City. She had scoliosis — sidewise curvature of the spine. Her muscles couldn't keep her sitting up in her wheelchair, and she was a goner. The surgery straightened her out and prolonged her life by twenty years. I fought with the state insurance company for years about the

149

operation, and they kept saying they wouldn't pay for it. Then it finally happened."

Joe smiled and glanced toward the bar to see if the drinkers were paying attention to Latta's sudden burst of emotion. They weren't. But Shawna looked over with sympathetic eyes, taking it all in.

Latta wiped roughly at his eyes with a bar napkin, and Joe didn't stare.

"Shit," Latta said. "I didn't mean to get all gooey on you. It's just, when I talk about Emily, I just fuckin' lose it."

"It's all right," Joe said. "I've got daughters of my own. I can't even imagine what it would be like to be in your shoes."

"It wasn't easy. It still ain't."

Joe said, "I'm glad the insurance company came through."

Latta looked up sharply. "Who said they did?"

Joe was confused. "You said you fought them for years . . ."

"It wasn't them that came through. If it weren't for a damned good-hearted individual, it wouldn't be a good story at all."

"That's great," Joe said. "Who is the individual?"

"Mr. Templeton. He owns half this county."

Joe felt a thump in his chest as he nodded. "I've heard of him. Good guy?"

"A goddamned saint. If it wasn't for him —" Latta began, but then cut himself off. "Enough about Emily," he said roughly.

"I was asking about Mr. Templeton."

150

Latta's deadeye cop stare returned, and he trained it on Joe long enough for Joe to feel uncomfortable again.

Latta said, "I hope he's not why you're up here, Joe."

Joe could tell by Latta's tone that he was done talking for the night — that maybe he'd said more than he intended to. Since they'd be together over the next few days, Joe didn't want to push Latta out of his comfort zone. Yet.

"Well," Latta said, sitting back and helping himself to a fifth beer while Joe still nursed his first, "I better get going. I've got paperwork to fill out for the new damned director, and Emily ought to be home."

Joe nodded.

"Let's meet tomorrow for breakfast in Sundance at the Longabaugh at seven-thirty," Latta said.

He slid clumsily out of the booth and stood up. He wobbled slightly but steadied himself in a well-practiced way. Jim Latta wouldn't be the first game warden he'd met who had a problem with alcohol. And given the circumstances of his life, Joe thought he could forgive the man.

"Yeah," Latta said. "I'd like you to come see the house and meet Emily before you have to go back to the Bighorns in a few days."

"I'll cover the beers," Joe said.

"You don't need to do that."

"Happy to."

"Tomorrow, then," Latta said, clamping on his hat.

"You okay to drive?"

Latta barked a laugh. "Shit," he said. "I didn't even get *started* tonight."

Joe watched the game warden lumber toward the door. Shawna watched him as well, but turned her eyes away when he got close. The door opened just as Latta reached for the handle, and the game warden stepped back to let two men wearing camo come in.

By the way they were dressed and the way they grinned with contempt at Latta, Joe guessed there was history between Latta and them as well, but no words were exchanged. Latta seemed to give them a wide berth. They stood, smirking, while Latta left the bar, then approached Shawna and asked for two six-packs of Budweiser to go.

Before leaving as well, Joe checked his cell phone. No texts or messages from Sheridan, but one from Marybeth: *Are you at your hotel yet?*

Joe replied, *Not yet, will call soon,* and returned his phone to his breast pocket as he got to his feet.

The two men were still standing at the bar when Joe approached Shawna to pay the tab. He could feel their eyes on him. Shawna thunked their six-packs on the bar, and the taller one said, "Put that on my tab."

Shawna rolled her eyes as she turned to Joe and took his twenty-dollar bill. Before she could count out four dollars change, Joe said, "The rest is for you."

She grinned, although it looked like work. "Thank you, mister. You're fine-looking *and* generous."

Joe didn't know what to say.

"Damn," one of the men in camo said, "the last thing we need around here is another damned game warden."

Joe turned his head toward them. They were rough-looking men in their late thirties. The one who had spoken was dark, with weathered skin, a three-day growth of beard, and black curly hair sticking out from under his cowboy hat. The brim on his hat was folded straight up on the sides like he was some kind of 1950s Hollywood cowboy. He had light blue eyes. On the bar ahead of him were a pair of huge scarred hands. Joe pegged him for a logger or miner. *Former* logger or miner, based on what Latta had told him. The other man was taller, maybe six-foot-four. He was pale but also had outdoor skin. He had reddish hair peppered with gray that licked at his collar. He could be considered handsome, Joe thought, in a redneck-surfer-dude-gone-to-seed kind of way.

"Just visiting," Joe said.

"Well, don't let the door hit you in the ass on your way out," the dark man grinned. The taller man stifled a laugh and looked down at his hands.

Joe stuck out his hand toward the dark man. "Joe Pickett."

The dark man paused for a second, not sure whether to reach out. Joe watched his eyes. He was confused by Joe's gesture.

Joe thought: *Bill Critchfield and Gene Smith*. The taller one, Critchfield, confirmed it by introducing himself and his hunting partner.

Joe said evenly, "It looks like you're going hunting tonight, although it's already dark outside. What are you boys after?"

"Snipes," Critchfield said. It was meant as a joke.

Smith still wouldn't look up, but his shoulders were trembling with laughter.

"Yeah, I remember going 'snipe hunting' when I was twelve. A bunch of older guys took me up in the woods with my .22 and told me to sit there by a tree while they drove the snipes to me. Instead, they left me up there and went on a beer run. Good times," Joe said. "I'm sure you have your licenses and wildlife stamps, so I probably don't even need to ask."

Critchfield and Smith exchanged looks. They weren't intimidated by the question, Joe thought — they were trying to figure out how to deal with it.

Finally, Critchfield said, "Left mine at home."

"Me too," Smith said quickly.

Joe said, "So I guess you better run by your homes before you go out after those snipe."

Critchfield squared his stance. He was bigger than Joe. He said, "You know what? I think maybe you ought to talk to Jim Latta before you start throwing your weight around here. He knows us, and he knows the deal."

"There's a deal about hunting without licenses?" Joe asked.

"Yeah, there's a deal," Smith said, from behind Critchfield.

Joe noticed that two of the three drinkers who had been in the bar all evening were standing and tossing bills down on the bar to cover their beers. Apparently, Joe thought, they didn't have running tabs.

Shawna had watched the exchange like a tennis fan watching a volley. She said, "Just keep me out of this and take it outside."

154

"Nothing to take outside," Joe said, pulling on his vest. He looked up at the two men. "Right, Bill and Gene?"

"Call Jim," Critchfield said. "Then scoot back to where you came from."

He heard Gene Smith whisper, "You asshole."

"Nice to meet you both," Joe said. "I'll see you around."

"Better hope not," Critchfield said.

To Shawna, Joe said, "And nice to meet you."

Shawna looked back at him with dead eyes, but there was a slight tug of a smile on her face.

Outside, Daisy whined with recognition as he came through the door. The air was misty and cold, and there was a blue halo over the only streetlight in Wedell. Next to Joe's pickup was a muddy Ford F-250 with a four-wheel ATV in the bed and another mounted on a trailer behind it. He glanced inside the cab as he approached his truck. Shotguns, boxes of shells, handheld spotlights.

After he climbed into his pickup, he glanced through the wet windshield at the Bronco Bar. Critchfield and Smith watched him through a window from opposite sides of the Fat Tire Ale sign. Critchfield was mouthing something, and Smith was nodding.

As Joe backed out, the lyrics of Hank Williams Jr. ran like a ghost soundtrack in his mind.

155

CHAPTER
TEN

Medicine Wheel, Wyoming

The town of Medicine Wheel was seventeen miles north on a pot-holed county road, and it looked to Joe as if a strong wind might blow it away. There was a dilapidated gas station and convenience store — closed — on the entrance into town, and the only other business that seemed to be in operation was the Whispering Pines Motel, which was tucked away in a copse of trees on the top of a wooded rise a half-mile away from the town itself. It was easy to find because there were three brightly lit small signs on the sides of the road saying WHISPERING PINES MOTEL: YOUR ROADSIDE OASIS, WHISPERING PINES MOTEL: HOME AWAY FROM HOME, and WHISPERING PINES MOTEL: LIKE STAYING AT GRANDMA'S.

Joe was curious to meet Grandma.

The facility had a single-level home that served as the office, flanked by eight small cabins, four on each side. *No*, Joe thought, seven *cabins*. On the far east side was a small tangle of burnt framework. That's where the DCI agent had been.

The tiny office lobby had a counter with a key and a note that read: *FOR MR. PICKETT — Sleep tight*

156

and hit the bell if it isn't too late. Otherwise, check in tomorrow. Sweet Dreams, Anna B. All of the *i*'s were dotted with little hearts. The walls of the dimly lit lobby were smothered with country-themed kitsch — hand-painted farmers and their wives, doe-eyed cows with long lashes, lots of wooden signs with cute and precious sayings like MY HEART BELONGS TO MY GRANDKIDS, IF YOU CLIMB IN THE SADDLE BE READY FOR THE RIDE, MY GREATEST BLESSINGS CALL ME NANA, I'M A QUILTER AND MY HOUSE IS IN PIECES . . .

Joe sighed, uncomfortable with the cuteness, and pressed a buzzer on the counter while he grabbed the key. He heard a chime ring in a back room, and waited for a moment.

"Mr. Pickett?"

"That's me."

Anna B. emerged from the shadowed hallway with a wide grin and eyes that sparkled behind steel-framed glasses. She was doughy and round, and looked like a caricature of a country grandmother — tight silver curls, apple cheeks, an overlarge sweatshirt with hearts appliquéd on the front.

She dug out an old-fashioned registration form from a stack under the counter and handed it to Joe along with a pen with a taped plastic rose on it, apparently so Joe wouldn't have the urge to take it with him.

"Please fill out all the lines," she said. "I've got you in cabin number eight. It's our coziest and roomiest, since your reservation said you'd be here for a week."

"Thank you," Joe said, filling in his name, address, and license plate number.

"Is it your first time here?"

"Yup," Joe said.

"So what brings you to Medicine Wheel?"

"Business," he said. "I'm with the Game and Fish Department. Helping out Jim Latta for a few days."

"Oh," she said, pressing her fingertips to her lips, "that poor, poor man. He's such a nice man. It's so *sad* about his family."

"Yup, it is."

"That little girl of his — she's *such* a pistol. She doesn't let a little handicap hold her back."

He completed the registration form and handed it to her with his credit card. She rammed it through a manual slider with surprising determination, he thought.

While she did, he noticed a decades-old certificate on the wall behind her recognizing Anna Bartholomew as Medicine Wheel County Businesswoman of the Year in 1991.

"Are you Anna?" he asked.

"Why, yes."

"Are you related to the judge?"

"He's my brother," she said, with the smile still firmly in place. But her eyes were probing. "Do you know him?"

"Not yet," Joe said.

"If you're around here, you'll probably run into him," she said. "There aren't many of us left."

He looked at his key. "What happened to cabin number one out there?"

"Oh," she said, as if overcome by the question, "it burned to the ground in the middle of the night. It was horrible, just horrible. It's so sad, because Mr. Thompson was in it at the time."

"What caused the fire?" Joe asked.

She shook her head and waved away the dire implications of the question. "They still don't know for sure, but the investigators said he was smoking in bed. We have a strict rule about not smoking inside our units. You're not a smoker, are you?"

"No."

"Well, good. It was so tragic what happened. Mr. Thompson was *not* a nice man, but he didn't deserve what happened to him . . ." She caught herself and shook her head. "I shouldn't say such a thing about him. I didn't know his heart, so I shouldn't say something not nice about him."

Joe nodded.

"Just in case, we've had all our wiring updated and inspected since then," she said, assuring him, "and everything is shipshape. The sheriff's department did a thorough investigation and determined we weren't to blame in any way. So there's nothing to worry about."

"I wasn't worried."

She paused as she separated his receipt from her original credit card form. "I see your ring. Are you married?"

"Yes."

"Children?"

"Three girls."

"*All girls,*" she said, practically singing. "That must be wonderful for you. Children are such a blessing. And wait until you have grandchildren! They are the most wonderful treasures. Do you have any yet?"

"Not close."

"Yes, you do look too young. I have four," she said. "Four little angels that *love* their nana."

Joe smiled and chinned toward her many grandma items on the walls while she reeled off their names and ages. The oldest was twelve. She began to tell him about young Josh, and he listened for five minutes.

Finally, she reached across the counter and gave him a friendly swipe on his arm. "Oh, you don't care about hearing all about them. You're probably tired and want to get to your room."

"Well . . ."

"It's okay," she said. "I'm just happy you're here. You're our only guest tonight."

"I see that."

"This place used to be quite busy," she said with a defensive edge to her voice. "We used to be filled with coal miners and loggers for most of the year. That's why every cabin has a kitchenette. But these days, with the economy and gas prices . . ."

"It's tough," Joe said, working his way toward the door.

"Thank God for Mr. T.," she said. "He sends a few of his hunters here from time to time — plus people who come here to meet with him about something. I know he doesn't need to do that, because he owns the largest hotel in the county, so I know he does it out of the goodness of his heart. Otherwise, I don't know what we'd do."

"Mr. T.? Wolfgang Templeton?"

"Oh, yes, he's a wonderful man. Wonderful, wonderful, *wonderful* man."

"I've heard he's generous," Joe said, recalling what Latta had told him.

"He's our savior, almost. This county would just die without him."

"That's quite a compliment," Joe said.

"And every word is true," she chirped. "You know, the day after the fire, he showed up here himself with rolls and coffee, and he had some of his men help clean up. Some of his maintenance people worked with the sheriff to make sure the wiring was good in all the rest of the cabins, and he never even sent a bill. I didn't even know him very well — not like my brother — but he said he'd heard about our tragedy and wanted to reach out. That's the kind of man he is."

Cabin number eight had a long list of rules on a laminated piece of construction paper mounted over the desk and written in Anna B.'s hand. Joe tossed his bag into the spare room while the ancient electric heater under the window clicked and hummed and filled the cabin with the smell of burning dust and miller moths. He wondered how long it had been since another guest had used it.

While Joe poured two shots of bourbon from his flask into a cheap plastic cup, he tried to check his email only to discover that the motel — and possibly all of Medicine Wheel — had no Internet access.

He called Marybeth on his cell and they talked for twenty minutes. Marybeth had heard nothing from Sheridan, either, and was frustrated that the computers were down at the library most of the day and she'd not found out anything on Erik Young. April was still sulking in her room, and Lucy was at play practice. Rojo had a mysterious patch of hair missing from his forehead that must have come from scraping it against the corral door.

Joe told her about the pheasants, meeting Jim Latta, and the Whispering Pines Motel.

He said, "It's really . . . cute."

"Would I like it?"

"Probably not," he said, leaning back and looking around his room. The prints — old C. M. Russells — on the walls were decades old and faded.

Then he asked her to look up a couple of names and another item the next day when she went to the library, provided the network was back up.

"The names Bill Critchfield and Gene Smith," Joe said. "I checked dispatch and they have no priors, but I'm wondering what else is out there. And see if you can find out what it costs to perform major scoliosis surgery."

He felt guilty for even asking.

"That's an interesting list," she said. Then: "Joe, you're keeping your distance, right? Like you promised?"

"Of course."

Although he was exhausted, he couldn't sleep. The first night in a strange place was always a long one. When the heater kicked on to ward off the chill, it moaned to life and ticked furiously. When it was off, the silence outside was awesome, filled only with a slight breeze through the branches of the pines.

Twice he heard the crunch of gravel from tires on the road outside. When headlights swept through the thin curtains of his cabin, he sat up straight in bed. He'd brought several of his weapons into the room with him before locking his pickup, and he felt for where he'd propped his 12-gauge Remington Wingmaster in the corner near his bed. It was loaded with double-ought buckshot. But whoever had driven into the motel alcove had turned around and left, as if doing a drive-through.

He wondered if it was simply a wrong turn or if someone was checking out where he was staying.

Then he thought about what it must be like to wake up to find the cabin burning up around him, and he got dressed.

It was one in the morning when Joe located the isolated logging road in the hills below Wedell. He made the turn into the dark timber and saw fresh tire tracks in the mud in the ruts ahead of him. Sleet sliced down through his headlights, and he switched them off in favor of his under-the-bumper sneak lights as he drove up the hill he had taken that afternoon with Jim Latta.

When he got to the top of the meadow, his precautions turned out to be largely unnecessary, because below in the trees there was a slaughter going on.

He stayed in the cab of the pickup but lowered the side windows. Down near the tree line was a hastily parked pickup with an empty trailer behind it. Inside the trees were the percussive blasts of shotguns and high whines from ATVs roaring around. Periodically, he saw the flash of headlights through the trunks as a four-wheeler spun around, and the red spouts from the muzzles of the guns. Once he saw the inverted teardrop shape of a rooster pheasant shoot out of the trees, only to explode into feathers and bounce along the grass like a kicked football. It landed near the parked truck.

There were shouts: *"Got you, you motherfucker! Ha!"*

The only bouts of silence were when they had to reload.

Joe pulled out his cell phone and called Jim Latta's home number. It went straight to voicemail.

"Jim, Joe. I'm up here where we released those birds this afternoon and there's a firefight going on. I'm pretty sure I see Bill Critchfield's truck on the lower part of the meadow and I can hear four-wheelers racing around and plenty of gunshots. I figure these guys want to poach out all those pheasants while they're still bunched up."

He paused. Then: "This is your district and I don't want to big-foot, but I hate guys who do things like this. I'll wait here until two. Call me back if you want to hook up and make an arrest. Otherwise, I'll head back to town."

164

A few minutes later, he left the same message on Latta's cell, then called in his location and situation to dispatch. The reception was scratchy, and he wasn't sure the night dispatcher understood him, but at least they'd have something to go on if he disappeared off the face of the earth.

The shotgun blasts continued.

Finally, Joe grabbed his shotgun, told Daisy to stay, and got out of his pickup. He wished his request for a night-vision lens for his digital camera had been approved, but he'd been told at the time that an employee with his record of equipment wreckage couldn't be trusted with $7,000 surveillance hardware.

So he used the camera on his cell phone. He snapped photos of the pickup — it was the F-250 that had been outside the Bronco Bar — as well as the license plate, the boxes of shotgun shells inside the cab, and the muddy tracks of the ATVs from the pickup to the trees. Joe leaned over and got a good photo of the mangled pheasant that had dropped in the meadow after being shot from inside the trees. The coloring on the ring-necked rooster was vibrant in the flash: gold, vermilion, beaded with droplets from the sleet.

Before he left, he placed one of his business cards under the windshield wiper of the pickup so they'd know he'd been there. Then he trudged back up the hill. While he did, he looked over his shoulder to make sure the four-wheelers hadn't emerged from the timber to chase him down.

Inside the cab, Joe reached over and patted Daisy on the head and said, "Yup, it's a whole different world here."

CHAPTER
ELEVEN

Sand Creek Ranch

The next morning, high above the ranch headquarters on a timbered south-facing slope, before the visitor arrived, Nate Romanowski straddled the peak of the roof of a hundred-year-old line shack and fitted a new six-inch inner-galvanized pipe into the top of an ancient rock chimney. A ladder was propped against the eave, and his weapon hung within reach from the top of the right leg of the ladder.

The sky had cleared from the snow and rain the night before, but the air still smelled of wet spruce and damp forest floor. From his vantage point on the roof, Nate could see dozens of miles in every direction — soft wooded hills stretching south and west to the plains, and east to the border of South Dakota. The lone distant conical spire of Devils Tower shimmered in the morning sun to the northwest.

The headquarters for Sand Creek Ranch was a mile away and a thousand feet lower in elevation than the line shack. The collection of buildings stretched along the contours of the creek itself on the valley floor. The compound comprised twenty or so buildings, including guest cabins, barns and sheds, corrals for horses, and the magnificent castle-like lodge itself. On mornings when the air pressure was low like it was now, a pall of woodsmoke hung above the headquarters until the temperature warmed enough to release it into the atmosphere. But the compound itself, with all its people and intrigue, was far enough away that Nate often was able to forget it was there.

The first thing he'd built on the grounds of the old log shack was a sturdy mews for his falcons inside a loafing shed once used by cowhands. The birds perched with hoods on their heads and jesses hanging from their talons — a redtail, a prairie, and his peregrine that had somehow found him in the Black Hills and returned more than a year after she'd flown away. He was surprised to see her because returning falcons were extremely rare in his experience and in the falconry literature, but there she was. Their reunion had been unsentimental — she simply cruised down from a thermal air current from the west and roosted on the roof of the line shack. When he recognized the raptor by the mottled pattern of her breast feathers and raised his forearm, she floated down and landed on it clumsily, talons biting into his sleeve for balance.

He'd said: "You again."

Nate still wasn't sure what to make of it. He wished she didn't remind him so much of his previous life and circumstances, and he brushed away any thoughts that her return *meant* something, because if so, he wasn't prepared to grasp the implications.

‎ ★ ★ ★

Over the previous three months since he'd found the old structure up on the ridge, he'd built the mews, replaced the doors and windows, chinked the logs, shingled the roof, and reinforced the rafters. He was pleasantly surprised to find out how sound the rock-and-concrete foundation was, and how well constructed the fireplace turned out to be once he cleaned the birds' nests from the chimney and sanded the facing rock clean of soot.

The cowboys who had built the place decades before knew what they were doing, he thought, which was rare for cowboys. There was a permanence about the place that defied cowboy logic.

Nate had a propane tank delivered, as well as a propane-powered electric generator that was housed in an ancient meat cellar, where it could be run almost soundlessly. Inside, the wiring was still exposed and the woodstove needed to be cleaned, blacked, and leveled, but he was days away from renovating the place well enough to withstand the winter, which was coming.

And so was the visitor. He caught flashes of a vehicle moving up the old logging road in the trees, and he narrowed his eyes and reached out to touch the grip of his revolver. When the pickup got closer, he recognized it as a white Sand Creek Ranch GMC. There was a single occupant inside. He knew from the profile who it was, and he went back to fitting on the pipe.

"Ah," she said, parking the truck next to the loafing shed and getting out. "It's peaceful up here. No wonder you stay away from the ranch. It's a madhouse down there, and this morning . . . *whew!*"

Her name, Nate had learned the first time he met her, was Liv Brannan. He guessed her first name was short for Olivia, but he hadn't asked. She was trim, compact, and athletic, with a thick dark shock of ebony hair pulled back in a heavy French braid. She had mocha skin, a heart-shaped face, a wide mouth, and startling green eyes. She wore tight faded jeans and a red down coat with the ranch logo — the outline of the castle lodge — and SAND CREEK RANCH embroidered underneath it.

He assumed Brannan was some kind of executive assistant to Templeton and had been in place for a number of years. There was no doubt she was competent, efficient, and well connected. Other staffers showed Brannan deference, although he never saw her throw her weight around. When he asked about ordering building materials for the line shack and the delivery of a tank, propane, and the generator, she knew instantly who to call and had said, "Consider it done." Other than Liv Brannan, Nate had no interest at all in the workings of the ranch itself, or the hierarchy and inevitable infighting of the staff.

His arrival was the first and last time he'd seen the ranch executive staff in one place — ranch foreman "Big" Dick Williams, Liv Brannan, Guest Services Manager Jane Ringolsby, the man who ran the Black Forest Inn and game-processing facility, and the two locals who headed up Sand Creek Ranch Outfitting Services, Bill Critchfield and Gene Smith.

170

Whip was not there at the time and no one mentioned his name. Whip lived by himself in the largest of the guest cottages. Liv had offered Nate the second largest, but he'd turned it down. So far, Nate and Whip had managed to avoid each other on the grounds since he'd been hired.

"I heard you were back," she said, crossing her arms and leaning against the front fender of the truck.

He felt no need to respond to such an obvious statement. The pipe was fitted on tight, and he grunted as he turned it slightly so he could line up the holes he'd drilled in the pipe and chimney fitting. He dug a sheet metal screw out of his jacket pocket and started it into the first hole, twisting it with his fingers until it caught the sleeve inside and was tight enough that he could reach for the screwdriver.

"I heard the plane come in two nights ago," she said. "I kind of looked around for you at breakfast the last couple of days, but then I remembered you don't ever show up. So I figured you were up here working on your cabin."

"I am," Nate said, screwing in the first screw. "So now you can leave."

She laughed in response. "No way," she said. She had a pleasant southern accent — Louisiana? — and would slip a bit into dialect when she was making a point. She knew she was attractive and, given the location, extremely exotic. "I'm not going back down there until the smoke clears. So you're stuck with me for a while."

"Oh, good."

171

"I see three birds in that cage of yours," she said, pointing at the mews. "I swear there were only two the last time I was up here."

"There were."

"How'd you get another one?"

Nate sighed. "She just showed up. We were acquainted with each other a couple of years ago."

Liv Brannan closed one eye and contemplated that, then said, "A bird you owned just *found* you?"

"A falconer doesn't own his bird. A falconer and the falcon are partners," Nate said.

"Kind of like a loyal bird dog or something?"

"Not at all. More like hunting partners."

"How do you make them come back when they fly?"

"You don't."

"Then why do they come back?"

He sighed. "I don't have time to explain an ancient art right now. have a cabin to fix before the snow flies."

"So the bird just kind of shows up," she said. "Kind of like *me*."

"Except the bird doesn't keep talking," he said, flapping his fingers and thumb together in the air to mock her.

She ignored him. "I'd like to see what these birds do one of these lays. Are you gonna invite me to come watch?"

"Not likely."

She laughed again. "Is it true sometimes you climb up a tree and just sit there naked? That's one of the rumors going around down at the ranch."

172

Nate paused and looked up. "Too cold right now," he said.

She whooped and clapped her hands together. "So it's *true*. Don't you get bark-burn or something on your tender white skin?"

He didn't respond. He had the second screw secure and shifted his balance so he could put some muscle into twisting the screwdriver.

"Tell me again where your people come from?" she asked.

"I didn't tell you the first time."

"Mine are from Houma, Louisiana, in the Terrebonne Parish. Five generations' worth. We've got some real characters down there, too, but nothing like the folks that've been coming around here. Especially this morning. That's why I needed to get some space from 'em.

"So I decided to come up here and see you," she said with a flourish.

Nate grunted.

She laughed and shook her head from side to side, as if amazed. "Most men usually don't try to get rid of me so damn quickly."

"Well, there you go," Nate said.

She pushed herself off the bumper and approached the cabin. Nate thought for a moment she intended to climb up the ladder and join him on the roof. He didn't like that idea. Instead, he saw the ladder move and he snatched his weapon from where it hung before she carried the ladder away and leaned it against her truck.

"Now you *have* to talk to me," she said with a sly smile.

"No, I don't."

"Then you'll just have to listen," she said with a laugh. He liked her laugh, *and* her smile. He wished he didn't.

He *really* wished he didn't. It was one of the main reasons he had decided to renovate the line shack — so he wouldn't have to see her every day. There'd been an instant attraction from the moment he first met her that was as jolting as it was unexpected. He'd tried to ignore it. But it was obvious from her visit she felt it, too.

She said, "You know, it's funny. I don't have any problem talking to you. Ask anyone down there and they'll tell you I'm kind of stuckup and, you know, *aloof*. They know I've been with Mr. T. for a long time and they don't know what to think about that. But I know you won't tell anyone else what we talk about because you're not a talker. And you can't tell me I'm wrong, can you?"

Nate said nothing.

"If Mr. T. says he trusts you to be his second earner, *I* trust you. Simple as that. Lord knows we need another earner around here."

Nate didn't like the word *earner*.

"There's a *lot* of stress down there," she said, after a few minutes. "Tension and stress. Living on a ranch is like living in a big dysfunctional family. It's not like we just see each other during the day, you know, like a regular job. We have to eat together and see each other

174

in the evenings — there isn't much personal space. I don't know how Mr. T. stays calm all the time. If it was me, I'd tell 'em all to stop their whining and get the hell back to work. Or back to town. I don't know how he does it, I really don't. I just know how much I admire that man, even if he brings a little of it down on his own head. That's why I stayed with him when he moved out here in the middle of freakin' *nowhere*. When I told my people I was moving here, my aunt didn't even know where it was. She thought Wyoming was somewhere by Nevada."

He continued to circle around the stovepipe, securing it with the screws.

She put her hands on her hips and said, "I don't know if you've noticed, but there isn't exactly a big population of sisters around here in these hills to gossip with."

Nate responded by not looking at her but raising his hand and opening and closing it even faster than he had the last time.

"Stop it with the hand," she said. "I'm on a roll. You know those two women down there in the castle, the ones with the fake boobs? A redhead and a blonde? Do you know who I'm talking about?"

"No."

"Well, he told them it was time for them to go. He did it in a nice way, like he always does. He offered them their golden parachutes and all, standard operating procedure. But they are none too happy about it, so there's lots more bitching than usual. That blond one, her name is Adrian, I never liked her anyway. She should have been gone months ago, if you ask me."

After a while, Nate thought, her voice was like anything else: the breeze through the trees, birds chirping. Other things he'd learned to filter out. But he grudgingly admitted to himself that he enjoyed the timbre and cadence of her voice and found it beguilingly musical.

She said with a conspiratorial whisper, "Mr. T.'s getting the place ready for someone new. I've been working for him long enough that I think I can recognize that Mr. T. is in *love*."

Nate couldn't help himself. He looked at her. She showed no signs of jealousy. In fact, she seemed delighted by the prospect.

"That's right," she said, nodding. "He's getting the walls painted and replacing old furniture. He got a nice proper poster bed to replace the decadent round one he's had forever, so I was wondering what was up. I used to ask him, 'When you getting rid of that white-trash Hugh Hefner bed?' and he'd just say it was in the castle when he bought it, which it was. But when he sent those two bimbos away and asked me to help him pick out a nice new bed to order, I just knew it. He's bringing in a new lady. I couldn't be happier for him. I think he's been lonely. Those bimbos weren't exactly interesting conversationalists, you know. So this new lady — she must be something pretty special."

Nate went back to the chimney pipe.

"So in the middle of them bitching and whining at breakfast about having to pack up their stuff to be out

176

of here by tonight — one of the staff is driving them to the airport in Rapid City — two of our local redneck employees show up and *demand* to see him. Usually those types come in the door with their hats in their hands, acting all docile because they want something from him. But these two walked straight into the breakfast room and said they needed to talk to him right away. They had no manners, just like most of the people around here. They were muddy and dirty, and they had blood and feathers stuck to them. It was disgusting," she said, making a face.

"I escorted them into Mr. T.'s office. He was calm and cool as always, but they were all worked up. They said they had a big problem, and like always they expected Mr. T. to fix it. They started going on and on before I even left the room. You know, Mr. T. can't fix every damn thing there is around here, even though some of those people seem to think he can."

She muttered to herself and shook her head back and forth before continuing. "But they said they knew Whip was back, which is something no one is supposed to talk about. None of the staff is even allowed to say his name, just like they aren't supposed to say yours. *No one.* Those rednecks said they wanted Mr. T. to send Whip to take care of their stupid problem."

She wagged a single finger in the air. "That just isn't done. You don't ask Mr. T. to send Whip. You just leave Whip alone and don't look at him or meet his eye or talk to him. Those are the rules. You just *leave that man alone.* Those fools don't know what they're doing even mentioning his name, and they don't know what kind of . . . man . . . they're dealing with. Whip —" She caught herself. Then: "He's the coldest alive, and not someone to mess with. Not for something like this."

She paused, and Nate waited.

"Did you hear what the problem was?" Nate asked.

"Not the whole thing," she said. "Something about a new game warden."

The screw slipped out of his fingers and rolled down the length of the roof and fell to the dirt below.

"You dropped something," she said, advancing again to pick it up. "Hold on a second, and I'll bring it up to you."

"It's okay," he said. He thought: *Game warden?* "I've got another one."

Liv retrieved it anyway, moved the ladder back, and climbed up. When she reached to hand him the tiny screw, their fingers touched and Nate felt it deep inside like he was afraid he would.

"Time to go now," he said.

"You know, Mr. Falcon, you're a hard man to flirt with."

"Good."

"You gonna tell me what the problem is?"

"No," he said, turning away.

CHAPTER
TWELVE

Sundance, Wyoming

Jim Latta was over an hour late arriving for breakfast at the Longabaugh Café in Sundance, and Joe checked his wristwatch and ordered a second refill of coffee. He needed it, since he'd slept only three hours after returning to the Whispering Pines Motel.

The Longabaugh was located on Main Street, across from the post office, and was the only business on the block open that early in the morning. Mud-splashed pickups were parked outside, and Joe had chosen a corner booth next to the kitchen bat-wing doors with his back to the wall so he could observe the patrons and greet Latta when he showed up. When Joe arrived at seven, the place was filled with road crew workers en route to a highway construction project on I-90 — men who wanted big breakfasts of chicken-fried steak, three eggs, and gravy to drown it all in. There was plenty of grumping about the weather and their bosses before they all got up and left en masse with box lunches at seven-thirty.

While he waited, Joe checked his phone — no calls or messages from Sheridan — and read about the history of Longabaugh on the back of the menu. Harry

179

Longabaugh was a fifteen-year-old Pennsylvanian who had come west in 1887 in a covered wagon as far as Sundance, where he decided to steal a horse, saddle, and gun from a local ranch. He was caught immediately and arrested. During his year-and-a-half jail term, he'd adopted the name the Sundance Kid.

After the construction crew left, locals filtered in. A young, dirty couple in their late twenties or early thirties took the largest table in the center of the room and situated three children under six in the other chairs. The kids were loud and wild, and the mother cursed at them to shut up. The father wore a battered Carhartt barn coat and he took it off to reveal a black heavy metal T-shirt and sleeve tattoos. He was obviously not in a hurry to get to work that morning, Joe thought.

When two of the boys threw packets of jam at each other from a container on the table, the father reached over and swept the condiments away from their reach with his arm, lit a cigarette, and looked away.

"Still waiting?" the waitress asked Joe. She was heavy, with pink hair, and she wore cargo pants and a hoodie. There was a small silver hoop in her left nostril that Joe found hard not to fix on.

"A few more minutes," he said.

"Waitin' on Jim Latta?" she asked, nodding toward Joe's red uniform shirt.

"Yup."

"He'll be here," she said. "He comes in most days. You want to order while you wait?"

He ordered the Wild Bunch — three eggs, bacon, and toast.

There was the old iconic photograph of Harry Longabaugh, Butch Cassidy, and the Wild Bunch over the counter of the cafe. In it, the Sundance Kid wore a suit, tie, handlebar mustache, and bowler hat. Joe wished idly that criminals still chose to dress well, but thought: *Nobody* did anymore.

He was reaching for his phone to check on Latta when the game warden entered the café. Latta nodded to Joe in a brusque manner and said to the waitress, "The usual, Steffi."

He sat heavily in the opposite seat and leaned forward toward Joe. Latta's eyes were bloodshot and hooded, and a hundred tiny veins were visible on his nose and fleshy cheeks. He looked like he'd got about as much sleep as Joe had.

"I got your messages this morning," Latta growled.

"I was wondering," Joe said.

Latta shook his head, almost in sorrow. "I wish you wouldn't have gone up there."

"Couldn't sleep," Joe said.

"This is my district, goddamnit."

"I know that."

"Then what in the *hell* were you doing?" Latta asked, angry and pleading at the same time.

"My job. *Our* job."

Joe drew out his phone and brought up the camera roll. "Here," he said, handing it over to Latta. "I've got 'em in the act. Scroll through there and you'll see their truck, the license plate, and some dead birds. You can

181

even see hatchery bands on one of their feet if you zoom in. The time stamp nails down when it happened."

Latta frowned as he scrolled through the shots. He grumbled about having trouble figuring out the features of the phone to zoom in on individual shots. He complained that his thumbs were too big for the modern world.

"That's Critchfield's truck, isn't it?" Joe asked.

Latta grunted an assent, then put the phone down in front of him.

"Jesus, Joe," he said, shaking his head from side to side. "Next time you can't sleep, why don't you play solitaire or jerk off like everybody else?"

Joe chose not to reply.

"Why didn't you tell me you were going to go back up there last night?" Latta asked.

"I tried," Joe said. "You didn't pick up."

Latta said, "Shit, you stirred up a damn hornet's nest."

Joe was puzzled. "I did?"

The game warden turned his deadeye cop stare back on. "You left your card on their *windshield*."

Joe nodded. "So you heard about that already? What, did they call you? Is that why you're late this morning?"

"Never mind that," Latta said. "This is my district and I deal with things in my own way. I don't need you around here pissing in the pool."

"Sorry you feel that way," Joe said through tight jaws.

Before Latta went on, the waitress delivered their plates. Both had the Wild Bunch in front of them.

"I'll try to smooth things out," Latta said, "but in the meanwhile, I don't need any more of your goddamn help, okay?"

"Smooth what out?" Joe asked.

A gust of cool air blew through the cafe as two men entered. One was obviously the sheriff, judging by his beige uniform. The sheriff had narrow shoulders and a potbelly, and wore black squared-off boots. He had a sunken, weathered face and looked bemused, and he held his gaze on Joe for a beat longer than necessary. The other wore a tie and slacks and a long gray topcoat. Both men glanced their way as they entered — two redshirts were always a curiosity in hunting country — but settled into a booth across the room. The older man in the topcoat had a large square head, silver hair, and a serious expression on his face. When Joe nodded a hello, the sheriff looked quickly to his companion as if he hadn't seen it.

Joe noticed Latta had seen them enter as well, and the game warden's face seemed to have drained of color.

"Who are they?" Joe asked as he stabbed the yolk of an egg with a point of his toast.

"Sheriff R. C. Mead and Judge Bartholomew," Latta said in a low tone, not wanting to be overheard. "Don't stare at them."

"So that's Judge Bartholomew," Joe said. "I met his sister last night. I see the resemblance."

Latta said, "Let's eat and get out of here. You and me have to talk."

183

Joe nodded and ate. He was starving. He didn't even look up when a packet of jam thrown by one of the dirty boys hit him in the leg.

"Had to meet the physical therapist at the house before I could get going this morning," Latta said through a mouthful. "That's why I'm late."

Joe thought: *It took you a while to come up with that one.*

After they'd paid their tab, Jim Latta left the restaurant with his head down the same way he had left the Bronco Bar the night before. He said he'd meet Joe outside. The fact that Latta didn't acknowledge the judge or the sheriff said more, in a way, than if he had, Joe thought.

On his way toward the door, Joe skirted the table with the family and intentionally neared the booth with the sheriff and judge. Neither raised his head to acknowledge him.

As he passed, Sheriff R. C. Mead said to the judge, "And there he goes, off to enforce the game regulations for the great state of Wyoming."

Joe paused next to them and looked over. The judge seemed to be fighting a grin.

Mead said to Joe, "If you find somebody out there engaged in major criminal activity — like with too many mourning doves in their coat pocket or something — you make sure to call 911 so I can call up our SWAT team, you hear?"

"I think I could handle that one on my own," Joe said. "But thanks for the offer, Sheriff."

"That's why I'm here," Mead said, exchanging glances with the judge.

"Joe Pickett," he said, extending his hand.

"I'm Judge Ethan Bartholomew," the judge said, dismissively shaking Joe's hand. "I hope you enjoy your stay at the Pines."

"So far, so good," Joe said.

The judge paused for a moment, then said, "And don't go smoking in bed. Poor Anna can't afford to lose any more units."

"I'll keep that in mind," Joe said. Then he clamped his hat on his head and said to both of them: "Morning, gentlemen."

The judge nodded back. Mead said, "I know all about you, you know."

Joe raised his eyebrows.

"Bud Barnum and Kyle McLanahan were friends of mine," Mead said, letting the names drop like lead weights. When Bartholomew looked to him for clarification, Mead said, "The last couple sheriffs of Twelve Sleep County, where Joe Pickett here comes from. He was a pain in the ass to both of them, they said. Barnum dropped off the face of the earth and McLanahan died in a mysterious fall. I'm sure you heard about that."

"I heard about it," Bartholomew said, then looked up at Joe as if seeing him in a different light.

Mead said, "There's a new sheriff over there, some cripple. I don't know him very well yet. But my guess is he'd agree with the other two how the local game warden doesn't know how to keep his nose out of

185

sheriff department business. That's what they told me, anyway."

Joe said, "His name is Sheriff Mike Reed. He's a paraplegic because he got shot in the line of duty. He's a good man who needs a wheelchair. There's nothing crippled about him."

Mead said to Joe, "Just keep out of my way in this county. I really don't want to run across you again. You seem to be bad luck when it comes to sheriffs."

He said it as a mock joke, but Joe could tell he wasn't joking.

"And I'd appreciate it if you would stay out of my courtroom," Bartholomew said. "My court has enough on the docket without a bunch of frivolous game violations."

"You mean like locals who poach pheasants at night?" Joe asked innocently.

Something flashed through Judge Bartholomew's eyes. Mead managed to act as though he didn't understand what Joe had alluded to.

"That's what I mean," Bartholomew said with finality. "I don't want to waste my time with trivialities."

When the waitress arrived with their breakfasts, Joe stepped aside.

"Nice meeting you," he said as he went out the door.

Jim Latta stood between their two pickups, shuffling his feet nervously. He had Joe's phone in his hand. "You forgot this."

"Thanks," Joe said, taking it.

186

"What were you talking with them about in there?"

"Just saying hello."

"That's all?"

"That and the fact that everybody in this county seems to know where I'm staying and what happened last night."

"It's a small place," Latta said. "Everybody talks. That's what I was trying to tell you."

"Except you," Joe said, standing close to Latta. "You don't seem to have a need to talk to anyone around here. You move through them like you're a ghost, I've noticed."

Latta looked over his shoulder as if checking for spies and said, "That's what we need to talk about. Why don't we drop your rig and your dog by the motel and you can go out with me today? You can tell me all about establishing some public walk-in areas, like we talked about."

Joe hesitated, then agreed.

When he got behind the wheel to follow Latta out of Sundance, Joe checked his phone for messages he might have missed. There were none.

But the photos had been deleted.

Joe followed Latta's truck east out of Sundance toward Medicine Wheel. The long grassy mountain meadow they drove across was empty of other cars. Wooded hills bordered the flat on both sides and a narrow creek meandered in and out of view on the right side, its bank choked by heavy brush. A small herd of white-tailed deer grazed in the grass near the creek and didn't bother to look up as the two pickups sizzled by.

He let Latta build a comfortable lead before scrolling through his phone for Chuck Coon's private cell phone number. When he found it, he punched the number with his thumb and put his phone on speaker and lowered it to his lap. Joe didn't want Latta to see him talking with anyone if the game warden checked him in his rearview mirror.

Coon answered on the second ring. "Make it quick, Joe. I'm on my way down the hall right now for a meeting with some D.C. honchos."

"Just checking in as instructed," Joe said.

"Anything to report?"

"Not a lot," Joe said. "Except everyone I've met so far seems to know I'm here."

"But do they know *why*?"

"I don't know what they know, but it's like walking into a bar full of regular customers — I stand out. But I can tell you Wolfgang Templeton seems to be well regarded around here. I haven't met anyone yet who doesn't sing his praises."

"Interesting," Coon said. "But will anybody give you something we can work with?"

"I don't know."

"Has anyone indicated they're aware of Mr. Romanowski in the area?"

"Nope. But I haven't asked specifically, either."

"Do that."

Joe grunted.

"So no whistle-blowers as yet," Coon said.

188

"Not yet," Joe said. "But there seems to be a lot going on up here I don't understand."

He told Coon about delivering the pheasants, then being there when they were being poached out in the middle of the night.

"You left them your card?" Coon asked incredulously.

"Yup."

"Joe, you were supposed to keep a low profile. We talked about that and you agreed."

Joe said, "Chuck, they already knew I was here. Now they know I'm a real game warden. They aren't thinking of me in any other way."

Coon paused for a moment, then said, "Okay, I see the sense in that. It establishes your cover."

"It's not a cover," Joe said. "I *am* a game warden. But what I can't figure out is why these two low-life poachers seem to be above the law up here. The local game warden doesn't want to roust them, the sheriff doesn't want to hear about them, and the judge doesn't want them in his courtroom."

"How do you know that?"

"They all told me."

"All this has happened already?" Coon asked. "You haven't wasted any time."

"I'll text you the names of the locals when I get a chance," Joe said. "Maybe you can run them and find something."

"Roger that."

Joe said, "The game warden up here seems to be hiding something. I think he knows a lot more about what goes on than he's let on to me so far."

"Are you on good terms with him? Will he talk?"

"I don't know yet," Joe said. "I've got to be real careful because he seems a little suspicious. He's not happy with me for identifying those poachers for some reason. I don't really like spying on a fellow game warden, you know. It doesn't feel right."

"Oh well," Coon said. "Get what you can out of him and let me know."

"Thanks for the sympathy and understanding."

"My pleasure."

Joe could hear Coon's shoes tapping out a cadence as if he were marching down a hallway. He was slightly out of breath when he spoke.

Joe said, "Hey — do you have anything for me regarding Erik Young? The name I asked you about?"

"I gave that to an agent," Coon said impatiently. "I haven't seen the agent yet today and I don't know if he sent me an email on it."

"You'll let me know, though, right?"

"Yeah, yeah. Okay, I've got to go. Keep me posted."

Joe punched off. When he looked up he could see Latta watching him in his rearview mirror.

Anna Bartholomew met them in the courtyard of the Whispering Pines with a platter of hot cinnamon rolls. She said she'd just baked them.

"We just ate breakfast," Latta said to her with a grin while Joe led Daisy back to cabin number eight. "But if it's okay with you, I'd like to take one or two along for later."

190

"They're best when they're warm," Anna said with a chirpy voice. "But I can get some paper towels and wrap them up for the two of you. You men must get hungry out there, driving around the countryside."

Joe rejoined Latta with his coat and the leather briefcase from his truck while the game warden waited for the cinnamon rolls.

"Walk-in area guidelines and paperwork," Joe said, lifting the briefcase.

Latta nodded and said, "She makes the best damned cinnamon rolls in the state."

"I like cinnamon rolls," Joe said. He sounded simple even to himself. But what he was thinking was, *How did she know we were coming back here?*

Latta's agency pickup was of a newer vintage than Joe's, but the contents of the single cab were remarkably familiar — GPS mounted on the dashboard, radios underneath, evidence kit, reams of maps held together by rubber bands on the floor console, empty shell casings and spent sunflower seeds on the floor. An M14 peep-sight carbine was secured to a mount in the center of the cab and a combat shotgun was wedged muzzle-down between the bench seats.

"Feels strange being a passenger," Joe said, climbing in and shutting the door.

"I bet," Latta said, taking the road out of Medicine Wheel.

Latta seemed preoccupied, Joe thought. No small talk about the weather, where they were going, anything.

191

Something was on his mind and he was trying to figure out how to present it.

Joe finally said, "The photos are gone from my phone."

Latta wouldn't meet his eyes as he drove, but he said, "What do you mean?"

"They've been deleted. I think you know that."

Latta said, "I might have pushed the wrong button when I was looking at them this morning. I told you I have trouble with those damn things." Then: "Damn, that's too bad."

Joe said, "We both know it doesn't matter. We could find feathers, blood, and other evidence in Critchfield's truck and send it to the forensics lab in Laramie. That is, if we really wanted to nail him. But it's your district and it's your call."

Latta started to respond, then caught himself. After a few miles, he let out a sigh. He said, "I might have pushed something that said 'reformat this camera' when I was scrolling through the pictures, I guess."

"Gee, you think?" Joe said with sarcasm.

"Okay, okay," Latta said. "Now is not a good time to cite Critchfield and Smith. It's complicated, but it's something that just isn't worth it, Joe. You've got to trust me on this."

"Are you building a case against him?"

After a pause, Latta said, "Something like that."

They took the winding state highway through timbered hills to get to the access road that would lead them to the Sand Creek Ranch headquarters. In addition to

192

spruce and ponderosa pine, Joe noted swaths of scrub oak in the valleys. As they passed, he saw deer and wild turkeys on the floor of the forest.

The truck approached a Y junction in the road and Latta bore left. Joe saw another historical marker whiz by. On a flat below a creek, he was surprised to see a huge red structure of sorts with turrets and a gabled roof. Two dozen four-wheel-drive vehicles were parked outside the main building. The southern wing looked empty except for two aging pickup trucks parked side by side.

"What the heck is *that?*" Joe asked. The building looked remarkably out of place. A sign read: THE BLACK FOREST INN.

"Used to be the home of the owner of the coal mine," Latta said. "He built it to look like some kind of European château. Up until a few years ago, it was in bad shape. Some guy tried to turn it into a hotel, but he didn't know what the hell he was doing. The only crowd he got there were the bikers on the way to Sturgis, and they beat it up even more."

"It looks restored," Joe said, noting its clean lines, new asphalt parking lot, and new roof.

"Pretty much," Latta said. "About ninety percent of the rooms are refurbished, and they're filled with hunters this time of year. It's pretty convenient for them because that structure on the south end is that wild game-processing facility I told you about — the only one in the county. It gets busier than hell."

"I saw a couple of trucks."

"Locals," Latta said. "When they're butchering game, they employ five or six people from around here. It's a damn fine processing outfit — one of the best I've ever seen. You know how some of those places are. But down there, you could eat off the floor. All the saws and equipment are stainless steel, and the cutters wear white coats and aprons. It's high-quality enough I take my own deer and elk there to get it packaged. We could swing by there on the way back and pick up some German sausage, if you want. They make great sausage."

"Who owns it?" Joe asked, already knowing the answer.

"Templeton. He saved the place," Latta said.

"I wish I'd known about it," Joe said. "I could have stayed there instead of the Whispering Pines."

"The bar gets pretty rowdy," Latta said with a grin. "Especially now, during hunting season. So you're better off where you're at."

Joe nodded. He said, "Since we're going to see him, what can you tell me about Wolfgang Templeton?"

"What do you want to know?"

"You seem to like him. Everybody I've met seems to like him. That's not always the case with big landowners who move in and buy everything up."

Latta agreed and said, "If it weren't for him, I don't know what this county would be like."

As they drove, Latta said Templeton had been a generous and selfless philanthropist since his arrival years before.

194

"You name it," Latta said. "When our six-man high school football team needed new uniforms, Mr. Templeton paid for them. When the county museum needed a new roof, Mr. Templeton paid for the materials and sent his men to fix it. When the medical clinic was just about to close because the mines shut down and hardly anyone had medical insurance anymore, Mr. Templeton was able to recruit a doctor from Pakistan — Dr. Rahija — and made a big donation to upgrade the place. He just helps people, Joe," Latta said, as if that explained it all.

"He's the biggest employer in the county by far," Latta continued. "He employs out-of-work loggers and miners as guides, outfitters, cowboys on his ranches, cooks, even those meat processors back there. Three-quarters of this county owe their walking-around money to Mr. Templeton."

"Interesting," Joe said.

"Yeah, I don't know what we'd do without him. Government checks and EBT cards only go so far."

"EBT?"

" 'Electronic Benefits Transfer.' The Feds issue 'em now instead of food stamps. They're kind of like debit cards. Food stamps gave the recipients a sense of shame, I guess."

Joe looked over to see if Latta was being facetious, but he didn't appear to be.

"Plus, he helped you and Emily," Joe said.

"That's right," Latta said, and turned to Joe. "Who else would do something like that out of the goodness of his heart? I mean, he found the best surgeon in

South Dakota and flew me and Emily to Rapid City in his plane so she could get that operation. Think about that."

"He has his own plane?" Joe asked.

"A couple of them," Latta said, which confirmed what Coon's file had said. "The ranch headquarters has an airstrip on it, and Mr. Templeton keeps his planes in a hangar there. See, he's a pilot. He actually flew us there himself. And when Emily was released from the hospital, he flew back over and brought us home."

"I've got to ask," Joe said, as conversationally as he could manage. "Where did he get all his money to do these things?"

Latta turned back to the road. He said, "Beef, of course. And he grows lots of hay on a couple of his ranches."

Joe said, "Still, there seems like there has to be another source. All the ranchers I know are land-rich but cash-poor."

Latta continued: "Then there's all the outfitting and hunting operations, the wild game-processing plant . . ." His voice trailed off.

Joe let the question just hang there, and it did.

"I don't know," Latta said, finally. "I heard he used to be some kind of big-shot financial whiz back east. He probably banked a ton of money away during the boom years."

As he said it, Latta turned from the highway onto a well-graded gravel road. They passed under a magnificent wrought iron archway that identified the property as THE SAND CREEK RANCH.

As they passed through the arch, Joe noted small closed-circuit cameras mounted to the wrought iron columns on each side.

"Why the cameras?" Joe asked, pointing them out to Latta.

"Cattle rustlers, I'm sure," Latta said quickly.

"Is that a problem around here?"

"Sure. Beef prices are up, you know. That's why the ranch shut down all the old access roads except the main one a few years ago. Rustlers can bring their cattle trucks in only one way: through the main gate."

"Interesting," Joe said.

"Mr. Templeton thinks of everything," Latta said with a nod.

"Tell me," Joe said, "in your visits out here, have you ever run into a falconer? Big guy, with a blond ponytail?"

Latta looked over, puzzled. "No, why?"

"Just wondering."

"Who is he?"

"Just a guy I'm always on the lookout for," Joe said. "We have some history."

Latta let it drop.

Joe looked ahead. The road followed the contours of a narrow but deep stream. He could see trout rising to the surface to sip at a mid-morning hatch. The concentric circles were substantial, meaning the fish were big. As a fly fisherman, Joe felt a tug in his chest and wished he'd packed along his rod and waders.

197

"We might catch Mr. Templeton himself," Latta said, "but more likely we'll talk to his ranch foreman about the walk-in areas."

Joe tried to contain his disappointment.

"But if we talk to Mr. Templeton, Joe, I've got to ask a favor of you."

"What's that?"

"Let me do the talking," Latta said. "You tend to ask too many questions."

Joe thought it over, recalling the admonition from Coon and the promise he'd made to Marybeth, before saying, "It's a deal. This is your district, after all."

The hills on both sides closed in as they drove up the gravel road and entered the shadowed mouth of a canyon. Joe kept glancing at the stream itself but also noticed the condition of the ranch: straight and tight barbed-wire fences, obvious habitat restoration work on the waterway, smart culverts and cattle guards, no ancient husks of spent vehicles or ranch equipment. The vast property was impressive, he thought, and well managed.

The road began to serpentine and narrow as it rose into the canyon, hugging the left side of the red canyon wall. When he glanced ahead, Joe could see the outward corners of four upcoming turns.

Coming around the farthest turn, more than a quarter of a mile ahead, was a flashing glimpse of the grille of an oncoming pickup.

"Oh shit," Latta whispered, slowing down immediately.

Joe narrowed his eyes. The oncoming vehicle was already out of view as it rounded the turn. But he'd recognized it as well.

"That's Bill Critchfield's rig," Latta said urgently. "Get out now."

Joe looked over for clarification.

"If he sees you . . ." Latta said.

"What if he does?"

"Just get out," Latta said. He pointed his finger toward a thick stand of ponderosa pine on the other side of the creek about two hundred and fifty yards upstream. "Meet me there. I'll pick you up in a minute."

"But . . ."

"*Go*," Latta hissed, his eyes flashing.

"It's your district," Joe said as he threw his door open and jumped out. The grade on the side of the road was steep and the ground was loose, and he danced his way down to the bottom. When he was able to stop and look back, he saw Latta's arm reach out from the cab and close the passenger door, then ease his truck up the road.

Confused, Joe pushed his way through heavy brush until he reached the creek. The air smelled of juniper and sage. He could hear both pickups on the road above him as they met. He imagined Latta and Critchfield stopped nose-to-tail in the road to exchange pleasantries. Or something.

Although he was too far away to make out any words, Joe heard Critchfield's voice bark sharply. He paused and listened and waited, hoping there wouldn't be trouble. Joe wished he'd brought his shotgun along, and he instinctively reached down to brush the grip of his service weapon with the tips of his fingers.

The stream was narrow enough at one point that he was able to jump across it, although he barely made the distance. Both of his boot heels sank into the mud of the opposite bank as he landed, and he windmilled his arms forward to keep his balance so he wouldn't tumble back into the water.

Joe stopped to pause and listen as he walked upstream, keeping to the heavy brush so they couldn't see him from the road. Again, he heard Critchfield's voice rise and fall. He got the impression Critchfield was yelling at Latta, or making some kind of emphatic point. Probably about the business card he'd found on his truck, Joe thought. He was still taken aback by how panicky Latta had acted, and he wondered what Latta thought Critchfield would do if Joe had stayed in the truck.

Latta, Joe thought, had some explaining to do.

Around a long, lazy bend of the stream, with the dark stand of pine looming ahead of him, Joe found out he wasn't alone. What he didn't expect was to stumble upon a man who appeared to be a refugee from *The Great Gatsby* searching for a tennis game.

CHAPTER
THIRTEEN

Sand Creek Ranch

"Hello there," Joe called out. "Are you having any luck?"

At the sound of Joe's voice, the man upstream froze in midcast. He didn't jump or wheel around but his fly line dropped and pooled unceremoniously around his ankles. As it did, he slowly turned his head, but his expression was stoic.

Joe had encountered enough fishermen over the years to know the reaction was unusual. Usually, anglers were startled and immediately started talking or reaching for their licenses when they saw his red shirt. Only once had it been otherwise, four years before in the Sierra Madre, and what led from that response had been harrowing.

The man was young, trim, and athletic-looking, although like the red stone structure on the way up, he seemed out of place. The fly fisherman wore British Wellington boots instead of modern waders, form-fitting cargo pants, a crisp button-down long-sleeved shirt, and a cream-colored sweater-vest with a V-neck. Joe thought he looked like a Hollywood actor, with his high cheekbones, slicked-back dark hair, and intense

201

blue eyes. The fisherman held an expensive-looking bamboo fly rod and wore a throwback wicker creel over his shoulder.

"How's fishing?" Joe asked.

"Fine, sir," the man said. The word spoken was southern and syrupy: *fahn.*

"I saw some big rises on the water a while ago," Joe said. "Are they still coming up to the surface?"

"Yes."

"Nothing better than fishing for big trout with dry flies, is there?"

The fisherman was still locked in place, the rod suspended in the air. He slowly lowered it and said, "No, there isn't. Even in the fall there are mid morning hatches. But I believe, sir, you might be trespassing."

Joe said, "Maybe so."

High above them, Joe could still hear the sound of voices from Latta and Critchfield. Apparently, they were still parked on the road. Joe shot a look toward the slope to confirm that he was still out of their view due to the angle, as was the fisherman.

"My name is Joe Pickett. I'm a Wyoming game warden."

"Ah," the fisherman said with a nod, "the misplaced game warden."

"Misplaced?"

"Back home, we'd call you a conservation officer."

"Where's home?"

"Not here."

"Meaning you're a newcomer here," Joe said.

"But not misplaced," he said with an edge.

202

So he was aware of him as well, Joe thought. Joe stepped a few steps to the side. The move was intended so he could observe the fisherman from a three-quarter angle from the back. He didn't appear to be packing any weapons, although it was hard to discern what was under the sweater-vest.

"Mind if I take a look at what you've got in your creel?"

Something flickered across the fisherman's face: a look of disdain. "This, sir, is highly unusual. May I ask you why you want to know?"

"Sure," Joe said. "I just wanted to make sure you're legal, which I'm sure you are. I'm guessing anyone who uses a twelve-hundred-dollar bamboo rod and an eight-hundred-dollar vintage creel would also be in full compliance with the fishing regulations."

The fisherman kept his gaze on Joe as he approached. He said, "You don't know your rods like you think you do. This is a Lyle Dickerson Model 8013. It was built in 1959 and it cost me $9,750." He paused for effect, then: "It's worth every penny on a narrow stream like this. It doesn't have the action of a modern graphite, of course, but it has touch and restraint I've learned to appreciate."

Joe whistled as he approached the man.

"Stop right there," the fisherman said, hardening his voice. As he did, Joe sensed danger in the man's stillness.

"I just want to take a look," Joe said. "It's up to you to let me. I won't force you. But if you refuse to let me see what's inside that creel, we may have issues."

"Issues?"

Joe nodded.

"You, sir, are trespassing on private property. These are private waters."

Joe paused and leaned back and hooked his thumbs through the belt loops of his jeans. He said, "I'm sorry, but this a free-flowing stream, not a private pond. There's a strange thing about Wyoming laws, and I can understand your confusion. See, in this state, the landowner owns the ground — even the streambed — but not the water itself. The water belongs to the public and so do the fish, which means Wyoming Game and Fish regulations apply even on private land.

"We don't want to make this difficult. So, if you don't mind, I'd like to take a look in that creel. It looks heavy. It looks like you're doing really well with that bamboo rod of yours. I'm a fly fisherman myself, and I'm always in awe of a real pro."

The fisherman didn't respond, although Joe sensed he enjoyed being referred to as a pro.

The man raised his chin, but his unblinking eyes never wavered. When Joe looked directly at them, he got a chill on the back of his neck. There was something about this man that made Joe wish he'd never encountered him. Something deeper and more serious than he'd anticipated.

After a beat, the fisherman reached down with his free hand and untied the leather strap on the creel and raised the cover. Joe noticed there was a word or name tooled into the strap that said WHIP. He stepped forward and peered inside. The heavy brown trout inside looked like brightly speckled lengths of burnished copper. They were nested in long, moist grass plucked from the bank to keep them cool.

"Impressive," Joe said, counting heads. "Ten of 'em, and not a one less than fourteen inches. You're quite an angler."

"I took up the sport a few years ago," the fisherman said, the edge on his voice dulling a bit more. "I find fly-fishing surprisingly relaxing."

Joe gestured to the creel. "Is that your name? Whip?"

"It's a nickname."

"What's your full name?"

"That, sir, is none of your business right now."

"Have you ever considered catch-and-release?" Joe asked. "That way, someone else might get the chance to catch one of these beauties."

"I've never considered it," Whip said flatly. "Letting a fish go after you've stalked it and landed it with the perfect fly and perfect cast seems incomprehensible to me. Letting a fish go after all that surveillance insults the fish itself, like making a silly sport out of something serious. Does that make any sense to you, sir?"

"No."

"You're not going to tell me I'm over my limit, are you?"

"Nope, because you aren't," Joe said, leaning back again and refitting his battered Stetson on his head. "You can have twelve in possession, and you're two shy. But there's a problem."

"What?"

Joe sighed, feigning sadness. "You can have twelve in possession, but only one can be over twelve inches. It looks like every one of those big trout is oversized."

Whip didn't move or speak.

Joe said, "Let's clear the air, and start with letting me confirm your license and habitat stamp."

The fisherman made no move to reach for his wallet.

"Maybe you didn't hear me," Joe said. "I need to verify your license and stamp. It's routine procedure."

"What are you going to do?" the man asked in a whisper. "Arrest me?"

"Probably not," Joe said. "But you may get a ticket. And if you don't have a proper license or refuse to comply, you may wind up in more trouble than either of us wants."

The man was still but smoldering. Joe mentally rehearsed reaching for his bear spray with his left hand or his weapon with his right, but he hoped it wouldn't come down to either.

He could barely hear Whip when the man said, "You have no idea what you're doing."

"Actually," Joe said, withdrawing his citation booklet from the back pocket of his jeans, "I've done this before. I can write you a ticket for violating fishing regulations and for not having your license and stamp in possession, but I'll waive the last charge if you produce your documentation. So for now, let's start with your name . . ."

Before Joe could reply, his name was called out from above.

"Joe!" It was Latta. He sounded alarmed.

Joe turned his head up toward the road. In the distance, he could hear Critchfield's truck making its way down the canyon. Whatever Critchfield and Latta had been talking about for so long was apparently resolved.

Latta was out of his truck and peering down into the meadow with his hands on his hips.

"Joe! Goddamnit, Joe!"

"What, Jim?"

He could see Latta looking from Joe to the fisherman and back to Joe. He was waving his arms. His tone was high-pitched and panicked.

"Joe, get the hell up here now. Leave that man alone and *get the hell up here.*"

Again Joe was confused. When he looked over at the fisherman, he saw the man smiling slightly, but in a malevolent way. As if he'd spared Joe, but Joe was too dense to understand just how closely he'd flown to the sun.

To the fisherman, Latta shouted, "I'm sorry this happened. He's not from around here. He has no idea what he's doing."

"No, he doesn't," the fisherman said, more to Joe than to Latta. Joe was stymied and angry. "Jim . . ."

"Get up here."

Joe took a deep breath and swallowed hard. He said to the fisherman, "Obviously, I've touched a nerve."

"Obviously, you have. Now please go so I can get on with my morning." Whip leaned forward and began to retrieve the line at his feet. He said, "There are fish to catch."

As Joe climbed up the slope toward Latta with his ears burning hot from anger and humiliation, he heard the fisherman behind him purr, "I'm sure I'll be seeing you around, Mr. Joe."

Inside the cab of the pickup, Joe slammed his door shut and said to Latta, "What the hell was *that* about?"

"We're here to see Mr. Templeton," Latta said through clenched teeth, "not to hassle his guests or employees."

"I wasn't hassling him," Joe said. "I was doing my job."

"In *my* district, on *my* watch, goddamn you," Latta said, slamming the truck into gear and lurching forward. His face was flushed, and Joe noticed a necklace of sweat beads under his jaw as if he were wearing a choker. He said, "I'm trying to do this, Joe, I'm trying to be a good host and a colleague. I'm fucking *trying*. But this is the second time you've left a turd in my punch bowl. I don't know how much longer I can keep this up."

"Keep what up?"

Latta's eyes flashed. "Keeping you from getting yourself hurt or killed, that's what."

"Why don't you just forget about that," Joe said. "How about coming clean with me instead?"

"It's for your own good."

"So who was that guy down there? Whip? Why is it so important to protect him?"

"I don't know his full name," Latta said.

"Then why did you warn me off?"

"He's not someone you want to mess with, believe me."

Joe said, "What kind of name is *Whip?*"

"Don't ask me questions like that."

Before Joe could ask another, the canyon opened up onto a vast green hay meadow bordered by timbered hills. The hay had been recently cut and lay in thick rows across the carpet of late-season grass. Sand Creek, choked with close streamside brush, meandered through the meadow.

Joe could see an older man below in a battered straw cowboy hat, riding a four-wheeler through the rows of shorn hay with his back to them. He wore worn jeans, irrigation boots, and a torn and faded chambray shirt. A shovel was attached to the back end of the ATV with bungee cords.

"That's Mr. Templeton out checking his final cutting of the year," Latta said. Joe noted the tone of admiration in his voice.

CHAPTER
FOURTEEN

Saddlestring, Wyoming

At the same time, behind her desk, Marybeth Pickett breathed a sigh of relief when both the RMIN (Rocky Mountain Information Network) and the FBI's ViCAP (Violent Criminal Apprehension Program) came up on the Twelve Sleep County Library system computer. She leaned back and glanced around to make sure no patrons or staff were close enough to see what was on the screen, then used her cell phone app to recall the usernames and passwords she'd been given years before from her friend Dulcie Schalk, who was also the county prosecutor. Dulcie had given Marybeth the keywords in the midst of a frantic investigation when she needed her help and had either forgotten — not likely, knowing Dulcie — or chosen to look the other way afterward. Both databases were supposed to be accessed only by authorized law enforcement personnel. Because Marybeth was married to one, and often was asked to perform research for him for free, she managed to justify why she kept the information.

For the first hour and a half that morning, she'd been too busy to access the system to see if the high-speed network was working again. The Internet in the old Carnegie library was often down and the IT man on staff could never seem to keep it live. Something about power surges, he claimed. But when she'd arrived that morning to open, there he was, assuring her that it was back up. The early-morning newspaper readers now lounged in the periodical section, several of the older locals napping. She'd inventoried returned books dropped off during the night, and spent the next hour answering emails and queries. A staff meeting was scheduled at eleven, which meant she had nearly an hour of practically free time behind the desk.

Before diving in, Marybeth did what she always did and ran through a mental checklist of her immediate family. She knew she couldn't proceed without knowing where everyone was, what they were doing, and when she'd talk to or see them next.

Lucy was in school but would be late getting home due to play practice.

April would go straight from high school to her shift at Welton's Western Wear for the evening, then return home enraptured, if Dallas Cates had called or stopped by, or in a sulk otherwise.

Sheridan should be in her third-hour class at UW, hopefully feeling safe, secure, and studious. Perhaps she'd even call that evening.

And Joe was hundreds of miles away, probably getting himself into some kind of trouble.

Marybeth glanced down at the scribbled list next to her keyboard, briefly debating who to look up first. No question, she thought, the first would be Erik Young. Erik with a *k*.

She was always worried that the usernames and passwords had changed since the last time she accessed the databases, and that by keying in the old ones she'd be flagging an investigation of some kind. So far, though, they'd remained the same and no G-men had shown up to question her.

She keyed in the usernames and passwords and she was in. Both the regional and national databases responded with prompts and search criteria.

She typed in "Erik Young" and listed "Los Angeles area" for a location in ViCAP, holding her breath while the search was conducted.

Four Erik Youngs had criminal records. None was younger than forty-two. She did the same search in RMIN, speculating that perhaps he'd done something in the region. No hits at all. She whispered, "Whew," took a sip of coffee, and realized the search had hardly been helpful. Erik would be, what, nineteen, twenty, twenty-one at most? In that case, if he'd done something before leaving California, his records would be locked away in a juvenile database she had no access to.

There were other problems with her approach, she knew. Sheridan had told Joe he was "Erik Young from Los Angeles." But there was no way to verify if Erik was actually his first name, a second name, or a nickname. Could "Young" be "Jung" or some other derivation? The only way to confirm his actual name would be to

212

crosscheck it with the university student database or ask Sheridan to get involved.

But there had to be a way to avoid that route, she thought. If nothing else, she could eliminate all the possibilities before she contacted the university or Sheridan. There was always a solution if she kept calm and thought it through.

Within a minute, she leaned forward and minimized both the ViCAP and RMIN windows and called up a national people-finder locator site and entered the same criteria.

There were forty-five Erik Youngs listed in California and sixteen in the Los Angeles area alone, although there were hundreds of Eric Youngs with a c. Marybeth concentrated just on the sixteen Eriks. There were four in Covina, two each in Anaheim, Hermosa Beach, Huntington Beach, and Torrance, and one each in Monterey Park, Playa del Rey, Rialto, and Venice.

Methodically, she accessed each location. The database listed the name, of course, but also the street address, the value of the person's home, and an approximate age — sometimes given as "unknown." Marybeth eliminated all the names with ages listed as thirty or above, and that left her with seven possible Erik Youngs, all designated "age unknown."

She isolated the list of seven. The site provided maps of each specific address as well as Google Earth satellite photos of each home. They ranged from a $2.8 million mansion in Playa del Rey to Apartment C in Venice to a post-office box in Covina to an "unknown" address in

Torrance. She assumed that a family in a multimillion-dollar home would not send their son to a state university, and crossed that one out. Likewise, she assumed families living in apartments or listing their address as a post-office box would likely not have the means to send any children out of state to college. Of course, she thought, she could always revisit the top and bottom tiers if the middle didn't pan out.

That left three possibilities: the $708,000 home in Covina (likely the parents of the P.O. box holder in the same suburb), the $565,000 home in Monterey Park, and the $268,000 home in Rialto.

She felt her pulse quicken as she looked at the likely homes that produced Erik Young and sent him to far-off Laramie to attend the University of Wyoming.

It took only a few minutes to access the L.A.-area white pages to obtain all three telephone numbers.

Surprisingly, two people answered — a housekeeper in Monterey Park and a stay-at-home mom in Rialto with a heavy Mexican accent.

She began with, "Hello, I'm calling to find out if this is the home of Erik Young who is a student at the University of Wyoming in Laramie . . ." She was careful not to misidentify herself or pose as either a law enforcement or university official.

Both said she was on the wrong track. The Erik Young in Monterey Park was a student at UCLA, the housekeeper said. The Erik Young in Rialto was incarcerated at the California State Prison in Corcoran. As the woman told Marybeth, she began to cry.

Marybeth apologized in both instances.

214

At the Covina home, she was asked to leave a message by a recorded female voice that sounded to be about right for the mother of a college-aged student, Marybeth thought. She left a message and asked to be called back on her cell phone.

But she was thinking: *Covina.*

When she had more time, she decided, she'd do an in-depth search of "Erik Young" and "Covina." Perhaps she'd find where he'd participated in school activities, or been mentioned in blog posts or newspapers. Maybe she'd find where he had been thrown out of school for wearing a long black trench coat or arrested for torturing small animals. The thought of the possibility of cracking it so easily left her shaking her head.

She hoped that after the staff meeting and lunch she'd have another extended period at the desk when she could do the additional research.

The RMIN database went off when Marybeth entered the names William Critchfield, aka Bill Critchfield, and Eugene Smith, aka Gene Smith, of Medicine Wheel County, Wyoming.

She whistled as she scrolled through the list of priors: issuance of a bad check, several counts of DUI, breaking and entering, aggravated assault and battery, wanton destruction of a game animal, fishing without a license, and several parole violations. They seemed to operate as a team, because all of the charges except the check kiting and DUI had been filed on the same dates.

She whispered "Jackpot" to herself while cutting the text from the site into a Word document to send to Joe.

It bothered her that Joe had asked her for research help so quickly after he arrived, and she wondered if he was keeping his vow to simply observe and report back. But she knew the answer to that question because she knew Joe so well. Her hope was that by providing him with the information he'd requested, he could leave and come home more quickly.

As she built the document to send, she noticed there had been no charges or convictions for either man for the previous five years. Given the frequency of criminality prior to that, she checked her search criteria and ran it again. But no new activity showed up.

As the other librarians and support staff gathered in the conference room for the weekly meeting, Marybeth logged out of the criminal databases and deleted the history of her searches on the Web browser.

Her cell phone vibrated as she was about to place it into her purse, and she checked the screen: UNKNOWN CALLER.

Covina, she thought, and turned her back to the open conference room door so none of the others could hear her.

"Yes?"

The voice was hesitant. "Did you call me a little while ago?"

It was the female voice that was on the outgoing message at the Covina home, although more distant and suspicious.

"Yes, that was me."

"Why were you calling me? I didn't listen to the message, but I saw that 307 area code . . ." She didn't finish.

"I'm calling from Wyoming," Marybeth said.

"I know," the woman responded. She sounded both weary and cautious, Marybeth thought.

Before Marybeth could explain, the woman said, "I knew this call would come someday. My God, what has he done?"

Marybeth felt a chill shoot up her back.

CHAPTER
FIFTEEN

Sand Creek Ranch

"Follow my lead and keep your mouth shut," Latta said over his shoulder to Joe as the two game wardens walked across the shorn meadow to where Templeton had parked his ATV in the shade of a huge river cottonwood.

"Got it," Joe said crisply but with resentment. He was still angry with Latta and getting tired of his constant admonitions.

Latta was several strides ahead and moving faster than necessary, Joe thought. There was no doubt Latta wanted to get to the ranch owner before Joe did.

Looking ahead over Latta's shoulder, Joe could see Templeton stiffly climb off the four-wheeler. The rancher raised his long arms to stretch, then lowered them and put his hands on his hips and leaned slightly forward to receive his visitors.

He'd aged from the last photographs Joe had seen of him. Despite the beat-up ranch clothing, Templeton maintained his patrician bearing. He was even taller and leaner than Joe had guessed from the photos, and his short hair was now silver streaked with black rather than black streaked with silver. He had sharp, intelligent eyes that revealed nothing. His once-thin mustache had grown in acreage and now covered his full upper lip and drooped down slightly on the sides, giving him an almost Marlboro Man appearance. He was a memorable presence, Joe thought: the kind of man even men looked at twice.

Joe felt his phone vibrate in his breast pocket and paused to retrieve it. There was a text message from Marybeth reading: *Call me when you can. Info on E. Young.*

He paused, weighing whether to call her immediately, but decided since she hadn't indicated it was an emergency it could wait a few minutes. Especially now, with Templeton right in front of him. Joe knew he might never get the chance to see the rancher in person again, and by doing so, his assignment might be near completion. He slid his phone back into the pocket. In his peripheral vision, he saw that Latta had used the opportunity to gain more distance on him.

Latta closed on the rancher and the two shook hands and exchanged greetings, and Latta leaned forward and whispered something into Templeton's ear. Templeton had no reaction to whatever Latta had said, but eased Latta aside and stepped forward to meet Joe.

"I'm Wolfgang Templeton," he said, grasping Joe's hand in a huge dry grip. "I own most of this country around here." He had a flat, authoritative voice.

"Pleasure to meet you," Joe said after introducing himself. "It's nice country."

"It's more complicated than it looks, that's for sure," Templeton said, turning his head toward the hills.

Joe got the impression there was more to Templeton's statement than the obvious.

But before he could find out, Latta intervened, literally stepping between the two.

"Mr. Templeton, remember we talked a while back about establishing a couple of public walk-in areas downstream on Sand Creek, where the county road ends . . ."

Latta went on to explain the parameters of walk-in areas, the benefits for the public as well as the landowner, the goodwill that could be established, on and on, Joe thought. He'd never heard Latta talk so much or so quickly. Joe let him and didn't interrupt. He assumed it was because Latta was nervous and perhaps intimidated, and instead concentrated on trying to read Wolfgang Templeton.

Joe had learned from Marybeth to trust his instincts upon meeting a man for the first time, and he'd honed the ability over the years when encountering fishers, hunters, and other loners in the outdoors. His immediate impression of Templeton was that he was a man with both the drive to achieve what he wanted and the patience to get it done. He was also a perfectionist who personally checked not only the fences, roads, and culverts of his ranches himself but also the hay crop. Templeton listened to Latta without a word, appeared to be engaged, but Joe doubted it. He seemed like the kind of man who had heard thousands of pitches in his life and could cut through the verbosity of the proposal to its bare essence within half a minute, and sum up the presentation in a sentence better than the presenter could ever dream of — for better or worse.

Joe had been in the presence of evil men — outright violent criminals and those with hidden motives and agendas — and Templeton didn't give off that vibration.

There was also something in Templeton's demeanor that suggested weariness and exhaustion. As if he had too much on his plate to spare the time for Latta, even if the game warden's intentions were good.

Templeton nodded slightly as Latta went on about access and agreements with the state, but his eyes drifted first toward the rows of cut hay and then to Joe himself, where they locked on Joe just long enough to make him uncomfortable.

While Latta was in mid-sentence about the property-tax benefits of establishing a walk-in area, Templeton cut him off and said, "Okay, we'll do one."

That seemed to take Latta by surprise. Again, he began to explain the benefits.

"I said we'd do one," Templeton said with finality. "Send all the paperwork to Mr. Williams, my ranch foreman. Deal exclusively with him to establish the boundaries. I'll let him know you and Mr. Pickett here will be in touch."

"That was easier than I thought," Latta said, beaming. "I thought you'd have questions and concerns —"

"I said yes even though, believe it or not, it's not the highest on my priority list," Templeton said. Then, to Joe: "Some people have trouble taking yes for an answer. So you're new to the area?"

Joe nodded.

"Where's home?"

"The Bighorns."

Latta said, "He'll only be here for a couple of days. He's done this walk-in area thing a few times, and —"

Templeton waved off Latta and turned a shoulder to him. To Joe, Templeton said again, "It's fine country, isn't it?"

"Yup."

"Only a settler or two away from pure wilderness," the rancher said. "What you see around you in this county is the first edition, even though it's crumbling away. Think about that, how new it is even though it looks old. Most civilizations build for centuries on top of themselves. Not here. What you see is the first version of an attempt to tame wild country and draw a living from it: Black Hills 1.0. I'm not counting the Sioux and Cheyenne — they were here first. But they hunted here and passed through. They didn't leave anything permanent except a few tipi rings."

Joe nodded.

"You don't talk much, do you?"

Joe nodded to Latta and said, "He thinks I talk too *much*."

Templeton took in a deep breath and exhaled it slowly through his nose.

"Strange how many people here feel they need to protect me in some way. I used to find it charming."

Joe had no idea how to respond or what to say.

Before Latta could interject again, there was the sound of another vehicle roaring up the ranch access road toward the highway.

222

All three men paused to look up at the late-model white Suburban with the SAND CREEK RANCH logo on the door. It was traveling so fast, Joe thought, it might cause a head-on collision if someone was coming the other way around the tight curves. The tires kicked up a large plume of dust.

As the Suburban shot by, Joe saw three forms inside — the driver in front and two women in back, each in their own row of seats. Although the windows of the vehicle were darkened, he saw a pale hand wave good-bye to Templeton through the smoky glass.

Templeton raised his hand and waved. "There they go," he said. "Off to the airport in Rapid City to return to where they came from."

"Who were they?" Joe asked. He could feel Latta's glare on the side of his head but didn't acknowledge it.

"Visitors," Templeton said. "Visitors who forgot they were visiting."

Templeton watched them go. As the Suburban curved around the last hill, his face softened as if a weight had been removed from his shoulders, Joe observed.

"You've got quite a few visitors," Joe said.

"I do," the rancher said. "Some are better than others."

"I assume those two in the car are who you're talking about," Joe said.

"Yes. But someone very special is replacing them."

Joe arched his eyebrows.

Templeton continued, "It's an amazing fact of life that no matter what your situation and current circumstances, you can suddenly meet a special someone who looks you right in the eye and sizes you up and opens herself up to you and everything else just melts away and you just know she will be a part of your life. Maybe even a big part. When that happens, it's important to reassess."

Latta's mouth dropped open. He was obviously unsure how to respond, and a little shocked that Templeton spoke to Joe that way.

"You realize it's time to clear out the detritus," Templeton said. As he did it, he raised his hand and flicked his fingers at the memory of the passing Suburban.

He said, "After I'd met my special woman and returned back to the ranch, I couldn't even look at those two anymore. It was the difference between dining on caviar and champagne and returning home where someone is opening a can of Spam for dinner. So it was time for them to leave and clear the air."

"When will this special lady get here?" Joe asked.

"Anytime now," Templeton said, almost in reverie.

"I met another one of your visitors down the creek," Joe said. "He was an interesting guy who called himself Whip. He was fishing with a vintage bamboo fly rod. I don't see many of those."

Templeton seemed to snap back to the present. "That would be an important colleague of mine."

"He wanted to ticket him," Latta interjected. "Luckily, I saw what was going on and put a stop to it."

Templeton nodded with approval. "That's for the best."

Joe said, "If I catch him fishing again with too many big fish or without a license, I'll ticket him for sure. The same with your other guests, so you might want to let them know what the rules and regulations are."

Latta moaned.

Templeton turned to Joe. He said, "I hope you'll give that some real thought. My colleague, well, you don't want to get on his bad side."

"I got that message loud and clear," Joe said. "Do you have other guests I should look out for, so I don't ruin their day?"

Templeton smiled as if he were wise to the game that was afoot. "Other guests?"

"You know," Joe said, "other colleagues of yours who might be out and about without paying any attention to Game and Fish regulations. Fishing without a license, for instance, or shooting pheasants out of season. Falconry without a permit — things like that."

There was a tiny twitch at the corners of Templeton's mouth at the word *falconry*, Joe noted.

"Why do you ask?" the rancher said.

"Joe, we've got to go," Latta said.

Templeton said, "Yes, I've got to get back to inspecting my hay-fields. If we don't have rain, I can start baling that cut hay tomorrow. It's the last cutting of the year, you know."

Latta thanked Templeton profusely for his time as well as for agreeing to the trial walk-in area, and grasped Joe's arm to pull him along.

"It was a pleasure meeting you," Joe said to Templeton.

"Likewise," Templeton said, coolly looking Joe over as if for the First time.

His demeanor remained serious when he told Latta, "Don't contact Mr. Williams until tomorrow about your project. He's busy tonight organizing a welcome reception and dinner for my very special guest."

"Okay, Mr. Templeton," Latta said.

To Joe, Templeton asked, "I hope the accommodations and the Whispering Pines Motel are okay for you."

Joe nodded. Of course he knew. But how much?

"What in the hell was that all about with his guests?" Latta shouted when they climbed back into the cab of his pickup. "What did I tell you about keeping your mouth shut and letting me do all the talking?"

"You did plenty of that."

Latta thumped the steering wheel hard with the heel of his hand. "He's talking to you all neighborly-like, and all of a sudden you start bringing up his guests and grilling him on his own land."

"*Grilling* is a strong word," Joe said.

"And what was that about someone doing falconry? I oversee the falconry permits around here, and no one has applied. What was that all about?"

Joe shrugged. "Just popped into my head."

"Jesus Christ," Latta said with disgust.

"Who is this special woman he's importing?" Joe asked.

"I have no idea," Latta said. "Why do you think I would know or care? That's not my business, and it sure as hell isn't yours."

226

"She must be something," Joe said.

"It doesn't matter!" Latta thundered. "It's his personal life. There have been plenty of females in the past. There is this black one — sorry, African American — from down south who is an absolute friggin' knockout. I don't know if she's still there or not. I don't care about any of them, and neither should you."

"He brought it up."

"He was just talking. Trying to be nice. And you screw it all up."

"Maybe I don't want him to get his hooks into me the way he's got them into you and everybody else around here," Joe said.

Before Latta could respond, Joe said, "Tell me what's going on around here. You like to talk, so talk. Tell me what it is they have on you, and why there's a group of people in this district that are above the law. Tell me what they've asked you about me, and what you told them."

"I can't," Latta said with heat.

"Then we're done. Take me back to my truck."

"You're goddamned right we're done," Latta said. "I can't protect you anymore. You just do whatever the hell you want in my district."

"I don't want or need protection," Joe said. "What kind of place is this that you even talk that way? Why is it that everyone here knows me and knows my business?"

"I already told you," Latta said, doing a jerky three-point turn on the gravel road so he could aim his pickup back the way they came. "It's a different world here. It's obvious you don't belong."

Joe said, "For once, I agree with you."

They rode along in silence for a few minutes, each consumed with his own angry thoughts. Joe put off calling Marybeth until he could be clear of Latta. He didn't want the game warden knowing anything about anything.

When they reached the state highway, Latta said, "If I were you, I'd pack up your dog and your stuff and head home tonight. Forget about helping me with the walk-in area. I can handle that on my own."

"Still protecting me?" Joe asked. "From who? From what?"

"Hell," Latta said, "I'm protecting myself, too. I've got Emily to think about."

His tone had softened into uneasiness and anguish, Joe thought. He felt sorry for him.

"We're done," Joe said, "but that doesn't mean I'm leaving right away. But whatever I do, it won't involve you."

"It better not," Latta said, inhaling a long and trembling breath.

When they approached Medicine Wheel, Latta said, "You aren't going to write up a report on all this, are you?"

Joe didn't respond.

"Tell me this will be between us. Just a misunderstanding between a couple of fellow game

228

wardens. I don't know our new director at all, and I don't want her getting the wrong impression."

Joe said, "I'm not planning to send in a report to her." It wasn't a lie.

"Don't," Latta said. "Because it's one thing if we're through and I'm off to the side. It's another thing if you make me your enemy, too."

Joe looked over at Latta. There was a mixture of fear and determination in his eyes. And there was nothing worse than that.

Latta dropped off Joe without a word of good-bye in the parking area of the Whispering Pines Motel and roared away. Joe's pickup was the sole vehicle in the lot, and he assumed he was still the only guest. As soon as Latta's rear bumper strobed away through the trees on the side of the road and vanished, Joe called Marybeth.

"What did you find out about Erik Young?" he asked.

"He doesn't have any priors I could find, although I can't access juvie records. But I think I located his mother."

The clouds had scudded off to South Dakota and the noon sun was straight overhead, warming the asphalt. Joe leaned against the grille of his truck.

Marybeth told Joe in detail about her experience that morning. She said, "If someone cold-called me and asked, 'Are you Sheridan Pickett's mother?' or 'Are you Lucy Pickett's mother?' the first thought that would probably come into my mind is *car wreck*. Or some kind of horrible accident."

"Really?" Joe asked.

"Really. That's how a mother's mind works."

"Gotcha."

"Thank you," she said. "But if a stranger called out of the blue and asked, 'Are you April Keeley's mother?' well, a bunch of other scenarios would immediately come to mind. I'd probably picture her in a jail cell or in the back of a squad car or something. I hate to admit this, but it's true."

Joe nodded, knowing that he wouldn't come to any of those conclusions without hearing more.

Marybeth said, "So for Mrs. Young to blurt out, 'I knew this call would come someday. My God, what has he done?' scares me, Joe. This woman knows Erik is capable of something awful. Trust me — a mother just knows. It convinces me Sheridan is on to something."

Joe took a deep breath. He said, "What did she say next?"

"Nothing," Marybeth said with a sigh. "She hung up the phone."

"Did you call back?"

"No. I thought if I called right back I'd spook her. She obviously didn't want to talk to me or hear anything I had to say about her son. Just think: What if I was the police chief in Laramie or the head of university security calling? Mrs. Young didn't even want to hear who I was or why I was calling before she blurted out what she said."

Joe asked, "Do you think you could call her again later tonight and get her to talk? You know, mother to mother?"

"That's my plan," she said. "She may see the area code again and not answer, but who knows? Maybe she will have talked to her son by then. But all I can do is try. Meanwhile, I'll keep digging. Young's path from California to Laramie might include some other stops where he might have made a mark. Plus, I haven't dug into social media yet. He's got to have a Facebook page, and he might have a blog or sites where he posts."

"Keep me updated," Joe said. "I'll keep my phone close."

"Oh," Marybeth said, "you asked me about two other names . . ."

She went on to detail the extensive rap sheets of Bill Critchfield and Gene Smith.

"Nothing at all in the last five years?" Joe asked.

"Not that I can find."

"That's odd," he said. "I didn't get the impression they'd reformed."

"I thought that, too," she said.

Joe paused, thinking it through. Then he said: "You know that wealthy rancher I told you about? He moved into this county five years ago."

There was a pause. Marybeth said, "What's the connection?"

"I can't say for sure, but I don't think those two became model citizens all of a sudden. But obviously no one arrested them. You'd think they would have had run-ins with the town cops or the sheriff, or Jim Latta."

He said, "I think maybe those two either work for the rancher or have something on him. But I'd guess the former."

"Then steer clear of them, Joe," Marybeth cautioned. He nodded, but of course she couldn't see it.

"Joe?"

"I got it."

"Joe, how are things going?"

He said, "They're heating up. It's probably good I won't be here much longer."

As he said it, he glanced up at the motel office to see Anna quickly back away from the window, where she'd been watching him.

"Good work," he said. "You've produced more results than the FBI at this point. But that shouldn't surprise me."

"Just get done and hurry home," she said. "I'm worried what I might learn from Mrs. Young, and you may need to get to Laramie in a hurry."

CHAPTER
SIXTEEN

Medicine Wheel, Wyoming

Joe finished his conversation with Marybeth and dug in his back Wrangler pocket for the key to cabin number eight.

As he reached for the knob, he paused as a thought came to him about what Anna B. had said. Daisy must have heard him outside, because she was snuffling up against the inside of the door, dying to say hello. But he didn't slide the key into the lock.

Instead, he backed away and speed-dialed Chuck Coon's private cell phone.

Coon picked up in two rings.

"Great job getting me that intel on those three names I gave you," Joe said, as a greeting.

"Look," Coon said with quiet irritation, "I'm in the middle of something. We all are. The state highway patrol stopped a van last night on I-80 going east filled with nine illegals who came over the border. That in itself isn't a big deal, but only four of them are from Mexico or South America. Three are from Yemen, and two are from Chechnya. As you can imagine, we've got all hands on deck trying to figure out what's what. I'm sorry I had to pull my agent off your inquiries, but —"

"Never mind," Joe said. "Marybeth got it all. But that's not why I'm calling."

"I've got maybe a minute," Coon said, lowering his voice. Joe imagined the agent-in-charge excusing himself from a room full of men in suits and stepping out into the hallway.

"That's enough time," Joe said. "I'm going to call you back on your office landline number in twenty minutes."

"But I won't be at my desk."

"Just as well," Joe said. "I don't need you to be there. I assume the incoming call will be recorded on your server, right?"

Coon hesitated, then: "Yes. But that's not supposed to be public knowledge."

"Come on," Joe said. "Everybody knows you Feds record everything. Anyway, just make sure you get a copy of the call and get it transcribed in case you need to send it over to the governor's office. You might need to refer to it later when you need to build a case."

"Joe, what have you learned? It sounds explosive."

Joe smiled to himself at that. He said, "Nothing has exploded yet, but I might be lighting the match."

"What are you talking about?"

"It's time to jump-start things."

"Uh-oh . . ." Coon cautioned.

"You've got to get back to your meeting," Joe said. "I'll explain later. I'll give you a call on your cell."

"Remember our deal —"

"Thanks again for the timely intel. You guys have been really helpful so far," Joe said, and terminated the call.

He let Daisy out to allow her to blow off some steam and relieve herself in the copse of trees behind the unit. While she loped around and through the tree trunks, he inspected the back of cabin number eight where the power and phone lines entered the exterior walls and compared the wiring with other cabins in the row. He tried to do it without looking obvious, in case Anna had found another place in her office to spy on him.

While he ran his dog he heard the sound of a vehicle enter the parking lot. He stayed back in the trees but peered around cabin number eight to see a Chevy Silverado with Michigan plates pulling a trailer with two ATVs strapped on behind it. The bed of the pickup was filled with hunting and camping gear, and two large bearded men in camo climbed out, stretched, and went inside the office. Obviously hunters checking in, Joe thought. So there would be some company besides Anna at the motel after all.

After a few more minutes of tossing a plastic dummy for Daisy to retrieve, he thought it was time to go in. He was surprised to see the Michigan truck swinging around in the lot and heading back out. He wondered if the hunters didn't like the motel or the rate — or if they'd been turned away — and why.

Inside, he again sat at the makeshift desk and scribbled notes to himself in his spiral. After he'd gone over his script a third time, he punched Coon's office phone number into his cell.

As Coon had warned, it went straight to voicemail.

Joe said, "Is this the Division of Criminal Investigation? Yes, well this is Wyoming game warden Joe Pickett. I need to talk to Director Don White. Sure, I'll wait."

Joe sat up straight in the hard-backed chair and counted to ten, then: "Don? This is Joe Pickett. As you know, I'm up in Medicine Wheel County, and I've spent a couple of days poking around like you asked."

He paused as if being asked a question, and said, "Yeah. I wanted to alert you that I'll be sending along a report soon that you'll probably want to hand-walk over to the attorney general's office. It's as dirty up here as you said it might be and maybe even worse. That grand jury idea you had might be the ticket for something this big and this wide-ranging. The whole county seems to be rotten to the core."

He checked his notes and did another count before proceeding.

"Right," he said. "Anyway, I'm no lawyer or prosecutor, but by tomorrow afternoon I think I'll have enough hard evidence of a criminal conspiracy for you to get some subpoenas and indictments going. I'm meeting with a confidential informant later this afternoon, so I can get the statement on tape, and another CI tomorrow morning who is on the inside. Both have given me enough to go on, but I need to do this formally for the report. Are we okay proceeding

236

without me putting their actual names into the document?"

Joe looked over at Daisy, who was sitting on her haunches, watching the phantom conversation take place with great interest. He waggled his eyebrows at her, and in response her tail swept back and forth across the floor.

"Okay, good," he said, turning back to his notebook. "They don't want their names out there for fear of reprisals. And up here, that's something that I wouldn't put past them. Everybody up here seems to be in communication.

"So as long as I have your word the CIs will be protected for now, I can assure them they can talk. But from what I'm getting so far, at the very least you'll have a RICO case to start that will probably include a bunch of other charges once you force them to testify in front of the grand jury.

"Okay, you said you wanted some names so you could get the paperwork started. I'll spell them when we're done. Ready?"

Joe gave it half a minute. "The first is William 'Bill' Critchfield. He's a local thug with a long rap sheet that ended five years ago.

"Eugene 'Gene' Smith is an associate of Critchfield's. Same deal with him. Both of them, I believe, are employed by Sand Creek Ranch to keep the locals quiet and pacified. They do it through intimidation. In addition to my two CIs, I think we'll find plenty of people around here who will testify to what Critchfield and Smith have been up to the last five years. Once you've got them in custody where they can't hurt or threaten anyone, I'm guessing we'll have some more folks come forward.

"Okay, next there's County Sheriff R. C. Mead. He seems to know everything that's going on around here, except he shows a blind eye when it comes to Critchfield and Smith. I'd suggest getting a subpoena going so you can look at his bank records. I wouldn't be surprised to find some payments coming in other than his salary. He's a slick old coot and he knows how the game is played, so he'll be slippery. But I think he'll wise up if he's actually facing jail time. No former sheriff wants to wind up in Rawlins with inmates they may have put there.

"Judge Ethan Bartholomew is next. Oh, you already know how to spell his name? Good. The judge is in cahoots with Mead. They work together to make sure connected guys like Critchfield and Smith are allowed to operate without any interference from other law enforcement who might not be in on the take. Yes, a judge. That's how deep it goes. Check his bank records also, as well as his court docket. It will be interesting to find out what cases *weren't* brought before him, or were brought and dismissed outright.

"Sheriff Mead may turn on Bartholomew, or the other way around, in exchange for some kind of deal. But that's up to you."

Joe took a sip of water — too much talking — before continuing.

"Two more," he said, rolling his eyes to himself but cognizant of the importance to continue to play it straight. He only had one take, and it had to be credible. "James 'Jim' Latta. He's the local game warden, it pains me to say. I don't know about payments, but there is definitely some quid pro quo going on that may raise to the level of bribery.

"There's another guy," Joe said, letting his voice rise with speculation, "a guest of the Sand Creek Ranch. He's a southern gentleman who comes across as snooty and out of place. I don't know what his role is, but he's obviously close to the big guy. He fishes with a cane rod, and you know how expensive those things are. He goes by the name Whip, which might be short for something. I don't have his full name yet, but I'll have it by tonight or tomorrow. It's just my gut saying this, but I think once we look into him we might find some surprising things. You should run that aka through your databases and see if he turns up. Can't be that many guys named Whip.

"Yeah, that's a lot," Joe said. "And it's possible I might add to that list or need to revise it. I think we both know how high it might go.

"In fact," Joe said, "I met the man himself today. You couldn't meet a nicer guy. But I'll bet you dollars to donuts that when the indictments start coming down on their heads, one or more of these guys will crack when you start squeezing them individually. They'll deal and point the finger higher up.

"So that's it for now," Joe said.

Then, after a beat: "Thank you, Don. I appreciate that. Just keep an eye on your email inbox, and happy reading."

Joe discontinued the call. He realized he was covered with a thin film of sweat, even though the room was cool. He closed his eyes and replayed his words, hoping he hadn't tripped himself up, but realized — and feared — there wasn't much he could do if he had.

After changing out of his uniform into a worn snap-button cowboy shirt and black fleece vest, he threw all of his clothes and possessions into the duffel bag on the bed. He left his shaving kit in the bathroom, though, so it would look like he was staying the night. All he'd have to do was snatch it and toss it into the duffel if he had to make a quick exit. While he glanced around to make sure he'd gotten everything, he found it hard not to look up at the ceiling.

Joe called Daisy and went outside to his pickup and let her bound into the cab. As he left the Whispering Pines for the afternoon, he noted Anna watching him from the office window.

CHAPTER
SEVENTEEN

Sundance, Wyoming

An hour and a half later in Sundance, after parking his very identifiable green Ford pickup underground in an unused outdoor bay two blocks away behind a closed auto repair shop, Joe strolled through a row of used three- and four-wheel ATVs at a ranch implement store on the outskirts of town. The business seemed to sell just about anything as long as it had an engine and was used — tractors, backhoes, utility vehicles, riding lawn mowers, and haying equipment. The gravel lot was stained with oil and the air smelled of hydraulic fluid.

In a small office a woman with a bouffant watched him carefully while she talked on the telephone, her cigarette bouncing up and down while she spoke. He waved hello to her and gestured to the row of ATVs, and she responded with an *I'll-be-there-in-a-minute-so-please-don't-leave* dance of her free hand. He nodded that he understood.

A sign above her office read: NO RETURNS, NO EXCHANGES, ALL SALES FINAL.

Joe's phone vibrated in his pocket — a text message — and he pulled it out and checked the screen. It was from Chuck Coon's private cell phone: *Heard your message. What the f*ck was that?*

Joe smiled and texted back: *Stand by for call.*

He was pocketing the phone when the woman in the small office emerged, shaking her head.

"Sorry about that," she said. "I seen you out here, but I couldn't get that banker off the phone. See, I'm trying to get a revolving credit line to keep this place alive, and the crap they keep asking me is ridiculous. It's like they want my firstborn son, but I told them he was twenty-eight. They blame the Feds, but I blame *them*. It would just be easier to close up shop and go on welfare like the rest of 'em around here."

She was short and solid, and the egg-shaped helmet of hair reminded Joe of something the English guards would wear outside Buckingham Palace. She wore a bright floral-pattern blouse, too-tight jeans, and scuffed red cowboy boots.

"I'm Kelli Ann Fahey," she said, sweeping her open palm over the row of ATVs. "I own this place, and I can see you're a hunter. I'll bet you're interested in something that will get you into the woods and help you drag that deer or elk out."

"Something like that," Joe said.

"This is a good time of year to buy one of these," she said. "Hunters come here from all over the country and you'd be surprised how many of 'em want to dump their equipment instead of towing it back home to Ohio or wherever. So we have plenty of inventory."

"I see that."

"Anything you particularly have your eye on?"

242

Joe nodded toward a newer model green Polaris Sportsman. The body and frame were dinged, but it had four new knobby tires and was set up with saddlebags on the rear rack and a heavy-duty rifle scabbard across the front deck.

"Wow," she said, stepping back as if to steady herself. "You just walked right up and picked out the best deal on the entire lot.

"No kidding," she said. "This was just turned in by a local rancher. Hardly any miles, and enough horsepower to get you where you want to go and drag anything out. The rancher used that saddle thing for his irrigation shovel, but I bet it would be perfect for your hunting rifle."

"That's what I was thinking," Joe said.

She reeled off the fuel capacity, wheel-base measurements, and four-stroke engine specifications. Then she mounted the ATV, started the engine, and cranked back on the accelerator on the handgrip. The engine whined until it was earsplitting and the air filled with acrid blue smoke. Then she shut it off.

"And," she said, leaning forward and resting her elbows on the handlebars and hushing her voice to him as if sharing a secret, "I could let it go for five grand as long as you promise not to tell anybody that you practically stole it from me. If you tell the locals, they'll bum-rush this place and want deals of their own."

Joe liked Kelli Ann Fahey. She was a good saleswoman.

"I need to check first," he said, raising his phone.

She smiled knowingly. "Tell your wife she can ride it to go to the store, or to the mailbox, or whatever. Tell her she'll feel twenty years younger when she's zooming this baby around the block."

"I'll be right back," Joe said, walking to the edge of the lot.

"I'll be in my office," she said with a wink, and climbed off. "Let's hope some other hunter doesn't walk up and steal this out from under you while you're negotiating with the home front."

Chuck Coon was incredulous when Joe reached him. He said, "I listened to your message three times and I still can't decide if you're serious or delusional."

Joe said, "I'm not sure, either."

"Explain."

"Okay," Joe said, turning slightly to make sure Fahey was in her office and not two steps away, handing him a title to sign. "A couple of things. As you know, I decided to stay at the Whispering Pines because that's where the DCI agent stayed. I am literally the only guest there. But it's hunting season up here. As you know — or maybe you don't — Wedell is one of those little towns that only has traffic during the fall. A lot of hunters aren't that particular where they stay, so it seemed strange to me I was there by myself. This morning, I saw some hunters get turned away. There are a bunch of hunters at a place called the Black Forest Inn. That's probably where the guys who got turned away ended up.

244

"The owner herself told me Wolfgang Templeton is her biggest referrer of business. Apparently, he likes to send people there who come here to do business with him in one form or another. She thinks he's wonderful. Everybody does."

"Can you trust her?" Coon asked.

"I don't know," Joe said. Then: "I doubt it."

"Anyway . . ."

"The motel has seven cabins left, and the owner told me that after the fire Templeton sent his maintenance crew to make sure the wiring was okay in the remaining units. That got me to thinking."

"Always dangerous," Coon said sarcastically.

Joe ignored him. "Last night I talked to Marybeth on my cell phone inside my cabin. I mentioned the same names to her that I sent to you: Critchfield and Smith. Then this morning, Jim Latta got spooked when he saw those two coming down the road we were on and made me get out of his truck before they saw me."

Coon said, "Couldn't that have to do with the fact that you braced them last night? That you left your card on their window?"

"That's what I thought at first, but I think there's more to it than that," Joe said. "I think Latta wanted to avoid a confrontation with them that would have been more than them just complaining. Chuck, I think the motel cabins are wired for sound and maybe video. I think they're *bugged*. Somebody heard me talk to Marybeth and mention their names and let those two know about it."

Coon paused. "So you think Templeton was listening? Is listening?"

"I have no idea who is on the other end," Joe said. "But a few hours after I talked to Marybeth and went to bed, a vehicle showed up at the motel. I didn't see it, but I heard it. I think someone was checking me out, making sure my pickup was still there and I was in my room."

"That's not much to go on," Coon said sourly.

"I know that."

"In fact, it sounds paranoid. No offense, of course."

"All I know is what's in my gut. Everybody I run into around this county seems to know something, and they all seem connected in unexplainable ways. I think they briefed Jim Latta bright and early this morning, which is why he was late to breakfast. I think the sheriff and the judge were at the restaurant to keep tabs on me and overhear what I said to Latta. And I think Latta took me out to the Sand Creek Ranch as much for Templeton to size me up as for me to meet Templeton."

Coon sighed a long sigh. "So a big conspiracy is what you're thinking. I don't know. Nothing you told me is actionable."

"Nope."

"So what is it you're up to, Joe? Remember our deal. Your job is to poke around and gather information. It sounds like you've let the place get to you."

"I told you already," Joe said. "I'm seeing if any of what I left on that message to you turns out to be true."

"'Lighting the match,'" Coon repeated.

"That's what I do."

"All the names you left on the recording may or may not be involved?"

"No idea," Joe said. "But I wouldn't be surprised if *most* of them were. And if I'm right about the cabin being bugged, this will smoke them out. It might start turning one against another."

Coon said, "We could maybe send up one of our tech guys to check out the wiring in your room."

"How long would that take?"

"A couple of days."

"Forget it," Joe said. "By then this will be over, one way or the other."

"Joe," Coon said, "you've implicated the local sheriff *and* the county judge. Not to mention your fellow game warden. And Templeton himself — his name came up. This is dangerous territory if that's all you have on them."

"It is," Joe said. "But think about it. I haven't made a single official charge at all. In fact, if that cabin isn't bugged, I haven't done anything but talk to myself and leave you a crazy phone message to the wrong person. What have I really done if I'm all wrong? Nothing, except to get you all hot and bothered."

"This is not exactly by the book," Coon said. "I'd never approve an agent in the field doing what you did."

"I don't work for you."

"And thank God for that." Despite Coon's words, his voice had softened. Joe could almost visualize Coon's mind spinning, taking in the implications of what he'd been told so far. Coon asked, "If your speculation is correct, how long do you think it will take to prove it true?"

"Fast," Joe said. "I purposely left it hanging out there on that message to you that I should have what I need by tomorrow. So if they hear it, they'll know they won't have much time. They'll either have to act or scatter."

"That's what I'm afraid of," Coon said. "What if the situation explodes?"

"Then I can get out of Dodge," Joe said. "I don't want to spend a single hour longer up here than I have to."

He reminded Coon about his daughter at college, how he may have to react in an instant.

"I forgot about that," Coon said. "Sorry. That name you asked us about. We've had a lot on our plate . . ."

"The Middle Eastern terrorists," Joe said. "Yeah, yeah, I remember."

"We can't call them that," Coon barked.

"Gotcha."

Coon said, "So do you really have a couple of informants, or was that your paranoia at work along with everything else?"

"I have no CIs," Joe said. "I wish I did. There's got to be somebody around here who doesn't think Wolfgang Templeton hung the moon."

"Another question," Coon said. "What's this about this southern gentleman you talk about? Where does he fit in?"

"Who knows?" Joe said. "But I couldn't leave him out. He might be a guy you'll want to talk to. There was something about him that gave me the willies, and I'm

248

pretty sure I wasn't supposed to run into him like that. Both Latta and Templeton seemed worried about it."

"And what about your pal Romanowski?"

Joe shook his head. "I've got zero leads on him."

"Honestly?"

"Honestly."

"Good, I guess," Coon said. "Is there anything you're holding back?"

Joe didn't answer right away. Then he said, "I need your authorization to buy a used Polaris Sportsman. My Game and Fish budget is shot and I'm not authorized to purchase any more vehicles. I know you guys have slush funds for things like this. It's a steal at five thousand dollars, at least according to the saleswoman. A drop in the bucket for a big-time Fed like you."

"A *what?*" Coon asked.

"It's an ATV," Joe said. "An all-terrain vehicle."

"Aren't they dangerous?"

In the tiny office, Joe handed over his credit card to Fahey, who ran it through her machine. He hoped the FBI could reimburse him by the end of the month so the family finances wouldn't go into the red, and he made a note to himself to warn Marybeth about the upcoming charge. Joe was grateful the governor had arranged for a bump in salary, but he knew the increase wouldn't cover the cost.

"So where are you hunting around here?" she asked, although Joe got the impression she was just making conversation while she waited for the authorization.

"I have permission on the Sand Creek Ranch," he said.

She looked up sharply. "Really?"

Joe nodded, hoping he hadn't taken the conversation in a direction he couldn't back out of.

She said, "It's a *huge* place. The owner moved here five or six years ago and just started buying up everything. Other ranches, old buildings, you name it. Most of the people around here either work for Mr. Templeton or owe him."

"That's what I hear," Joe said, hoping she would go on.

She said, "I was scared to death for a while, because there was a rumor he was going to put in a farm-and-ranch store that sold implements. Obviously, that would compete with me and drive me out of business. This isn't exactly a booming economy around here."

"But he hasn't," Joe said.

"Not yet, anyway," she sighed. "I wouldn't put it past him, though. He doesn't look real kindly on independent people around here, and believe me, I'm an independent woman. I'm a single mom who raised two boys on my own and never took a dime of welfare."

"So he doesn't like you?" Joe asked.

She barked a laugh. "I'd guess he doesn't even know I'm alive. But a couple of his flunkies do, and they might suggest to him that a nice new dealership would go real well in Sundance."

Joe thought: *Critchfield and Smith.*

He asked, "What's he like?"

250

"Mr. Templeton?"

"Yes."

"He does a lot for the community," she said without enthusiasm. "Very little happens around here that he doesn't sponsor or fund in some way. So why do you ask? Do you know him? Are you on his payroll?"

The question surprised Joe. "No and no."

"Just checking. If you're not, you're one of the few. You and me have that in common, I guess."

"So he's got his fingers into everything?" Joe said.

"Everything."

"What's wrong with that?" he asked. "It's got to be a good thing to have a local philanthropist."

She stared back, puzzled.

"A guy who pays for and sponsors things," he explained.

"Yeah," she said. "But honestly, sometimes I wonder. I guess I'm just a suspicious person, but I wonder if he does all these nice things for the county because he has a good heart and plenty of money or if he does them so he can be in control. I think I'm about the only one asking that question anymore. There used to be others that agreed with me, but he's picked them off one by one and now they're all on his side. That's what money can do, I guess."

The credit card machine came to life with an approval, and a length of paper rolled out of it like a tongue. She ripped it free and handed it over to Joe for his signature.

As he signed, he asked, "What does he do to make all this money when he flies off in his plane?"

Instead of answering, she laughed unconvincingly and shrugged. She was done talking.

A few moments later, Joe drove the ATV down a weedy alley to where he'd hidden his pickup. Using a pair of collapsible ramps he'd purchased from the hardware store earlier, he drove the four-wheeler up into the bed, lashed it down tight with straps to a couple of eyebolts on the interior walls, and shut the gate.

He wondered if he'd found his CI.

On the way out of town, he stopped at a convenience store to top off the gas tank on his truck and to fill the ATV. He wanted to make sure there was enough fuel in his new purchase to get him to the headquarters of the Sand Creek Ranch and back.

CHAPTER
EIGHTEEN

University of Wyoming, Laramie

Between classes, Sheridan Pickett rode the elevator alone to the fourth floor of White Hall. She stood in the corner of the car, clutching her textbooks — *Introduction to Criminal Justice* and *Chemistry 1020* — to her chest. She liked her criminal justice class as much as she hated chem. Criminal justice, she thought, was in her wiring.

Before the doors opened on four, she took a deep breath and put on her game face, which was a smile. Being the resident assistant meant she could no longer be anonymous, the way she had been her first two years of college. Now she knew all the students on her floor — and a few of the busybody RAs — kept an eye on her. Her residents followed her lead in regard to behavior, and she made sure she was never observed bending the rules.

She heard male voices down the hall as the doors hummed open, but no one was standing in front of her to get on. She glanced over her shoulder in the direction of the voices as she made her way to her room and saw a pair of roommates at the end of the hall, gesticulating wildly. Sheridan paused.

Their names were Matt Nicol and David Hansard, both freshmen from Cody. They'd each started the year paired with a roommate they didn't get along with and found each other. They occupied the corner room at the end of the hall, one of the larger dorm rooms, and they seemed to Sheridan to be normal, red-blooded Wyoming boys who wore hoodies, caps cocked sidewise, and baggy jeans. They liked to hunt, fish, and drink too much. And they were having a loud argument of some kind. She'd never heard them raise their voices before.

It wasn't Sheridan's role to intervene, but at the same time she didn't want the argument to escalate. She thought that by standing in the hallway looking in their direction she would send the signal they were being observed. Often, that alone cooled things down.

Nicol saw her, mid-rant, and went suddenly quiet.

She waved at him.

Hansard, who had stomped away from Nicol into the room and couldn't be seen, suddenly appeared around the doorjamb to see what had made Nicol stop speaking.

She waved at him, too. "You guys okay?"

Nicol looked to Hansard instead of answering, but Hansard grinned and said, "Oh, yeah. Everything's fine," and reached out and shut their door.

Sheridan gave it another half-minute. If they were still having a conflict, they were doing it quietly. That was good enough, she thought.

Then she heard a shuffle of feet directly in front of her. The sound would have been masked by the yelling if the yelling was still going on, and when she looked up she realized she was standing less than two feet from Erik Young's door. There was a thin stripe of light beneath the door, punctuated by the shadows of two feet.

He was right there, she thought, standing on the other side of the door. Listening to her, listening to what was going on in the hallway. There were no other sounds from behind the door — no video games, no television, no music. If it wasn't for the door itself, she realized, she'd be eighteen inches from him.

Quietly, she said, "Erik?"

No response.

A little louder: "Erik?"

The shadows vanished from beneath the door. He'd backed quietly away.

She shuddered and turned for her room, and it felt good to her to close and lock her door.

She dumped her books on her desk and scrolled to a Pandora classic country channel she'd created on her computer. For reasons she couldn't really explain — maybe it had to do with where she came from — the twang of George Strait, Chris LeDoux, and Patsy Cline always made her feel comfortable when she was trying to sort out her feelings. As if Pandora could read her mind, Chris LeDoux's "Look at You Girl" came on. She never listened to that channel with anyone else around, though. Too uncool.

On her wall was a collage of framed photos, most of them selfies with her and her girlfriends mugging for a camera phone. Then there were family photos — a formal one with everyone wearing stiff clothing where she looked particularly photogenic — and an informal one taken two summers before by a friend near their corrals. Her dad, mom, Lucy, and she glanced toward the camera from where they perched on the corral rails behind their house on Bighorn Road. Her mom was in jeans — her riding outfit — and had just ridden Rojo. April stood off to the side, looking annoyed. And in the background, looking out from behind the barn like some kind of burglar, was Nate Romanowski. She loved this photo for its candid nature. No one was posing, and Nate had been caught by surprise. It was the only photo she had of Nate, her mentor in falconry. She was sure he would rather it had never been taken.

When there was a knock on her door, she quickly doused the music on her computer and leaned into the peephole. If it was Erik Young, she wasn't sure what she would do.

But it was Matt Nicol and David Hansard, both with their hands jammed into their pockets, both looking at their feet.

"Hi, guys," she said, opening her door.

They grumbled a hello.

"What can I do for you? I've got a few minutes before I head to lunch."

Nicol looked to Hansard to take the lead, and Hansard did. "Can we talk to you for a minute?"

"Of course."

"Can we come in and close the door?"

She hesitated for a few seconds, then backed up and stepped aside. Neither had been in her room before — they weren't the type to share concerns with her. Both entered cautiously, looking around at the photos and decorations. She was glad she didn't have any underwear lying around.

"We can trust you, right?" Hansard said. "Everybody says you're cool."

She shrugged and said, "It sort of depends. If it's something really bad —"

"It is," Nicol said gravely.

"Maybe," Hansard countered, shooting a *shut-up* look to his roommate.

"What is it?" she asked.

"You said during orientation that your door was always open. I remember that. If we can't trust you, we might get kicked out of school."

It was a dilemma. She wanted to know, but she didn't want to know something that would put her — and them — at risk.

"All I can tell you is I'll be fair," she said. "If you guys tell me you committed a felony or something, well, I can't just not report it. But if it's something else —"

"See?" Nicol said to Hansard. "I told you we shouldn't have come here."

Hansard said, "She isn't a dorm Nazi, like some of the others."

"What is it?" she asked.

Hansard and Nicol exchanged looks again, and Hansard said, "Our guns are missing."

257

She gasped and covered her mouth with her fingertips. She didn't want to, but she did. "What do you mean? From where?"

"We had them under our beds," Hansard said. "We know you're not supposed to have them in the dorm. We're not idiots — we know how to handle guns, and they weren't loaded or anything."

"Mine was," Nicol corrected.

"Except for his, I guess," Hansard said, looking anywhere but at her face.

"Okay," she said, leaning back on her desk. "You know you aren't supposed to have them in university housing. You signed a resident agreement saying you wouldn't bring any firearms into the dorm, and we talked about it at orientation."

Nicol and Hansard grumbled in agreement. Guns *were* allowed at the university, but only if they were stored at the UW Police Department. Every student was allowed up to three weapons plus a bow on campus as long as they were checked in and left in storage. A photo ID was required to store them or check them out.

"We screwed up," Hansard said. "We went out target shooting a few weeks ago and got back late at night. We *meant* to take them to the station, but we never got around to it."

"How many guns are we talking about?" she asked.

"Four," Hansard said. "My 12-gauge shotgun and Ruger .357 Magnum revolver. Matt has a .223 Bushmaster and a 9-millimeter semiautomatic pistol."

"The pistol was the one that is loaded?" she asked.

258

Nicol nodded sheepishly.

"How long have they been missing?"

"Who knows?" Hansard said. "Anytime in the last three weeks. Neither one of us even checked until just a few minutes ago — that's what we were arguing about. I wouldn't have even realized they were gone except I dropped a can of Copenhagen and it rolled under the bed. When I went down to get it, all I could see was dust bunnies."

"I really need that pistol back," Nicol said. "It belongs to my grandma."

Hansard said, "The shotgun belongs to my dad. He'd kill me if he found out I lost it."

"Does anyone have a key to your door besides you?" she asked.

They both shook their heads. Nicol said, "We thought about that. The thing is, as you know, our room is kind of a party room. We leave the door open all the time on Friday night and on the weekends. Sometimes we go to someone else's room and just leave it open. Everybody knows we always have beer in our fridge, and people just go in and grab one. Anybody could have gone in there and taken them."

Sheridan closed her eyes and tried to think of what to do besides the obvious: call the campus police. But that might trigger an over-reaction. There had already been one all-campus lockdown earlier in the semester when someone reported an untended backpack in the commons. It turned out the backpack was full of textbooks and granola bars.

"What I hope," Hansard said, "is that we've been punked. Maybe one of our friends took them just to watch us flip out."

"Is that possible?" she asked.

"You don't know our friends," he said, rolling his eyes. "One of them shit in Matt's bed once and he didn't realize it for two days."

"Shut *up*," Nicol said, red-faced.

"We don't want to get kicked out," Hansard said.

"Okay," Sheridan said. "Here's what I'm willing to do, but no more. Right now, I'm as guilty as you are since you told me. I'll give you forty-eight hours to try and find out who took them. Talk to *all* of your friends. Email them, text them, whatever you have to do. If one of them punked you and fesses up, you can get the guns back and check them where you're supposed to, and we can forget about this as long as you don't do it again. But if those guns can't be found . . ."

"We're in the shit," Hansard said.

"We're all in the shit," she said. "It isn't like somebody stole your iPod."

After they'd left, she realized she'd lost her appetite for lunch. She was angry at herself as well. The easy thing would have been to call the police and let the chips fall where they may. But she hated to be responsible for the expulsion of two students. They weren't bad, just stupid. Like just about every other freshman.

She stared at her phone and contemplated calling her dad for advice. Maybe even her mom, except she'd probably freak out.

260

Nicol and Hansard were like most of the boys she'd grown up with around Saddlestring. Guns were a fact of life.

And she thought of those two feet under Erik Young's door.

Sheridan reached over and pressed PLAY on the Pandora window. Chris LeDoux again, with "Hooked on an 8 Second Ride."

CHAPTER
NINETEEN

Sand Creek Ranch

Late that afternoon, Nate heard another vehicle coming up the mountain toward his line shack. He was installing the final new glass and window frame into the south-side wall — a difficult task because the opening was out of square. He strapped on his shoulder holster before stepping outside to see who it was.

"You again," he said, as Liv Brannan braked to a stop in the ranch pickup and climbed out. She had a square white envelope in her hand.

She smiled slyly, then it morphed into full beam. She seemed to enjoy antagonizing him, he thought.

"This time I'm here on official business."

She approached and handed him the envelope. Because the day had warmed, she no longer wore the red down coat she'd covered herself up with earlier. She looked attractive and businesslike in a crisp white button-down shirt with the collar open and a loose string tie. He wished she'd put the coat back on.

He took the envelope, addressed to simply *Nate R.*

"The lady herself — I call her 'Herself' because I don't know her name yet — is due to arrive tonight on the late flight into Rapid City. Apparently, she's flying in from overseas, so she'll need some rest. But Mr. T. wants to have a big ranch welcome dinner for her tomorrow evening, and he'd like for you to be there."

"So there's no need opening this, then?" Nate asked.

"You should open it. You can RSVP to me right now in person."

"What if I'm busy?"

She widened her eyes and blew a puff of air out her mouth as if there had been a bug in it. "Busy doing *what*?"

"Fixing up my place. Or locating pigeons. I think I have a line on some."

"Pigeons? Aren't they urban birds?"

He shook his head. "Not necessarily. Pigeons hang out in old structures, usually in the rafters. I spotted some old buildings on the far end of the ranch — a couple of barns — that look like pigeon heaven."

"And you want them why?"

"To train my falcons."

"So the pigeons are targets," she said flatly.

"Yes."

"You'll need a better excuse."

"What if I don't *want* to go?"

She waved that off as if he hadn't said it. "Remember when he welcomed you here? It's like that. When a new VIP arrives, he wants everybody there so the VIP can feel like a welcome part of the family."

Nate grunted.

He opened the envelope and looked at the card inside.

"I thought we had a deal," he said.

"This is special. This is for *Herself*." She stifled a smile at the word *herself*. Nate wondered if deep down she was jealous. Not sexually, but because a new woman at the compound might threaten her autonomy and access.

"Do I have to wear a tie?"

"No."

"Jacket?"

She said, "I'll find one for you. You don't have to go out and buy one."

He shook his head.

Brannan reached out and grasped his arm. "It's important for you to be there. Mr. T. really wants you there. He said so himself."

"So it's nonnegotiable."

"I'm afraid so. Can I take that as a yes to the RSVP?"

Nate took a deep breath and sighed. She was persuasive. He could feel the warmth of her fingers on his forearm through the fabric of his shirt. He didn't want her to let go. And that smile . . .

"Oh," she said, "Mr. T. would like a few minutes of your time after dinner. Not long — he's got *Herself* to entertain, after all. But he specifically asked me to ask you to linger a few minutes after the dinner breaks up."

"Does he have another assignment for me?" Nate asked.

"I don't get involved in those things," she said.

"Right, I believe *that*."

Her nostrils flared at being questioned, and she let go of his arm and thrust her face at him with her hands on her hips. "Okay, mister, I may handle details on the

264

back end. Travel arrangements, cash advances, false IDs — that kind of thing. And I'm damned good at it. But I'm *not* involved with setting up the assignments. Mr. T. handles those all on his own."

"Okay," Nate said, holding his palms up. "Back off."

"You are a frustrating individual," she said, cooling off. "No one else around here insults me and sticks around very long."

He almost took her right then. He fought an overwhelming urge to pick her up in his arms and carry her into his line shack. He knew she wouldn't object. The back-and-forth had been subterfuge — both knew what was sparking. But . . .

"One thing," she said over her shoulder, as she sashayed toward the pickup. "Mr. T. said no weapons."

Nate's eyebrows arched.

"Mr. Whip will be there," she said. "I told him the same thing."

Nate cringed. Then: "How did he take it?"

"He was much more gracious than you," she said. Then, with a flip of her hair, "Mr. Whip will do anything I ask."

So that was it, Nate thought. He smiled cruelly at her.

"It's not like that," she said. "He's not my type. Too preppy. As far as I'm concerned, he's just a very important colleague. He'd like it to be more, but that would be unprofessional. Mr. T. would frown on it."

"One question," Nate said. "Does Mr. T. know you come up here sometimes? Not on official business?"

Brannan got in and shut the door. Before starting the motor, she said, "No, and I'd appreciate you not mentioning it. He'd frown on that, also."

"I guess I'll see you tomorrow night," Nate said.

"Try to be nicer and more pleasant to *Herself* than you are to me," she called out, spinning gravel as she backed out.

CHAPTER
TWENTY

Wedell/The Black Forest Inn

It was late afternoon when Joe pulled off the highway and bounced down an untrammeled grassy lane that wound through an old apple orchard two miles from Wedell. As he stopped, hundreds of fat birds lifted from where they'd been feeding on dropped fruit. It was obvious it had been years since anyone tended to the trees or pruned them, and a third of the orchard was gnarled black skeletons. An ancient farmhouse had smashed-in windows and the open front door looked like a ghoul face saying *Boo*, he thought. But there was no one around.

Joe set up the ramps and backed the four-wheeler out of his pickup onto the grass. The fat tires crushed apples and made the air tangy. He hid the ATV even deeper in an impenetrable tangle of Russian olive bushes on the side of the abandoned house. Joe transferred his shotgun into the ATV's saddle scabbard and filled the saddlebags with extra ammunition, a few bottles of water, binoculars, spotting scope, tool bag, Maglite, camera, evidence kit, handheld radio, a roll of topo maps of the county, and his Filson vest.

Then he climbed back into his pickup.

* ★ ★

Anna B.'s face appeared at her office window as he drove into the parking area and stopped in front of cabin number eight. When he got out and looked over his shoulder, she was gone.

Again, he tried not to look up at the light fixture as he yawned and stretched theatrically and shuffled into the darkened bedroom. The bed was out of view from the light fixture, if indeed there was a camera in it. Joe fell back onto the bed, making the bedsprings creak.

He waited an hour, then checked his watch: five-thirty. Rolling silently off the bed, he opened the hasp on the rear window and tried to open it, but it wouldn't give. Apparently, they'd painted the window shut when it was refurbished. Joe wondered if it had been intentional or a careless mistake.

He wedged the long blade of his Leatherman tool between the window and the wood frame and carefully sawed down the seam. He had to do it on the sides as well.

Finally, using his legs to give him more momentum, he pressed the palms of his hands against the bottom of the upper window frame and shoved. There was a wooden-sounding *pop* as it opened. Had it been too loud?

Nevertheless, he swung one leg across the sill and bent forward so he could squeeze his shoulders and head through the opening, and he dropped to the ground. His knees barked in pain as he landed, and he paused to let it recede. It did, somewhat. He thought to himself that he wasn't yet used to aches and pains

268

where they didn't used to be. And, he thought grimly, it would only get worse.

When he looked up, he saw Daisy staring sadly down at him, her front paws on the sill.

"Stay," he whispered. She moaned and dropped back into the cabin. He hoped she wouldn't start whining. He hated to leave her.

Joe gathered himself and stood on his tiptoes to close the window behind him as quietly as he could. He left it open an inch in case he'd have to reenter his cabin the same way he'd left.

Then he turned and entered the copse of pine trees. His boots crunched on the carpet of dried needles. He had the key to the four-wheeler in his front pocket. His phone was muted, but he was aware of it in his right breast pocket in case he received a text or call from Marybeth or the FBI.

Or Sheridan.

There were hundreds of old logging roads through the spruce and ponderosa pine forest. He wasn't even sure he'd need to consult his topo maps to find his way to where he wanted to go.

Joe mounted the four-wheeler and started it up and raced through the gears on an overgrown logging road in the general direction of the Black Forest Inn.

The terrain was steeper and more heavily wooded than he had anticipated. Deadfall blocked the old road in several places, and he found himself picking through brush around hazards on the ATV. The temperature dropped twenty quick degrees as the sun nosed over the western hills and the light choked off the dappling on the tops of the trees.

It took thirty-five minutes to navigate the wooded hills to the northeast. Twice, he emerged from the timber to note the distant ribbon of the state highway. He encountered no hunters or other ATVs on the old logging road, although as he neared the Black Forest Inn he saw day-old tire tracks on the trail.

As he wound down the trail through a thick stand of aspen, he sensed heavy forms within the trees to his right that weren't trunks. A small band of elk — a bull, a spike, three cows, and a calf — stood like statues in the trees as he passed. He wondered how many other elk hunters had been down the trail that day who simply hadn't seen them. He'd heard of some elk learning to freeze instead of run when being hunted, although he'd never encountered it before. To reward them for their adaptability, he didn't slow down and gawk but kept his eyes forward until he could no longer see them in his peripheral vision.

At dusk, the trees thinned and he slowed his ATV to a crawl. On a massive grassy bench below him were the winking lights of the Black Forest Inn. The turrets on top looked oddly medieval against the burnt-orange sunset as he descended from the hills. It was almost dark enough for headlights, but he didn't want to turn them on and draw any more attention to his arrival than necessary.

The parking area was filled with four-wheel-drive vehicles with license plates from states as far away as

270

California and New York, as well as a kind of unofficial corral of muddy ATVs in the crushed grass on the north side of the inn. In the parking lot, a few scruffy hunters leaned against their vehicles, drinking beer. A bearded man raised his bottle in salute.

On the south side of the inn, three pickups waited their turn on the roundabout that served the meat-processing facility dock. Joe looked over as he passed. Two hunters in camo and blaze orange had backed their truck with Michigan plates to the loading dock. Meat-cutters in bloody white aprons helped the successful hunters jam meat hooks through the back hocks of two big buck deer and swing the carcasses inside. The game had been gutted but not skinned, and Joe instinctively checked for white paper license tags on the bodies. They were there — wired to the tines of the antlers. Because he wasn't in uniform and not on official duty, he was glad he didn't have the dilemma of illegal deer being received right in front of his eyes.

Joe parked his ATV among twenty others on the north lot and climbed off. His inner thighs and palms tingled from the vibration of the two-stroke engine and he'd picked up enough road dust, pine dust, and mud on his clothing to appear as he hoped to appear — as just another hunter.

The air smelled of fall in a Rocky Mountain hunting camp: cool air, pine, mulch from the forest floor, gasoline and diesel fumes from the vehicles, and the metallic bite of spilled blood, wet hides, and raw meat.

Bathed in yellow neon light from a Coors beer sign in the window, he paused at the entrance to the saloon and breathed it all in and settled into its familiarity.

The saloon was dark, smoky, and raucous. Old dusty mounts of mule deer, elk, bighorn sheep, mountain lions, and pronghorn antelope covered the walls. Strings of tiny white Christmas lights were looped through the tines and curls of the horns and antlers, and gave the room the feel of being roped in by a twinkling lariat. Hunters still in their hunting clothes crowded the bar or stood together in knots throughout the tables. A few still wore holstered sidearms on their belts, and most had sheathed knives and saws. A harried waitress waded through them with a full tray of beaded beer cans and shots. Joe smelled cigar and cigarette smoke and fried hamburgers from a small grill behind the bar manned by a dour gnome-like man with three missing fingers on each hand. With the exception of the harried waitress, there were no women in the saloon.

His first concern on entering was the possibility of being recognized by locals he had met who could identify him, but he confirmed quickly the hunters in the saloon were from out of state. These men were on *vacation*, or, as he'd heard the term once in Saddlestring, on a "red holiday."

A few hunters saw him enter and nodded hello, and he nodded back and went to the bar. He knew a lone hunter was odd but not unusual, although he glanced expectantly at the door several times to pretend he might be waiting for a buddy to join him. Behind him, he heard loud but good-natured ribbing about missed shots, getting stuck, and poor Ritchie from Indiana who had literally been caught with his pants down and his rifle out of reach when two large bucks broke from the timber right in front of him and continued on.

"Bob Pulochova," the bartender said in greeting. "Everyone calls me Pulo."

"Coors Light, please," Joe said. Pulo was gaunt and toothless, and had a white inverted horseshoe of hair beneath his shiny bald head.

"Get your deer yet?" Pulochova asked as a greeting while reaching down into an ice-covered bucket and placing the unopened bottle on the bar.

"I'm an elk hunter," Joe said. It wasn't a lie.

"I don't see blood on your hands," the man said with a wry smile.

"Good reason for that," Joe sighed, leaving it vague. "Say, are there any rooms in this place? It looks pretty full."

"There might be, but you'd have to check up front with Alice. I think a couple of guys from Pennsylvania got their elk and cleared out today, but don't quote me on that. This place fills up fast with hunters."

Joe nodded to his beer. "I might leave this here while I go check."

"You can take it with you. Want another one? Or a shot to go with it?"

"I haven't even opened this yet," Joe said.

"It's happy hour," the bartender said. "Two for one for the next twenty minutes until seven."

"That's okay," Joe said.

"Suit yourself," Pulochova said, rolling his eyes. "Want to know the menu?"

"Sure."

"Hamburger or cheeseburger, single or double," the bartender said, chinning toward the gnome. "That's the menu, unless you want to go into the restaurant down the hall. They got everything in the damn world to eat down there, as long as it's beef."

Joe smiled and said he wanted a double cheeseburger.

"Double cheeseburger coming up!" Pulo shouted out without looking over his shoulder.

The registration desk was no more than an ancient knotty pine lectern in the main lobby. The lobby had high, tin-lined ceilings and smelled of hundred-year-old woodsmoke. A flinty woman with bleached yellow hair stood behind the lectern, sucking on a cigarette and squinting through the smoke. She wore a name tag that read ALICE PULOCHOVA.

"Do you have any single rooms available?" Joe asked, nodding toward the open ledger in front of her.

"Did my better half send you here?" Alice asked, meaning the saloon. Apparently, the bartender was her husband.

"Yup."

"Well, we got a room on the top floor that just opened up, but it ain't cleaned out yet, so I can't rent it to you."

"I'll take it," Joe said.

274

She looked put-out. "My housekeeping folks have left for the night."

"I'll still take it," Joe said, reaching for his wallet. He could tell by the set of her mouth that she was about to turn him away. "Do you take cash?"

Her eyebrows arched conspiratorially, and she said, "Yes, that would be fine." Meaning: she could keep him off the books and pocket the cash and not enter the rental in her ledger, and there wouldn't be a credit card trail to tie either one to the transaction.

"It'll be a hundred," Alice said.

Joe counted out five twenties, leaving only thirty dollars in his wallet.

"This means I'm gonna have to go up there myself when I get a break and take care of it. So the room won't be available for a few hours."

"That's fine."

She gave him a registration card. He filled it out and handed it back.

"Here's the key," she said, reading the card. He wondered if she'd ball it up and toss it in a garbage can the second his back was turned. "Welcome to the Black Forest Inn, Mr . . ." She struggled with the pronunciation of the last name.

"Romanowski," Joe said. "Nate Romanowski."

"Like I said, give me a few hours to get up there. Unless you want to wallow in the empty beer cans and assorted filth from the last guests."

"No thanks."

"How long are you staying, Mr. *Roma-nooski*?"

Joe shrugged. "Maybe just tonight."

She cackled at his answer. "You must be pretty sure you'll kill something tomorrow, then."

He nodded, and said, "I think I'm on their trail."

An hour and two Coors and a double cheeseburger later, the south interior door of the saloon opened inward and three men shuffled in. Joe glanced at his watch — eight-thirty. It was a half-hour after the wild game-processing facility had closed to receiving, and the men were obviously employees just off the clock. They looked exhausted. Joe recognized two of them from when he entered the lot before nightfall as the workers who assisted the Michigan hunters with their deer. One large man with a full red beard still wore his blood-covered apron. Small bits of bone, like cracker crumbs, nested in his beard from sawing off limbs and cracking through pelvises and rib cages. The red-bearded man and a second meatcutter took two adjacent barstools, and the third wandered Joe's way, looking for a place to sit.

Joe had empty barstools on both sides of him, and he nodded toward the approaching meatcutter that it was okay for him to have a seat. The worker nodded back, sat down on Joe's left with a heavy sigh. He was short and round, with thinning black hair and had the bulbous red nose of a drinker.

"Want a beer?" Joe asked, gesturing toward the five full cans and three whiskey shots sitting in front of him. "Guys keep buying rounds for the house and every time I look up, there's another one in front of me. I don't even want to try to drink 'em all."

The worker looked over, assessing Joe's intentions. *Free beer from a stranger?* "Are you kidding?"

"Nope. Somebody back there came up with a rule where anyone who got his deer or elk today had to buy a round for the house. I was just sitting here minding my own business, and the drinks started piling up. Feel free to have one . . . or two."

"Hell of a deal," the worker said with a grin, and quickly drained half of a Coors in a long pull. "Damn, that's good after the kind of day I had."

"Lots of work back there?" Joe asked.

"Jesus, you have no idea," the man said, shaking his head. "I think we took in something like thirty deer and seven elk today. I'm worn out from lifting those things from the back of pickups and carrying quarters to the butcher tables, I'll tell you. I couldn't wait until closing time."

"I'll bet," Joe said as the worker finished the beer, crushed the aluminum can as if pronouncing it dead, and started to reach for another.

He paused: "Are you *sure*?"

"I'm sure," Joe said. "I'm going out early tomorrow and I don't want to be hungover."

"I wouldn't come to work any other way." The man laughed as he slid another beer toward him from Joe's collection.

His name was Willie McKay, he told Joe over the next half-hour and three beers. An unspoken deal was struck: he'd keep talking as long as Joe provided the free alcohol. It was a part-time job, he said, that supplemented the limits of his EBT card, and it was a good deal for him, tax-wise, because he and the other meatcutters were paid off the books in cash. He'd once been a logger, McKay said, before that industry went "all to shit."

Joe brought the conversation back to the facility. He said, "I'm considering bringing my elk here if I kill it tomorrow. Between you and me, if it were you, would you bring game here to be processed? I'm real particular about how it turns out."

"Shit," McKay said, "I'd bring my kill here in a heartbeat, and I don't even hunt. You can't do no better than this place, I swear it."

"What about keeping track of my elk?" Joe asked. "It wouldn't get thrown in with someone else's animal?"

"Not a chance in hell," McKay said, slightly offended at the question. "Part of my job is to tag the quarters of every carcass that comes in. We make damned sure we never mix the meat — even the hamburger. You get back what you brought in, one thousand percent."

"That's good to hear," Joe said. "So your hours are from six in the morning to eight at night?"

"Long fucking day," McKay said, sighing and reaching for Joe's last spare beer. He didn't feel the need to even ask anymore. As he did, Joe signaled the bartender for two more.

McKay said, "If you want one-inch steaks and chops, that's what you'll get. If you want the steaks butterflied, well, it'll cost you a little more in labor, but that's what you'll get. And if you want some of the trim ground into burger, sausage, or jerky, well, we make the best there is."

278

"Is it just the three of you?" Joe asked, nodding toward the other two meatcutters who had set up a few stools down.

"Sometimes there's as many as seven," McKay said. "We were supposed to have more help today, in fact, but the guys they hired didn't even bother to show up. That's why I'm so beat. What is it with young people anymore?" he asked. "Don't none of them have a work ethic at all? They'd rather play video games or jerk off to their iPads or whatever it is they do, because they sure don't want to work hard."

Joe shrugged.

"Hey," McKay said suddenly, as his new beer arrived, "you want to see the shop? You'll see I'm not blowing smoke."

"You mean a tour?" Joe asked.

"Like that," McKay said.

Not really, Joe thought. But when he saw through the crowd of milling hunters that Bill Critchfield and Gene Smith had entered the saloon by way of the lobby, he said, "Let's go."

"Now?" McKay asked, with the beer halfway to his mouth.

Critchfield and Smith seemed to be very well known among the hunters, and several stepped forward to shake their hands and tell them about their day — as if seeking approval from them. Joe realized why: most of the men in the room had booked their hunting trips through the two local men who had access to Templeton's game-rich private land.

"Now," Joe said to McKay, quickly turning on his stool so his back was to Critchfield and Smith. He didn't think they'd recognize him without his uniform shirt but couldn't afford to take any chances. "Bring your beer along. I'll pop for another one when we come back."

"Hell of a deal," McKay said, turning and dismounting from his stool. He hopped down with more energy than he'd shown when he entered the saloon, Joe thought, as if the beer had served as nutrition.

Joe kept his back to Critchfield and Smith as he followed McKay through hunters toward the south door. The red-bearded meatcutter raised his eyebrows as they passed by, and McKay said to him, "He wants a tour."

"Don't mess anything up," the bearded man said. "And make sure the lights are off and everything's locked back up when you leave."

As the door wheezed shut behind them, Joe let out a long breath of relief.

The wild game-processing facility was larger than he had anticipated, and as clean and sterile-looking as advertised. Long stainless-steel counters ran along the side walls, and a stout steel table stood in the middle. A worn but spotless butcher block bristled with knives and cleavers, and an assortment of bone saws hung from hooks on the wall. It smelled of ammonia from being wiped down, and there was an absence of the metallic meat and blood smell in the air that lingered in similar shops Joe had experienced. The large accordion door to the receiving dock outside was closed tight and locked with a chain and padlock, Joe noted.

"What do you think?" McKay asked with pride as he lowered his beer.

"Impressive," Joe said. "You guys seem to take a lot of pride in your work."

McKay shrugged. "We don't have a choice, really. It gets crazy during hunting season sometimes. But somebody complained to Mr. T. himself, and he showed up here one night a couple of years ago and he ripped each one of us new assholes and fired the foreman. He said he wanted this room to look like a surgical suite in a hospital from then on, and we never know when he might pop in and start firing people — or worse — if we screw up."

"That would be Wolfgang Templeton?" Joe asked.

"Yeah, he's the owner of this whole operation: the rooms, the restaurant, and the wild game-processing facility. Like I said, he pays in cash and he pays well. I don't want to lose this gig and neither do the others, so we keep the shop spotless."

"What did you mean when you said *or worse?*" Joe asked.

McKay leaned close enough to Joe that Joe could smell his beer breath. He said, "Did you happen to notice those two guys who just came into the bar out there a minute ago? Guys wearing cowboy hats and acting like fucking lords of the manor or something?"

"I saw them," Joe said.

"They work for Mr. T., running the guiding and hunting operation, and throw their weight around. I don't think Mr. T. knows what assholes they are."

"Like how?" Joe asked.

"They're thugs," McKay said, shaking his head. The alcohol had loosened his tongue. "It ain't unusual for them to take somebody outside and whip their asses if they think he ain't doing his job or if he gives them any lip. That's one reason, I think, it's getting harder and harder to get new employees. The word is out that if you screw up, you might get your ass kicked."

Joe shook his head in sympathy.

McKay said, "I keep my nose clean around those yay-hoos, I'll tell you."

"Probably a smart plan."

"You bet it is. Hey, do you want to see the whole plant?"

Joe figured Critchfield and Smith were likely still in the saloon, so he agreed.

He followed McKay through the refrigerated meat-hanging lockers while the cutter kept up a nonstop dialogue. Joe was astounded at the quantity of hanging skinned carcasses. There were so many, and they were packed together so tightly, that he couldn't wade through them without thumping his shoulder into meaty hindquarters, which bumped into adjoining quarters and set them all rocking slightly. The exposed meat and tallow had taken on a veneer like translucent wax due to exposure to air, but beneath the dry exterior the lean muscle had plenty of give. He noted the multiple tags on each carcass indicating who had brought it in, just as McKay had said.

As McKay explained the process, Joe noted another large steel door on the back wall. As McKay shifted his weight during his monologue, Joe could see a sophisticated keypad near the doorjamb behind him.

"What's in there?" he asked.

McKay paused and turned. "Oh, that room is reserved for the ranch."

"What does that mean?"

"They don't want their beef mixed up with all this wild game," McKay said. "So they hang beef in there."

"And they need a keypad lock?" Joe asked.

"I guess they don't want none of the employees pinching any of it," McKay said with a shrug.

"This place is quite an operation," Joe said.

McKay finished his beer and crushed the can. "You still buyin'?" he asked.

"Yup," Joe said.

He paused at the south door after McKay went through it to confirm that Critchfield and Smith had left. Then he bought McKay another beer, excused himself, and went outside.

Joe walked along the loading dock to the east side of the facility, re-creating in his mind where the freezer room was, and where the hanging lockers were located. There, on the other side of the stone exterior wall, was Templeton's private meat locker. There were no windows or openings to indicate what was there.

He squinted and rubbed his chin.

CHAPTER
TWENTY-ONE

Sand Creek Ranch

With a pair of snips from his tool bag, Joe clipped the holding wires of the three taut strands of barbed wire on the steel T-post that delineated the western border of the Sand Creek Ranch. He'd strapped on a headlamp to be able to see what he was doing. The ATV idled in the trees behind him.

After flattening the loosened barbed wire to the ground with two downed logs, he climbed back on the four-wheeler and drove the vehicle over the top, then rolled the logs away. He loosely restored the fence behind him with baling wire he always carried with him.

Joe glanced around at the terrain and hoped he'd be able to find the entrance he'd created on his way out. There were no landmarks or characteristics to the endless pine forest all around him except for the faint old logging road he'd taken to approach the ranch from the west. He'd decided early on he couldn't risk driving through the entrance gate again where the closed-circuit cameras were located.

Over the years, Joe had rarely trespassed on private property. But the few times he'd had to — to find a wounded animal or rescue a hunter or fisherman — were the reason he always carried cutters and wire for a quick repair.

Nevertheless, his conscience nagged at him. There he was, out of uniform and trespassing on a private ranch without invitation and with only the vague authority of the governor of Wyoming — who would likely plead ignorance if Joe was caught or arrested. This was *after* he'd registered under a false name at a hunting lodge.

As he picked his way up the mountain on the ATV, he kept the speed low and his eyes wide open so he wouldn't overrun the pool of yellow light from the four-wheeler's headlights. The old road he was on hadn't been maintained and at times was blocked by brush and fallen logs. Several times, he looked ahead to see twin sets of green eye dots in the blackness ahead — deer or elk eyes reflecting back. For a mile or so, he followed fresh elk tracks and pellets on the two-track ahead of him until the herd eventually broke off and plunged into the forest.

He had no idea where the old road would end, but it was going where he wanted to go: east and up. Joe hoped that when he found the spine of the local Black Hills he'd be able to get his bearings, see below into the timbered valley, and possibly get a cell phone signal to check messages and communicate.

The department had never replaced the handheld GPS he'd left in his old pickup on the top of the mountain in the Bighorns, and until this moment, Joe hadn't missed it. Judging by the rounded peaks ahead under the star-washed sky, he *thought* he was headed in the right direction. If he was correct, he should be able to see the ranch headquarters below him through his binoculars and get a better understanding of the layout.

When he crested the ridge, a line shack appeared in his headlights so suddenly Joe didn't have the opportunity to kill the motor or douse his lights before he was upon it. Instinctively, he braked and froze while a swirl of dust from the knobby tires of the ATV curled through the beam.

Joe recovered from the surprise of seeing the structure fifty feet in front of him and snatched his shotgun out of the saddle scabbard. He dismounted and took several steps to the left into the trees and waited for the door of the shack to open or the curtains behind a window to rustle.

What would he tell the occupant about why he was there? Joe was a poor liar. He could only hope he'd be instantly mistaken for a lost hunter.

He cursed to himself as he pressed the slide release of his Wing-master, ready if necessary to defend himself by racking in a 12-gauge shell filled with buckshot. He could feel his heart whump in his chest, and he tried to hear over the roar of blood in his ears.

Nothing happened.

The shack looked occupied: there was fresh lumber and building materials stacked on the side of it, there were tire tracks in the ground on the edge of the cut grass, and bright multicolored electrical wires were stapled to the exterior logs. A new galvanized tin

286

chimney on the roof didn't even have soot on it yet, and it gleamed in the lights from his ATV.

After a few minutes of waiting, Joe cautiously approached his four-wheeler and shut it off and killed the headlights. Was it possible, he wondered, that whoever was inside hadn't heard him coming in the dead of night? He considered rolling the ATV back down the hill until he was far enough away to start it and retreat off the mountain, but instead he was drawn to the shack first. Did a Templeton ranch hand stay there? Was anybody home?

He muted his headlamp down to a faint glow and carefully circumnavigated the structure while staying in the trees. There was no doubt the old cabin was under construction, but no way to tell from the outside if anyone was inside. He found no vehicles in the timber beside it, but he did see a crate-sized box raised on stilts just inside the tree line. There was rustling from inside.

Joe approached the construction and leaned into it. The front was open and covered with wire mesh, and when he twisted slightly on the lens of his lamp the three hooded falcons came into view. They were perched on dowel rods and facing him, aware of his presence. A redtail, a prairie, and a peregrine that looked startlingly familiar. He recognized the tooled leather hood and leather jesses from the last time he'd seen the bird in person.

"Nate," Joe whispered.

And he turned back to the line shack.

Joe took a deep breath, approached the closed front door. He stood to the side of the doorjamb and rapped on it with his backhand knuckles, in case Nate instinctively grabbed his weapon inside and decided to fire through the door.

"Nate. It's Joe Pickett."

There was no reaction from inside. He knocked again — harder — and said: "Nate. Let me in. We need to talk."

Nothing.

Joe thought the likelihood of Nate blasting him was remote. Nate wasn't one to panic. Even so, he wasn't the kind of man to surprise, either.

Joe reached down and turned the knob. Unlocked. He pushed the door open and entered, using his headlamp to see inside like a Cyclops.

After thirty seconds, Joe had no doubt who lived in the line shack. Falconry gear — hoods, jesses, bells, lures — was scattered on the tabletop. Ancient books on falconry were stacked on a single bookshelf next to volumes on war, military tactics, and Special Operations. And in a small frame on the end of the bookshelf was a five-year-old photo of a young girl with a falcon on her arm. Sheridan, fifteen years old, grinned awkwardly at the camera with strands of her blond hair whipping across her face in the wind. The photo tugged at Joe's heart: both that it was a younger and more awkward Sheridan, and that Nate displayed it.

Joe took a deep breath and tried to regain control of his heartbeat and breathing.

He'd found him. But now what?

Nate was obviously gone, but who knew how long? His weapon and hat were missing, and there was no vehicle outside. Folded clothes on the bed indicated he was around, and fresh-skinned grouse marinating in the refrigerator indicated he was coming back soon.

His friend lived in his own world, Joe knew. Nate was prone to midnight sojourns, sitting naked in a tree for hours, and sometimes submerging himself entirely in a river or pond with a breathing tube just to experience what it was like to be a fish. Nate didn't keep regular hours, and except for feeding and flying his falcons, there was no routine. He could show up at dawn, or within the minute.

Or he could be outside, watching silently to see what Joe was up to.

Now that he'd found Nate's location, Joe wasn't sure he wanted that conversation after all. If his friend was at Sand Creek Ranch, it confirmed to Joe that Nate was hooked up with Wolfgang Templeton. And if what the FBI suspected was true, the surveillance video from the Scoggins compound in Montana might turn out to be enough to place Nate at the scene. Kidnapping and murder were crimes Joe couldn't overlook.

He stood in the cabin for ten more minutes, running scenarios. He could slip out, wait, or set up an ambush. None felt right.

In the end, Joe extracted a single shotgun shell from his pocket and stood it brass-down on the table. Nate had once left a .50 round in Joe's mailbox to signal he was in the area. Nate would recognize the shell and know he'd been there, and draw his own conclusions.

Maybe, Joe thought, Nate would come to *him*.

At the edge of the clearing, with the line shack behind him and an access road cut into the hillside below, Joe set up a short tripod and mounted his spotting scope. Lights from the ranch compound winked below. In the star- and moonlight, Joe could make out the silhouette of the lodge itself — it indeed resembled a country castle with turrets and peaked roofs — as well as an assemblage of outbuildings, barns, sheds, and guest cabins. The entrance road to the compound was illuminated by soft yellow pole lights. The dark ribbon of Sand Creek itself serpentined through the valley floor.

Although he'd viewed the satellite photos of the ranch compound on Google Maps back in his cabin, the shots displayed on his screen had been taken in midsummer, when the main lodge and outbuildings were obscured by trees. Now that the leaves were clearing from the branches, he got a better idea of the layout.

He was no expert at night photography, but he was surprised by the clarity of the digital photos he took of the compound below under the lights. He doubted at that distance he'd be able to capture individuals, though, especially if they were moving. But he used the camera display and the long lens to zoom in on the vehicles parked on the side of the castle and snap uselessly away at them in the hope that a computer

290

whiz at the state crime lab could determine license plate numbers.

More important, for Joe, was simply understanding the large scale and scope of the ranch headquarters itself. He'd been to many in the past, but never one as regal or elegant in design and construction.

Joe's ears pricked when he heard a shout from below, then a slammed door. Floodlights came on and illuminated the huge lawn in front of the castle and a paved circle drive Joe hadn't noticed previously in the dark. The back of the castle blocked his view from whoever had shouted and come outside, and he crawled the scope along the edges of the structure to try and catch a glimpse of who was there.

He could only hope that the reason for the sudden activity was not his presence above them at the line shack. Then, in his peripheral vision, he saw oncoming headlights flashing through the trees on the road to the headquarters. Someone was coming, and it seemed whoever had hit the lights knew of their imminent arrival.

Joe rocked back from the camera and lens so he could see the whole of it. He caught a glimpse of a woman in a white shirt or jacket emerge on the lawn for a moment, gesticulating to people out of sight. He leaned in and rotated the focus ring and saw her clearly and briefly for a second before she walked out of view toward the front of the building, but it happened too quickly to take a shot. She was young, attractive, black — the woman Latta had mentioned. She waved her arms at someone with the authority of a woman in charge.

A long white SUV with the SAND CREEK RANCH logo on the front doors cleared the trees on the road and turned onto the circular driveway. Joe swung his lens over and shot several rapid photographs as the vehicle approached the castle and went out of view in front of it, blocked by the building. A few words of greeting — happy in tone — floated up from the valley.

Whatever was happening, whoever had arrived with such fanfare, couldn't be discerned. He checked the display on the camera and moaned. The shots of the vehicle under the floodlights were blurry and pixelated. From that distance and in the poor light, he couldn't tell who was in the SUV — or how many.

"I," he said to himself in a whisper, "am a lousy spy."

Three-quarters of a mile away, on the bank of Sand Creek on the valley floor, in a stand of thick river cottonwoods and red buckbrush, Nate Romanowski watched it all. He clutched a writing burlap bag filled with pigeons he'd trapped in the loft of an unused barn farther down the river to feed to his birds.

He had no reason to expose himself, and had stopped cold when the floodlights went on in front of the castle. Instead, he'd stepped farther back into the shadows.

He'd watched as ranch staff poured out of the front door, directed by Liv Brannan. She made them stand shoulder to shoulder along the edge of the circular driveway like a scene out of an English drama. Seeing her in action caused a tug in his chest. As she assembled them, Wolfgang Templeton appeared. He was framed by the huge double doors and backlit from inside for a moment before he stepped outside on the portico.

Nate could see Templeton's starched white open-collared shirt, his silver-belly Stetson. He looked stiff and formal, as if he were about to receive royalty.

The white Suburban slowed as it took the circular driveway and stopped in front. A staffer Nate didn't recognize opened the driver's door and strode back to open the door for his passenger.

Because the SUV was between Nate and the front steps, he couldn't see the woman when she was escorted out, but he did see Templeton's reaction. After a momentary pause, he skipped down the steps to greet her. The staff offered their welcome and parted, and Nate watched as Templeton escorted his new woman up the stairs. Templeton towered over her, and guided her up the steps with his hand on the small of her back. She wore a dark skirt and matching jacket and had shiny dark hair.

At the top, the woman turned to thank the staff, and Nate saw a wide mouth and glint of perfect white teeth and her porcelain doll-like face in the porch light.

It was as if someone had punched him in the stomach.

CHAPTER
TWENTY-TWO

Wedell, Wyoming

After finally locating the red baling twine ties, Joe secured the wires he'd lowered so he could pass through. That he'd located Nate disturbed him. Although he wanted to see his friend again, he didn't want to encounter him, given the circumstances.

He was pleased he knew more about the Sand Creek Ranch itself, and wondered if the arrival of Templeton's love interest would cause them to lower their guard for a few days. He doubted it. He wished that at least a few more of his shots had come out more clearly than they had, and he hoped the techs at the FBI could find something on them to help establish probable cause for a raid. But he doubted that, too.

The night cooled considerably as he rode the ATV back down the mountain, and he'd stopped to pull on his buckskin gloves and Filson vest. When he reached the Black Forest Inn, it was dark and quiet except for randomly lit windows and the thumping bass from the jukebox in the saloon.

Joe skirted the inn grounds and kept to the trails in the trees until he was halfway between the hunting lodge and the town of Wedell. He braked and shut off the engine and drank half of a bottle of water and looked at his watch.

Midnight.

He was surprised how much time his sojourn had taken. It was too late to do much more than text Marybeth that he was okay and would call tomorrow when he could. Obviously, if she'd learned more about Erik Young, there would have been a series of voicemails or messages.

With his thumbs punching the letters clumsily in the cold, he wrote to Chuck Coon: *Templeton has thousands of acres to bury bodies. What do you need for PC to search it?*

PC meaning "probable cause."

He wondered if Coon would see the text before morning.

Joe parked the ATV at the abandoned orchard and walked the rest of the way to the Whispering Pines. He was exhausted. His intention was to open the back window, retrieve Daisy and his packed duffel bag of clothes, and drive back to the Black Forest Inn to stay the night. He figured he'd have one day while the Game and Fish truck sat out in the parking lot before they'd realize something was off — maybe he was sick or injured or awaiting instructions in his room? — before trying to smoke him out. Joe wondered who they'd send to check on him and thought Anna would be the most likely.

By then, he hoped, Chuck Coon and his special agents would have enough background and probable cause to swoop northward to take over the investigation. As far as Joe was concerned, it wouldn't be soon enough.

But there was a problem, and at first he thought his tired eyes were playing tricks on him.

Through the last trees and brush before he reached the back of his cabin, he could view his pickup parked by itself in the lot under the illumination of a single blue-white pole light. Someone was underneath it, on their back with arms extended, reaching up toward the engine.

He shook his head and rubbed his eyes and looked again. Yup.

Joe dropped to his haunches. He reached out and used the palm of his hand to bend a caragana bough down far enough to see over it. Not only was there one man beneath his truck, he could see the ankles and boots of another who was standing or squatting on the other side of his vehicle, as if keeping watch on Joe's cabin. He could see neither man clearly enough to make an identification.

Joe heard the clink of metal on metal from beneath the undercarriage. The man underneath was using hand tools.

Why else would someone be underneath his pickup after midnight? They were obviously dismantling a part in his motor or drive-train . . . or installing something to his vehicle, whether a tracking device or explosives.

He thought, *They couldn't burn me out like they did the DCI agent*. It would be too obvious. So this time they were trying a new tack. Which meant his suspicions about the electronic surveillance in his cabin had turned out to be correct and had roused the attention of . . . somebody.

He shifted until he could see the whole of the parking lot. Anna B.'s Jeep was parked where it always was on the side of the office. No lights were on in her rooms. There were no other vehicles in the lot besides his. Yet . . .

Whoever it was doing something to his truck couldn't have simply walked there, he thought. No one walked in Wedell. No one walked in *Wyoming*. Their vehicle had to be parked nearby.

Keeping low, Joe scrambled backward until he was sure he was out of view from the lot. Then he stood up and looked around. He cursed himself for leaving his shotgun in the scabbard of the ATV, and wished he hadn't removed the .40 Glock he'd tucked into his belt on the small of his back earlier because it was uncomfortable to ride with.

He moved cautiously toward the access road to the motel, sidestepping from tree to tree. The brush on his side of the borrow pit was thick enough to keep him concealed from the road, although he feared the dry fall leaves would rattle as he pushed his way through them.

He could see a vehicle parked in the dark on the far side of the road. It was a blocky SUV pointed uphill. It was located in deep shadow under a canopy of pine so even the stars and moon couldn't reach it. It was too dark to see if anyone else was inside, but he could tell it was light-colored and had a bike or luggage rack of some kind on the roof.

Joe waited, worrying about himself and his dog. If Daisy heard or sensed the men outside and started barking, it could scare them off and confirm in their minds he was inside. But he feared for her life if she barked. The men might panic and enter the cabin to shut her up. He couldn't sit back and let them. If that happened, he knew he'd risk exposing himself — and his lack of weapons — to them.

There was a shaft of blue light from the pole lamp on his side of the borrow pit about seventy feet up the road where the turn-in for the motel was located. When the men at his truck were finished with whatever they were doing, he thought, they'd have to return to their SUV that way. He doubted they'd bushwhack their way back in the dark.

If they returned to the vehicle on the road, he'd see who they were. Joe waited. Daisy didn't bark.

Ten minutes later, Joe saw two forms enter the light shaft on their return to the parked SUV. He recognized the distinct brim fold in the taller man's cowboy hat as the one worn by Bill Critchfield. He could see a three-quarter's glimpse of Gene Smith's profile as he entered and exited the light. Smith was carrying a small toolbox in his hand and swinging it slightly forward and back with each step.

298

Joe tried not to breathe as they neared him, and hoped they couldn't somehow hear the beating of his heart, as he could.

Critchfield and Smith crossed over the road and surprised Joe by not opening the front doors to climb in. Instead, they split up at the front bumper of the vehicle and walked to the back doors and opened them. They'd used an unfamiliar vehicle to get to the Whispering Pines instead of Critchfield's pickup.

When the doors opened, the dome light inside came on. In the near-total darkness, it was almost blinding.

But in the second or two it took for Critchfield and Smith to swing open their doors and slide in, Joe could see they weren't alone.

Sheriff R. C. Mead sat behind the wheel. Next to him on the passenger seat was Jim Latta in civilian clothes. Latta's expression was blank.

Joe closed his eyes and sighed. *Latta*.

Mead started the truck but kept his headlights off. Instead of pulling a U-turn, he backed into the road, bathing Joe in red backup lights, then cranked his wheel and rolled downhill. As he did, Joe heard muffled words being spoken from inside the vehicle but couldn't make them out. Not until the SUV was out of sight below in the trees did its headlights flash on.

It wasn't a luggage rack on top of the SUV, Joe realized, but the light bar of the sheriff's department GMC Yukon.

First Nate, and now Mead and Latta, Joe thought. Who else would reveal he was on the wrong side tonight?

Joe was no mechanic, but it was obvious what they'd done to his pickup when he rolled under it with a mini Maglite in his teeth.

Smith had attached a cheap prepaid cell phone — the same make and model Joe had noticed at the Sundance convenience store — to the undercarriage of his pickup. It was secured with strips of electrician's tape that had been rolled around the front axle. The phone was powered on but inert, and there were two wires — one red, one white — that snaked out from its plastic shell. Joe followed the wires from the phone as they looped around and through steel undergirders toward the mid-rear of the vehicle. There, they were jammed into what looked like a fist-sized lump of light gray clay that had been pressed against the outside sheet metal wall of the gas tank.

He stared at the assembly and thought about it. The clay was obviously plastic explosive, likely C-4 or Semtex. The wires fed into a thin silver tube — a blasting cap — inserted into the lump. The idea, he guessed, was to leave the bomb under his truck until they decided to trigger it with a remote call to the cell phone, which would activate the explosives in back and blow his truck in half using its own fuel. They wouldn't even have to tail him — just be sure he was driving the roads of Medicine Wheel County, preferably on a series of steep switchbacks with cell reception — and hit the speed dial.

Then: *Boom.*

Conceivably, Joe would be injured or killed instantly or lose control of the vehicle and plunge off the mountain. The gasoline fire would consume the truck and melt away the components and render the cell phone unrecognizable.

Still, he thought, it was a sloppy and desperate act. There were holes in the plot. State and federal forensics units could determine the origin of the explosion, the specific brand of plastic, and maybe find the wires and cell phone detonator. The prepaid phone could possibly be traced to where it was purchased, and by whom.

Joe knew he'd gotten their attention. His first inclination was to go right back after them. Bill Critchfield and Gene Smith weren't hard to find. But what would he do — arrest them and take them to the county jail, which was run by coconspirator R. C. Mead? Or in front of Judge Bartholomew, who also was likely in on the act?

And he didn't dare try to call any backup. Latta was involved, and likely the town cops and sheriff's deputies. A request made by dispatch through channels would be instantly heard by all the players.

In the past, he knew who he'd call for help: Nate Romanowski. But Nate had apparently crossed over as well.

Then he recalled his promise to Marybeth, and vowed to leave Medicine Wheel County the next day. The Feds and state boys could follow up.

The question, though, was whether he could keep himself safe until the big guns moved in to take over.

A thought hit him. What if the explosive had been planted not to kill him while he drove, but to be activated remotely to warn him off? And what if they decided to call the number on the cell phone *at that moment*, once the four men were far enough away not to be tied to the scene?

Joe felt his gut contract, and he stared at the cell phone, willing it not to light up with a call. He quickly scrambled back to the gas tank and reached up — his movements seemed incredibly slow in his mind — and pulled the blasting cap out of the lump. Then he switched ends and cut the cell phone loose from the tape and powered it off. If they tried to call now, he thought with relief, nothing would happen.

"Sorry, girl," Joe said to Daisy on the bench seat of his truck as he drove out of the parking lot. "You've been cooped up all night. But you're a lousy watchdog."

She responded to the tone of his voice and not his words with a rhythmic thumping of her tail on the inside of the passenger door.

The bomb components were in a large plastic evidence bag on the floor of the cab. The cell phone was off and the wires and blasting cap weren't attached to anything, but Joe was nervous about the lump of explosives. He drove extra-slowly to the apple orchard, avoiding potholes and rocks. He blew out a breath of relief when he reached his destination and killed the engine. But he made it a point not to slam his door shut, and eased it closed.

The move would puzzle his enemies, he figured. Anna would no doubt call them at dawn to report Joe missing, his pickup gone. A quick check of his room would reveal that he'd packed up and left during the night.

He wondered what they'd do. Would they try and locate him before calling the number on the cell phone under the pickup? Or would they panic and hold off until they knew it would be a clean kill? Either way, he figured, they'd be confused . . . and alarmed.

Joe convinced Daisy to hop up on the rear platform of the ATV. The key to his room at the hunting lodge was in his front pocket, and he couldn't think of a better place to bunker in and get some sleep. He started the four-wheeler and began to pull away from his truck when a thought came to him that made him grin.

Then he cranked on the handlebars and returned to the pickup. If the C-4 was stable enough not to explode on the ride to the orchard, it was stable enough to survive a trail ride as well, he thought. But all the way to the Black Forest Inn he drove slowly and cautiously, avoiding rocks and bumps, in a cold sweat, despite the freezing air.

Overhead, a thick wall of storm clouds extinguished the stars as it advanced from the northwest.

There was no one at the front counter when Joe led Daisy into the lobby of the old hunting lodge, just as there had been no one about outside. He removed his hat and whapped it on his thigh to clear the half-inch of snow that had gathered on the brim. The door to the saloon was shut and locked, and the interior lights were muted. If the decades-old bull moose head on the wall could have seen through its dusty glass eyes, it would have beheld a dirty and disheveled man with a pair of ATV saddlebags over his shoulder, a shotgun in his hand, and a tired yellow Labrador on his boot heels.

Joe circled behind the lectern and checked the guest registry book. No Nate Romanowski. He saw where Alice had written *Maint* next to room 318, which corresponded to the key she'd given him. He guessed *Maint* meant "maintenance," the reason she listed for not renting it out. All the other rooms in the lodge were full.

He nodded at his luck. For the hundred dollars cash that was now in Alice's pocket, he had inadvertently gone off the grid.

Room 318 was small, dark, and smelled of carpet fungus and historic flatulence. The walls were fake wood-grain sheets of paneling that were blistered from a leaking roof or broken ceiling pipe. The double bed sagged in the middle and was lit by a naked low-wattage bulb that hung from a cord. The curtains were pulled across a tiny window, and they looked like they were made of lace. Obviously, Joe thought, Templeton's men hadn't renovated it yet.

Joe parted the curtains to find a view of the parking lot. The window opened roughly, but it was too small to climb through if it came to that.

The bolt on the lock didn't fit snugly into the doorframe, despite Joe's putting his shoulder to it. So in addition to attaching the chain lock — which was lamely held by two small screws to a three-quarter-inch strip of plywood — Joe wedged the top of the only hard-backed chair in the room under the knob. He dropped the saddlebags on the seat of the chair to give it some weight.

He plugged in his cell phone to recharge, then jacked a shell into the receiver of his shotgun and propped it in the corner near the headboard. The .40 Glock went on the floor on the right side of his bed so he could reach down in the dark and raise it quickly if necessary.

The bedsprings moaned as he flopped back on the bed fully dressed. It was two-thirty in the morning and the inn was quiet except for snoring sounds through the thin wall behind him.

If he was going to try to get some sleep, he thought, he had a three-hour window before hunters started getting up and pounding on one another's doors and wrestling guns and gear down the hallways.

Joe shut off the light and closed his eyes but couldn't will himself to sleep. Nate was in the hills, there'd been a bomb under his pickup, and in the morning Templeton's minions would be looking for him.

He settled in for a short and miserable night.

CHAPTER
TWENTY-THREE

Black Forest Inn

"What do you mean, not until tomorrow?" Joe said angrily to Chuck Coon.

"Realistically, it may be a couple of days."

"Are you sure? In a couple of days, I may be dead."

"Have you looked outside?"

He grunted as he swung to his feet and limped to the window. His lower back ached from sleeping on the sagging mattress.

Fifteen inches of snow covered the ground outside, and it was still coming down. The pine forest had been transformed into two tones: white and gray. Trees looked ghostly through the falling snow, and the hills looked quiet and muted — as if everything was on hold for a while.

"It's worse in Cheyenne because the wind has kicked up as usual," Coon said. "Everything's closed — the airport, the interstates, the schools. Half my guys didn't even make it in this morning. What a freak damn storm. They didn't even predict it. It's just like you wake up and it's a whiteout."

Joe groaned.

306

He'd spent the previous thirty minutes on the phone with Coon — pausing only to take a quick call from Marybeth to say he'd call her back — recapping all that had gone on the night before and what he suspected. Coon admonished him for dismantling the bomb instead of leaving it intact for forensics, but he was as intrigued as Joe was about locating Nate Romanowski. In fact, the agent-in-charge seemed almost jaunty — which rubbed Joe the wrong way. Joe's story had energized Coon to a surprising degree, Joe thought. The man was *on the hunt* now, armed with real evidence. Joe understood the feeling but couldn't share it because of his circumstances. The dreary hotel room, lack of sleep, and growing fear that he'd be found by Critchfield and the others didn't allow him to share Coon's enthusiasm.

Coon spoke as if he were thinking out loud: "We finally have actionable evidence on the operation up there, thanks to our midnight bombers. You can personally identify the four of them, right?"

"Right."

"Did you get any photos?"

"No."

"I wish you had."

"Chuck, I didn't even think of it at the time, and I'm not sure I could have risked it." Joe paused and said, "But *they* don't know that."

Coon chuckled. "We might be able to suggest you did, is what you're saying. Something like, 'What would you say if you found out that Joe Pickett took a camera-phone shot of the four of you together in the sheriff's SUV?' And see what they do."

"Yup."

"If we can get somebody to talk — and we now have four suspects — one or more of them might give us something we can build on. I'm particularly interested in sweating this Bill Critchfield. He might be our link between the bomb under your truck and Wolfgang Templeton."

"That's why I made that stupid call to your voice message yesterday. I was trying to flush them out."

"And just maybe it worked. I still can't condone all your methods, though."

"Oh well," Joe said.

They talked about sending state DCI and federal evidence techs to search the ranch with sonar for buried bodies.

Coon said, "That makes it even more important we do this right. From what you're telling me, we need to storm that county with every man we've got and grab them all at once before they know what's happening, so we can isolate the four bombers from each other. We can't pick them up one by one or they might warn the rest in the food chain. So that means we need at least four arrest teams and maybe even extra manpower from South Dakota or Montana. I need my full forensics team to go over that motel cabin to pull out the spy gear you say is there, and the bomb experts to go over that device you found. We need to get approval from D.C. for an operation on that scale."

"How long will *that* take?" Joe asked.

"Like I said, a couple of days. You know how the bureaucracy works — or doesn't."

"I want to get out of here as soon as I can," Joe said, parting the moth-eaten curtains with the back of his hand to look outside again. Most of the hunting vehicles were long gone. Nothing excited hunters more than fresh snow to track game. "Everybody knows everybody around here. It may not take them long to figure out where I am."

"I'll make some calls," Coon said. "I'll call you back after I've talked to D.C. Guys are slowly making their way in here now, so I'll have a better idea of what kind of manpower we've got by this afternoon. I'll also give the heads-up to Rulon that his range rider might have broken this thing wide open. He'll need to give us his blessing to proceed, because he's said in the past — *many times* — that he'd arrest any federal official who takes action in the state without his approval."

Joe noted the disdain in Coon's tone, and it made him smile.

Coon continued, "I don't think there'll be any problem this time, since he was the one who sent you up there. But keep in mind even if everything goes perfectly, it's still five hours from here to there on the roads. There's no way we can fly up there in this weather. So you'll need to just lie low and stay off their radar until we can get there."

"I thought I was supposed to make my report and go home," Joe said. "That was the deal."

"That deal is no longer operable," Coon laughed. "Now we need you to stay. It'll make a big difference

309

that you're with us when we brace those four bombers — especially that other game warden. They need to see your face and know that you can place them at the motel last night. That'll turn the heat up on them. Make sense?"

"Yeah," Joe said, discouraged.

Coon mused, "I'm thinking that even without the definitive photo of them together from you, we can still pull trace and DNA evidence from inside the sheriff's vehicle that will put them at the scene. Not to mention fingerprints and trace from the bomb itself. Where did you say it was now?"

"In a safe place," Joe said.

Coon paused. "What does that mean?"

"I hid it someplace they won't think to look for it. That's all I'm going to say."

"But what if —"

Joe finished Coon's thought for him. "What if they get to me and by the time you get up here, I'm not around to show you where it is or place them at the scene? Well, maybe that'll give you another reason to get things moving on your end."

Coon chuckled. Joe didn't appreciate it.

"Whatever you do, Joe, don't engage them. Just stay where you are and don't let yourself be seen. We can't risk them finding you and blowing the case before we can move on it."

"That's thoughtful of you," Joe said.

"Yeah — it didn't exactly come out the way I wanted it to sound," Coon said, his voice contrite.

"But it's what you meant."

Joe took Coon's silence as agreement.

"I'm trapped here for the moment," Joe said, explaining that his pickup was miles away through the forest and he wasn't sure when he'd be able to retrieve it.

"There's something else," Joe added. "I need money."

"We all need money."

"No — I need cash. I'm tapped out, is what I'm saying."

Coon said, "The governor didn't give you a budget?"

"No."

"Well — this is uncomfortable," Coon sighed.

They worked out a way that Coon could transfer seven hundred dollars from a bureau emergency fund directly into Joe and Marybeth's bank account. Joe could draw it out from the saloon ATM when it cleared, which he hoped would be soon.

"You'll have to pay that back," Coon said.

"Talk to the governor about that."

Coon groaned but agreed.

"I'll call you back as soon as I know when we can move," Coon said.

Before Joe could speed-dial Marybeth, his phone lit up again. Coon calling back.

"That was quick," Joe said.

"Ha-ha. No, I just remembered I had something to tell you. I forgot about it until now. Didn't you say this fancy southern guy you ran into was named Whip?"

"Yes."

"We might have something on him. The photo we've got matches your description, and I'll send it to your phone in a second so you can ID it."

"So who is he?" Joe asked.

"He might be named Robert Whipple, originally from Charlotte, North Carolina. My guys did a search of FBI databases and got more than a few hits on him. If it's this Robert Whipple, you need to not run into him again."

"Thanks for the advice," Joe said. He could hear Coon shuffling through paperwork so he could summarize it over the phone.

"Robert Whipple, aka Whip, was a CIA Black Operator during Operation Desert Storm. He was with an off-the-books rendition and interrogations unit, but his cover got blown by a whistle-blower in the same unit who claimed Whipple murdered a couple of Iraqi Republican Guards who wouldn't cooperate. The whistle-blower said Whip shot one of the Republican Guards in the back of the head with a .22 pistol in front of the other. The scared Iraqi told Whip everything he wanted to know, but it turned out the information was bad. Whip supposedly came back the next week and put a .22 round into that man's head as well.

"Let's see," Coon said, reading further: "By the time the whistle-blower made his allegations, Whip had vanished into thin air. He's never been arrested, and his whereabouts were unknown — until possibly now. But his name was associated with several high-profile disappearances, kind of the same deal as Templeton himself. Dirty people seem to know his name — *Whip*

— but they didn't give enough information to tie Whipple directly to any murders."

Joe felt his chest constrict. Again, he parted the curtains on the window. There were no new vehicles in the lot.

His phone chimed and he opened the photo message sent from Coon.

"Yup," Joe said. The dark features, hooded eyes, and feminine mouth. "That's him."

"Man," Coon laughed, "there is a nest of dangerous outlaws up there. I may end up getting a promotion out of this."

Joe sighed and terminated the call.

Before he could call Marybeth, there was a rapid knocking on his door. Joe froze for a second and took a step toward his shotgun. The knocking was frantic, and sounded like a woodpecker hammering.

"Housekeeping." A female voice Joe recognized as belonging to Alice from the front desk. Daisy barked at the sound.

"Why start now?" Joe asked her through the door, looking around at his armpit of a room.

"What did you say?" she asked suspiciously.

"Never mind. I don't need anything."

"Was that a dog I heard in there? Dogs are an extra twenty-dollar surcharge."

"I'll pay it."

"Aren't you going hunting today?" she asked. "Everybody else is gone. It snowed during the night and it's still snowing."

"Yup."

"So you're just going to stay in your room all day? Do you need any towels or anything?"

"No."

"Are you sick?"

"No."

"You can slip that extra twenty for the dog under the door, then."

Joe rolled his eyes, dug out his wallet, and found his last twenty. As he slid it under the door, she snatched it with the speed of a change machine.

"Something else, Mr. Roma-nooski. If you're staying in this room again tonight, you need to pay in advance. You can just slip that under the door like you did the other."

Joe took a moment to think. If she wanted cash on the spot, he assumed he was still off the books and their unspoken arrangement could continue.

"I'll have it for you tonight," Joe said. "I've got to get some cash from the ATM."

"You said cash, right?" she asked.

"Yup."

She paused and seemed to be thinking something over. For a moment, Joe feared there might be someone with her. The door didn't have a peephole so he couldn't check that out.

"Look," she said, her voice much lower. He had to lean toward the door to hear her. "Couple of guys came by this morning and asked whether I'd seen a man who kind of looked like you. They didn't mention no dog, though."

Critchfield and Smith, Joe thought.

"I told them you weren't registered, which is the truth."

"Thank you," Joe said, not sure if he believed her. But then he thought she must be telling the truth or he would have already had visitors.

"I don't like them two guys," she said. "Never did. It goes back years. But I thought you'd want to know."

"I appreciate it," Joe said. "I really do."

"Of course," she said conspiratorially, "that means the price of this room just went up."

He winced. "How much?"

"I'm thinking five hundred a night, two-night minimum — in advance."

Joe said, "So a thousand."

"That'll be good," she whispered.

"I'll give it to you tonight," Joe said.

"I think you'd better," she said. Then: "Sure you don't want some clean towels?"

He quickly texted Coon to make the loan at least twelve hundred dollars and "no less." Then he imagined the special agent blowing his top.

When he reached Marybeth, he tried not to convey his growing sense of panic. There was no need worrying her when there was nothing she — or he — could do about it at the moment. She said it was snowing there, too, but it was supposed to clear up by late afternoon. The Twelve Sleep County Library and schools were closed due to the weather, but both would likely reopen the next day.

And, she said, Mrs. Young in California wouldn't pick up.

"I'm guessing she sees the 307 area code and just won't answer the phone," she said. "I'm really frustrated."

She said she was equally frustrated by the fact that she couldn't locate a Facebook page or blog she could tie to Erik. That alone made her uneasy, since she assumed he was on the Web — *he had to be* — under a false name.

When she asked what he'd been doing the previous night, Joe said he'd been out scouting and left it at that, and quickly changed the subject: "Have you heard anything from Sheridan?"

"The university's closed today, too," Marybeth said. "I texted her and asked how things were going. She sent me an answer that everything was fine. That's all she said, and I didn't ask any more. I may call her later today, though, since she's likely just hanging out in her dorm room."

"Let me know," Joe said.

"I will."

"So the girls are home with you today?"

"Yes, yes, they are," Marybeth said. "Lucy got up, heard school was closed, and went back to bed. April's making breakfast."

"How's *that* going?"

Joe heard the muffled sound of Marybeth covering the mic on the phone, and he waited until she was someplace — probably the hallway — where she felt free to talk. Her voice was a barely audible whisper.

"I don't know what's happened, but she's been an angel. The good April is back. She even smiled this morning when she heard there was no school."

"What brought on the change in her outlook?"

"I'm not sure, but I'm not going to ask yet. I'm stuck in the house all day with her, after all."

"That's good news," Joe said. "Maybe she's kind of getting over this Dallas Cates thing."

His wife snorted and said, "*That's* not likely. But I don't know — maybe he's getting a clue and not pressuring her to follow him on the rodeo circuit or something. Whatever it is, she's not sulking and slamming doors, which is all I ask."

Joe nodded to himself. He said, "I'm hoping to be home in a couple of days at the most. I'm ready to get out of this place."

"Yes," she said, "it will be good to have you back."

"Marybeth, I love you and the girls." It just came out.

She paused and said, "Are you okay?"

"Fine."

"Exactly what Sheridan said, and I'm not sure I completely believe either one of you. Now you've got me scared."

"Don't be," Joe said. "I can't tell you everything yet, but the FBI is manning up to get up here and take over. This should be done soon — or at least my part in it."

"Good. Remember your promise."

"I have," Joe said.

"Joe," she said, "did you try to call me last night? From a pay phone or something?"

"No," he said, narrowing his eyes. "I saw your text, but I thought it was too late to call back."

"Oh."

"Why?"

"Someone called my cell phone last night. I missed it because I was in the shower, but it had a Medicine Wheel County prefix. They didn't leave a message or anything, but I thought it was curious."

Joe asked, "What time?"

"A few minutes after midnight."

Joe thought back. He'd been on the ATV, retreating from the Sand Creek Ranch.

"It wasn't me," Joe said. The second he said it, he had a possible explanation.

She beat him to it, and said, "Joe, I had this premonition. What if it was Nate?"

"He's here," Joe said.

She paused and her voice rose. "And when were you going to tell me that little fact?"

"Soon."

"Have you seen him?"

"No. But I think I found where he lives on the Sand Creek Ranch."

"I hope he's not . . ." she began to say, but didn't finish the sentence.

"Me too," Joe said.

"But if it was him, I wish I knew what he was calling about."

Joe wondered the same thing, and was about to say something when he noticed Daisy had gone rigid and was staring at the door. Her growl came out as a low, cautionary rumble that ended with two heavy barks that shook the thin walls.

Joe said, "Gotta go." Someone was outside in the hallway.

As he tossed the phone on the bed and reached for his shotgun, he heard the clumping of retreating boots.

He kept the shotgun aimed at the door for thirty seconds until Daisy calmed down and there was no more rustling outside. Then he went to his window and parted the moth-eaten curtains. They weren't made of lace after all.

"Oh no," Joe said aloud.

There, out in the parking lot, was Jim Latta walking from the inn toward his pickup. His shoulders were bunched and hands jammed in his pockets against the falling snow. His vehicle was idling in the lot, exhaust billowing from the tailpipe. When Latta opened his door, Joe caught a glimpse of a passenger — a young girl. His daughter, no doubt.

What he didn't see was Latta opening his phone to call anyone.

Yet.

CHAPTER
TWENTY-FOUR

Black Hills, Wyoming

By the time Joe gathered his gear bag, unlocked the door, called Daisy, thundered down the stairs through the empty lobby — no sign of Alice, who was no doubt hiding after ratting him out — and swept ten inches of powder snow from the seat of his four-wheeler, Latta's pickup was gone.

He mounted the ATV and it roared to life, and he gunned it and turned 180 degrees to follow the fresh set of tire tracks in the snow of the parking lot. As he cleared the Black Forest Inn property, he tried not to think of the cold already seeping into his clothing or the sting of heavy flakes in his eyes. He had to head Latta off before the game warden blew his cover. What he didn't know was how he was going to do it.

The tracks were in the middle of the road, which said to Joe that Latta was driving cautiously on the unplowed highway. There might be a chance to catch up with him — but then what? He couldn't — and wouldn't — try to force Latta off the road. Not with Emily inside.

Within five minutes of leaving, Joe saw a faint pair of pink taillights through the heavy snowfall ahead. He

320

knew it was Latta because there was no one else on the highway. Joe recognized where he was — on the flat stretch prior to the series of switchbacks that would climb the mountain on the way to Wedell. Now, for sure, there was no way to get ahead and ease Latta to the shoulder.

He maintained a cushion with the taillights in sight, hoping Latta wouldn't see him in his rearview mirror or get on his phone yet. Joe put himself in Latta's place and prayed the other game warden would wait to place his call when Emily couldn't overhear. Wedell was eight miles away.

Joe thought: *Use your tools and the terrain to your advantage.*

Then he turned his head and called over his shoulder, "Hang on, Daisy," and slowed the four-wheeler. He scoped out the timbered slope on his right for an opening in the trees, and when he found it, he turned the wheel. The path was little more than a game trail.

The front end of the ATV rose in his hands on the hill and he stood up from the seat and leaned into it. He could feel Daisy's warm bulk against his back as he downshifted into a lower gear for the climb. Plumes of snow shot out from the fat rear tires, along with clumps of soil and grass when the treads ate through the ground cover. He flattened a dozen small treelings, and his front wheels glanced off downed timber and rock outcroppings.

Halfway up the hill in the deep timber, the ATV began to stall, wheels spinning madly, before his right rear tire found purchase on an exposed knob of granite and shot him farther up the hillside. Since he couldn't risk spinning out again or even slowing down in the deep snow, Joe kept the throttle open and just tried to stay on, as if riding a runaway horse. Black wet tree trunks shot by him on both sides and he blasted through a low-hanging bough that dumped a foot of snow on him so he was temporarily blinded.

He slapped the snow from his face as he climbed, but his collar and cuffs were packed with it. He could feel small rivers of melted ice water course down his backbone into his Wranglers. His feet and hands were numb.

At the top of the hill, he burst through the brush in a white explosion and found himself straddling the untracked center of the highway. He sat for a moment, his heart pounding.

Daisy licked the snow off the back of his neck with a warm, wet tongue.

He squinted through the snowfall to his left and saw the yellow glow of headlights around the second switchback turn. Joe hoped Latta would be able to see *him* in the middle of the road.

Latta's truck didn't stop until it was so close Joe could see the man's troubled face through the windshield. Even with the wipers sweeping the glass, he could see Emily mouthing, *Who is that, Dad?*

Joe simply sat there on the ATV in the middle of the road with his engine idling, squinting against the snow.

Finally, Latta jammed the gearshift into park and opened his door. He left his pickup running so Emily wouldn't get cold, Joe guessed. So he could hear better, Joe reached down and shut off the engine of his four-wheeler.

"Joe!" Latta called out. "What the hell?"

He was trying to sound naturally surprised, Joe thought. But he didn't perform very well.

"Where the hell is your truck? Why are you out on a day like this on top of an ATV? And why are you in the middle of the damned road?"

Joe said, "To stop you."

Latta paused between the grille of his truck and Joe.

"I take it that's Emily with you."

Emily had light brown hair parted in the middle and stylish black-framed glasses that showcased her large brown eyes. She looked guileless and quite sweet, and Joe couldn't detect her physical impairment by looking at her.

Latta said, "Yes. They canceled school this morning, so she's hanging out with me today."

"I used to do that with my daughter Sheridan," Joe said. "She used to ride along."

Latta nodded, eyeing Joe carefully.

"Jim, I saw you in the sheriff's SUV last night when Smith and Critchfield put those explosives under my truck. I kept hoping you weren't involved with them up until that minute. But you're dirty, Jim, and we both know it. What I don't know is how dirty."

Latta's face didn't flinch, but Joe could detect a quick slump of his shoulders, as if someone had let some air out of him.

"The FBI and DCI are on their way up here now," Joe said. "They have a list of names and you're on it."

"Jesus," Latta said.

Then Latta reached up and unzipped his parka. He brushed the right front of his coat back so the fabric hooked behind the butt of his sidearm. His right hand hung there within inches of the Glock. Unlike Joe, who treated his handgun as an afterthought and rarely kept a round in the chamber, Latta likely adhered to protocol and would be able to draw it and fire fourteen rounds quickly without racking the slide.

Joe chinned toward Emily and said, "What are we going to do here? Have a Wild West shootout in the middle of the road? Neither one of us wants her to see this, Jim."

Latta's expression was blank, his eyes flat. He said, "Everybody in the agency knows you can't hit shit with your weapon."

"That's why I pack this," Joe said, and nodded toward the exposed stock of his shotgun in the saddle scabbard. Latta's eyes followed Joe's gesture. Melted snow beaded on the varnished butt.

Joe let the silence between them take over. If Latta drew on him, he was prepared to lunge forward, pull the shotgun out, and fire while falling backward behind the ATV for cover. He wished the grille of Latta's pickup — and Emily's searching face — wasn't directly behind the game warden in case his aim was off. And

324

he couldn't recall if he had racked a shell into the chamber previously or would have to pump in a round. He prayed silently Latta wouldn't make a desperate move.

Joe said, "She's wondering right now what's going on between us. I can see her face. You don't want to shoot at me in front of her and I don't want to have to shoot back. She's confused about what's going on."

Latta said, "So am I, goddamnit. You might have destroyed my life here. She thinks I'm a good man. What's going to happen to her if I end up in Rawlins? What will she think of me?"

"I understand," Joe said. "Believe me. But you can use your head now. If you work with me, the Feds will likely take it easy on you. If you tell them what you know and cooperate, there might be a way for you and Emily to stay together. You know how these things can work."

"Sometimes they work. Sometimes they don't."

"It's your only chance, Jim."

Latta said, "What you don't understand is what Templeton's men do to people they consider turncoats. Family isn't off-limits, and they'd go after Emily first."

"Not if she's in protective custody," Joe said. "Not if all of them are in cages."

Latta paused and took a deep breath that shuddered out when he exhaled. He was making his decision.

Joe said, "How about I ditch the four-wheeler and you give Daisy and me a ride? We can work out terms along the way."

"I don't want Emily knowing anything she doesn't have to," Latta said. Then: "Jesus, I can't think of anything worse than to disappoint her. Life wouldn't be worth living if that happened."

Joe rose from the ATV and retrieved his shotgun from the scabbard. He handled it casually so Latta wouldn't perceive a threat. Before propping it against the trunk of a tree on the side of the road, he glanced down at it. There *was* a shell in the receiver.

He turned to Latta and said, "Help me push this ATV off the road and we can get out of here."

Latta stood for a moment, then zipped his coat and joined him. They each placed their outside hand on the handgrips of the machine and leaned into it to roll it over the side of the switchback. It rolled quickly out of sight but made plenty of racket crashing through snow-laden trees until it came to a stop out of view.

"C'mon, Daisy," Joe said. Then, to Latta as they walked to his pickup, "Good choice, Jim. For sure they'll check your house first. Do you have a place we can go to wait things out? A place where Critchfield and Smith and the others wouldn't think to look?"

Latta grunted. "There's a cabin on the other side of the mountain. Belongs to a guy who only lives here in the summer. I know where he keeps the keys."

"That ought to do for now."

Joe slung his bag into the bed of Latta's pickup, and it nestled in between the metal gear box and Emily's collapsed wheelchair.

★ ★ ★

In the cab, Latta immediately had to turn the interior fan on high to combat against the fogging windows. Joe's clothes were soaked and steaming. He fought against trembling until he warmed up. Emily sat between Latta and Joe, with Daisy crammed tight between Joe's knees on the floorboard.

After Latta said, "Emily, this is Joe Pickett. He's a game warden like me and a friend of mine," most of Emily's attention was focused on Daisy, who licked her outstretched hand.

"Daisy is a sweet dog," Emily said.

"She doesn't smell so good when she's wet, though," Joe said.

"I don't mind."

To her father, Emily asked, "Where are we going now?"

"A place I know of. We can hang out there for a while until the weather gets better."

Emily considered the answer, then said, "Okay, I guess. I've got my homework with me. Will Daisy be with us?"

"Yeah," Latta said.

"Okay, then."

Joe felt relieved but cautious. He couldn't trust Latta yet, but he thought it unlikely the game warden would turn on him now with his daughter wedged between them. In a sense, Joe thought with dismay, Emily was a kind of hostage. He didn't like that at all.

Latta engaged the four-wheel drive and turned his pickup off the highway onto a rough two-track that would take them over the mountain. Joe asked if he could borrow his phone.

Latta was suspicious but handed it over. Joe punched it on and scrolled through the record of activity, and as he did Latta understood what was going on and moaned.

"What's wrong, Dad?" Emily asked.

"Nothing," Latta said, quickly resuming his game face.

Latta had been called by Critchfield six times the previous night — from nine p.m. until two a.m. — and four times that morning. In turn, Latta had called both Critchfield and Smith three times, and Sheriff Mead twice. Joe checked the time stamps of the activity. He was relieved Latta hadn't contacted any of them after finding Joe at the Black Forest Inn.

Joe removed the battery from the phone, pocketed it, and handed the phone back to Latta. They both knew what it meant, Joe thought. Critchfield and Smith — or more likely the sheriff — couldn't track them using the internal GPS in the phone. And Joe couldn't trust Latta enough to run the risk of Latta placing a call.

Joe reached down and turned the power off on Latta's radio, then unscrewed the connection to the mic and let the cord dangle. No doubt if either of them tried to call dispatch, Sheriff Mead or one of his people would overhear.

"We need to go dark for a while," Joe said. "Jim, do you have any other phones or radios on you?"

"No phones, but there's a couple of handhelds in the gear box in back."

Joe nodded. He'd deal with them later. Then he thought of something else. The agency had recently equipped all game warden vehicles with a GPS tracking device mounted out of view under the driver's-side seat. The idea was if a warden was taken by gunpoint and forced to drive — or the truck itself was stolen — dispatch could locate the vehicle.

"Excuse me," Joe said to Emily, while he bent over her lap. He reached under the seat and jerked out the wires to the GPS unit.

"Never even thought of that," Latta said. "And there you go damaging state equipment again."

"My specialty," Joe said.

Joe tried to keep his promise not to let Emily know too much. She was very smart. Fortunately, she was distracted by Daisy, who was making cow eyes at her.

"So you haven't told them," Joe said to Latta.

"Didn't get a chance."

"Did they know where you were going?"

"Not necessarily. I think we were all covering the same ground, and the inn would obviously be on the list."

"Finally, a lucky break," Joe sighed.

Emily asked, "What are you two *talking* about?"

"Just business stuff, nothing important," Latta told her. Then to Joe: "Where did you get the ATV?"

"Bought it."

"I'm surprised we didn't know about it. Usually, there isn't a transaction done in this county without them knowing about it."

"The dealer isn't on your team."

"Ah," Latta said with a nod. "Kelli Ann Fahey. She can be stubborn."

"I'd call it honest," Joe said.

Latta shrugged.

"Have they located my pickup?" Joe asked.

"Not that I know of. But they wouldn't necessarily tell me right away. I'm not exactly at the top of the food chain. But I'm surprised you drove it away."

As far as Latta knew, Joe thought, the bomb was still under Joe's pickup and ready to be triggered.

"I hope nobody does anything stupid," Joe said.

Latta grinned bitterly and shook his head. "That's *their* specialty."

Joe asked, "Does this place we're going have cell service?"

"Probably not."

"Does it have a landline?"

"I think so — assuming the owner pays the telephone bill when he's not here. He seems like the kind of guy who would."

"Let's hope so."

Latta's pickup ground up the road through the heavy trees.

Emily said to Joe, "I thought at first you two were going to fight or something. I'm glad you're friends, because I really like Daisy."

Joe and Latta exchanged glances.

"She likes you, too," Joe said to Emily. "She's used to being surrounded by girls."

Latta said, "This ain't going to work forever, Joe. Those guys track everything that goes on in this county. It won't be long before they figure this thing out."

"Figure *what* thing out?" Emily asked.

"I told you, honey," Latta said, with an edge in his voice, "it's just business."

Joe said, "We've just gotta hope the cavalry arrives in time."

An hour and a half later, they found the cabin. It was a two-story log structure with a green steel roof and an impressive rock chimney. The cabin was located on the far end of a small meadow that had drifted over in the wind and snow. A few of the drifts were three feet tall. Latta's pickup began to lurch from drift to drift, and Emily looked up in alarm.

"Dad, are we gonna get stuck?"

Joe wondered the same thing, although Latta was an experienced four-wheeler.

"Nope," the game warden said, hitting his brakes on a small patch of dry ground between drifts. "This is as far as we go. We'll have to hike the rest of the way in."

Joe inadvertently glanced down at Emily, and felt ashamed for doing so.

"I'll carry Em if you'll bring her chair from the back," Latta said.

"Deal."

"Let's hope the owner didn't change the place he keeps the keys."

He hadn't.

The old-fashioned rotary-dial telephone inside the cabin had a dial tone.

While Jim Latta set about starting a fire in the fireplace and Emily murmured her love to Daisy, Joe checked in with Chuck Coon and Marybeth and gave them his new callback number.

Coon said the skies were clearing over Cheyenne and the snow-plows were out on the highways. His strike team was assembling and would be ready to go within hours, provided the roads were reopened.

Marybeth said the Internet was out at the library — likely storm-related — and that she'd made no more progress finding an online profile of Erik Young.

As the fire crackled to life, Latta announced with foreboding that the electricity to the cabin was out, probably the result of wires that had been taken down by snow-laden tree branches somewhere in the forest. Joe and Latta combed the cabin for kerosene lamps and fuel, and found both.

By midafternoon, it was warm enough inside that Emily removed her coat.

Joe and Latta sat facing each other at the kitchen table.

After twenty minutes of painful silence, Latta looked at the front window as if he expected to see armed figures approaching.

"This won't end well," Latta said softly so Emily wouldn't overhear.

CHAPTER
TWENTY-FIVE

Sand Creek Ranch

Nate arrived at the Sand Creek Ranch lodge for dinner and walked through the parking lot with a bad attitude and Joe Pickett's 12-gauge shotgun shell in his pocket.

The snowfall had lost its intensity at dusk but continued to sift down through the sky and trees like flour. There were small openings in the cloud cover where the stars shone through, but the moon was still obscured and there was little ambient starlight, which made the lodge look as if it were blazing from every pore.

There were rows of vehicles in the lot and Nate could see the silhouettes of people milling about through the ground-floor windows. He remembered what Liv had told him about weapons, so he skirted the lot and stashed his .500 and shoulder holster at the base of a thick caragana bush on the side of an outbuilding.

Liv met him at the door with a gracious and relieved smile. She looked magnificent in a purple flowing blouse, tight gray slacks, and shiny black pumps.

"I'm so glad you came," she said. She was standing just inside the door. There was a clipboard in her hand; no doubt the guest list and the agenda for the evening.

"Didn't think I had a choice," Nate grumbled.

"You're right!" she said with a laugh. "And you look very presentable."

Nate wore jeans and boots, a white shirt with an open collar, and a buckskin-colored jacket. His hair was tied into a ponytail by a leather falcon's jess.

"Didn't think there would be so many people," Nate said. "I hate these kinds of things."

"Close your eyes and think of England," she said.

He grunted.

"Look," she said, stepping close to him and lowering her voice before he could enter the great room, "here's how these things go. There's an order to the evening's events. Mr. T. wouldn't have it any other way."

Nate paused and tried to listen, but he couldn't get past her eyes.

She said, "First, there's the cocktail reception. The crowd is a mix of important locals, potential new clients, and ranch staff. Mr. T. likes to have the locals out once or twice a year to impress them. It tells them they're on the inside and reminds them how much they depend on Mr. T.

"Your role is to mill around and casually meet the guests. I'm guessing you won't be very good at that."

"Correct."

"Then dinner in the dining room. There's a seating chart, so just look for your name on a card above the china. It's important to Mr. T. who sits where, so please don't break the protocol."

Nate said, "I want to sit next to you."

The corners of her mouth rose in a slight smile, but she continued on, businesslike. "You'll need to sit where your card is located, and it's not next to me. But I'll be straight across the table."

"Good. We can make eyes at each other."

"We will *not*. Then, after dinner, a few of the guests will leave and there will be a short business meeting."

"Can I leave with them?"

"No. I told you, you need to stay."

Nate screwed up his face.

"Mr. T. said it was important. It's about a new assignment. You'll be involved."

Nate nodded. It seemed strange to him that he'd spent weeks keeping her at bay, but now that he was at the lodge with two dozen strangers, he wanted to wrap her up and take her home. And he could tell by the way she stood so close to him and repeatedly touched him on the arm while talking to him that she was feeling it, too.

"So, go," she said, stepping aside. "Mingle. Try not to kill anyone. And make sure you meet *Herself*. Her name is . . ."

"Missy," Nate said. "Is she going by Longbrake, Alden, or Vankueren?"

Liv looked up, alarmed. "You *know* her? How is that possible?"

"Our paths crossed a few times, but I know all about her. Her showing up here fits the profile."

"What profile?" Liv asked, equally alarmed and intrigued.

"She's the mother-in-law of a friend I haven't seen for a while. What I know about her is that she trades up."

Liv's eyebrows arched and she said, "Trades up?"

"Men. Husbands. Each one is wealthier than the last. I've lost count how many there are, but the last one was found swinging from a chain tied to the blade of a wind turbine."

"My God," Liv said, raising her fingertips to her mouth in alarm.

"Then she vanished. I don't know the story, but I've always had my suspicions. She's supposedly been on a world cruise ever since. But I see she's landed."

"Do you think Mr. T. knows any of this?"

Nate nodded. "I'm sure he knows some of it, but with her personal spin on everything I just told you. The fact that she's here means he bought it."

Liv moved back in and whispered, "What kinds of problems will this cause?"

Nate said, "Hard to say. But I'll tell you one thing: whatever you think of her — she's worse than that."

She studied him closely. "You're not kidding, are you?"

"Nope."

He left Liv Brannan stammering in the doorway. She began to pursue him, but a newly arriving couple filled the doorway and she turned to them reluctantly, her well-practiced hostess smile lighting up again like embers in a fresh breeze.

336

Sheriff R. C. Mead met him in the hallway before Nate could enter the great room. Mead was in his khaki dress uniform with dark-brown breast pockets and epaulets. His service weapon was in its holster on his right hip.

"Hope you don't mind," he said, quickly but thoroughly running his hands down inside Nate's jacket, on the inside of his thighs, and along the shafts of his boots. Nate gritted his teeth and never took his eyes off the sheriff.

"Okay," Mead said, satisfied Nate was unarmed. "Mr. Templeton always asks me to check. Enjoy your evening."

"I will," Nate said. "But there's one thing."

"What's that?"

"Touch me again and I'll tear both of your ears off and hang them from my rearview mirror."

Mead grinned at first, then realized Nate was serious and his face went blank.

Without another word, Nate shouldered around the man and entered the great room.

People stood in loose knots throughout the massive great room under the dim light of three wagon-wheel chandeliers. Nate didn't know most of them but assumed they were the locals Liv told him about — town councilmen, county commissioners, bankers. There were lots of clean cowboy hats and reptile-skin boots, and the women were wearing their most formal western wear and showy jewelry. He could smell hair products in the air. Several of the wives' eyes lingered a bit too long on him and he broke eye contact.

He got a neat double Wyoming Whiskey from the bar and surveyed the crowd. Whip was entertaining a couple of men in sport coats in the corner, obviously telling fishing stories because he was false-casting in the air without a fly rod.

"Who are the men listening to Whip?" Nate asked the bartender. He'd seen him around the ranch before in his day job as a horse wrangler.

The wrangler said, "Well, the one on the left is Judge Bartholomew. The other one I don't know, but I guess he flew in from San Francisco this morning."

The man to Whip's right was in his mid-sixties and reeked of money and arrogance: loose-fitting jeans, boat shoes without socks, blazer worn over a black silk shirt, and a $400 haircut. Nate thought, *The potential client*.

He heard the man as he introduced himself to Whip as Rocco Biolchini. The name was vaguely familiar, Nate thought. Biolchini was some kind of high-profile social-media mogul. A movie had been partially based on his life, but Nate hadn't seen it and couldn't recall the name of the film.

While Biolchini talked about himself, Whip's attention wandered and he acknowledged Nate with a nod. Nate nodded back. There was no reason to do any more, he thought.

And there in the corner of the great room, framed by floor-to-ceiling bookshelves, were Wolfgang Templeton

338

and Missy Vankueren, surrounded by admiring guests with sloppy smiles on their faces. Templeton towered over everyone, looking, Nate thought, like an out-of-place aristocrat. Because Missy was tiny, she was hard to see through the well-wishers. But when the crowd parted, there she was: stunning in a tight white-and-gold dress that hugged her figure. If Nate hadn't known better, he would have guessed her age at forty — over twenty years off the mark. She had a perfect porcelain face, high cheekbones, and blood-red lipstick.

She hadn't seen him.

Nate finished his drink and handed it back to the bartender for another. When he turned around, Templeton was waving for him to come over. Missy was still engaged with a couple as Nate approached.

"Missy," Templeton said, "there's someone who works for me I'd like you to meet. Nate Romanowski, this is Missy Vankueren."

It was subtle, very subtle, but Nate noted the bolt of terror that went through her upon hearing his name. She didn't wheel around or drop her wineglass, and her knees didn't collapse. It was more of a full-body twitch. She didn't even turn immediately. But he'd seen her reaction, even if no one else noticed it. Then it was over.

Damn, he thought. *She's good.*

"Nate!" She beamed with all her mouth, but her eyes remained cold and meant solely for him. She held her free hand out and he grasped it.

"It's been so long! How have you *been?*"

339

"A lot has happened."

"No doubt," she said, shifting her smile from Nate to Templeton before Templeton could react. "Nate and I were acquaintances in a different world . . . long ago and far away, as they say in the movies."

Templeton was obviously confused but not alarmed, given the warm reception she'd shown to Nate.

"Nate was close to my daughter when I lived in Wyoming," she told Templeton. "She thought the world of him. We haven't seen each other in what — two years?"

Nate said, "Something like that."

"Does Marybeth know you're here?"

"No."

He saw a glimmer of relief in her eyes. She said, "You're the *last* person I thought I'd see here."

Nate grinned in a way he'd been told was cruel. He said, "You too."

"He's one of my best men," Templeton said to Missy with enthusiasm.

She grinned up at him. "No doubt, Wolfie. I don't doubt that at all."

Wolfie? Nate thought.

"We met in Davos," Templeton said to Nate as he drew Missy in close to him. "She was spending some time in Europe between cruises and we found out we had some mutual friends. It's almost like a small town at that level — everyone knows everyone. We hit it off *immediately* — especially once we realized we both shared a love for this country out here and the lifestyle."

340

Nate said, "Sure."

"It's the first time it ever happened to me," Templeton said, shaking his head. "Love at first sight."

"What do you know," Nate said.

"And here she is, right back where she belongs. Isn't that right, Missy?"

She blushed in a well-practiced way and said, "I don't want to come across as, you know, *too easy.*"

It was said as a joke, and Templeton roared in laughter. Nate looked from him back to her. Before he could say another word, Missy shrugged away from Templeton and told him, "Let me catch up with Nate for a few minutes and I'll be back."

Templeton agreed reluctantly. "There are still people to meet," he said. "I want to show you off."

"You are *so* sweet," she said while batting her eyes at him, then grasped Nate by his arm and led him down the expanse of the bookcase to an unoccupied corner.

Her face retained its pleasant glow and her smile was fixed even as she asked, "Who have you told about me?"

"No one yet."

"Do you swear you haven't let Marybeth know I'm back?"

"Haven't had the chance." Meaning: She didn't pick up.

"No one knows but you?"

"Nope."

She softened a little. Ever the seductress, he thought. "Can you keep your mouth shut?"

He didn't respond because he didn't like threats.

"Let's put it this way," she said softly. "Wolfgang and I are very close. *Very* close. He listens to me and I'm much better at this kind of palace intrigue than anyone you've ever known. Do we understand each other?"

Nate took a sip of his drink.

"See that woman over there?" she said, chinning almost imperceptibly over Nate's shoulder. He turned his head and saw Liv across the room, checking her clipboard. "The dishy one? She's worked for Wolfie for years. But one word from me? *Gone*. And when it comes to you: same thing."

He took another sip. How could she know his feelings toward Liv, other than Missy's innate intuition and lizard-like genius for self-preservation?

"I think we understand each other, right?" she smiled chillingly.

"I think I understand *you*," he said.

"So as far as you and I are concerned, we're acquaintances from another time. I'm not aware of your questionable background, and you know very little about my . . . history."

It was said as a statement, not a question.

She said, "I better get back to our guests. It was nice seeing you, Nate."

With that, she turned to rejoin Templeton.

Nate said, "By the way, Joe's here, too."

It froze her for a second before she turned back around. He knew he'd hit the target. She took a breath, gathered herself, and said, "Joe is on the *ranch?*"

"He's working in this county."

She narrowed her eyes. "Keep him away from me."

"He probably feels the same way about you."

"And keep him away from Wolfgang."

With that, she turned away to sidle up to Templeton again. Her smile hadn't lost any wattage.

Nate returned to the bar and found himself eyeing Liv closely, imagining her . . . *gone.* He thought that very soon this new world he had entered would blow up. His sudden goal was not to blow up with it.

Or Liv.

Or Joe. Damn him for showing up.

CHAPTER
TWENTY-SIX

Bearlodge Mountain Cabin

Twenty-two miles away, Joe and Latta were outside the cabin in the dark, gathering wood from a snow-covered half-cord under the bobbing glow of Latta's headlamp. Without electricity, there were two sources of heat inside: the fireplace and a woodstove in the master bedroom. They needed enough of the soft pine to get them through the night, and each had already delivered an armload.

The windows of the cabin glowed with warm pinkish light from the kerosene lamps inside. The sky had cleared and the starlight turned the snow on the ground from white to aquamarine. Emily waited inside at the window, watching them, her head a silhouette. Daisy was beside her with her front paws on the sill and her nose pressed against the glass.

"First real cold night," Latta observed.

"Yup."

Since they were out of Emily's earshot, Latta asked, "So we can expect the task force to show up tomorrow morning?"

"That's what Agent Coon told me," Joe said. He needed to knock the snow off each length of wood before stacking it in the crook of his arm. "Midmorning is more likely. He said they're arming up and getting the vehicles ready tonight and the DOT promises the roads will be open and clear an hour after sunrise."

"Assuming there's no wind," Latta grumbled. "It's never just the snow. It's always the damned wind."

"Yup."

Latta paused and looked hard at Joe. "What do you think? Am I gonna be okay after this?"

Joe said, "Probably not. You'll lose your job, for sure. But if you cooperate with the Feds you might stay out of prison. That's probably the best you can hope for, I'd suspect."

"What about my pension? You think they'll let me keep it?"

"I don't know, Jim. Director LGD has her own way of doing things."

"I've heard," Latta said, shaking his head. "I'm surprised I made it all the way up to badge number six in seniority. Now I'll get busted and you'll move up a notch."

"I really don't care about my badge number," Joe said.

"Well, this ought to work out for tonight," Latta said, nodding toward the cabin as if to reassure himself as well as Joe. "We're lucky he keeps some food in the place, even though you took care of that tonight."

Two hours before, Joe had tracked a wild turkey in the pine forest on the east side of the cabin and killed it with a blast from his shot-gun. For dinner, the three of them had roast turkey breast, canned potatoes, and half a jar of green beans. Latta had located the owner's liquor stock as well and had placed an unopened bottle of Evan Williams bourbon on the counter for later.

"We'll have to keep track of everything we use so we can repay the owner when this is all over," Joe said. "I might even pay him a visit to thank him in person."

"He's a prick," Latta said. "He's got a nice place, but he's one of those rich guys who bends your ear telling you how much better everything is in Florida. And on and on about the damned weather. I don't care that it's warm in Florida. It's also humid and filled with bugs. Just send him a check."

"Why does he come here, then?"

"Who knows? Maybe Daytona Beach isn't so wonderful in the summer."

Joe looked toward the cabin and asked, "Do you think Emily is doing okay?"

"Yeah, she loves it. It's like camping. You're going to have a tough time getting your dog away from her, though."

"You should get her a dog, Jim."

"I have enough trouble in my life as it is," Latta said, grunting as he stood erect with his load of wood.

"Yeah, I guess you do."

As both men trudged from the woodpile toward the cabin they heard the phone ring inside. When Joe looked up, Emily was gone from the window.

"Who in the hell is calling?" Latta asked in a desperate whisper.

"Maybe Coon or my wife," Joe said. "I gave them the number here."

"But what if it's someone else?" Latta said, and let his load of wood clatter to the snow. Then, shouting: "Em! Don't answer the phone!" He sidestepped the dropped wood and ran toward the cabin.

Too late. Joe could see her straining her arm up from her wheelchair and bringing the receiver down to her face.

When Joe came inside with his load of wood and closed the door behind him by leaning back against it with his butt, Latta appeared panicked and Emily frightened by her father's reaction.

"Tell him what you told me," Latta said to his daughter.

"Some man called."

"Did he identify himself?" Joe asked. "Did he ask for me?"

"No. He asked if my dad was here and I told him he was. He asked if we were okay."

"What did you tell him?"

"I told him we were fine."

"Did he ask who was with you?"

"Yes. I told him there was another game warden here — my dad's friend Joe."

Latta said, "Jesus, Emily."

She was hurt. "Dad, if I did something wrong . . ."

"It's okay," Latta said. "You're not in trouble. Just think back to every word that was said. Think, Em, did he say his name?"

"No. But he seemed happy to hear we were here. I asked him if he wanted to talk to you and he said no, he just wanted to make sure we were safe."

Latta and Joe exchanged looks.

"He said to stay here until they could send someone to help," she said, looking from Latta to Joe. "He said not to tell you so it would be a surprise. Then he hung up."

CHAPTER
TWENTY-SEVEN

Sand Creek Ranch

While the bartender was getting ice, Nate slipped behind the bar and made his own drink: tea, ice, and water. It looked close enough to what he'd been sipping to pass, he thought. He needed a clear head as the guests were shooed by Liv into the cavernous dining room.

There was a preordained hierarchy to the seating plan.

Templeton and Missy sat at the head of the table side by side. Nate located his card — to the right of Missy at the end of the table. Whip was directly across from him, so the two of them were literally displayed as Templeton's right- and left-hand men. Rocco Biolchini was sandwiched across the table between Whip and Liv.

Nate winced as Sheriff Mead took the seat to his right. Next to Mead was Judge Bartholomew, then the Wedell chief of police, Dale Miller, in his dress blues. Miller was infamous for the speed traps he maintained on both ends of town that served as his department's primary source of outside income. The rumor was Miller took a personal cut as well. He was red-faced and crude, and had started pounding beers long before he arrived at the ranch, judging by the flush in his face and his glassy eyes.

Locals occupied all of the rest of the chairs on both sides of the long table, but two seats were empty. Nate noted the cards for the missing guests: Bill Critchfield and Gene Smith. He thought it was odd, and wondered if an explanation would be offered.

It was raucous: dozens of individual alcohol-fueled conversations going on at once among locals, ranch staff, and the people Templeton had positioned nearest to him. Nate didn't say a word to anyone and he noted Liv was silent as well. She was attentive to all that was going on and busy surveying the guests to make sure everyone was in their correct place and the discussions were quasi-civil.

Jane Ringolsby and the ranch staff quickly served the first course: small grilled mourning dove breasts shot by Templeton himself and sausages from Templeton's own processing facility. Red wine was poured into every glass. Nate glanced down the table. It was obvious many of the locals were nervous and thrilled at the same time — and drinking too much. He saw one woman instructing her husband which fork to use first.

Missy simply glowed while she followed Templeton's every word. He was telling a slightly bored Rocco Biolchini how white-tailed deer were kicking the remaining native mule deer out of the Black Hills. She seemed entranced with him, Nate thought, and very well practiced in the art of alert subservience. She tittered at his jokes and shook her head solemnly while he told a story about encountering a wolverine while bird-hunting. Only once did she slip, when her eyes darted away from Templeton to Nate. Nate grinned back at her as if to say, *I'm on to you.*

Rocco Biolchini was deep into his story — one he had no doubt told many times — about his undergraduate years in an Ivy League university, his lack of success with athletics or the opposite sex, his early infatuation with computers and the Internet, his desire to connect similarly minded geeks into a network where they could make fun of the jocks and arrogant handsome pricks who sucked up all of the oxygen in every room — without any of the golden boys knowing about how they were being mocked. The website later morphed into in a social-media empire with millions of users.

Nate thought Biolchini spoke as if he were used to being listened to, as if the listeners were of course as fascinated by Rocco Biolchini as Rocco Biolchini was. He paused at the end of passages for listeners to say "Wow" or "Oh my God" but didn't invite questions or urge others to add anything. It was a monologue, not a dialogue. While he went on through the salad course, Nate noticed two figures skulking outside the dining room in the great room, looking furtively around the doorframe.

The two men, Smith and Critchfield, weren't dressed for dinner. They wore heavy coats still glistening from outside snowfall and their cheeks were flushed from the cold. They looked inside the dining room, imploring someone to invite them in, it seemed.

Nate observed what followed as Liv spotted the two men and excused herself with an exasperated smile. She strode toward the two men and walked past them so they had to follow her into the great room and farther from the guests. There was a heated exchange, with Liv refusing something at first and pointing toward the front door as if ordering the dog to go outside, but she soon relented as they continued to gesticulate. She put her hands on her hips and told them to wait where they were for the time being, then reentered the dining room and whispered a long message into Templeton's ear.

Templeton's eyes narrowed, but his face gave nothing away. Halfway during the message, he glanced up at Smith and Critchfield and shook his head, then looked away with annoyance. The cacophony in the room never wavered — no one else was paying attention to what was going on. Nate saw that Missy had her eyes averted from Templeton but her head cocked in a way that indicated she could hear everything that was said.

When the message was delivered, Liv paused for a response. Templeton took a deep breath, sighed, and turned toward Missy and had a whispered conversation. Then, with a tiny sour nod, he indicated, *Okay.*

Liv left him crisply to return to Critchfield and Smith. In a moment, the two men were gone. And when Nate looked across the table, so was Whip. He hadn't seen him slip away.

When Liv sat back down, her eyes were downcast and there was a concerned set to her face for a

352

moment, but she quickly recovered when one of the locals said something to her.

Nate had no idea what had just happened.

Rocco Biolchini was now into his entrepreneurial phase in the Silicon Valley, where his once-trusted partner was beginning to "put the screws to him" by turning his corporate board and the *Wall Street Journal* against him . . .

"You and me, we're okay, right?" Sheriff Mead asked Nate, while Nate tried to put together all the nonverbal clues as to what had transpired among Smith, Critchfield, Liv, Templeton, Missy, and Whip.

"*What?*" Nate asked, annoyed by the interruption.

"I mean, what you said after I searched you for weapons. We're okay, right? After all, we're all on the same team here."

"I'm not on anyone's team."

Nate didn't want to engage in conversation with the sheriff. He'd seen the man down four quick glasses of wine and the main course hadn't even arrived yet. Mead seemed like the type who would just get louder, although even Mead would have trouble out-trumpeting Chief Miller or Biolchini, who was reciting some of the charges his bastard partner's lawyers had made against him in their first epic legal showdown . . .

"Excuse me," Nate said. "I'll be right back."

He got up without fanfare and passed the locals, who seemed not to notice he was leaving the room. The din died as he stepped outside onto the front porch and closed the door behind him.

The sky had cleared and the moon now had a halo. Thick bands of stars were brushed across the sky. He could smell the fireplace smoke as the coming low pressure tamped it down. It would be a very cold night.

Smith, Critchfield, and Whip were long gone.

"Are you all right?" Liv asked, startling him. He hadn't heard her open the door.

"Fine," he said. "I needed a break. When the air is that thick with bullshit, I have trouble breathing."

She laughed and said, "I've seen worse. Sometimes the locals get completely out of control and we need to drive them into town. They seem more restrained than usual tonight — probably because of *Herself.*"

Nate grunted.

"It's probably time to come back in. The steaks are ready to bring out."

"What happened in there?" he asked her sharply. "What did Templeton agree to?"

She paused. "I really can't say."

"Sure you can. It seems like an odd thing to happen during a dinner that supposedly requires mandatory attendance."

"I told you — I can't say. I've already told you too much about what goes on around here. Besides, I didn't think you cared."

"I don't. But I'm stuck sitting there with the sheriff on one side, Missy on the other, and Biolchini going on and on right across from me. It's my idea of hell on earth. If anyone's going to bolt this place, it ought to be me."

354

"Oh dear," she said. Then: "Hold on for a second. Don't leave. I've got to clear something with Mr. T."

Nate nodded.

When Liv withdrew and closed the door, Nate acted quickly.

He was back on the porch when the door opened again. But instead of Liv, Wolfgang Templeton stepped out on the landing and closed the door behind him.

"It's going to get cold, isn't it?" Templeton asked, looking up at the sky as Nate had.

Nate didn't respond.

"Liv said you saw something going on in there and it bothered you. I thought rather than have her play go-between, we could talk about it briefly ourselves."

Nate nodded.

"Whip has been with me for a lot of years. There would be problems if I didn't reach out to him first in an emergency situation. I hope you understand that."

Nate squinted at Templeton in the dark. Templeton seemed to think Nate was miffed he hadn't been chosen to go with Smith and Critchfield. Nate let him think it.

"So what's going on?" Nate asked.

"Just a local problem," Templeton said with a sigh. "There seems to be more and more of them all the time and they're making me weary. I despise these situations and I'm frankly *sick of dealing with them.*"

Templeton spat out the last few words with the kind of vehemence Nate had never experienced in him before.

"When I moved here, this county was like some kind of transplanted backwoods Appalachia," Templeton said. "The people were lazy, unemployed, and without hope. You've never seen so many EBT cards floating around. The responsible citizens were leaving in droves. It touched me and I wanted to help those who stayed, but I had no idea what kind of monster I was creating. They've become totally *dependent* on me for everything. No one has any drive or ambition — they just want to suck on the tit of Wolfgang Templeton.

"At first, I admit, it felt kind of good to be held in such regard. Every man wants to be liked and admired and looked up to. I helped everyone I could — entire families! But by helping them — giving them what they said they needed to survive — I created my own entitlement state. The more I give them, the more they want. They don't seem capable of solving their own problems anymore, and whenever one comes up, who do they come to? Me!"

Templeton shook his head. "In the most bizarre and unexpected way, I find myself being held hostage to them. If I don't give them what they ask, I fear they'll turn on me. On *us*. They'll keep our secret as long as the trough is full, but they keep demanding more of me. I can hardly keep up."

Nate said, "That's why you brought me on. To double your output."

"*Our* output," Templeton said. "We're in this together. I thought that by stepping up what I could give them, I could live a more comfortable life without all these constant problems. But it hasn't worked. In fact, it gets worse every day. And in order to keep up, I have to become less discriminating in the kind of work I accept. I used to turn clients away if what they asked didn't feel right. But now . . ."

"Now we've got people like Rocco Biolchini," Nate said. "Who just wants to get revenge on his business partner."

"Exactly," Templeton said, his eyes suddenly moist. Nate was surprised by the honest emotion. "Exactly, Nate. In the past I wouldn't have even invited him here. But now I'm weighing the payoff over the justification of the assignment. I used to take only jobs when I knew we were the only people professional and thorough enough to get to a bad guy who was above the law because of his wealth or connections, and leave no trace. It is a *righteous* line of work. We right wrongs and make the world a better place. We take out the most expensive garbage. I firmly believe that."

"So do I," Nate said. "At least I used to."

"It can be like that again," Templeton said wistfully.

Nate repeated, "Go out and do some good."

Templeton smiled sadly. "That's what it was all about. After all, even the president has his kill list. We're private sector, and the private sector is always better at everything than the politicians. But I never thought it would come to this . . ." he said, gesturing vaguely toward the lodge and the guests inside. "They're all leeches who could turn on me any minute. If there were any way I could do this all again, well, I'd do it differently."

"So what's the latest problem?" Nate asked.

Templeton shot out his sleeve and looked at his wristwatch. "We have to get back inside — we're keeping everyone waiting. And if we don't eat, they'll drink even more and I'll have to blast them out of here with TNT."

Templeton opened the door and held it so Nate could join him. The din of conversations coming from inside were even more out of control than before. "I know this isn't your idea of fun."

"It isn't."

"Stick it out for me, please. We need to listen to Mr. Biolchini's proposal after the guests clear out and make a decision — without Whip — whether we'll take the assignment based on how much he'll compensate us. I'll do that part of the negotiation — so you'll be free to go."

His plea was almost childlike, and Nate was taken by it.

As Nate passed through, Templeton threw an arm around his shoulder to guide him back toward the dining room.

"Thank you, Nate."

"So about the local problem?"

Templeton sighed again. "Nothing momentous. Those idiots Gene Smith and Bill Critchfield got tangled up with a game warden who is new to the area. It's their fault — they think they're above having to pay attention to the game laws around here and they invite this kind of trouble by being stupid. They are a couple of local thugs I decided to bring inside the operation so they'd work for me instead of against me, but it hasn't really worked out. It was a miscalculation. Thugs are thugs, just like zebras can never be horses."

"A game warden?" Nate asked, his throat dry.

"Yes. I met him the other day and he didn't seem particularly sharp. Certainly not clever enough to be the kind of danger to me those fools seem to think he is. But the situation escalated, and now they desperately needed to locate him. Unlike what *we* do, it's a clusterfuck out there, with no one knowing who is where or what's going on. This game warden seems to have stymied them. They came and asked for my help finding this man and eliminating the problem. They're pretty sure they know where he is: some remote cabin twenty miles from here."

Nate felt something cold inside that seemed to spread to his extremities and harden them, like a protective suit of armor.

"So I sent Whip to be there and make sure they didn't screw things up again. One of our trusted locals is with this game warden, but so is his daughter. I don't want the local or his daughter harmed or compromised. Whip said he'd see to it, and he seemed eager for the job, although he hates working with others. Apparently, Whip had an encounter with this game warden that didn't set well with him at all, so he jumped at the opportunity to settle the score. I hate to mix our business with local affairs, but this time I didn't see where I had a choice in the matter."

Nate didn't respond. The light in the room seemed to have gotten much brighter than it was when he'd left it. The conversations, if possible, seemed even louder.

"Missy overheard some of it and agreed with my decision," Templeton said. " 'Best to nip this in the bud,' she said."

Nate sat down to his steak and ignored the imploring look Liv gave him from across the table.

He felt himself being transformed from within. At one point, he looked up to find Liv staring at him. She looked terrified.

Yarak.

It took a long hour for the locals to finish their steaks and desserts and clear out. Liv had to practically hoist several men and women from their chairs and point them toward the door, where ranch staff held out their coats to reclaim.

Missy had left as well, saying she was still tired from jet lag and that she'd meet Templeton in their room soon. To Nate, she said, "It was wonderful to see you again."

Nate was grateful when he saw Liv walk away with Missy toward the stairs.

The sheriff, judge, and chief of police remained at the table to Nate's right. Biolchini was directly across the table, lighting a Cuban cigar.

And Templeton sat at the head, glaring at Mead, obviously wishing for the sheriff to go and take the other two with him. Mead didn't get the message, it seemed. Nate guessed that Templeton had to deal with the three law enforcement officials with kid gloves and couldn't simply pry them out of their chairs as Liv had with the other locals.

Judge Bartholomew got the message, though, and said to Mead, "R.C., I think it's time to call it an evening."

"After I finish my drink," Mead said. He slurred his words.

Templeton smoldered for a moment, then said to Nate, "I'll go get my notebook for our meeting with Mr. Biolchini." He said it in a way that it was clear he expected the three locals to be gone when he returned.

A moment later, Mead turned to Nate and said, "Hey — quit prodding me with your finger."

Nate said, "It's not my finger."

Mead's eyes got wide when he looked down and saw the muzzle of the .500 pressed into his ribs. Nate had retrieved it earlier from the brush outside the lodge. Mead's sudden silence caught the attention of the judge and Miller, who turned to see what was going on.

Nate said, "If I pull this trigger, the slug will go through all three of you. I've dropped two men with one shot before, so this would be a personal best."

Biolchini couldn't see the handgun under the table on the other side. He said, "What is happening here?"

Nate ignored him. To the three men sitting side by side next to him, he said, "Ease your weapons out and put them on the table in front of you. Then slowly stand up and back against the wall."

"Please," Mead whispered to Bartholomew and the police chief. "He's not kidding."

"Slowly," Nate said.

The semiautomatic service weapons of the sheriff and chief clunked on the white tablecloth, and their hands withdrew from them quickly. Nate was mildly surprised to see the judge surrender a snub-nosed .38 as well.

"Now stand and back up."

"What the *fuck*!" Biolchini said loudly. "Does everybody here pack heat?"

Nate shushed him without looking over. He kept his weapon leveled at the three men, who were doing what they'd been told. It was oddly silent in the room.

"You too," Nate said to Biolchini. "Up against the wall with them."

"But . . ."

"I said," Nate whispered, "go over there with them."

When the four of them stood shoulder to shoulder, Nate got up and marched them into the great room.

Judge Bartholomew said, "Mr. Templeton would not approve."

"No talking," Nate said. He ordered Mead and Chief Miller to sit on the bottom two steps of the staircase, and Biolchini and the judge to stand on the other side of the thick iron railing.

"Take out your cuffs and give me your keys," Nate said to the two law enforcement officers.

After collecting the keys, Nate told the men on the stairs to snap one of the handcuffs on their outside wrists and pass their arms through the railing. Biolchini rolled his eyes, as if he weren't going to participate in the game, but Nate cocked the hammer back on his revolver and raised it to fire.

Biolchini and the judge scrambled to lock the open cuffs on their own wrists.

As they did, Templeton entered the room holding a leather notebook. He assessed the situation and said to Nate, "You've completely ruined the evening."

Nate said, "Clear out your shit and be gone by the time I get back here. I'm giving you this one chance only."

The reaction on Templeton's face was one of regret.

"Yeah," Nate said. "Me too."

He caught a movement out of the corner of his eye and wheeled toward the men on the staircase. Miller was clumsily hiking up his pants leg to reach for a small semiautomatic in an ankle holster.

Nate blew his leg off.

Miller screamed and tried to stanch the blood from the stump, and Biolchini simply fainted to the floor.

As he walked through the great room toward the door with his weapon in his hand, Nate kicked Miller's detached shin and throw-down across the floor. From the level above, he heard Liv scream and Missy call out, "Wolfie, is everything all right down there? *Wolfie!*"

Liv appeared at the top of the stairs. She said, "Nate, what happened?"

He stopped and ejected the empty casing and replaced it with live .500 caliber cartridges. "I ended the dinner party."

Her hand flew to her mouth. "Is Mr. T . . . ?"

"He's all right," Nate said, glancing toward the dining room. Templeton still stood holding his notebook in stunned disbelief. He shook his head slowly to an internal monologue.

Nate said, "He'll be leaving this place soon because everything has just blown up. It's over. You better pack up as well."

Missy joined her, wearing a purple silk bathrobe. Her face was set in cold rage.

"You son of a bitch," she seethed. "I should have known this would happen. You're no better than Joe."

Nate said, "Actually, he's better than me."

Liv said to Nate, "But what about *us*?"

"There is no us. Every time there's an us, I lose somebody who didn't need to die. I'm toxic, and you deserve better."

Liv's eyes flashed. "So that's the decision you've made?"

"I'm afraid so."

"What if I don't agree with it?"

Nate said, "I wish you'd trust me on this. All of this is over, including you and me."

He forced himself to turn his back on her as he walked to the door.

Behind him, in the saddest voice imaginable, he heard Templeton say, "Somebody get a hacksaw."

CHAPTER
TWENTY-EIGHT

Bearlodge Mountain Cabin

"Hit me again," Latta said to Joe after spitting blood out of his mouth into the snow, "and this time make it count."

"You're kidding me, right?" Joe said, feeling nauseated. He'd already used the butt of his shotgun to pop Latta solidly in the nose. The dull crack of bone sickened him. The blow had staggered Latta, but the game warden straightened up and stepped forward and asked for more.

"No," Latta said. "Lay me out. The only chance Em and I have with them is if they're convinced you jumped me and got away. So it has to look like you *really* jumped me. And damn it, Joe, do it before Emily hears us and looks outside."

Joe winced and drew the shotgun back, the butt aimed at Latta's bloody face. He hesitated.

"Do it! Pretend I'm somebody else. Somebody you hate."

Joe searched his memory for anyone who could call up that kind of violent urge. His mother-in-law, Missy, flashed through his mind, but he knew he could never bash an older woman — even her — with a shotgun.

Nevertheless . . .

It had been Latta's idea they fake an assault so Joe could escape alone. Better that, he thought, than the three of them fleeing down the mountain on the only access road and running into Templeton's men on their way up. Latta told Joe that Sheriff Mead's office was probably already on the radio getting a team together to raid the cabin. Joe was astonished to hear that law enforcement in Medicine Wheel County operated in the open when it came to dealing with threats to Templeton and that Latta was just a cog in a much larger machine. Knowing this, Joe agreed to the strategy although it meant he had to trust Latta — as well as get off the mountain on his own.

Joe insisted on an addition to the plan: that Latta tell Templeton's men that Joe was headed for the Black Forest Inn to gather his belongings and regroup. Latta agreed with the strategy. Joe didn't tell Latta the reason for the wrinkle.

"What about Emily?" Joe had asked earlier in the evening. They were at the dinner table with the open bottle of Evan Williams between them. Daisy was curled up on a rug in front of the fireplace and Emily was sleeping in the bedroom. "Can she lie well enough to pull it off? She seems like a bad liar to me."

Latta assured Joe that Emily *was* a bad liar.

"So are my girls," Joe said. "Two of 'em, anyway."

"She can do it if I explain to her what's going on. If she knows that if she gives up the game, they might kill me and hurt her. I'll be honest with her."

366

Joe was skeptical.

Latta said, "She's gonna find out about what her father did one way or another. I'd rather it be from me, so she at least knows why I did it. She needs to know I made mistakes but now I'm making it right."

Joe reluctantly agreed because he couldn't see a better option. He didn't want to try and make a stand at the cabin. Templeton's men could fill it full of holes or burn them out. And it would put Emily in harm's way. Also, if the three of them tried to get down the mountain and encountered the thugs, there could be a bloodbath. He jotted down the cell phone number for Chuck Coon on a napkin and slid it over to Latta.

"Call him and let him know what's going on. Tell him where I'll be, because I doubt I'll have any cell service on the way down."

Latta agreed.

Latta had located an ancient snow machine — a 1989 Polaris Indy Sport 340cc — in a shed next to the cabin. It was in bad shape, but they were able to get it started by spraying fuel directly into the carburetor. It was now fueled up and ready to go. Joe found a moth-eaten snowmobile suit and a pair of bulky boots that fit him hanging inside the shed.

"Let's go outside," Latta said with resignation, after taking a long pull of the bottle.

Joe said, "I can't do it. You're already bleeding like a stuck pig. You're hurt bad enough to convince them, I think."

Latta rolled his eyes and said with contempt, "Good. Don't do it, Joe. Get me killed and Emily, too."

Joe grunted and hit Latta hard in the chin with the butt of the shotgun. Latta went down to his knees holding his face in his hands. Streams of blood pulsed between his fingers and darkened the snow in front of him. He said something garbled that Joe translated as, "You busted my jaw."

"Sorry, Jim," Joe said through clenched teeth.

He heard Latta clearly when the man wailed, "Now go!"

The old machine started again with a cloud of blue smoke and sounded like an angry electric shaver. Joe roared out of the shed and didn't look back. He found out a mile away from the cabin that the gauges and electronics were shot and the single headlamp flickered on and off. It was a clunky, wedge-shaped machine, and the brakes were bad and the windscreen was cracked down the middle. Mice had eaten away most of the seat down to bare metal.

It ran, though, and he picked his way through spruce trees parallel to the road. He didn't want the distinctive snowmobile tracks to be seen easily by occupants of a vehicle coming up the mountain. Joe and Latta had decided that the assault scenario would also include Joe stealing the snow machine. Eventually, Templeton's thugs would be in pursuit. If they didn't see him on their way up, Joe could buy an hour or two of time.

That was the plan, anyway.

The suit was warm, but the cold air stung his face. His shotgun was secured to the front of the machine by bungee cords and the ATV saddlebags were strapped to the back. Daisy sprawled on her belly across what once had been the seat. He could see her hind end under his left arm and her head under his right. She looked out at the passing trees with a kind of stoic dumbness unique to Labradors, and he was grateful he owned a dog not bright enough to be frightened. Fine powdered snow covered her snout.

The snow was deep and soft in the trees, and he was scared to stop moving, in fear the machine would sink and he'd be stuck. Like a shark, he kept moving — even when he couldn't see a clear path ahead and when the headlight flickered off. Eventually, he found the switch to the light and flipped it off — better to navigate by the light of the stars and moon than by the unreliable lamp.

If he were to bet on it, Joe thought, he'd wager the Polaris wouldn't last the trip down the mountain and back to his pickup in the orchard. The engine seemed to be running especially hot, he thought, and who knew the last time it had been overhauled? Snowmobiles of that vintage, Joe knew, used to be equipped with extra fan belts, spark plugs, and tools for fixing the engine in the field when it stopped performing. Present-day over-the-snow machines were much more reliable. But the old Polaris was all he had, and it didn't have any extra parts in the compartment beneath the seat where they should have been.

Joe prepared to simply leave it when it stopped and hike the rest of the way. Every mile it ran, though, was a mile he wouldn't have to walk in deep snow.

He found himself praying and thinking of his daughters and Marybeth.

Joe would never forgive himself, he thought, if he got himself killed in such an inhospitable place.

He'd been gone nearly an hour when he noticed a splash of gold in the trees to his right where the road wound through the forest. Because he'd been running dark, his eyesight was especially tuned to any glimpse of artificial light, and he immediately reached down and killed the engine. He didn't dare let himself be seen or heard from the road.

Once he stopped, the snow machine listed to the left and sank into the snow. He was grateful it wasn't as deep as it had been at higher elevation, and hoped that if he could get the engine started again — a big if — he'd be able to continue.

Joe swung his leg over the seat and the dog and crouched behind the machine in the dark.

Daisy stared at him, confused.

"You too," he whispered, and she clambered down next to him and sat on her haunches. The engine ticked manically in the cold. Joe rubbed the snow from her eyes.

There was another splash of yellow on the trunks of the trees near the road, then the sound of a pickup engine. Joe hugged Daisy to him so she wouldn't bound toward the road to greet new friends. He hoped there wouldn't be a turn in the road that would hit him with the headlights and whoever was at the wheel didn't have a spotlight at the ready.

His muscles ached from the vibration of the machine, and his ears hummed from the high-pitched drone of the engine. The legs of his snowmobile suit were spattered with hot oil from somewhere beneath the faded plastic cowl.

Bill Critchfield's pickup crawled up the road in four-wheel drive and was soon in plain sight through the trees. Joe could make out two people inside — Smith, too — as well as the barrels of two long rifles sticking up between them. They were looking ahead and not to the side, and they continued on. Joe waited until the taillights faded to pink and eventually blinked out. When he stood up, he could barely hear the pickup in the distance.

"Whew," he said aloud.

But he was frightened for Latta and Emily when the pickup arrived at the cabin. Would Critchfield and Smith believe Latta's story? Had Latta followed through making the call to Agent Coon? Thank God, he thought, the landline worked despite the fact that the rest of the power was out.

Joe mounted the machine and reached down for the key when he heard another low rumble from the road and looked over.

The light was amber this time, and low to the ground. It belonged to a Range Rover that crawled up the mountain minutes behind Critchfield's pickup. The driver kept the headlights out and used only the running lights — probably so he wouldn't be detected by the men up ahead.

Joe squinted and the profile behind the wheel was unmistakable as belonging to Whip, Robert Whipple, the snooty man with the bamboo fly rod he'd rousted on Sand Creek. Unlike Critchfield and Smith, though, Whip proceeded up the two-track as a hunter would. He drove slowly with his windows open so he could listen. It took a full minute for Whip to pass by. Joe's heart was beating so hard he wouldn't have been surprised if Whip suddenly stopped and turned in his direction. But he didn't.

So now, he thought, there were *three* of them after him. Two mouth-breathing thugs and another one much more sinister.

He waited ten minutes — he didn't want Whip to hear the snowmobile — before holding his breath and turning the key.

The engine caught.

"Let's go, Daisy," he said against the whine of the snow machine.

The machine lurched to a stop three miles from the orchard, and Joe climbed off and shed his oil-soaked suit. There was a burnt smell in the air from beneath the cowl of the machine and he didn't even bother to look at what had caused it.

As he trudged in the snow with Daisy at his heels, he shot out his arm and checked his watch. He should make it to his pickup an hour or so before dawn, he guessed. He *had* to.

372

Once the sun was up, he could no longer elude the men who were after him. His tracks — first the tread from the machine on the snow and then his boot tracks — would expose his whereabouts the same way the elk and deer would be revealed to the hunters out there.

He drew out his cell phone. There was a faint signal and two text messages appeared that had been sent during the night.

One was from Chuck Coon and it simply read: *It's on. Is there room to land choppers at BFI?*

Latta had come through. Joe paused and texted back: *Hurry. Yes.*

The second was from Sheridan. It said: *Saw EY in the elevator. He's creeping me out and I need your advice.*

When he called, her phone was off — of course — and he left a message for her to call him back immediately.

Then he picked up his pace.

He'd never been so happy to see his battered green Game and Fish pickup where he'd left it in the orchard.

CHAPTER
TWENTY-NINE

Black Forest Inn

A half-hour before the first shafts of dawn sun would laser through the pine tops of the eastern hills, Joe watched the activity below through his spotting scope.

He'd taken the two-track road he'd discovered two nights before on the ATV and had parked his pickup in a heavy stand of snow-covered spruce overlooking the Black Forest Inn. From his perch, he was able to observe the structure lighting up window by window as hunters arose. Men eventually emerged, blowing clouds of condensation in the early-morning cold, and dozens of rigs sat idling as guns and gear were loaded inside. A haze of gasoline and diesel fumes hung over the lot. Occasionally, he could hear a shout or catcall from one of the hunters as they loaded up. The scene reminded him of a military deployment, but with dozens of private armies.

One by one, the hunters left the lot and went either north or south on the highway. Streams of taillights seemed to hang in the dark.

Joe could only sit and wait in complete silence. He was shut off from the world. He'd turned off the radio and powered down his phone an hour before, after responding to the two messages he'd received. If the local sheriff's department was in fact monitoring radio traffic, he couldn't risk connecting with either dispatch or Chuck Coon. And if Medicine Wheel County law enforcement were on their game, they would have procedures in place to monitor any cell phone calls made in the area, and with the help of the phone company they could triangulate his location. Joe found it disconcerting to be on the other side of the law and its technical capabilities. But he'd never encountered a thoroughly corrupt department before. The thought made him angry.

He speculated on the progress — or lack of progress — of his plan. He'd set it in motion with Latta on one end and Agent Coon on the other, and things would play out right in front of him — or they wouldn't. Everything was now out of his control. He shivered from both the cold and from outright fear of what might transpire. One thing he'd learned about plans was they rarely worked as envisioned.

While he waited and watched, he imagined Coon and his team charging north while trying to reach him and coordinate the raid. He imagined Sheridan trying to return his call. And he imagined Marybeth trying to touch base, only to find out he was off the grid. So many things could be happening out there, and so many things could be going wrong . . .

Although he was getting colder — thank goodness for Daisy's warm head on his lap — he didn't want to start up his pickup and run the heater. Someone could hear the motor or see the puffs from his exhaust pipe and know he was up there. Plus, the vibration of the engine made it impossible to sharpen the focus of his spotting scope.

He watched the highway in the distance for approaching vehicles and the sky for FBI helicopters. The only sounds were from heavy clumps of snow falling from the pine boughs to the forest floor. That startled him every time.

Bill Critchfield's pickup appeared on the highway approaching from the north, followed by Jim Latta's green Game and Fish truck. Joe raised his spotting scope and focused on both as they slowed at the entrance to the inn and turned in toward the parking lot.

Critchfield was alone and behind the wheel of his vehicle. Behind him, Gene Smith drove Latta's rig. Latta himself was slumped against the passenger window as Emily, between the two, comforted her dad.

At least he was still alive, Joe thought. And Emily appeared unhurt. He guessed Smith was driving because Latta was too beaten up. Joe felt a sting of guilt and hoped Latta had held.

The two pickups drove around the inn and parked nose-to-tail along the outside wall of the processing facility. They faced Joe's direction, although he doubted they could see him up in the shadowed forest over five hundred yards away.

Critchfield jumped out of his pickup. He held his cell phone to his head and stomped around in a tight circle while gesticulating wildly with his free hand. Joe guessed he was furious about something, and figured it was probably that Joe himself was still on the run.

He sat back from the spotting scope and surveyed the highway. He thought, *Where are the others?* Where were Sheriff Mead and his deputies? He doubted big shots like Judge Bartholomew or other county officials would show up, but he hoped the law enforcement types under Templeton's control would arrive. Joe's hope was that all of the armed conspirators would assemble in one place — the Black Forest Inn — when Coon and his team arrived. The Feds could corral them all at once. Once the locals were in custody, it would be easy to send a couple of agents to pick off the judge and others who weren't present in their homes.

Most of all, Joe wondered why Whip wasn't there. Where had he gone?

As he leaned forward into the lens of the spotting scope, he had a thought. Whip had shown his tactics as a hunter. Joe had spent hundreds of hours during his career doing what he did now: perching on high ground and patiently observing the landscape around him and noting the moving pieces, whether they were wildlife or hunters. And he realized Whip would likely be doing the same exact thing.

He scooted back on the seat and dislodged Daisy so he could have a better angle. He swung the scope up out of the lot into the heavy forest above it and directly across from him and readjusted the zoom to greater distance.

377

The terrain through the lens was a mirror of his own: dark, densely packed trees, shadowed hillside, pine boughs bent down as if offering their heavy payloads of snow for collection.

And there he was.

Partially hidden in a copse of spruce trees, Whip watched the activity in the parking lot far below him through a pair of long-barreled binoculars. The back end of the Range Rover was obscured from view by the forest as well as the front bumper, but there he was.

Joe knew that if he could see Whip, Whip could see *him* if he looked up. The realization shot through him, and he instinctively reached down for the key to start the truck and move it back out of view.

The second before he did, though, Joe caught a movement — a flash of color — on the other side of Whip's vehicle. In a world of dark blue-green trees and pure white snow, that glimpse of light brown between two tree trunks was an anomaly.

He drew back his hand from the key and concentrated on Whip's vehicle. Joe focused the scope beyond Whip, over his head, through the passenger window on the far side into the wall of trees where he'd seen the flash of color.

Nate Romanowski pushed himself through the pine boughs toward Whip, who was still scoping the valley floor through his binoculars. Nate looked to be dressed up for dinner, which was bizarre. He was wearing a sport jacket of some kind. Nate's weapon was out, a hank of hair hanging from the long barrel alongside his thigh as he closed in on Whip. Then Nate threw open the passenger door and reached inside for something on the seat.

Whip had no chance. He'd lowered the glasses and turned toward the open door when Joe saw his head jerk back once, twice, three times. His grip on the binoculars gave way and they dropped to the snow outside. Whip slumped forward, his face resting on the steering wheel. As Whip slumped forward, it revealed Nate grinning his cruel grin and clutching a small pistol.

Barely discernible because of the distance, Joe heard a delayed *pop-pop-pop*.

Nate had apparently killed Whip with his own gun, because if Nate had used the .500, everybody would have heard it. Still, since Joe had heard the shots, he was afraid Critchfield had as well. Joe swung the scope back down to the parking lot. Critchfield was still pacing, still talking. If he'd heard anything, he didn't react as if he had.

Joe was thrilled to see his old friend, even though he couldn't put into context what he'd just observed. But no doubt Whip was now out of the picture.

Behind Critchfield, Alice Pulochova was assisting Latta around the building so he could go inside. Alice pushed Emily through the snow in her wheelchair. Gene Smith leaned back against the grille of Latta's pickup with his arms crossed, waiting for marching orders from Critchfield — or whomever Critchfield was talking to on the phone.

Joe waited until Latta and Emily were safely inside before he said to Daisy, "Here we go."

The pickup shot quickly down the mountain, the front bumper pushing snow, fantails of snow shooting out from the wheels on both sides. Joe had little traction and winced as he sideswiped a tree that dumped a heavy load of snow on his windshield, but he didn't slow down and hit the wipers on high to clear it.

By the time he emerged from the trees and could see again, Critchfield and Smith were two hundred yards away.

Critchfield heard him and lowered the cell phone as Smith shouted and pointed toward Joe's oncoming truck.

Joe gunned it.

While he closed the distance between them, Smith ran back to Latta's pickup and backed out of the cab with a black rifle of some kind with a long magazine. Critchfield warned Smith off, and jogged to his own pickup and reached in through the open passenger window.

Instead of a weapon, Critchfield emerged with a new cell phone in his hand. He opened the passenger door and stepped behind it. Behind him, Smith scrambled and did the same.

Joe kept going, closing the gap to a hundred yards. He felt himself start to pucker . . .

He could see Critchfield duck down below the open window of the door. The cell phone rose to fill it, Critchfield's thumb on the speed-dial button.

The explosion came from the outside wall of the processing plant next to Critchfield's truck — the concussion like a thunderclap as the wall erupted in flame and smoke. Joe felt his pickup buck from the shock waves and ducked down to his right as chunks of the stone wall smashed into the grille of his vehicle. The windshield imploded and thousands of tiny cubes of glass, like ice, covered the inside of the cab.

Joe stomped on the brake and the truck slid to a stop in the snow. His ears rang from the explosion and all he could hear was a low humming sound inside his head. Daisy was covered with glass, and tried to shake it off as if it were errant beads of water.

He climbed out of his pickup with his shotgun but realized as the smoke cleared he wouldn't need it. Critchfield had been cut in two. His bottom half was behind the open door of his vehicle. The blackened top half was fifteen feet away and smoldering, as was the driver's-side door that had been blown through the cab like a giant scalpel. Somehow, Critchfield's cowboy hat had gone undamaged and was crown-down in the snow.

Smith was writhing on the ground in his death throes, both arms and one leg severed completely from his body, bleeding out so fast that he'd be dead within seconds. Joe gagged at the sight. He turned and ordered Daisy back into his truck. He didn't want his dog sniffing the body parts.

Despite the steady hum in his ears, Joe heard the thumping of approaching helicopters as they skimmed over the southern horizon. He looked up to see a convoy of speeding SUVs on the highway coming from the south with lights flashing.

Everything had worked according to plan, except there was no one alive to arrest. Except Nate, who was suddenly standing beside him. He hadn't heard him walk up through the fog in his head.

"Are you all right?"

"Just great," Joe said. "And you?"

"Dandy." Then: "How did you know there was a bomb inside the wall?"

"I put it there. Critchfield thought it was still under my truck."

"How did you know he'd park there?"

"I didn't," Joe confessed.

Nate said: "See that?"

Joe followed Nate's outstretched arm. Most of the stone wall of the processing facility had collapsed in the explosion, revealing the contents of the locked-up room. Which was why Joe had planted the explosive there in the first place. The bomb had served as a kind of search warrant made up of C-4.

"Oh God," Joe said. He'd suspected what he was seeing when he thought his darkest thoughts, which was why he'd hidden the bomb in the wall.

Two thick male human bodies hung head-down from meat hooks. They swung back and forth from the aftershock of the concussion. The bodies were naked but covered by stained white cheesecloth, the kind used by hunters to cover big game animals they'd skinned and hung from trees. Both corpses had visible wounds:

382

one with five or more small gunshot wounds in his face and neck, the other a gaping chasm.

"The one on the left is Henry P. Scoggins the Third," Nate said. "You know the other one."

"Jonah Bank," Joe whispered. "Anybody would recognize him."

Nate shrugged. "I always wondered what they did with the bodies we brought back."

Joe was speechless. But it hit him like a hammer. "They're being *aged*," he said in a whisper. "They sell sausage to the public and dole it out bit by bit to every hunter who gets his game processed here. Critchfield was the butcher."

"I've always heard humans taste like pork," Nate said with a whistle. "I guess that's right. Damn, I kind of liked that sausage, too."

Joe said, "Which means the Feds won't be able to pin more murders on Templeton unless he confesses. The remains of all the other victims have been . . . *consumed*."

He had trouble saying that last word. Then he looked straight at Nate.

"The only way you get out of this, maybe, is to become a state witness," Joe said. "I know the Feds want to nail Templeton really bad. That's why they sent me up here. Tell the Feds everything you know so they can build a bigger case against him. They might make a deal."

Nate scowled but didn't respond.

Joe squared up against Nate and raised his shotgun to parade rest. "If you don't, I'm going to have to arrest you right here. I don't like it any more than you do, but you really crossed the line this time."

"You'd do that, wouldn't you?"

"Yup."

"That's something I've always admired about you, Joe."

Joe gestured toward the highway. The federal convoy was making the turn onto the road that led to the Black Forest Inn. Above, the helicopters were stabilized and lowering from the sky to land.

"So you trust them?" Nate asked.

"The Feds? Not at all," Joe said. "Not one bit. Too many of 'em these days are no better than government thugs. But I trust Agent Coon. He's always been straight with me."

Nate said, "It won't be the first time I worked with the Feds."

Joe closed his eyes briefly in relief. The last thing he wanted to do was try to arrest Nate if Nate didn't want to be taken. Joe said, "I know about Whip. I saw what happened up there. But where are all the others? The cavalry is here and they don't have anyone to arrest. All I can figure is someone must have tipped them off."

"Probably."

"So where are they?"

Nate said, "The sheriff, judge, and chief of police were all manacled together the last I saw them. But they've probably cut themselves free by now."

"Who cuffed them together?"

"*Moi.*"

Joe was stunned. "I'm glad you didn't . . ."

"I'm not a murderer, Joe."

"Glad to hear that, Nate."

The roar of the first helicopter landing drowned out any more conversation. Joe reached up and clamped his hat on his head so the rotor wash wouldn't send it away.

Agents in black tactical gear and helmets poured out of the helicopter before it settled on the grass on the skirt of the parking lot. They carried Heckler & Koch MP5 submachine guns and shotguns and jogged to where Joe and Nate stood.

For a moment, Joe thought the agents might start firing, and he threw his shotgun aside and raised his hands. Nate did the same with his revolver.

The lead agent paused and made a hand signal for the agents to swarm the inn around him. As the second helicopter landed, more black-clad agents ran across the parking lot into the inn. When they were dispersed, the lead agent raised his face shield. *Coon.*

Joe noticed that Coon glared at Nate with obvious contempt.

The conversation was heated and held mostly in shouts. Joe shouted that Critchfield, Smith, and Robert Whipple were dead, Latta and his daughter were inside, and as far as he knew the violence was over. The sheriff and judge were likely on the run. Then he gestured toward the missing wall of the processing facility.

"Jesus Christ," Coon said. His face blanched white as he recognized the bodies. "We've broken this thing wide open. But Jesus, that's disgusting."

"You don't know the half of it," Joe said.

"What about him?" Coon asked.

"He's working with us," Joe shouted to Coon. "He's going to help you build the case, same as Latta. You'll need them."

Joe insisted Nate had inside information and had in fact saved his life by confronting Whipple and taking him out. Coon yelled back that Nate was as bad as Whip, and just as guilty. Nate didn't say a word.

Finally, as the helicopters wound down and they could speak normally, Coon turned suspiciously to Nate and asked, "Will you help us throw Templeton into federal prison for the rest of his life?"

"I'll tell you what I know," Nate said. "The throwing-into-a-cage part is up to you."

Coon stepped back and shook his head, as if having an argument with himself. Then he looked up and asked Joe, "You'll vouch for him?"

"I trust him with my life and the lives of my family."

"I can't promise anything," Coon said to Nate. "You know that, right?"

Nate nodded.

"We'll see what we can do. The U.S. attorney will make the final call, not me. Now, if you'll both just hang tight, I'll go inside and set up a command center and coordinate a raid on the ranch to get Templeton, and a couple of more teams to go after the sheriff and the judge. Then we'll all have a real long talk."

The morning air smelled of smoke from the explosion and the exhaust fumes of two helicopters and a dozen

SUVs. It was warming up nicely, though, and snow was sliding off the pitched roof of the inn to the ground below.

Joe leaned against the damaged front of his pickup as the adrenaline dissipated. He felt suddenly exhausted, and tried to count the hours since he'd last slept. He couldn't.

He didn't even note the high-pitched sound of an airplane overhead in the sky until he saw Nate had his head back, looking at it with interest.

"There he goes," Nate said.

"Who?"

"Wolfgang Templeton and his new squeeze, Missy Vankueren."

Joe nearly lost his footing. "*What?*"

Before Nate could explain, Joe felt a vibration from the phone he had just turned back on in his pocket.

It was Sheridan, and she was panicked. "Dad, someone just saw Erik Young going up the stairwell to the roof with a rifle."

Joe said with anguish to Sheridan, "I'm five hours away."

Nate asked, "What's going on?"

CHAPTER
THIRTY

Laramie, Wyoming

Past Douglas and somewhere over Laramie Peak in the Cessna Turbo 206H Stationair that belonged to Wolfgang Templeton, Joe said to Nate: "I didn't know you were a pilot."

"Officially, I'm not," Nate said. "But I've spent a lot of time in small planes. Plus, I observe how birds fly."

Joe put his head in his hands. He was grateful they'd be able to quickly cover the 320 miles to Laramie. Nate had reported they were traveling at 220 knots, which meant nothing to Joe. Arriving in less than an hour and a half meant everything.

"Can you land it when we get there?" Joe asked.

"We'll see."

There were three passengers in the plane. In addition to Joe and Nate was a woman named Liv Brannan who had been standing on the edge of the private airstrip in tears with a duffel bag and a suitcase. Joe hadn't heard the conversation that went on between Brannan and Nate — he was on his phone with Sheridan — but he was surprised when Nate said they'd have company.

When the federal strike force arrived at the Sand Creek Ranch earlier, Templeton's Gulfstream jet with Missy inside was long gone. While Agent Coon and his agents swarmed the ranch headquarters and gathered the confused staff, Nate had commandeered a ranch ATV and driven Joe to the airstrip. The air had been heavy with smoke from the burning lodge, which added enough confusion to the raid that they were able to slip away.

As the Cessna gathered speed on the strip and ascended, Joe looked down. The massive old lodge was engulfed in flames. By the time the rural fire department arrived there would likely be nothing left. Templeton had covered his tracks. Nate asked Brannan what had happened with the four men inside. Joe didn't pay any attention to the conversation. It could be sorted out later, he thought.

Over the radio, Joe could follow the progress of the FBI raids throughout Medicine Wheel County.

Judge Bartholomew was arrested in his home while he ate his morning oatmeal.

Sheriff Mead was stopped and arrested as he tried to escape in his personal Lincoln Continental.

Police Chief Dale Miller was in custody, but being flown to the Rapid City hospital due to massive blood loss.

All of them claimed they had no idea where Wolfgang Templeton had gone. In fact, they said they barely knew the man.

* * *

Before losing his cell signal, Joe had been able to learn from Sheridan that the university had been locked down and all dorm residents had been ordered to stay in their rooms. She had talked to the student who'd seen Erik Young in the stairwell and reported it to campus police. The student knew nothing about guns, but said the rifle "kind of looked like a toy." Joe guessed from that description that Young had the stolen Bushmaster, because that semiautomatic rifle had plastic composite stocks. It also had a high-capacity magazine filled with .223 rounds.

The Laramie Police Department and campus police had been called. The rumor mill was up and running. There were posts on Facebook and Twitter about up to a dozen victims thus far, but Sheridan said she'd not personally heard any shots from the roof of her building, and her floor was close enough, she thought, that she should have.

From her dorm room window, she could see police setting up a perimeter and sealing off the streets to traffic. The rumor was that a SWAT team was being assembled to storm the dormitory, but she couldn't see any signs of them yet.

Joe was proud of how calm Sheridan was, given the situation. He hoped *he* could hold it together as well as Sheridan had until they arrived.

But he wasn't sure what he'd do when they got there.

"She just held her hand out and said, 'I don't think so,'" Liv Brannan said to Nate. "I was handing my bags

390

up to Mr. T. on the steps of the plane when she said it. At first he seemed confused. But he didn't argue with her. He just said, 'Sorry, Liv,' and handed my bags back."

"Sounds like her," Nate said. "Doesn't it, Joe?"

Joe had half heard the conversation. He was thinking that instead of landing the plane at the airport west of town, they could buzz the dorm building itself. From their vantage point, they might be able to actually see Erik Young on top of the roof. He didn't think the Laramie PD had any helicopters of their own to put into the air, and if they had to call one in it would have to be from Cheyenne or Fort Collins, Colorado. Nate would no doubt have the Cessna on the scene before the choppers could arrive.

"I said, sounds like Missy, eh, Joe?"

Liv recounted for Joe the scene where Missy kept Liv out of the Gulfstream after Templeton had destroyed all his records and ordered the lodge torched.

"It does," Joe said. "I still can't wrap my mind around the fact that Missy was right there on the ranch. I'd hoped she was out of our lives forever."

"You should have known better," Nate said.

"I should have, but I can't think about it right now." To them both, he asked, "Where do you think Templeton is headed? I doubt he filed a flight plan."

"You can count on that," Nate said, rolling his eyes.

Liv said, "I wish I could tell you, but I can't. Mr. T. knows people all over the country and all over the world — wealthy people with private airstrips. I know because I've been with him for years and gone on plenty of trips with him. He'll be able to get to wherever he's going without getting close to any kind of commercial airport."

Nate nodded. He said, "Templeton gave Whip and me a list of safe havens to go to if something went tits-up during an operation. We were supposed to stay there until the heat was off and he could come get us. The list is of Templeton's contacts: former clients, mostly. It reads like the society column in the *New York Times*. With that list, the Feds should be able to close a lot of cases. And no doubt they'll find Templeton."

"So you do have something to bargain with," Joe said.

"I do. I feel guilty about it, though. All those old operations were justified."

Joe shook his head and didn't comment.

Joe could see the wheels in Nate's head were suddenly turning.

"Don't do it, Nate," Joe said. "Don't even think about it. You gave your word and I gave mine. We shouldn't even be in this airplane right now. If you're thinking of skipping out after this . . ."

Nate shrugged.

Liv said, "What about Missy?"

Joe said, "What about her?"

After the longest hour of his life, Joe could see Laramie laid out before them like broken glass winking in the brown prairie. The snow-covered peaks of the Snowy Range rose to the west and the mountains of the massive Gangplank rose to the east, cradling the little college town between them. Nate lowered the altitude of the aircraft and aimed toward the small cluster of buildings on the eastern side of town. The University of Wyoming.

"That's where we're headed," Nate told Liv. "The tallest building in Wyoming."

"You're kidding!" she said with a whoop.

"Please," Joe said sharply.

There were no other aircraft in the sky.

"We're going to be the first people to get a visual of the roof," Joe said to Nate. "Let's not buzz him too close on the first pass. Let's see what we can see."

"If the little bastard shoots at us, he's history," Nate said, leveling on the approach.

White Hall seemed to be rushing toward them now, filling the cockpit windshield.

"There he is," Nate said, tilting the Cessna so Joe could see clearly through the pilot's-side window over Nate.

Erik Young was wearing the long, dark coat Joe recognized from before, and he was stalking across the top of the gravel-covered roof with a long rifle. The top of the building was flat except for large utility boxes and a cinder-block structure in the corner with a door in it, where Young had obviously accessed the roof. Young was moving from box to box and peering around them as if looking for adversaries.

What he *wasn't* doing was aiming at students below over the short wall abutment along the sides of the roof.

"What in the hell is he up to?" Nate asked.

"I don't know," Joe said, confused. "He looks like he's hunting imaginary bad guys."

"Does he even know we're up here?" Brannan asked from her seat directly behind them.

"Doesn't look like it," Joe said.

"He better not raise that rifle," Nate hissed.

"I'm getting a bad feeling about this," Joe said.

After they'd zoomed by the campus, Nate began a long, sweeping bank in the sky to return.

"Lower this time, right?" Nate asked.

"Yes," Joe said. "If nothing else, we can help keep him distracted until the SWAT team is on the roof."

The radio in the Cessna crackled with bits of dialogue. National Guard choppers were on the way from Cheyenne and would be there momentarily. The officer in charge on the ground asked the chopper pilots if the single-engine aircraft in the sky over Laramie was with them, and the pilots responded that it wasn't.

"So who is flying that plane?" the officer asked.

"Air Romanowski!" Nate shouted in response. But he hadn't used the radio.

Joe grabbed the mic.

"This is Wyoming game warden Joe Pickett in the single-engine aircraft."

There was a long pause.

The officer asked, "What are you doing up there?"

Joe said, "My daughter is in the building," and signed off.

"Do you have a visual on the suspect?"

"Yes."

"What can you tell us?"

"I'm not sure what to say," Joe said. "He looks . . . confused."

As they approached the dormitory from the south, Nate pointed out the black-clad SWAT officers running into the ground-floor lobby from several white vans. The streets on all sides of the building were filled with police cars, sheriff's department vehicles, and campus police with lights flashing.

"I've seen enough storm troopers today to last me awhile," Nate grumbled.

They neared the roof again at lower elevation. Joe could see Young even more clearly than before. He was still moving from box to box, hunkering down, peering around corners. He seemed blithely unaware not only of the Cessna but also of the police presence twelve stories below.

There was no way, Joe thought, Young could not know about the dozens of SWAT officers thundering up the stairwell.

Young raised his rifle. Whatever he was aiming at was on the roof itself. And he wasn't pointing toward the access door where SWAT would emerge but directly away from it.

What looked like confetti rose from the corner of the roof where Young had been aiming. Joe was momentarily confused, until he realized it wasn't confetti but a big flock of pigeons.

"Oh no," Joe said, his stomach clenching.

"What?" Nate asked.

Joe grabbed the mic: "Stand down, stand down! He's not shooting at students. He's hunting *pigeons*."

"Oh shit," Nate said, as the access door blew open and a swarm of officers emerged on the roof with their weapons raised. Young apparently heard them and swung around, his weapon up. A dozen orange stars burst from the muzzles of automatic weapons.

Joe saw Young's long coat flutter up behind him as dozens of rounds passed through his body. Erik Young crumpled to the roof with his gun beside him.

The officer on the ground said, "Come again?"

"Too late," Joe moaned, and slumped against the side window.

CHAPTER
THIRTY-ONE

Saddlestring, Wyoming

"It seems like a month since I've seen you," Joe said to Marybeth. "You're a sight for sore eyes."

"It does seem like a month," she said from behind the wheel of her minivan, "but it's only been a few days."

"Still," he said.

"I agree."

"That poor boy on the roof," she said. "I feel sick just thinking about it. I wish we could have saved him somehow, or connected with him. Was he really just hunting pigeons?"

"Yes," Joe said. "He never stole the missing guns — their so-called friends did it to punk them. No, Young bought the pellet gun that morning at Walmart."

"If his mother would have taken my call, maybe . . ."

"It's not your fault what happened," Joe said. "You did what you could to prevent anyone getting hurt. Don't beat yourself up."

"I can't help it," she said. "It was such a huge overreaction."

"By everyone," Joe said. "Including us."

"Sheridan is doing a lot of soul-searching and second-guessing herself right now. She's devastated. I told her she'd done nothing wrong, but still . . ."

"She's not the only one," Joe said.

She'd picked him up in Gillette after his truck broke down on the way home. Shrapnel from the explosion at the Black Forest Inn had apparently penetrated the engine and had poked tiny pinprick holes in the coolant and hydraulic hoses. He hadn't noticed the damage until he was halfway to Saddlestring, although he'd have to admit later that his gauges were trying to tell him about it. His only excuse for not realizing what was happening was exhaustion from lack of sleep and the fact that he was overwhelmed by what had happened both in Medicine Wheel County and Laramie.

Joe left his vehicle at the state highway shop outside of Gillette, where Marybeth had agreed to pick him up. The vehicle maintenance man looked at Joe's pickup and simply shook his head.

"Another one," the man had said.

"Another one," Joe echoed.

Joe planned to spend the time filling her in on their drive back to Saddlestring, when he was interrupted by his cell phone.

He looked at the screen. "Rulon," he said.

"It sounds like you did it," the governor said, "but you weren't supposed to leave so many bodies behind."

"That wasn't all my doing," Joe said.

"Tell me everything," Rulon said. "I've got a press briefing in half an hour. They might ask me some questions about what happened up there, but I have a feeling the only thing they care about is what happened in Laramie this morning. There are already idiots calling for gun control. Ha! That poor bastard had a *pellet gun*!

"Anyway," Rulon said, cooling down. "Tell me what happened up there from the beginning. It sounds like a pretty wide-ranging criminal enterprise — even bigger than our federal government. And don't leave anything out — especially any details that might come back to bite me later."

Joe did. Marybeth listened as she drove, sometimes shaking her head. Finally, Rulon told Joe the "hounds were baying in the next room for his head" and hung up.

"You just can't do it, can you, Joe?" she asked when he was through.

"What?"

"Keep your distance. You just feel compelled to get into the middle of things, don't you?"

"They came after *me*," Joe said defensively. "Remember the part about the bomb under my truck?"

"And they forced you to put it in the wall of that building, too," she said.

He conceded the point by not responding. He was too exhausted to mount much of an argument. He envied Daisy, who was sleeping the sleep of the dead in the backseat.

"Is he going to be okay?" she asked after a few moments of silence.

"Nate?" Of course she meant Nate, he thought. "I don't know. If he plays it right and gives them enough information, he should get a good deal. But you know how the Feds are."

"They can be vindictive," she said. "He might have to go back to federal prison. But at least we'd know where he was and we can work on getting him out again. You working for the governor has its perks."

"Maybe," Joe said. Then: "I was proud of Nate today. He stepped back over the line and did the right thing. He's likely to have plenty of time to think about the direction he took."

"Will they allow visitors?" she asked.

They were discussing the horrifying return of Missy when Marybeth pulled up in front of their house.

"That's odd," she said, nodding toward April's Cherokee, which was parked near the detached garage. "She shouldn't be home now. School isn't out."

Joe wearily swung out of the van. He would take his weapons inside but leave his gear bag for later. All he could think about was taking a shower and getting into his bed. He hoped that when he closed his eyes he wouldn't see the last moments of Erik Young play on the inside of his eyelids on a continuous loop.

Before Joe could enter the house with his holster and shotgun, Marybeth burst out of it. Her eyes were wide and panicked.

"She's gone, Joe. April packed up and left while I was driving you back."

He stopped, stunned at the news. "But her Jeep is here," he said.

"She didn't leave in her truck," Marybeth said, suddenly angry. "She left with *him*. They've been planning this and waiting for the right time."

Joe was bone-tired but he reached up and clamped his hat on tight as if he were about to climb aboard a bucking horse in the chute. He said, "This rodeo just never stops, does it?"

Acknowledgments

The author thanks first readers Lauric Box, Molly Box Donnell, and Mark Nelson.

Thanks also to the support team of Jennifer Fonnesbeck (Facebook, Twitter, merchandise), Don Hajicek (website), Molly Donnell (graphics and images), and Templeton Rye.

It's an author's dream to work with terrific and sincere professionals in publishing at Penguin/Putnam in New York, including publisher Ivan Held, Michael (Cowboy) Barson, Kate Stark, Tom Colgan, and my legendary and brilliant editor, Neil Nyren.

Kudos, always, to my amazing agent and friend Ann Rittenberg.

Other titles published by Ulverscroft:

TO THE TOP OF THE MOUNTAIN

Arne Dahl

After the disastrous end to its last case, the Intercrime team — a specialist unit created to investigate violent, international crime — has been disbanded, their leader forced into early retirement.

The six detectives have been scattered throughout the country. Detectives Paul Hjelm and Kerstin Holm are investigating the senseless murder of a young football supporter in a pub in Stockholm, Arto Soderstedt and Viggo Norlander are working on mundane cases, Gunnar Nyberg is tackling child pornography while Jorge Chavez is immersed in research.

But when a man is blown up in a high-security prison, a major drugs baron comes under attack and a massacre takes place in a dark suburb, the Intercrime team are urgently reconvened. There is something dangerous approaching Sweden, and they are the only people who can do anything to stop it.

THE HANDSOME MAN'S DE LUXE CAFE

Alexander McCall Smith

Even the arrival of her baby can't hold Mma Makutsi back from success in the workplace, and so no sooner than she becomes a full partner in the No. 1 Ladies' Detective Agency — in spite of Mma Ramotswe's belated claims that she is only 'an assistant full partner' — she also launches a new enterprise of her own: the Handsome Man's De Luxe Cafe. Grace Makutsi is a lady with a business plan, but who could predict temperamental chefs, drunken waiters and more? Luckily, help is at hand, from the only person in Gaborone more gently determined than Mma Makutsi . . . Mma Ramotswe, of course.

CONCEALED IN DEATH

J. D. Robb

There is nothing unusual about billionaire Roarke supervising work on his new property — but when he takes a ceremonial swing at the first wall to be knocked down, he uncovers the body of a girl. And then another — in fact, twelve dead girls concealed behind a false wall.

Luckily for Roarke, he is married to the best police lieutenant in town. Eve Dallas is determined to find the killer — especially when she discovers that the building used to be a sanctuary for delinquent teenagers and the parallel with her past as a young runaway hits hard.

As the girls' identities are slowly unravelled by the department's crack forensic team, Eve and her staunch sidekick Peabody get closer to the shocking truth.

EXTRAORDINARY PEOPLE

Peter May

Paris.

An old mystery.

As midnight strikes, a man desperately seeking sanctuary flees into a church. The next day, his sudden disappearance will make him famous throughout France.

A new science.

Forensic expert Enzo Macleod takes a wager to solve the seven most notorious French murders using modern technology — and a total disregard for the justice system.

A fresh trail.

Deep in the catacombs below the city, he unearths dark clues deliberately set — and as he draws closer to the killer, discovers that he is to be the next victim.

THE BOOK OF YOU

Claire Kendal

Clarissa is becoming more and more frightened of her colleague, Rafe. He won't leave her alone, and he refuses to take no for an answer. He is always there.

Being selected for jury service is a relief. The courtroom is a safe haven, a place where Rafe can't be. But as a violent tale of kidnap and abuse unfolds, Clarissa begins to see parallels between her own situation and that of the young woman on the witness stand.

Realizing that she bears the burden of proof, Clarissa unravels the twisted, macabre fairytale that Rafe has spun around them — and discovers that the ending he envisions is more terrifying than she could have imagined . . .

UNSEEN

Karin Slaughter

Special Agent Will Trent has something to hide. Something he doesn't want Dr Sara Linton — the woman he loves — to find out.

He's gone undercover in Macon, Georgia and put his life at risk. And he knows Sara will never forgive him if she discovers the truth.

But when a young patrolman is shot and left for dead, Sara is forced to confront the past and a woman she hoped never to see again. And without even knowing it, she becomes involved in the same case Will is working on.

Soon both of their lives are in danger.